THE HEADHUNTER

By E.J. Gray

Published by New Generation Publishing in 2016

Copyright © Jerry Gray 2016

First Edition

The author asserts the moral right under the Copyright, Designs and Patents Act 1988 to be identified as the author of this work.

All Rights reserved. No part of this publication may be reproduced, stored in a retrieval system or transmitted, in any form or by any means without the prior consent of the author, nor be otherwise circulated in any form of binding or cover other than that which it is published and without a similar condition being imposed on the subsequent purchaser.

This novel is a work of fiction. Names and characters are the product of the author's imagination and any resemblance to actual persons living or dead is entirely coincidental.

www.newgeneration-publishing.com

New Generation Publishing

To Mio (E.I. Smakigo)
my Japanese daughter!

For my wife, Inge,
and all my friends from Search and Selection

It has been great having you to stay: hope you laugh at the book and good luck with your future postings.

xx

1. THE NEW BOSS

"The most trusted name in global leadership services, Russell Reynolds excels in finding uniquely qualified leaders for clients in all major markets. In a world that increasingly attempts to commoditize every service, our "one firm" approach, deep knowledge of major industries and unwavering commitment to client service make us stand out from other executive search firms."

RUSSELL REYNOLDS WEBSITE

Adam Noone, level with Lewins, had four seconds to decide whether to commit murder by wing-mirror. Four seconds was how long it would take for the brown UPS van, accelerating along Jermyn Street, to be upon them. His new boss wittered on as she strode unknowingly towards it, and to Noone, the large, shiny mirror loomed appealingly.

"You've got the presentation pack, the assignment stats, our track record and the sources list?" she demanded. No, I have come out for this important pitch we are making before brand-new, FTSE-100, potential clients without a moment's thought or preparation; stupid cow, thought Noone, viciously.

"Of course," he answered obediently, feeling like a schoolboy. His annoyance grew sharply; why should he, fifty-something years old with twelve years in the "profession", be treated as a lapdog by this jumped-up thirty four year-old? She was young, successful, incisive, confident, attractive and highly popular with the younger consultants, who luxuriated in the attractive glow of her success, incisiveness and confidence. They loved her extensive network of senior executives whom she called "darling" and her resultant ability to "rain-make": to conjure a seemingly endless supply of business from these great friends of hers. More experienced consultants like Noone, the old dogs to whom new tricks were proving difficult, hated her.

Calliope Brown had been born into a loving Black-country home where livid hatreds lurked, like whorls of cream being stirred into a dense, dark coffee. Dad had been a "postie" all his life, "a man of letters" as he described himself in a half-hearted effort to compete with the driving ambition of his wife. She was Gertrude Morel incarnate: father an engineer who never quite had enough money, married slightly beneath herself to this postman, having fallen pregnant through a midnight fumble against a wall after a disco, becoming increasingly resentful at her trapped social condition as the years passed. She was brighter than her husband and chafed at his good-natured lack of ambition. When the children came along, she bestowed her snobbery upon them by way of exotic names, Zamora for the boy (via a slushily-written travel article about Spain) and Calliope as a tribute to Manfred Mann. The siblings grew up intensely competitive, older brother adored, indulged, feted and encouraged whilst Calliope was used as "mother's little helper", condescended against and vaguely admired for her pretty innocence. Consequently, she nursed and honed a loathing for He Who Could Do No Wrong and relentlessly waged an undercover war of sabotage. When four and "too young to know better" she wax-crayoned all over his school books; at nine, she "accidentally" poured her mother's hair dye into his bath and turned his fledgling pubes, of which he was intensely proud, peroxide blond; at thirteen, with hormones raging, she had slipped crushed aspirin into his first "proper" girlfriend's cider, whose subsequent catatonic state ruined his attempts to get beyond the inviting barrier of her spray-on jeans.

Nevertheless, Calliope thrived at the local "bog-standard comprehensive" and with eight O' levels and A,B,C at A'level, she progressed proudly and defiantly to provincial university, graduating three years later with a

2:1 minus her virginity. From the milk-round, she selected the least boring presenter, made herself available to him for a drink, and having tempted him with a low-cut top and seductively-appointed mascara, persuaded him personally to deliver her application for the graduate trainee scheme to the Personnel Director the following week. She then cast him adrift into the night, coyly flashing her big, blue eyes with the promise of favours to come. He never saw her again.

United Food & Beverages was one of the country's largest companies, employing some 80,000 lackeys across numerous manufacturing sites and offices. Its products were saccharine and bland, mass-produced, mass-marketed and mass-consumed. They were promoted endlessly to the gullible public on cushions of catchy phrases supported by multi-million pound advertising budgets, creating abnormal, ad-fuelled desires in the target markets. Calliope loved it.

After an uncertain start, during which she was spun uselessly around various departments ("all part of the training") time too short in each to deduce exactly where the power resided, she ended up in the Personnel team. In those days, before Human Resources had been invented, those who could, managed real businesses and people, those who couldn't, ended up in Personnel. It existed to do all those jobs that the gabardine swine from Head Office, or the robber-barons in the business units, felt beneath them: payroll, car policy, terms & conditions, pension queries and it was a handy blame-pigeon when it came to discipline: "Sorry, Dave, it's company rules, talk to Personnel if you don't believe me." Personnel was a morass of mediocrity, a dumping ground for failures, unambitious waifs and strays, some cheerfully accepting, some sullenly resentful of their fate. It was perfect for Calliope: she could shine here.

Keen and eager to impress and be noticed, she was available for every pencil-sharpening exercise, smiling her white, bright smile at male superiors whilst appearing sincere and caring before the female ones. Her peers weren't fooled: they could see she was genuinely insincere, but they didn't give a toss. Not for them the Icarus-like ascent towards the light for they, poor timorous creatures, feared The Fall; Calliope was alone in her drive and her ascent was meteoric: Personnel Assistant, Assistant Personnel Executive, Personnel Executive, Assistant Personnel Manager and finally, the wholly, holy grail, Personnel Manager, which came with company car. And all this in six years: it was unheard of. She had become the youngest person to reach management grade since the last one, certainly the youngest female. She gloried in her position, began to shun her former peers, drove proudly around in her Ford Sierra with "United Food & Beverages" discreetly etched on each door and thought she had reached heaven. Within 18 months Calliope was bored.

She realised she could aspire higher, that Personnel *Director* sounded more suitable, especially as the incumbent was approaching sixty. He was kind, open, generous and desperate to be liked. He was confident that his job had meaning and he went home to his wife each night content that he had "made a difference". Secretly, however, he was afraid that he was too indecisive, weak and ineffectual to be taken seriously. He could always see all sides of an argument and changed his mind to agree with successive speakers, often voting against his original proposal. He lived in a constant welter of fear that one day he would be unmasked as useless.

Everyone thought he was useless. At company conferences he was deferential, quoted the latest employment legislation, earnestly discussed the minutiae of policy reform and was ignored by senior management. He was knowing and avuncular in Union negotiations, nodding mournfully as he agreed with the delegates' absurdly entrenched position, whilst blaming "The Executive" for making his position impossibly difficult. He usually conceded far more than the Union expected and sent the reps away happy, mistaking their incredulous smiles for respect and embryonic friendship. To foster team spirit, he would dispense encouragement to the younger, junior staff with bon mots and humorous anecdotes from his wealth of corporate experience, delivered in gentle, sonorous tones, a twinkle in his eyes and a toss of his white mane. Younger, junior staff were bored shitless by his boring, patronising interruptions. They wished he would leave them alone to abuse company time on personal telephone calls. By virtue of his length of service and resultant accumulated knowledge of the company's secrets, its petty politics and occasional scandals, the Board nevertheless considered him "part of the furniture", safe in his job until he decided to take retirement in a few years' time. In short, he was hugely vulnerable.

Calliope first needed to make him an ally. He was flattered when she asked if he would "mentor" her and gradually, willingly, he leached his knowledge to her. He admired her bubbly personality, drive and appetite for work and was charmed by her occasional coquettishness which always remained within the bounds of professional propriety. Mantis-like she drew him in and sucked him dry until she needed him no more. After Calliope had successfully represented the Company in a difficult tribunal hearing and then held the Union to a below-inflation pay increase, the Board needed no further evidence: she had become the real star, alongside whose brilliance the incumbent paled into liability. It was time for a change.

The old man, knife firmly between his shoulder blades, was pensioned off and Calliope appointed Personnel Director, based at company HQ in London, just before her thirtieth birthday. Her mother was ecstatic, defiantly boring acquaintances with the news that "our Cally is a director, y'know"; father, more taciturn and somewhat bemused, was nevertheless infused with a warm glow of pride. Zamora, by now an extremely average estate agent, didn't give a shit.

Calliope brought vision, purpose and action to the role and genuinely believed that "Human Resources", as she now called her department, would act as a partner to the business units. By streamlining the Company's hierarchies and "embedding" her team "in the line" she created a purposeful, dynamic and morale-boosting support function for business managers. The Board congratulated itself on her appointment and agreed that she was "a breath of fresh air". The business managers hated the new approach as it compromised the feudal control they were used to exercising. They could see power being centralised at Head Office in the name of "synergy", "best-practice" and "greater efficiency", with these obvious virtues insidiously imposed on their worlds. They were trapped: to resist risked gaining a reputation for being "difficult", or worse, "resistant to change" and once labelled, it was but a short step through the door marked Exit. Calliope always assisted her Chief Executive with such "separation interviews"; she was sympathetic with the individual, apologetic that his time had passed, and keen to assuage the pain he must feel at the loss of his job by paying him "in lieu of notice". Earnestly, she would look him in the eyes and repeat her well-honed mantra:

"I want you to know that we are not abandoning you; I am always here for you, should you ever wish to talk about anything, anytime."

In reality, she despised these yesterday's men with their grey personalities, outdated practices and misogynistic attitudes. If they couldn't see and embrace the coming of Calliope's brave new world, they deserved to die. Inevitably, they realised too late that they had become sacrifices upon the altar of her ambition and vanished one-by-one into their private wildernesses, ushered there with a flashing smile and a warm "Goodbye, and good luck".

By now consummately aware of the value of business relationships, Calliope also became active outside the

Company, networking with her HR peers at the Chartered Institute of Personnel Management conferences. Her youthful confidence and vivacious spirit attracted many admirers. She was asked to share her experience of "driving business change through HR", speaking alongside seasoned practitioners whom she flattered with a knowing flash of her bright blue eyes. Not infrequently, amongst the audience stupefied by the previous night's excess, someone felt that Calliope "had something" and noted her name for future reference. She became known. Assiduously she read about all prospective new employment legislation so that by the time a White Paper became enshrined as law, Calliope was already an expert: TUPE, the Working Time Directive, Discrimination in the Workplace on the grounds of Race, Colour, Creed or Disability, every change introduced, however obscure, was devoured and filed away in the dark recesses of Calliope's memory; she knew that knowledge begat power.

Then came the fateful day when a headhunter called for her. Of course, she was used to playing the game: listening detachedly whilst her secretary fended off a succession of recruitment consultants' pathetic attempts "to get something in the diary". It amused her to hear of their limp, predictable gambits ("your CEO suggested I meet up with Calliope to discuss how we can help your business") batted like long-hops into the jungle grass by one of her secretary's withering put-downs: ("I can only book people she knows into her diary"). Occasionally, if the caller was from a major search firm such as Korn Ferry or Russell Reynolds, she might receive the grateful lackey in her office for 45 minutes. They were all keen to tell her how different they were from the other firms and Calliope was continually amazed at how identical they were. Calliope used these meetings to impress on the consultants how interesting she found them and their propositions, and how it was only a matter of time before she would favour them with her gift of work. They would report back to their Partners' meetings that she was "a breath of fresh air", that there had been "a real connection" and that an assignment had been promised shortly. Calliope would keep them keen by accepting their subsequent invitations to lunch, at which she would dazzle them with her false friendship, petty confidences and increasing "darling" ratio. She racked up an impressive list of favourite restaurants at which she liked to be seen (Quaglino's, Langan's, Scott's and for something daring and different, Veeraswamy). Her male hosts would bid her a fond and reluctant farewell at the door, only slightly disappointed that she drank wine by the glass rather than bottle, and encouraged by a flash of those eyes and her breezy "'Bye darling"; female hosts were impressed that she was a trustworthy teetotaller and were equally convinced that the unspoken feminine pact that united them against the unfair tyranny of the masculine workplace would reward them in due course.

Then came that call from Dusti McFie of Marigold Associates. Disparagingly dismissed by the boys in the trade as "The Rubber Udders", Marigold was a three-woman boutique specialising in HR appointments. Although marketed as "a full-service search firm", in reality most of its work was word-of-mouth contingency stuff or advertising-led selection for middle-management roles. Just occasionally, however, it was awarded a senior-level search by a client overwhelmed by the heady credentials of sheer nylon, décolletage and expensive perfume submitted in pitches by the Marigold representatives. This was such an occasion, and Dusti had become the proud possessor of a search to find a new HR Director for Dogs' Dinners, an uncompromisingly-named petfood company. Ironically, the immediately-past Human Resources Director had been bitten by mosquitoes whilst on a Big Cat safari in Africa, dying of wounds enhanced by a particularly virulent strain of malaria which flourished untreated in a bush hospital. Dusti found Calliope on Marigold's database of "Ones to Track/Breaths of Fresh Air" and confidently assured Calliope's secretary on the phone that all three of them would benefit from Calliope's input into this highly confidential and important project. When she picked up the message, Calliope assumed this was bollocks, but nevertheless found her ego massaged and interest piqued. When her office had emptied at the end of the day, she returned the call. Dusti was embarrassingly happy to have a call returned: it didn't happen often.

"Ooo, Calliope, thanks so much for calling back; I'll tell you what it is; what it is is a job I am doing on behalf of a client that is looking for a high powered, but young and dynamic HR Director. They are a big, well-known company, it's a fantastic opportunity, do you know anyone who might be interested?" she gabbled. Dusti was a downmarket practitioner of the supposedly upmarket art of search, and it showed. Calliope cringed.

"If you really mean, 'would I be interested', probably not, but tell me more and we will see how I can help," she answered, neutrally.

Once the fencing formalities were over (yes, she would treat the information confidentially, no she couldn't recommend anyone immediately, yes she might be interested herself) and despite her initial misgivings (petfood, really, how interesting) Calliope allowed herself to be drawn in by Dusti's desperate enthusiasm. It helped that Calliope would apparently double her salary; also, that Dogs' Dinners was a multi-site FTSE 250 company employing several thousand people, which was growing rapidly on the back of its super-slick, patented process for turning low-grade animal carcasses into cost-effectively-rendered, beautifully packaged and relentlessly above and below the line-marketed dog food. The clincher, however, was that unlike the conservative United Food & Beverages, it deemed its HR Director worthy of *a seat on the Main Board*. To Calliope, still a relative fingerling compared to the old trout she was inevitably to become, this lure proved irresistible. The Dogs' Dinners Board found her a refreshing breath of fresh air, the job was offered and she graciously accepted, after persuading

Dusti that she needed an extra £20k on the salary to convince her to risk moving from such a venerable organisation as United Food & Beverages, where her future was assured, to Dogs' Dinners, which could be construed as a step down-market. Calliope's parents were overwhelmed at the news, although even the most loyal amongst their dwindling circle of friends became listless before Mrs Brown's airs and graces, brought on by large doses of Calliope-worship. Mrs Brown bought a new dress from George at Asda and forced her husband into a Moss Bros suit, "just in case Cally asks us to go with her to one of her functions." She never did.

Calliope was not replaced at United Food & Beverages, which, after a disastrous series of profit warnings, and the consequent collapse of its share price, hauled in a "company doctor" who split it up and sold it off, achieving a spirited ten pence in the pound for its less-than-grateful shareholders, of which only one, faced with the loss of his retirement fund, actually committed suicide.

Meanwhile, Calliope arrived triumphantly at Dogs' Dinners where she was duly hailed as a breath of fresh air. In two weeks, she allowed some of the stale air to escape from her own department by making the managers for Comp. & Bens. and Policy redundant: what expertise in these speciality areas Calliope didn't possess, she could easily buy in. Indeed, several weeks later, she persuaded one of these unfortunates to return for "a consultancy project" lasting sixty days. At a daily rate worth 50% more than his salary equivalent, why should he complain? Having set the example of downsizing her own team, Calliope spread the gospel widely throughout Dogs' Dinners: within six months she had assisted the CEO in reducing the workforce by one third. By concurrently dismantling outmoded "double-coverage" working practices in the face of feeble opposition from a Union emasculated by years of easy living, productivity per head soared, alongside Calliope's popularity with her boardroom colleagues. In five years, Dogs' Dinners trebled in size on the back of acquisitions and diversification: Cats' Suppers, Bunnies' Breakfasts, Parrots' Eat-'em-all, Reptiles' Repasts and other exotic subsidiaries were added to the menagerie. Dogs' Dinners would have continued its triumphant march through the shopping baskets of the pet-loving British public were it not for the unfortunate, fox-led outbreak of leptospirosis icterohaemorragiae of 1995, so deadly that legislation was nearly passed against dog ownership. Dogs' Dinners was left stranded by collapsing sales and began to haemorrhage itself.

Calliope, at the annual conference, exhorted employees "to pull together at this time of need". Inspired by herself as a charismatic, young leader she dramatically implored "Ask not what this company can do for you, but what you can do for it". She knew she had to get out quickly before her reputation was tarnished by the dog's dinner Dogs' Dinners was becoming. She accepted every recruitment consultant's call for lunch, during which she would casually imply that most of her tasks at Dogs' Dinners had been successfully completed and she might be interested in a new challenge. It didn't take long.

Adonis Fairweather, a languorous, foppish fellow from Overy, Cutt & Dribble ("Headhunters to the Stars") had watched Calliope's progress over the years and had become an ardent admirer. His long felt want hardened with the anticipation of giving Calliope a helping hand. In an inspired moment over lemon meringue at the Caprice, he asked her if she had ever considered becoming a headhunter. He could see the attributes she would bring: she was dedicatedly self-centred, determined, task-orientated, well-networked, money-focused. This needed translating into language she could understand:

"I think you'd be great: you are interested in people, you know how businesses work, you have charm and people like you," he told her. "I can arrange for you to meet our Managing Partner..." Calliope had wondered when he was going to suggest this.

"Oh darling, this is such a surprise. Do you really think so? I'm not sure really; I'll need to think about it. I'd never really thought about it before." Calliope pretended that she was flattered and amused but actually became slowly energised by the prospect, although she knew Adonis really only wanted to shag her. This she allowed him to do, whilst she plumbed his shallow depths for everything he knew about the work and the company. Seemingly reluctantly, she agreed to proceed, and, duly enticed by the prospect of six figure bonuses, joined Overy, Cutt & Dribble as a Consultant, anticipating the warm welcome, training and encouragement promised by Adonis.

Calliope was completely ignored. When she approached the Head of the Consumer Goods Practice, into which she had been nominally deposited, she was given an enlightening sermon in how it worked:

"It's like this luvvy; when we are very busy you may find work referred to you to transact; but basically, you eat what you kill, and if you don't kill, you will end up dead." Calliope instantly understood that this was far more of a dog-eat-dog world than Dogs' Dinners, and being tough, cute and highly self-motivated, she resolved to succeed at this dangerous new game. Having ingratiated herself with the Practice Head by taking on the marginal, low-level jobs for boring clients which no experienced consultant would deign to touch, she diligently began to mine her network of HR contacts. Inevitably, some thought she had "sold out" and joined the enemy, for recruitment consultants are often thought of as pond-life, swimming around in the stygian gloom alongside estate agents and insurance salesmen. Many, however, praised her brave move and felt she would bring a breath of fresh air to the somewhat fusty culture at OCD.

It wasn't long before she had landed her first assignment. A female HRD in a paint manufacturer was impressed by how Calliope empathised with the difficulties of doing her job in such a masculine environment, and her need to hire help in the form of a

Director of Organisational Development. For a career HR professional like Calliope, the assignment proved meat and drink, and she astutely realised that if she undertook the research herself, each call to a potential source or candidate would be enlarging her own network of contacts and lining her nest for the future. With little difficulty and copious quantities of "darlings", she persuaded a keen but callow fellow from Cadbury Schweppes to "broaden his horizons" and take the job, even if it did entail leaving his clingy girlfriend behind in Brentwood while he relocated to Bristol. Everyone was delighted: he was delighted to have had an exit route away from committing romantically to a prodworthy bird he only respected for a probe and drogue, the Client was delighted that a solution had been found so quickly, OCD was delighted that Calliope had recorded a successful, cost-effective completion on her first assignment and she was pleased with all these things but delighted that she had made many more useful contacts who now knew who and where she was.

In searching for possible sources on the company database, Calliope had also divined that there existed large numbers of senior executives with whom nobody from OCD had communicated for months, if not years. Possession being nine-tenths of the law, Calliope immediately actioned a schedule of calls to these as yet faceless folk who were unknowingly going to enhance her status. She rang them one-by-one on the pretext of being interested in finding out how they were progressing in their respective careers "since we were last in touch". None of them knew her from Adam, but all knew OCD and were flattered that this charming young lady had taken the time to enquire as to their wellbeing. Assuring all that she would bear them in mind "if anything interesting comes along", with several she was even able to sign off the conversations with an "okay, darling". Her spell was strong and alluring. She then set up a programme of follow-up invitations to lunch "to get to know them better" and few resisted her siren call. Naturally, from these intimate affairs, business began to flow, for it was unusual for any CEO, HRD or head of function not to have at least one problem over succession-planning or performance somewhere in their empire. How could they not respect Calliope's solicitous and generous offer of help? Once again, albeit in this different context, Calliope "began to be noticed", this time by the dry and austere Senior Partners in OCD. In short, they congratulated themselves on what was proving to be a highly successful hire. She had made it! Once again, Calliope basked in success and praise; once again, her peer group began to detest her.

Consultants began to find that when they finally got round to phoning somewhat neglected old contacts, they had recently spoken "to that nice, new lady, Calliope Brown: she was very helpful". Worse, some had even had lunch with her! It was outrageous: all of these "clients" had promised work at some stage and now she was stealing it behind their backs. A murmur of protest became a chorus (one feisty female consultant even threatened to "punch her lights out" if Calliope spoke to any of her clients without permission). The chorus reached the Managing Partner who reluctantly agreed to voice the collective concerns to Calliope. He disguised the reprimand by way of a celebratory dinner at the Lanesborough, congratulating her on her level of billing and impact on the Consumer Practice. There was just one small thing; could she possibly check the database to see if a contact had been assigned to a particular consultant before she picked up the phone? Calliope, anticipating this, demonstrated contrition and was apologetic. She had only been trying to improve OCD's hit-rate by tapping into its rich, in-house database resource and was devastated to think that others (perhaps a little jealous and small-minded?) could not appreciate her altruism. Of course she would apologise to the peevish few, would offer them a small "introduction" percentage for any new business emanating from one of "their clients" and would ensure that she asked them first before making an unsolicited approach to a contact in future. The Managing Partner, reassured by Calliope's understanding and obvious remorse and relieved that the evening had gone rather well, went home in self-satisfied contentment, having promoted her to Director. Calliope, seething, had no intention of changing her modus operandi and resolved to have revenge on those useless bastards she had to call colleagues.

She was by now the most adroit consultant-user of the database and was able to manipulate the entries to demonstrate that she hadn't been where she had been and vice versa. Inconvenient records (especially those belonging to The Enemy) were discreetly manipulated to provide an audit trail of her innocent and helpfully inclusive business development activities; in some cases they were ruthlessly expunged in unexplained system-errors. This clandestine war of attrition led to the inevitable casualties; here, a perfectly average consultant found him or herself eclipsed by Calliope's brilliance at business-generation and left for a haven of less intense exposure; there, a previously successful colleague found his or her revenue stream had dried up, only to discover it channelled by the client's higher authority through OCD's Key Account Director who turned out to be Calliope. Regrettably, with his billings falling as much as 50% below Calliope's, the Head of the Consumer Practice was quietly but forcefully encouraged to "find a new challenge" and Calliope was installed as the obvious successor. In just a few short years she had become one of the firm's highest billers and the OCD management team was keen to reward such conspicuous success. Calliope, with a team to control and a reputation for results burgeoning in the marketplace, allowed herself the luxury of pride, revelling in her power and position. She made a mental note to visit her parents soon, rather amazed to find that it had been two years since her last return home. Not that it was really home anymore: no, she was a truly cosmopolitan London girl now, with a flat in Fulham, a sexy soft-top Alfa Spider (thank God for aircon though, such a bore to lower the roof and frazzle her hair) and a small but vibrant circle of upwardly-mobile young professionals who called each other "darling" and jealously admired each other's material acquisitions. She valued her independence and took sexual gratification when she needed it from a succession of one-night-stands who were quickly dispensed with the morning after, like a spicy curry. She was at the peak of her powers, earning £400k a year and was confident of her ability to become a true icon in headhunting. How could it possibly go wrong?

It went wrong quickly. The ageing equity partners, wishing to realise their years of financial and personal investment at a time when the business was performing at a peak, sold out to a large, mid-market volume recruitment firm for a miraculous twelve-times-earnings ratio. The new owners congratulated themselves on their inspired bid and miraculous coup of obtaining such a prestigious brand which would take their business lucratively upmarket. Their Group CEO told the business press that "the capture of OCD validated our investment thesis of countercyclical asset acquisitions."

Much champagne was drunk on all sides, but whilst the vendors invested their well-earned gains in retirement Bentleys and Sunseekers, the purchasers were left with a bitter aftertaste. They had foolishly failed to safeguard their most important new assets, many of which walked within six months, disillusioned by OCD's loss of autonomy and move downmarket. The new owners' management team became pre-occupied with staunching the losses of personnel and revenue at OCD and lost focus elsewhere. Turnover nose-dived across the group, which, traditionally highly profitable, now slid into the red. The CEO and the FD judiciously elected to find new jobs elsewhere, spring-boarding off the public admiration of their OCD acquisition coup, whilst concealing the current trading situation. They were hastily and ominously replaced by a pair of buyout specialists, who began to pick over the group with a fine toothcomb to assess where value lay and where it did not.

Eventually, they reached Calliope. She had been quietly building her own Carthage whilst carnage raged all around: taking lost sheep under her wing, expanding her practice leadership to include all Industrial and Commercial clients, powering what was left of OCD by her own and her team's collective billings. By now, she was fond of claiming credit for all successful placements. "I have just recruited Philip Ball into BA" she would drop to prospective clients, without revealing that it was one of her young, adoring acolytes who had handled the transaction from the moment the client had awarded the assignment to Calliope. She was unstoppable.

The new CEO soon stopped her. He admired her dedication, attention to detail, strategic skills and indefatigable energy, marvelling at how all these commendable assets had been focused on self-promotion. She was a self-made woman who worshipped her creator. Surreptitious conversations with embittered leavers revealed to him how destructive and egotistic her behaviour had been. She was out of control and had to be brought back into line. He resolved to break up Calliope's empire and refocus her on the Consumer marketplace.

The showdown was illuminated by Calliope's virtual incandescence: How dare he suggest such a thing; was this the thanks she deserved for single-handedly holding the company together; and what about her billings, the highest in the firm by far? He was adamant. Knowing she was indispensable she played her ace:

"Let's get this straight; if you don't leave me alone, *I* will leave *you* alone, literally. You'd better believe it; I will walk out of here." That showed him: she knew they could not afford to let her go.

"Well if that's the way you feel, we had better see if we can make it as painless as possible for us all," she was stunned to hear him say. He *was* letting her go.

Quickly, Calliope phoned contacts in the other major

search firms, Korn Ferry, Russell Reynolds, Spencer Stuart, Heidrick & Struggles, ostensibly to ask how they were ("just touching base, darling") but letting slip that she had become disillusioned by "all the changes" at OCD and wondering whether her star should alight over a new home. None of them would touch her with a barge-pole; word from trampled-on, disgruntled former colleagues had fizzed round the headhunt fraternity, never the most discreet of clubs, and she had unknowingly acquired the sobriquet "Poison-Dwarf". Mischievously, however, one of these contacts in turn rang Bix Napier, the dashing head of the group formed around Aspallan, Bane Consultants, to tell him that a heavy-hitter from OCD was looking to move: she might be just the thing to lead ABC's own rebuilding programme.

Calliope, expecting an invitation from one of the big firms, was rather underwhelmed to receive the call from Aspallan, Bane, Consultants which she likened to a once-fine wine that had lain down for too long and become stale and musty, its rich, crimson glory days replaced by a dull, brown colour. Nevertheless, it would be churlish and short-sighted to turn them down flat. She would play hard-to-get. The first hurdle, ABC's worthy-but-dim and limited Managing Director Barry Bargewell was no match for her: he was charmed by her flattery, amazed at her client list, impressed by her billing record (casually mentioned en passant) and delighted that such a star would consider moving to ABC. Over the next few weeks Calliope had reeled him in to the point where he would match her current £175k salary, guarantee a first year bonus of 30%, give her equity and appoint her Managing Director, while he stepped back into a more non-executive, Chairman-like role. Bix Napier, who had prompted the whole scenario, had a quiet, assuring word with her.

"I can assure you," he purred, rather enjoying the Jehovah's stiffness he had inadvertently contracted whilst surveying the competitive advantage of the leisure facilities on Calliope's top shelf, "Barry will not be around for long after you have taken over, Calliope. There is no danger of him crashing your action, so to speak. You will be free to lead the business as you see fit. You have my word." She did not yet know that his word was as bonded as the Goodwin Sands.

It only remained for her to spirit out of OCD's office her personal papers, including client contact lists, CVs of key candidates, procedure manuals, examples of company documentation and anything else that might prove useful; which things having been achieved, she left after a subdued farewell party thrown by her grateful team. After three months' "gardening leave", during which she planned her triumphant entry to ABC, tipped off her clients as to her impending re-location and was in daily contact with the for-now-still Managing Director, Barry Bargewell, about which office and support staff she required, Calliope was eager to re-shape ABC in her own image.

By the time her garden leave had finished, Napier had already removed Barry Bargewell, so that he was able to introduce her to the company as ABC's new Managing Director. It sounded good. On her first Monday morning, Calliope stood before the gathered staff of Aspallan, Bane, Consultants.

"I can't tell you how thrilled I am to have joined a fine outfit with such an outstanding pedigree. I am tremendously encouraged by the quality of all the people I have met: it was one of the things which convinced me to come here, rather than Russell Reynolds or Egon Zehnder." These two consultancies were probably the pickiest of the bunch and the latter only hired consultants who possessed two degrees. She knew ABC people would know this, thus implying that she was more than qualified to join any firm she wished, which she wasn't.

"I intend to spend my first ninety days observing how you do things before I make any changes. After all," she lied with a coy smile, "you have been doing things pretty well for a long while now!" She looked around them all purposefully and finished positively: "I am convinced that we will do great things together".

Within a month, she had changed the company completely, forever.

Now, three months later, here were Noone and Calliope striding purposefully along Jermyn Street, she towards the glory of another successful pitch, he entranced by the huge wing-mirror advancing towards them at accelerating speed. He could see it was exactly the right height to collect her head just above the shoulders. Perfect: it would smash her fucking face in.

Three seconds to decide: he would manoeuvre to the inside of the pavement and as the UPS van reached them, he would accidentally slip and nudge her sharply into the path of that magnificent mirror. It was that easy; his troubles would be over and so would she. He felt a deep pang of regret: how had he managed to reach this low point in his headhunting life, when it had all begun so promisingly? His mind went back to the day when he had chanced upon the avenue to this strange but addictive world.

2. SHARON RIDELL

"As executive search professionals, the insights we bring, the advice we impart and the solutions we provide can have a significant impact on the businesses, careers and lives of others. We recognise these responsibilities and take them seriously. We adhere to a code of professional ethics with an emphasis on honesty and integrity — handling our relationships with clients, candidates and colleagues with great care. Above all, we value quality — the quality of the service we provide our clients, whether we have been retained to recruit a senior executive, advise a board or conduct a leadership assessment exercise. Our search process is thorough, efficient and tailored to meet the needs of each client".

SPENCER STUART WEBSITE

"WANTED-PREFERABLY ALIVE" the advertisement shouted, "SUCCESSFUL PEOPLE TO JOIN OUR GROWING TEAM." Noone was impressed at the first attempt at humour he had read that day. The Sunday Times Executive Appointments Section in March 1990 was invariably an arid desert when it came to fun and games, he had found. Sure, it was a very exciting place to be, with endless promises of challenging, life-enhancing jobs accompanied by alluring rewards including company cars. Twenty eight pages worth, to be exact, of unique opportunities to drive change through market-leading organisations, presented in densely-packed, self-satisfied prose. Noone was usually bored by these identical, tempting offers by page three, but on this one, he lingered.

Was he successful, he wondered? He had been a school prefect, scored the winning goal for his team in the final of the "House" football tournament, become vice-captain of school cricket and was useful and competitive at most sports except windsurfing, which he found irritating. He supposed that wouldn't cut much ice. Although he fancied cute, tricksy, little Nina from Accounts, he seemed to be successfully married, with a wife who said she loved him, and Noone knew that was unusual: after ten years of marriage, most wives had become disillusioned as their triumphant march down the aisle to marital bliss proved transitory. They hated their husbands' childish, manly habits, the constantly-left-up loo-seat, the thick, wiry pubes left behind in an unwashed bath, the occasional discovery of an ill-hidden stroke-mag and, particularly, the farting in bed, in which men delighted. So far, his wife hadn't complained too much about his performance in this area. What gave him confidence, however, was the fact that he had accidentally become a Chief Executive by the age of thirty-five. He had been stolen from the company which had taken him on and nurtured him as a graduate trainee by John Halstead, his current Group Chairman, and sent in to run Eezigaz, a small independent distributor of bottled gas. This was "the jewel in the crown" of Halstead's group of companies and Noone had been seduced by the extra £5k salary, the possibility of a bonus ("based on company profits") and the huge company Vauxhall Carlton. He keenly anticipated his own office and secretary and to driving the turnover up from £2.5m to £10m within five years: he knew he would love it and flourish.

After a day he hated it and over three years struggled to achieve anything meaningful: the combustible mixture of a sullen and uncooperative staff, dangerously dilapidated vehicles, and highly flammable product scared him shitless. The profitability of the business was wholly dependent on how many days per year the temperature fell below freezing. Noone was highly relieved when Halstead, uncannily prescient of impending global warming, apologetically informed him that he had sold Eezigaz behind Noone's back to one of the Oil Giants for ten times asset value. Noone was delighted to hear that the Oil Giant, clearly awash with spare CEOs, didn't require his services.

So here he was, wasting time at Head Office, admiring Nina's pert behind (Kylie had yet to be fully invented) awaiting Halstead's promise of another business to run "once we have invested the money from Eezigaz in an acquisition". Given the FT's eager anticipation of an approaching major recession, Noone was certain that this would not happen, and thus had begun to scan the job advertisements. Nobody seemed to mind.

"Find a nice juicy one for me, Adam dear," said Trudi, a late-middle-aged secretarial busybody, as she bustled past in a cloud of Clarins Eau Dynamisante. Trudi liked people to know how dynamic she was, and regaled the office constantly about her brilliant family, alluding coyly to a highly active sex life she had concocted for herself and her second husband, who was impotent. The office was united in the uncharitable hope that a car smash would wipe out Trudi's brilliant family. That would shut her up.

Returning to the advertisement, Noone read that this particular, unique opportunity was to join a fledgling subsidiary of the renowned search firm, Aspallan, Bane Consultants, of which he had never heard. Noone presumed that X, Y and Z surnames were frowned upon as being too far down the alphabet. It wanted successful people to help it "become pre-eminent" in its field. Noone understood why it wouldn't want unsuccessful people, with such a grandiloquent aim. As a successful Chief Executive, he had once hired a field salesperson through a so-called recruitment consultancy which had wanted to charge him money in advance. He refused, and the rather over-made-up female account executive had flounced out in a sulk, warning Noone that he would never find the right hire if that was his approach. The next day she called and agreed to a success-only fee of 15% of the first-year salary. Two weeks later she had gushingly presented two "top-class" candidates, one of whom didn't possess a licence ("just never got round to it, I s'pose") and the other a short, dumpy blonde who had sold advertising over the phone for Yellow Pages (which Noone had always regarded as shark-infested custard). Assured that these were the only two available candidates interested in the job (the implication being that Noone was at fault for conceiving such an unattractive role) Noone plumped for the plump one. Over the next three months, in an impressive whirlwind of activity, Plump One successfully consumed vast quantities of company time, petrol and expenses. She sold nothing and resigned two days before Noone fired her, for a job offering a better company car. Noone was therefore slightly suspicious of consultants.

The advertisement which had now caught Noone's interest with its humorous strapline encouraged those with a degree-level education and experience of running a business to bring their charismatic personalities, attention to detail, sales orientation and team ethic to this dynamic new environment. Boxes ticked, as far as Noone could see, no wucking furries. The clincher was the highly seductive "positions available in London or Uxbridge". London held no attraction, but Uxbridge was fantastic! He only lived a relatively short drive from Uxbridge. Admittedly Noone had never actually been there, and he had heard that it gave Slough a close run for its money in the "Come friendly bombs" category, but having worked in a Portakabin in Edmonton once, he had seen real horror and was undeterred. He quickly addressed a letter of application, as urged by the advertisement, to Hugo Reeve-Prior, Managing Director of Aspallan, Bane Consultants' subsidiary, AB Selection, and allowed the company to pay for the postage through the franking machine.

Having applied for a number of jobs recently, Noone expected to hear nothing for a couple of weeks, if at all. Initially he had felt anger when his carefully crafted submissions elicited silence, not even a grudging acknowledgement. Once he had phoned through after two weeks and harangued the woman who answered for her bad manners at leading supplicants towards a holy grail, only to leave them unattended at the altar, so to speak. She had deflated him instantly:

"Sorry love, I can't help you, I'm just a temp." Since then, and armed with the additional knowledge that there was seemingly an endless supply of candidates more suited to every position than himself (he wasn't trying out the Karma Sutra for God's sake) he hardly cared.

Imagine Noone's surprise, then, when a neatly word-processed Conqueror envelope dropped through his front door two days later, containing an equally neatly Conqueror-clad, word-processed letter thanking him for his application and indicating that it was one of several that appeared of great interest and relevance. If this remained the case once all applications had been carefully studied, then Sharon Ridell would be in touch. Noone was particularly impressed that his first name was handwritten in blue-black ink by the signatory, Hugo Reeve-Prior, as was a flowing "Yours sincerely".

The following Monday morning, Noone was having severe difficulty trying to hide the after-effects of the previous night's ill-judged ale and curry mix. The kitchen at "Delhi's Delights" ought to be commandeered by the MOD for its explosive and possibly lethal, ring-stinging concoctions. He marvelled that, despite severe pyroclastic flow necessitating three excursions to the Gents and a by now incredibly sore khaki buttonhole, his flatulence raged still and he was running out of corners to park its urgent sussurations. Trudi had just mentioned how her son had received yet another pay-rise, before wrinkling her nose and wondering whether the drains were blocked and Dynarod needed to be called, when mercifully, Noone's phone rang.

"Adam Noone?" a soft, warm, feminine voice enquired.

"That's me" he answered authoritatively, pretty sure it was him.

"Sharon Ridell, from AB Selection. I am ringing on behalf of Hugo Reeve-Prior; are you free to talk?" Flatulence aside, he was indeed. And talk they did, for some twenty-five minutes. She asked him about his career to date, the highs and lows, his occupations outside his occupation and why he was interested in joining AB Selection. Having applied on the whim of working close to home, Noone hadn't given this much thought, but, relatively gifted with the gab, he winged it, impressing her with his sincere desire to make a career change into the exciting world of recruitment consultancy. She began to wind up the conversation:

"Well Adam, I have enjoyed talking to you and your profile does seem to be a reasonable fit for what we are seeking; I presume you would prefer to work in London rather than Uxbridge?" This was a tricky one, so he hedged his bets.

"Actually, I don't mind. Uxbridge has some attractions." He heard a chuckle:

"You must tell me about them. Let's meet in my office there on Wednesday at, say, 1100 am? I will confirm in writing to you." She proceeded to give him directions and bade him a warm goodbye. Only after Noone had put down the phone did it dawn on him that Sharon was not Hugo Reeve-Prior's secretary, but the Manager of AB Selection's Uxbridge office. As he pondered whether he had committed any faux-pas through misunderstanding Sharon's status, he caught sight of a man in Dynarod overalls shaking his head as he talked to Trudi by the Gents. Gratefully, Noone noted his flatulent tandoori whispering had subsided at last.

On that Wednesday morning, Noone's pleasant drive through Denham Village was only interrupted by the abrupt onset of Uxbridge's utilitarian western approaches along the Oxford Road. Thence, a skirmish with the one-way system spat him out past a depressing line of unprepossessing shops, Indian and Chinese takeaways and launderettes at the far end of the High Street before he was able eventually to make his way to a squat, nondescript three storey building on Belmont Road, just behind the train and bus stations. To Noone, who had been used to the production line filth of a bottled gas (LPG) filling plant, it seemed perfectly acceptable and he was a little bemused by Sharon Ridell's profuse apologies for the office location. It was only temporary, she explained, as they had picked up the fag-end of a sub-lease which ran out next year; it was very handy for the station (although everyone drove to work, Noone discovered, except for little Irene, one of the two secretaries, who caught the bus from her parents' council flat in Hillingdon).

Sharon Ridell impressed Noone as they shook hands: she knew how to make the most of her average assets and presented herself with nicely bobbed, dyed blonde hair, a dark blue, sheeny, just-above-knee-length skirt and matching jacket from Debenhams which might have contained silk, a cream-coloured blouse, and patterned, dark, kitten-heels. The whole ensemble was topped off by a just-past pretty, well-made up face featuring bright red lipstick and mauve eye-shadow edged by finely-drawn eye-liner. It was a maturely seductive package and Noone suspected that men were quickly and helplessly drawn to make passes at her. Luckily, he didn't fancy her one bit. The overtly flirtatious flutterings of cute, tricksy, little Nina and her tiny waist pelmet were more to his taste.

Image was extremely important to Sharon. Initially, she hadn't run fast enough to escape her Essex-girl origins. Basildon had entertained her adequately enough for the first twenty two years of her life, by which time she had married good-old dependable Dave, who had patiently followed her around since school, knowing Sharon was meant to be "his girl". At sixteen, Dave had joined a local firm of Chartered Surveyors and, much to everyone's surprise, including his own, had proved rather good at the worthy but dull routines and absorbed the training so well that he achieved chartered status himself six years later. The firm sought to protect its investment by offering him a company car and Dave, overcome with joy, pursued Sharon with renewed ardour and an aggressive sports car to impress. In a moment of weakness brought on by the smell of leather from the Recaro seats in his new Ford XR3i, Sharon succumbed and agreed to marry him, finding herself safely ensconced in her Wimpey starter-home a year later, bored, lonely and frustrated.

Resolving to break her bond with Basildon, she furtively took a secretarial course in advance of announcing to Dave that she needed "to spread her wings" before settling down to have children. Joining a London secretarial agency, she shrewdly took a succession of temporary jobs to learn how office power and politics worked in different environments before happening upon a position at Diamond Chance, then the market-leading, US-based search firm. With a fearsome reputation for being able to shift the unshiftable, it had built up a considerable presence amongst the deal-doers in the City and was widely reviled by both competitors and clients for the arrogance of its consultants, one of whom was Hugo Reeve-Prior. It was a perfect grooming ground for Sharon, who had by now lost most of her Estuary English, only occasionally dropping an unguarded aitch when agitated or drunk. These days, of course, she was careful to be neither amongst work colleagues.

Dave was immensely proud of his wife's new airs and graces, the fact that she commuted daily to London, now wore clothes from Next rather than Topshop and had developed a taste for Italian food and Soave in place of the local curry house and rum & black. In all things, Sharon was increasingly influenced by Hugo Reeve-Prior, to whom she had initially been assigned as a temporary secretary following the sudden departure of Julia after the unfortunate incident with the black candidate. Sharon proved an efficient, speedy typist, was deferential and eager to please and impressed Reeve-Prior with her neatly-packaged figure and gamine good looks. Before long, he had invited her to go "temp-to-perm", convinced her to go blonde (both "collar and cuffs" for authenticity, he urged) advised her how "society gels" spent their time and money, given her a pay rise, and made it clear that there was a rise of a different sort available if she would care for it. This placed Sharon in a predicament: there was no doubt that she was outgrowing Dave, finding him dull and pedestrian compared to the brilliant butterflies amongst whom she now worked. And what did Basildon's bland suburban streets offer against the City's bright lights, wine bars and the girlie chatter of secretarial secrets? If she followed Hugo's brightly shining and ascending star, she could bathe in its reflected glow and her own career-path would similarly rise and shine; Hugo had promised this. Such a future appealed to her inner, suppressed Mr Hyde and greatly excited Sharon. But as for Dr Jekyll: she didn't want to hurt dull, dependable Dave and certainly didn't want to give up the security and future children which he offered and her bourgeois upbringing demanded. Sharon decided to cheat on him slightly, for a limited time, while she made herself indispensable to Hugo. One night, after working late with Hugo to complete a set of shortlist reports, she accepted his invitations to dinner, to a nightcap back at his Kensington flat, to a first tentative kiss and finally to his bed.

This consummation confirmed Sharon's place by Hugo's side at work, whilst allowing her Dave's side at home. Dave was content to reach his ceiling in the middle management sponge of his firm of surveyors, which had by now spread outwards from Essex and, thrillingly, conquered Kent, providing plenty of work for all who remained loyal. Hugo's plummy, upper-class confidence convinced an increasing number of clients to invest their trust in him and his name began to be whispered in the Members' Clubs of London, amongst old friends at the "In and Out" and new ones at the City of London Club. Enjoying her increasingly lucrative partnership with Hugo (he ensured she received the highest annual secretarial bonus) Sharon allowed her partnership with Dave to produce two children, Theresa and Daniel, in rapid succession.

Then came the day in early 1988 when Hugo quietly

confided to Sharon that he had been speaking to the impossibly grand doyens of UK headhunting, Archimedes Aspallan and Giles Bane, about establishing a subsidiary executive recruitment business to rival NB Selection, which was beginning to become noticed in the Sunday Times Executive Appointments Section as a purveyor of interesting sub-board level jobs for "people on the move". The eponymous employment of Aspallan and Bane's initials would steal a march by creating an alphabetically more advanced business moniker: AB Selection. It would make Hugo's decision considerably easier if Sharon would decide to join him as the second employee and *a director* in the new business. Further, it would be based in the West End and Sharon realised that she would be able to shop for clothes in Debenhams and Selfridges, even (during the sales) in some of the designer-labelled boutiques along Bond Street. She instantly agreed, suffering only a slight pang of guilt later that night when she remembered to tell Dave as he turned out the light.

So it was that from a small, two-roomed, un-serviced office in the basement of a best-before 1980 building in Stratton Street, the fastest-growing, most successful and most profitable executive recruitment business of the 1990s was born. Sensibly, because they were now serious people with a serious mission, Hugo and Sharon tacitly agreed to cease their occasional post-prandial, extra-marital trysts: they had too much to lose and too much to gain and the "affair" had only ever been driven by his lust and her expediency. Aspallan and Bane introduced them to a couple of "house" clients to get them started, and Hugo's contacts began to come through and offer him work, once they understood how serious he was about building the business. Sharon found the transition to managing assignments herself fairly painless, as Hugo had been an excellent mentor in every respect. Like him, she became a stickler for detail, ruthless with second-rate candidates ("I can assure you that this job is not right for you") and direct with clients ("Believe me, this candidate is the best the current market can offer"). Sharon began to feel quite accomplished and whilst she knew that she would never be Hugo's equal, at least she was now working in parallel, rather than under him, so to speak.

The business thrived and grew: as they hired new staff, they moved to bigger premises round the corner on Berkeley Street, which accommodated up to ten consultants in individual rooms, each with an attendant secretary. Christmas 1989 provided the first real office party and whilst it was still small and intimate enough for nobody to get out of hand, Sharon resisted the offer of "one for old times' sake" from Hugo. He did, however, confide in her that he was going to open a satellite office near to London ("in case it doesn't work and the troops have to be withdrawn") as part of the strategic plan to build AB Selection into a nationwide player. Sharon found herself volunteering to lead the project. It made sense: her ambition was not yet sated and she felt an increasing need to demonstrate that she could succeed on her own without, not because of, Hugo, for she had caught wind of whispers suggesting she owed her position as his confidante for reasons other than a strictly professional relationship; below sheets rather than above board. How dare they? She would show them! Besides, with Theresa and Daniel growing apace, she and Dave needed a bigger house and Sharon was determined to escape Basildon for good.

January saw Sharon in an ecstasy of activity, procuring both an office and a new home, the former in Uxbridge for its strategically pusillanimous proximity to London, the latter a four-bed detached with garden just outside St Albans, from where dependable Dave could still commute back to his firm in Basildon. There were good schools nearby, both state and private (Hugo urged her to send the children to private school, indicating that a portion of her annual bonus could be channelled tax-effectively by his accountant, should she wish to avail herself). The office was kitted out in AB Selection style (leather chairs, solid, faux-oak desks and occasional tables for the consultants, functional Staples-type furniture and grey steel filing cabinets for the secretaries). Sharon hired a "dragon-lady" as her secretary who in turn hired dowdy, downtrodden Irene to bully and to undertake the menial tasks that were beneath Dragon-lady. Dragon-lady preferred to be called Mrs Kinkaid, after her third and current husband (number one tragically taken early by cancer, the second by that bitch campanologist from the church circle) although she acknowledged a first name of Daphne to Sharon in a moment of weakness during her interview. Not that she was being interviewed, she told her husband, "it was more the other way round". Sharon also hired an aggressive "young turk", Gordon Sharpe, from Willard Wonks, the leading sales and marketing recruitment agency, before she and Hugo placed the advertisement which had brought Noone before her.

She reflected on their meeting as from her window she watched Noone reverse gently into a lamp-post before speeding hurriedly away. He had obviously failed as a Chief Executive, presiding over a grubby little business which he could not grow until he was bailed out by the plc selling it opportunistically from under him. He had been unable to find a job elsewhere so far, clearly was about to be made redundant and was probably getting desperate, so she would not have to offer him much more than his current salary. That was a plus. Also, he had been confident and articulate, a well-packaged product of a minor public school (vice-captain of cricket, no less) and red-brick university with the concomitant competitive sporting record, which Hugo would like. Compared to the other dross that the advertisement had flushed out of the sewer of Uxbridge and its environs, this guy shone like a diamond. They could do much worse: she would definitely ask Hugo to see him.

3. REEVE-PRIOR

"Heidrick & Struggles provides exceptional service and expertise to deliver effective leadership solutions for clients. We are the world's premier provider of senior-level executive search and leadership consulting services, including talent management, board building, executive on-boarding and M&A effectiveness".

HEIDRICK & STRUGGLES WEBSITE

Hugo Reeve-Prior was a very important man, even though he said it himself. Born into landed gentry and several hundred acres of prime Oxfordshire farmland, the silver spoon had remained firmly embedded in his palate as he gradually assumed his rightful place at the head of the family, as befits the number one son. The village school was "far too common", necessitating, from the age of four, a half-hour drive to Chieveley House, Pre-Prep School for Young Gentlemen. Usually Nanny undertook this vital daily task of transportation, although occasionally Daddy's Estate Manager, Dorridge, was entrusted with the valuable cargo. Duly pre-prepped, Hugo naturally went to board at St Trisstram's, aged eight, like his father before him and three preceding generations of the Reeve-Prior male offspring.

St Trisstram's was initially a shock to little Hugo's system: slight of build and stature, he never quite got on with the rough and tumble of rugger or its unique, boy-on-boy sport, Bully-Ho. He lacked ability in cricket and football (the latter was too coarse in any case) and as a result, was bullied for being "a bit of an outsider". One Flashman-like Fifth Former, Greville Sarky, made Hugo's life a misery for several terms. Hugo never forgot the black despair of lying in bed at night, fighting back the tears as he grimly anticipated the next day's relentless verbal and physical harrying. Until, that is, whilst making cocoa one night in the kitchen for his House Prefect, he persuaded a fellow Fag to allow him to slip caustic soda into Sarky's drink. The resultant throat burns necessitating two painful weeks in the San, quite distracted Sarky and he lost interest in Hugo thereafter.

St Trisstram's is a strange institution: primarily it presents a dog-eat-dog, merciless but ordered environment, honed by centuries of ritual, where the strong and roguish can thrive at the expense of the weak and principled; yet, simultaneously, it encourages eccentricity and provides a haven for the dilettante and the dandy. Across this dichotomy, it reveres manners and status and understands how important the social networks formed by the boys at school will be in their future careers. Boys were encouraged to send pictures of themselves to each other at birthdays, Christmas and at the end of the academic year, to cement friendships that would lead to connections "after school". To the visiting sports teams of lesser Public Schools, whose members were allocated one-by-one to an individual opponent, in whose room and amongst those smirking, simpering pictures the visitor had to change into sports kit, it was evidence that St Trisstram'sians were "a bunch of poofs". St Trisstram'sians knew better. Whilst incidents of sodomy may have been slightly over the national average owing to its single-sex status, above all, St Trisstram's taught them that they were *special*. They emerged unblinking into the real world aged eighteen or nineteen, protected by the knowledge that they were superior to the less fortunate plebs, over whom they were born to rule.

Over time, Hugo settled into the routine and found things at which he was less than hopeless. At home, Dorridge had taught Hugo how to shoot and by the time he was fourteen, there were few indigenous birds and beasts he hadn't killed. He had personally eliminated the local partridge population and knocked off several cats that had foolishly roamed within his sights. His prowess was soon spotted at St Trisstram's and he became a stalwart of the shooting team, becoming Captain in his last year. Similarly, his equestrian skills equipped him to ride with the school's pack of hounds and Sunday mornings were often pleasantly passed in pursuit of foxes to dismember. However, he discovered as a Wet-Bob, more precisely, as a cox, the talent which was to drive his career. Too small to become a genuine rower, he was placed in the stern of the boat by his Housemaster and there flourished. The large fellows who bowed and stroked, huffed and puffed, were boisterous but generally not very bright, and Hugo found they responded well to his terse commands and directions, delivered in the plummy voice which they had been bred to respect. It was positively Pavlovian. One of these hulking great brutes, Henry Ughyngton-Fitzhardynge (or "Huff" as he was gratefully known) became a firm friend.

On the constantly-changing, roiling and shapeless playing field of the Thames, Hugo developed a knack for knowing where the current would help or hinder, where the breeze might blow favourably and where speed-sapping eddies could destroy the carefully harnessed power of an Eight pulling in unison. Under his guidance, a succession of successful boats triumphed in Inter-House races, against local schools and finally, in the British National Schools' Championships. Hugo was no longer purely resented because of the good fortune of his birth but respected for his own achievements. It felt good, even though he knew it was his due.

The school ensured that all pupils were coached to maximise their potential for passing exams; its Guardians (Headmasters) were both proud of, and annually frightened of, St Trisstram's's long record of launching young men into the United Kingdom's finest universities. Despite its best efforts, some pupils were either naturally or wilfully academically disinclined; these had to go straight into Daddy's business, or dubious professions such as broking or reinsurance in the City, where the old school tie still spoke positively of its wearer and smoothly opened well connected doors. Though no intellectual, Hugo was close enough in his A'levels to be channelled down a well-worn St Trisstram'sian path to St Kitts College, Cambridge, whose Dons granted him first an interview and then a place, having much admired his sound breeding, coxing exploits and father's money, not necessarily in that order.

Cambridge was "great fun" for Hugo. He developed an eye for the girls whom he charmed with his deep blue, deeply English Alvis TD 21 drophead, deeply English voice and taste in fine French wines. Enthusiastically, Hugo lost his virginity to a jolly hockey player from Roedean and Girton in a punt moored against a secluded bank on a lazy June Sunday afternoon. Cometh the summer, cometh the man. He maintained his friendship with Huff, who had also gone up to Cambridge, and continued to cox, made the college First VIII in his second year and only just missed out on the seat in the Blue Boat to a wretched little fellow from Wolfson with a ghastly Birmingham accent. Although the History degree course did hamper his pursuit of pulchritude and bibulous pleasure, actually Hugo was interested in the derring-do which had made Britain great and created the Empire. He had been brought up to believe in the "God-given right of the Englishman" and as far as he was concerned, the world would be a better place if it were still predominantly coloured pink. Whilst it had always been assumed that Hugo would return to run the estate at some stage, there was also an expectation that he would "see a bit of the world first". The idea formed that it might be useful to see how bad it really was by serving in Her Majesty's Armed Forces for a while.

Armed initially with a third-class Honours "Gentleman's Degree", Hugo found to his dismay that the cavalry regiments, to which he was most inclined, no longer rode horses but tanks, to which he was most certainly disinclined: he couldn't possibly sit inside a tin can with the sweaty hoi-polloi. The elite outfits found him too small and the infantry definitely "wasn't him". The RAF were "Johnny-come-lateleies" and not worthy of his attention but the Senior Service decided he had potential as a submariner and offered him a commission. After some initial misgivings, during which he had to overcome a fear that he was heading for a tin can after all, Hugo convinced himself that being under water was similar to being on it, signed up and went below. Despite the gloomy depths at which he was trained to work and spent much of his time, Hugo's natural air of authority and rower-management skills served him well; he encouraged and rewarded teamwork, cracked down immediately and strongly on any breaches of naval or tinfish discipline and kept just far enough aloof from his fellow officers. He tolerated the inferior classes which made up "his men", vaguely nauseated by their constant swearing, tattoos and occasional earrings but he kept his own counsel, watched, learned and grew shrewd enough to turn an avuncular blind eye to their drunken and debauched onshore antics ("what goes ashore, stays ashore") and onboard proclivities such as his sailors' "spunk runs", the gaps beside the bunks where bongo mags, soiled grundies and tissues into which a man may have blown his hose, were kept. His rise was steady if unspectacular and in 1978 he became a Lieutenant Commander of a Churchill class nuclear submarine.

That was as good as it got. Just before the Falklands War, which would have catapulted him forward career-wise or killed him, disillusioned by the constant Defence cuts handed down by Governments horrified by the increasing Trade deficit, Hugo resigned his commission.

An un-buoyed ex-sailor who didn't sink the Belgrano was not a particularly valuable commodity in mid 1982. Despite the "tinfish" existence, The Navy had broadened Hugo's horizons and he was reluctant to go straight back to the estate. One night, he caught up with Huff in Town over a few drinks and a couple of willing ex-debutantes with large vital organs. Huff had "gone into banking" after Cambridge.

"The City is the place to be, old chap" advised Huff. "Trouble is, all you're good for is ridin', shootin', rowin' and blowing up Russia from underwater."

Hugo protested that he knew a fair bit about wine and farming.

"Yes, but you don't actually know anything useful. That was fine a few years ago, but nowadays they take barrow-boys from the East End and make 'em millionaires inside two years. And they are all ahead of you in the queue."

Hugo was forced to assess his prospects against the stark reality revealed by Huff and was beginning to think that the family estate was looking like the only option after all. But Huff continued:

"Why don't you have a look at one of these MBA things; they seem to be all the rage and add £20k to a chap's salary overnight."

This got Hugo thinking; he investigated the options and bought his way onto a one year course at Blandford, a forum for re-styling cast-adrift military types, which was delighted to accept a Cambridge graduate with money. It took hard-hitting, cynical, ex-officers and by feeding them a diet of budget creation, cash-flow breakdowns, cost control, P & L accounts, M & A scenarios, marketing plans and product life-cycle management all wrapped up in case-studies and spreadsheets, turned them into hard-hitting, cynical would-be Chief Executives ready to be unleashed upon a grateful world.

In reality, Blandford's graduates found themselves competing just as hard but at a slightly more exclusive level for the jobs for which they now considered themselves qualified. MBA schools were turning out their products in ever-increasing numbers and having invested not inconsiderable sums in pursuit of the keys to successful business leadership, these products felt they were owed the chance to put theory into practice. As ever, there were not enough jobs to go round. Once again, Hugo debated his prospects with Huff over dinner at Claridges and a pair of enthusiastic Sloane Rangers, whose rocket-sockets were primed to receive gentry such as Huff and Hugo.

"It's so bloody frustrating," complained Hugo, "I know I can run a business now, but nobody will give me a chance because I haven't run a business."

"Yes, that's the jolly-old Catch-22; perfect isn't it? Tell you what: why don't you think about doing what I am doing now- no previous experience necessary." Huff went on to explain that six months ago he had been rung up by a nice chap from Diamond Chance, a firm of "City headhunters" as he put it, which was looking for new consultants, preferably with a City background, to help cope with the avalanche of business "rolling in over the transom". This was a direct result of Margaret Thatcher's belief that a free-market economy operates best unfettered by regulation, self-correcting by market forces. This had unleashed a "greed is good" philosophy to howl through the financial and commercial sectors. Huff, beginning to tire of the long hours demanded by investment banking, had been immediately interested.

"They are a bunch of Septics, of course, but you have to admire their balls; they know what they want, they are good at what they do, and they are building a reputation." He had joined Diamond Chance and was enjoying himself immensely.

Hugo considered what he knew about Americans: to be avoided at all costs in live military engagements owing to gung-ho tendency towards "friendly-fire"; murder their own Presidents; vote in film stars as Presidents; cannot spell properly; no breeding or cuisine (although it seemed to have a fledgling wine industry). He also recalled a terrifying news clip from TV where a roving reporter had asked everyday Americans simple questions:

"Name a country that starts with a 'U'?" produced Yugoslavia, Utah and Utopia; nobody mentioned the

United States.

"What is the religion of Israel?" rendered Israeli, Protestant, Islamic and "Catholic probably". Buddhist monks were apparently also Islamic, America won the Vietnam War, Fidel Castro was a singer, a triangle had either no sides, four or one, and the currency of the United Kingdom (of which one interviewee had never heard) was possibly "American money" or "Queen Elizabeth's money". The portents were not good; Hugo was not sure they were really his sort of people.

"The fact you haven't actually done anything in the City won't matter," Huff told Hugo encouragingly, "they will like your breeding and contact network." He was right; Hugo barely had to lie about anything during the interviews and he enjoyed the awe he felt they felt in his presence. The CEO had been to Harvard and seemed sharp enough, whilst the UK Managing Partner was actually English, albeit from Wellington School. Despite his early misgivings, Hugo became a "Diamond Chancer".

Several short but profitable years rushed by, during which Hugo found time to marry Melissa Fortescue, a childhood sweetheart from the Young Farmers' Club whom he had savagely neglected during the sowing of his wild oats, but who had remained faithful to her dream of marrying him. Verdantly fertile, she rapidly presented Hugo with Lucinda and Candida and was then told to stop, Hugo fearing that the further pursuit of a son-and-heir might only lead to more daughters. His natural confidence and leadership skills helped him settle in at Diamond Chance and things were going pretty well until the unfortunate incident of the black candidate.

Julia, his secretary, had booked into his diary an interview with someone called St John Baptiste for the position of Director of Corporate Communications for an old-established, traditional English merchant bank. With hindsight, Hugo realised that the name sounded slightly foreign and the final "e" on the surname should have set alarm bells ringing loudly. Despite a decent-reading CV,

Hugo had been appalled to discover, when Julia had brought Mr Baptiste to the door of his office, *that he was black*. His client would have been horrified had Mr Baptiste appeared on the shortlist with Hugo's recommendation. After a difficult fifteen minutes during which Hugo asked meaningless questions about the wretched fellow's upbringing, he resolved to grasp the nettle firmly in both hands. After a pause to signify deep thought, Hugo leaned forward and looked Mr Baptiste straight between the eyes:

"I can see you are a man who admires plain-talking, aren't you?" he postulated, expecting the answer Yes.

"Yes," Mr Baptiste replied.

"Good," Hugo continued, "well, let me be plain: this job is not right for you. But," he continued smoothly, unruffled by Mr Baptiste's punctured expression, "why don't we spend some time considering what *might* be right for you?" Twenty minutes later, Mr Baptiste had left quite jauntily, resolving to look for more suitable positions in manufacturing companies in the Coventry area. Hugo had given Julia a rocket for wasting his time with an unsuitable candidate and she had resigned in tears on the spot.

Then, miraculously, Angel Temps had sent him his very own angel, Sharon Ridell. From the start, he had admired her efficient, no-nonsense approach, work ethic and desire to progress. Her neatly-packaged frame and gamine good looks were a bonus. Theirs was a relationship both of necessity and convenience and they invested equal shares, he the mentor, she his willing pupil. He was gratified to discover that his old bachelor touch had not been lost and that she yielded her knickers relatively readily when he knocked on that particular door. Their fortunes waxed at Diamond Chance until Hugo felt a reawakening of the desire to run a business, which had lain dormant since the post-MBA rebuffs. He believed there was a gap in the market for a high quality consultancy offering to fill executive positions for clients through striking advertisements placed prominently in the Sunday

Times Appointments Section. He had noted that NB Selection had recently emerged in this niche and stood out amongst the dross. Hugo felt this was a growing market with plenty of space and he wanted a piece of the action. Hugo took his plan, tidily packaged and presented thanks to his MBA training, to his American bosses, whom he felt were bound to receive his "out-of-the-box thinking" enthusiastically.

They were totally unimpressed by this strange cul-de-sac Hugo wanted to turn into and wanted nothing to do with it. Diamond Chance would remain a top-level search firm undistracted by faddish forays into uncharted waters that would only dilute the brand. Everyone in America knew that advertising didn't work, except at pond-life level.

"Forget it, buddy," the Harvard MBA told Hugo, "just stick to the knitting and do what we do best." Hugo resolved to prove to the ungrateful bastards that he was right and called Archie Aspallan, whom he had discovered was also an Old St Trisstram'sian. Aspallan, urbane, tall, fit, square of jaw and broad of shoulder was initially as appalled as Hugo's current masters at this down-market and rather tacky idea, although he didn't let on and promised to "run it through" Giles Bane, his business's co-owner. Bane, the more pragmatic of the two and closer to the wider commercial/industrial marketplace, surprised Aspallan by believing the idea had merit and asking to meet the upstart Reeve-Prior.

Although neither of them wished to have anything directly to do with Hugo's proposed new business, they became intrigued by his enthusiasm for it and purred at the thought of stealing a consultant from those arrogant Yanks at Diamond Chance. They could see little harm in bringing him under their umbrella, splashing him a loan to play with and allowing him to establish a bastard offspring. There were, however, strict ground rules: it must be kept separate from their search business with a different name and brand, could not offer search to its clients, must be self-funding and not expect any referred business from their clients. If Hugo succeeded in building something, great, the company would have a broader base and provide more profit for them; if not, they would quickly get rid of him. They assured him of their full backing, wished him good luck and agreed to his two-year business plan and budget. Between themselves, Aspallan and Bane agreed they would give him six months.

It was no surprise to Hugo that AB Selection flourished from day one, for all his upbringing, education and training had created in him an absolute certainty a) that he was a superior being, and b) that he was destined to be highly successful. Until now he had been held back by the strictures of, firstly, the hierarchical nature of the Navy and, secondly, by not yet being fully in charge of anything. AB Selection was that thing. He was now able to repay faithful Sharon (unfaithful only to her husband) by making her a fellow Director in the new business and was pleased that his careful grooming paid off as she began to flourish as a fully-fledged Consultant; the Essex girl had come a long way and was not going back. The connection with Aspallan, Bane Consultants was undoubtedly useful, as it allowed AB Selection to claim the pedigree of a well-regarded firm and, contrary to non-expectation, Archie Aspallan and Giles Bane each introduced a client in need of Hugo's new service.

AB Selection rapidly expanded in line with Hugo's ego from the basement in Stratton Street to the new premises in Berkeley Street. Radiating self-belief, passion and drive, Hugo found it relatively easy to attract those who lacked these attributes to his cause. Whilst casting Sharon off to her first management position in Uxbridge, Hugo was feverishly busy, planning other offices around the UK and interviewing personally every potential new recruit for the business. Hugo's control-freak tendencies had found the most perfect outlet to express themselves. His first major hire was his old friend, Huff, whom he snaffled from Diamond Chance as soon as he was able and placed in charge of developing Financial Services as a revenue stream: they both knew that that was where quick money was. He was also keen to build up a regional presence to rival that of NB Selection. Thus it was that he came to be interviewing Adam Noone in his office in Berkeley Street at the end of March 1990.

He had been reasonably impressed by Noone's CV and Sharon had told him that the trawl through the slough of Uxbridge and its environs had produced none better than Noone. In the flesh, the man was physically unimpressive and he lacked the outright arrogance that often signified a successful headhunter. He was self-deprecating to a point which obscured the competitive spirit he claimed to possess and at which his amateur sporting achievements hinted. The tinpot gas business which he had run sounded perfectly awful but it did demonstrate that he "had something", that he must be relatively well-organised and Hugo didn't blame him for wanting something different. He was personable and articulate enough, with a sense of humour and ready (perhaps too ready?) smile, so if he could sell, Hugo felt he would be able to shape him into a decent consultant. He asked his killer question:

"So why should I risk my reputation and hire you for my business?" Don't say Because I have always been interested in headhunting, he thought. No-one has ever "always been interested in headhunting".

"I suppose I have always been interested in headhunting," replied Noone, before attempting to justify this obvious lie. Time to slap him down.

"What we do at AB Selection is not headhunting," Hugo interrupted coldly. "It is advertising-led executive selection. It is applicable where the universe of potential candidates is large and unknown. Advertising allows them to self-select against a set of predefined criteria. Headhunting is only appropriate where potential candidates are known, either because the job is so senior or so specialised; we call it executive search and it is what Aspallan, Bane, our sister company, does. Incidentally, we do not use the word 'recruitment' either; that is what agencies do. We are management consultancies specialising in executive resourcing." Noone seemed unperturbed by the lesson in semantics.

"I see," he said, digesting this interesting and exciting comparison with Bain & Co, McKinsey and BCG. He hadn't seen recruitment in that light, but yes, "executive resourcing" sounded more upmarket and more correctly positioned in the exalted company of those paragons of strategic consultancy.

"Would you say you were a man of principle and conscience?" continued Hugo. Noone spotted a test of character when there was one.

"I sincerely hope so," he replied quickly.

"In that case I wonder about your suitability for executive resourcing," said Hugo. Noone was dumbfounded.

"But, but I thought that AB Selection and Aspallan Bane stood for quality..." he stammered.

"Never confuse quality with principles or conscience, Adam," replied Hugo tartly. "To succeed in this business you cannot afford to be too precious about principles or conscience. Our job is to challenge comfort zones, disrupt the status quo, elevate and promote 'movers and shakers', discriminate against the merely mundane. You must leave your conscience behind and learn to live with ambiguity. Do you think you can do that Adam?" Without hesitation, Noone said that he could.

Hugo reflected on this expectant, hopelessly naïve fellow in front of him. He seemed ready, willing and able to give this new career a shot and prepared to work from Uxbridge. Despite Noone's display of false eagerness, Hugo was inclined to give him the benefit of the doubt and offer him a job. First, however, he would let a couple of consultants meet Noone before allowing Giles Bane a casting vote; although Hugo was more than ready to make decisions, he was also a pragmatist and there was safety in numbers.

4. GILES BANE

"Korn/Ferry is a premier global provider of talent management solutions and delivers an array of solutions that help clients to identify, deploy, develop, retain and reward their talent. Korn/Ferry consultants... work closely with clients and candidates to craft successful human capital strategies and solutions. The firm's seamless global network, time-proven <u>search process</u> and broad industry and regional expertise provide the <u>competitive advantage</u> necessary to recruit and develop world-class leadership teams".

KORN FERRY INTERNATIONAL WEBSITE

Noone was a fast walker. He hated pavements filled with other pedestrians who got in his way, particularly American tourists and shoppers; they would meander aimlessly from corner to corner, consumed by meaningless chatter, often laden with an unnecessary number of conspicuously-branded shopping bags and invariably stopping to consult a pocket-map, so interrupting Noone's direct and purposeful strides. Oh to be Leslie Nielsen in Airplane, carving a picaresque and savage swathe with elbows and fists through hordes of peace-loving, orange-clad Hare Krishnas. As he manhandled his way up Davis Street towards the zoo of Oxford Street and Bond Street Tube, he reviewed the meeting with Reeve-Prior, seeing nothing to make him pause or falter. The more he heard and thought about this "not really headhunting" malarkey, the more he fancied giving it a shot. Reeve-Prior certainly took no prisoners: he had been focused, incisive and frank, answering Noone's questions in that rich, clipped, voice. Granted, he was a bit of a stuffed shirt and was very sure of himself; Noone wouldn't have been surprised if Reeve-Prior had been to St Trisstram's and he was sure he had been in the military. He had certainly put Noone straight about headhunting: Noone hoped that his naivety on that subject would be viewed by Reeve-Prior as understandable and forgivable, but the more he thought about it, the more he felt his faux-pas there would be given a black mark. As he reached the entrance to Bond Street Tube, his pace had slowed, reflecting his uncertainty.

Bond Street Tube, along with the entire Jubilee Line, was shut because of "passenger action". Noone could never forgive the selfish bastards who threw themselves under trains on the day he was travelling by public transport. If they had reached the decision to self-terminate, they should be able to do so free of moral encumbrances, but Noone was not happy for them to disrupt his and others' lives through the act of ending their own. They should have the decency to top themselves quietly at home. Maybe they should build a short, self-contained, suicides-only Tube line at Neasden with a train passing once every hour on the hour. The jumpers would be allotted places on the platform on a first-come, first-served basis, outward tickets only of course. The train would run through a giant washer at the end of the line to emerge sparklingly clean and ready for its next "passenger action".

Forced to share the Number 11 bus to Marylebone with The Great Unwashed, Noone reluctantly persuaded his mind to return to the interview from the contemplation of organising more efficient suicides. He felt he had been suitably enthusiastic about the prospect of working for Sharon Ridell in Uxbridge, but did that imperceptibly raised eyebrow from Reeve-Prior indicate that he had been *too* enthusiastic? Had he been convincing about his desire to change career track or was Reeve-Prior's fleeting smile a sure sign that he had been unconvincing? He burned with embarrassment at the thought of how gauche his conversation had been and arrived home convinced he had indeed been unconvincing. He told his wife "it had gone as well as can be expected" and resigned himself to the rejection letter.

The following day, Sharon Ridell called him at work and asked him how he felt the meeting had gone:

"Difficult to say, fine from my point of view," he lied, knowing he must remain upbeat whilst conveying his sincere and continuing interest. "Have you heard anything yet?"

"Well, yes actually," she replied seductively, "Hugo liked you a lot. He thinks you've got the right stuff. But he'd like you to meet Giles and a couple of the others just to make sure you feel comfortable taking this step." Noone was overjoyed that his fears had proved groundless and that Reeve-Prior had found him neither too enthusiastic nor unconvincing.

"Just a word of advice," Sharon continued smoothly, "Hugo felt you shouldn't be too enthusiastic in front of Giles or he will be unconvinced. Be interested but neutral, don't oversell." She went on to give him the number of Bane's secretary for him to arrange the appointment and confirmed that she would also line up a couple of the consultants for him to meet on the same day.

"Good luck; I really hope we can close this off quickly. 'Bye for now." She sounded very positive, thought Noone, feeling chipper and revitalised, as he replaced the phone. It was good that she seemed certain about him.

Sharon wasn't certain about Noone; Hugo had been unconvinced about Noone's commitment to becoming a recruitment consultant; surely he would miss the cut-and-thrust of running a business and the status of being a CEO? For her part, keen to build her mini-empire in Uxbridge, she needed a good hire but Noone seemed almost too good to be true. She would be interested in what Giles Bane had to say.

Giles Bane was in many ways the perfect foil to Archie Aspallan, or rather, the sabre to Aspallan's rapier. Where Aspallan was urbane, Bane brought Northern grit handed down by several generations of textile mill owners. Grammar school educated, he had entered the family business as it entered the relentless decline of the '70s. By the time he had become Managing Director, it was clear to him that its days were numbered and he sold it to Coates Viyella in the nick of time, securing a reasonable fortune at the expense of his workers' livelihoods. Not liking the industrial wastelands that were poisoning the life of the North, he had sold the family seat for a more modest, seven bedroomed manor house in Hertfordshire and joined the conglomerate, Chemicals International Limited, then the darling of the Stock Exchange, "because he could afford to". His blunt decisiveness, lack of regard for what others thought of him and early experience of ordering people what to do, stood him in good stead at the head of a succession of mergers and acquisitions, fuelled by ever-increasing profits, as CIL efficiently went about its business of quietly polluting the world. Eventually, this industrial juggernaut began to slow down with the onset of the downturn in the early '80s. The Board decided to extract maximum value by splitting it up and Bane found his remaining ambition of becoming a FTSE 100 Chief Executive thwarted. Rather than languishing in the rump of the businesses left behind, he resolved to get out with his head held high, implying in future that the top job "had been promised to him" until market forces had intervened.

One Friday, whilst lunching at Boodles, Bane bumped into Archie Aspallan over a post-prandial brandy and cigar in the Gentlemen's Lounge. He knew him quite well through the dinner parties of mutual friends and was aware of his pedigree and reputation as a smooth operator in the City. Someone who could get things done. However, he hadn't particularly warmed to his southern, aristocratic, superior air and was therefore a trifle surprised to hear himself being propositioned about a new business venture.

"Yes, I am getting bored with the City; once you've had the Porsche and the Bentley there is only so much you need to spend the bonus on, isn't there?" Aspallan drawled, off-handedly. "I'm thinking of cutting loose and setting up a show of my own with a few like-minded souls. What do you know about headhunting, Giles?"

Bane had had little experience of it, being a self-made man through the money he had inherited and then made from the sale of the family business and the carefully nurtured contacts which parachuted him into CIL. Having little experience of it made him an expert in his view:

"Bloody pariahs if you ask me. Just glorified estate agents or insurance salesmen."

"That's just where you are wrong," countered Aspallan, "they actually provide an immensely valuable service, making connections where none previously exist, allowing confidential approaches whilst protecting the identities of both parties, and, crucially, they broker the job and the offer negotiations to the mutual benefit of all. They work alongside the most senior captains of industry and can take a quiet satisfaction from placing this peer group into positions of extreme power and renown."

"But what if they get it wrong?"

"My dear chap, in that case it is always the client's or candidate's fault for moving the goalposts. But the most incredible thing is that they get paid an absolute fortune *even if they fail to find a successful candidate!*"

Bane was suddenly very interested. It sounded like money for old rope.

"The key to being a successful headhunter," Aspallan continued, "is to have an extensive network of friends in high places. And that is where I come in, and so do you, if you are interested." Aspallan went on to explain how it had dawned on him that he could use his network far more efficiently for the gathering of greater personal gain. Early soundings had suggested that this network would support him, were he to set himself up in executive and non-executive search. If he could find several others with complementary rather than overlapping networks, a powerful force would emerge, becoming indispensable to the British financial services, commercial and industrial communities.

"I have heard good things about you Giles: people tell me you are ruthless, very self-confident, independently-minded, thick-skinned and driven by money. These are key attributes. Most importantly, you also have an extensive network out there in industry to match my financial services clout. It's a dream ticket. Will you join me?"

Bane proved good to those attributes so prized by Archie Aspallan by initially playing hard-to-get, then driving a hard bargain, such that Aspallan had to concede an equal share in the business to him. So it came to pass in 1982 that Aspallan, Bane, Consultants became the first British search firm to set up defiantly in opposition to the established US contingent of Korn Ferry, Heidrick & Struggles, Russell Reynolds, Spencer Stuart and Diamond Chance.

Physically they were chalk and cheese: Aspallan tall, angular, broad-shouldered (rowing at St Trisstram's) and trim (owing to at least three hours of competitive squash per week plus some social tennis played for lunch or dinner); Bane shorter, jowly and softer round the edges, verging on corpulent. Any form of sport was to him "an-absolute-bloody-athema", a waste of money-making time, although he conceded that several hours could be utilised profitably on a golf course doing deals and had hired Peter Alliss once for personal tuition to manufacture him a socially-acceptable swing. Together, though, Aspallan and Bane proved unstoppable. They gathered a small coterie of well-connected friends, each with a productive network, hired a high-quality research team of Oxbridge grads to keep them abreast of every nuance and rumour in the markets (as well as informing where the rising stars were) and a complementary flock of top-class, purposeful secretaries with society backgrounds and polished, upper-crust voices. They blithely and unashamedly charged fees that were identical to the large American outfits: one third of the first year's anticipated package divided into three equal tranches payable on commencement, 30 days and 60 days. If the negotiated package turned out to be more than originally anticipated, then Aspallan, Bane would add a fourth "uplift" fee tranche of the balance to a third of the actual package. Expenses of 12% would be levied on every invoice. There would be no refund of any fee.

The amazing thing was that on the client side, executives tasked with senior-level hiring actually went along with this sort of daylight robbery. But then again, most recruitment was delegated to the dump marked "Personnel Department", where those who couldn't do anything else ended up. The Personnel Department was more than happy to spend money that didn't belong to it on finding someone else to blame if the recruitment exercise went wrong. It was called "armour-plating the corporate trouser". Headhunters were a convenient arse-cover for those afraid of making a real business decision. Unsurprisingly, given that sort of a licence to print money, the business flourished.

Within a couple of years they had relocated the office to a floor of some 5,000 square feet on St James's Square, situated, ironically Bane thought, next door to Chatham House, the home of the Royal Institute of International Affairs, whose famous Rule encouraged openness and debate. How different from headhunting, which was by nature covert and encouraged lies. One of Bane's early assignments opened his eyes to this: he had been asked by the Chairman of Floris, then a FTSE 25 mining company, to find a replacement CEO without alerting the incumbent to the fact that he was to be "terminated with extreme prejudice". If word had escaped into the market, the share price would have taken a severe dive. Bane had to sign a confidentiality agreement and not even his secretary was supposed to know. Of course, he couldn't operate like that but as he confided in her about the task, he warned, only half-jokingly, that he would have to kill her if she was indiscreet. He was not allowed any research help, couldn't mention the client company name to candidates and had to correspond with the company Chairman through a PO Box number. The client only ever phoned him at home in the evening. Amazingly, he had been able to attract three souls intrigued by "what this once-in-a-lifetime opportunity" could do for their careers. Their subsequent meetings with the client were held in hotels at weekends and one was duly appointed to the role. On the day that the announcement was made public, Bane had instructed his broker to buy shares in Floris at the moment they faltered at the news of the removal of its CEO. His replacement CEO performed well over the next two years and Bane was able to sell his shares at a tidy profit. His secretary, perhaps truly fearing for her life, left soon after. No sense of humour, Bane supposed.

It was a golden age for "the old school tie" networks and, pre-computer, mobile phones and email, one in which the headhunter's "little black book of contacts" ruled supreme. The traditional ties that created loyalty between employer and employee (a job for life with a final salary pension on retirement at 55-60 in return for a life of obedience and acceptance of the hierarchy) were loosening. The word "redundancy" had appeared like a miasmic alien presence and had created great fear throughout the workforce of UK plc. As a result, the more forward-looking executives had begun to seek a job-move before one was thrust upon them from an unwelcome, unanticipated and disadvantaging direction. This created the fertile ground into which the headhunters had seeded themselves, put down roots and from where they were now fruiting luxuriantly.

Aspallan, Bane developed a reputation for "getting things done" and was appreciated by its clients, most of whom had begun as close friends or business acquaintances, although they were referred to an increasingly wide audience. Tenacity became a watchword and Bane himself pioneered the tactic of finding out when potential candidates went on holiday, so that he could arrange to see them or call them the day after they had returned, when they were low in spirit and vulnerable to the temptation of a more rewarding job prospect. In those days, the Aspallan, Bane consultants did not delegate candidate contact to researchers and would make all the phone calls themselves. Bane would strike like a python, wrapping his coils of mellifluous promise around his victims until they were suffocated by the seductive squeeze of the job with more money, more challenge, more future. Slowly, they would surrender, recognising that Giles Bane was right: they were undervalued and hence underpaid by their current employers; they were being prevented from realising their true potential and their prospects looked meagre compared to the riches being offered by Bane's client. Bane was industrious and thorough; increasingly, amongst the denizens of FTSE boards, the receipt of a solicitous call from Giles Bane was appreciated with quiet, smug satisfaction, like a badge of honour, proof that even if your own company didn't recognise the great job you were doing, at least somebody did. Bane particularly enjoyed the thrill of a difficult chase, such as when a freight-forwarding company engaged him to find a new CEO for its Asia-Pacific region, where it was number two in the market. Bane was told not to bother approaching the CEO of the market-leader, as, although he was shit-hot, he would not be interested in this job. Of course, Bane could not resist making the call to this most obvious of candidates from whom he had been warned off, and, three months later, delivered him triumphantly like a turkey at Christmas to the astonished and ever-grateful client.

The only cloud on the horizon was the intense personal rivalry that had sprung up between Bane and Aspallan; it began as a relatively healthy annual race to achieve the highest billings. The loser would buy the winner dinner at a place of his choosing and in the early years Le Gavroche, Le Manoir aux Quat' Saisons, Petrus and the Waterside Inn were plundered of their finest food and wine with honours even. Then came the year of Aspallan's million-pound fee: with one phone call he moved the City's then-best fund manager from the world's largest hedge fund to the second largest for a guaranteed remuneration package of three million pounds. Naturally, Aspallan's fee was a third. The champagne flowed freely in the office that day, with everyone basking in Aspallan's extraordinary achievement. Bane was shattered; he could never achieve fees like that from the industrial sector. The canker of jealousy grew at Aspallan's great good fortune in working amongst the financial services community, where salaries were outrageously high (although not as high as footballers', admittedly) and the fees correspondingly mouth-watering. That year, having trounced Bane in the fee-race, Aspallan rubbed salt into the festering sore of Bane's resentment by choosing as his prize a trip to La Coupole on the Boulevard du Montparnasse in Paris, where he enjoyed the finest oysters from Cancale, followed by Edouard Artzner's whole foie gras in duck juice, with truffles, mustard seeds and spring onion, washed down by an elegant but persistent Moret-Nominé Puligny-Montrachet Premier Cru Foliatières and a velvety and harmonious 1966 Pessac-Léognan Chateau Haut-Brion, all at Bane's considerable expense. It was during this meal that Bane, watching his companion's esurient enjoyment of the epicurean spread, decided that he couldn't stand Archie Aspallan. Whilst he, Bane, conveniently ignoring the inheritance which had set him on his way, had worked hard in the "real world" to build up his network, Aspallan had merely been born into the right family and gone to the right school. Toffee-nosed bastard. The return flight to London, First Class, natch was untroubled by convivial conversation and thereafter, relations cooled to the point where communication between them was usually conducted through their secretaries passing messages to each other.

Nevertheless, the business continued to grow and when Hugo Reeve-Prior had arrived on their doorstep from Diamond Chance with his harebrained scheme for exploiting a downmarket niche in the market, realising that Aspallan was unimpressed by his proposition, Bane, on principle, decided to back him. Sure, Reeve-Prior was another "stuffed shirt", but he was so convinced by his own invincibility it was worth allowing him a little rope to hang himself. He persuaded Aspallan to give Reeve-Prior six months, told Reeve-Prior he had two years and sat back to watch the fun. Astonishingly, the business took off and flew; he had misjudged Reeve-Prior who wasn't an empty-headed, ex-navy yahoo after all, but a clever, prescient, astute businessman who was now contributing profitable additional revenue to their coffers. Bane and Aspallan were content to allow him to expand AB Selection as it had rapidly become self-funding. Reeve-Prior had opened an office in Uxbridge of all places (it was once said of its citizens "They will steal the very teeth out of your mouth as you walk through the streets.") and there was talk of adding a string of strategically-placed regional offices around the country. If AB Selection overtook NB Selection, they might actually be able to sell the whole lot on. Bane could almost smell the salty, sea air from his retirement yacht. He was happy to show willing from time to time by agreeing to interview PLSs (Possible Lambs to the Slaughter, as they called potential consultant recruits) and here he was, seated behind his huge mahogany desk reviewing the CV of Adam Noone.

Bane enjoyed his desk; its size demanded respect from those lesser mortals called before it, and Bane kept it free of clutter, the better to appreciate its wide expanses. In these pre-a-PC-on-every-desk days, a telephone, Rolodex business card holder, yellow writing pad, fountain pen and gold propelling pencil were the only artifacts allowed to sully its pristine acreage. His In-tray, Out-tray and other papers were banished to a sideboard running down the wall behind his plush, leather Georgian wing chair. Interviewing from behind his desk gave Bane a sense of immense power. Safe behind his desk, he stood up and proferred a pudgy but well manicured hand as Noone was introduced through the door by Bane's slightly superior secretary. In her view, working for Bane elevated her beyond those whom she ushered in to see him, in her brisk, brusque, efficient manner. Visitors found her overbearing and somewhat supercilious but Noone hardly noticed her cold, unsmiling eyes, impressed as he duly was by the size of Bane's room and the desk planted imposingly three-quarters of the way across its length. Having shaken hands, he sat down on the single straight-backed chair facing the aircraft-carrier of a desk, whilst Bane settled back into the embrace of a matchingly large, green, leather armchair.

Noone nervously observed an avuncular sort of chap with a large head, thick, almost-white hair and half-moon reading glasses. He surprised Noone by having a northern accent; somehow Noone had expected the fruity tones of a Reeve-Prior which he was beginning to believe was de rigueur for headhunters. Bane quizzed Noone about his career in a down-to-earth fashion before asking him if he had any questions.

"Well, I understand that the recruitment market is split into three segments, with database agencies at the bottom, selection in the middle and search at the top. What distinguishes the firms in each segment?"

Ah, that was tricky, thought Bane. All the firms spent money producing expensive-looking brochures printed on premium-grade paper and illustrated with high quality photographs, usually in black-and-white for effect. These brochures each demanded that the reader acknowledge how unusual and superior was the firm, whose logo was embossed on the front cover. In spirit and pretty much in fact, they were all identical. They all trumpeted how they treated clients individually, assignments originally, candidates professionally and everything under the sun, discreetly. All these firms possessed unique insights, first-class research and support functions, the best service ethos and the highest-calibre consultants in the market. It was all so much bullshit. Actually, the only difference was the personality of each consultant and the client either disliked you, in which case you would never win any work there, or liked you, which gave you a chance. Best not to disillusion him too soon, Bane thought; give him the standard patter:

"It all boils down to three things: the quality of your people, attention to detail and the desire to get the job done. We are the best because we hire the best, both for our clients, so they keep coming back, and for ourselves, so that we can provide the best service." Bane impressed himself by how sincere he sounded. He watched as Noone digested the import of these words before he raised another reasonable question:

"How long does it take to establish oneself as an executive resourcing consultant?" he asked, remembering Hugo's definition. Bane contrasted his own brilliant beginnings with the chances of the poor, eager fool in front of him, with no useful network of which to speak.

"Hugo and Sharon will pass you work to begin with so that you can develop your assignment handling and client and candidate management skills. It will take you two years to become properly self-sustaining." Bane knew that if it took that long, it was unlikely that Noone would remain employed by AB Selection. Grudgingly, he'd give him the usual six months. Gratefully noting, from the large wall-clock mounted strategically behind Noone's head, that half an hour had elapsed, he brought the interview to an end.

"Anyway, I am really just the rubber stamp; I understand Hugo and Sharon are keen to hire you, so I wish you the best of luck. If you want advice at any time, do call me, won't you?" he offered magnanimously, knowing it would never happen. He stood up, walked the mile or so to the front of his desk, shook hands again with Noone, ushered him to the door and called his snooty secretary to show Noone to the lift. Giles Bane, who prided himself on an uncanny ability to sum up people within five minutes (which as a headhunter he could never admit to, of course) marked Noone down as an eager-beaver who would probably be ok, but never a star.

Noone walked elatedly to Piccadilly Circus Tube, ignoring three beggars en route. He was in. Giles had said so. His new career was about to begin.

5. GORDON SHARPE

"Egon Zehnder International was founded in 1964 with a distinctive vision and structure aimed at achieving two basic goals - to place our clients' interests first and to lead our profession in creating value for our clients through the assessment and recruitment of top-level management resources. The most fundamental expression of our client-first vision resides in our structure, which is unique to our profession...organized around a single-profit center partnership. This is designed to eliminate competitive barriers between our offices. It allows us to operate seamlessly when engagements call for us to mobilize across many offices in a country or a region. Large or small, local or global, our clients benefit from our structure by having access to our most relevant resources and relationships wherever they may reside. We... are motivated solely by a desire to exceed our clients' expectations."

EGON ZEHNDER WEBSITE

The following day at work, Noone had commended Trudi for sorting out the problem with the drains and was flicking through her Daily Mail. He had alighted disbelievingly on the news that a baker, June Fothergill, had been ordered to rename her cakes because they had fallen foul of trading standards. June's marzipan likenesses of Kermit the Frog's nephew Robin were highly misleading and could no longer be called Robin Cakes because they contained no robin meat. The same applied to her Miss Piggy tarts, which were not made with pork and her Paradise Slice, which did not actually come from heaven. Noone felt great sympathy for the luckless, well-meaning June and a concomitant sense of outrage; how dare these idiot, petty bureaucrats interfere in our daily lives like this? He feared for his favourite pint of real ale,

Scruttock's Old Dirigible, which was bound to be banned for not being brewed from airships. Had there been any dogs left, the country would definitely be going to them.

The phone rang. It was Sharon Ridell.

"Hello Adam, I hope you enjoyed meeting Giles yesterday?" she enquired, rather leadingly, he thought. Can you really enjoy a meeting with a man who positioned his office furniture to your extreme disadvantage? He decided to play safe:

"Yes thanks, very much. He is a very interesting man." Interesting wasn't the word Sharon would have used to describe the self-important old fart, but still.

"Well, he agreed that you didn't have two heads and I have just spoken to Hugo. Are you ready for some good news?" she asked, a tad too coyly for Noone's liking.

"Congratulations, we would like to make you an offer." She paused for effect and went on to outline the details: £5k more than his current salary, potential for a discretionary bonus of 30%, car, pension scheme, family private health cover, life assurance and critical illness insurance. Noone was delighted and had no hesitation in accepting, forgetting in his eagerness to ask for time to consider the offer, so missing the chance to negotiate an extra £3k on the salary, which was the upper limit Reeve-Prior had allowed Sharon. She happily reported back to him that she hadn't needed to offer the extra.

"That's worrying," said Reeve-Prior," it doesn't say much for his selling or negotiation skills."

Noone phoned John Halstead to tell him that he was about to lose a senior executive; regrettably, he would be resigning, having received an offer he couldn't refuse. Halstead was subdued, understanding and confided that he was extremely disappointed to be losing one of his more able protégés, of whom he had high hopes.

"Thank fuck for that" he said to his secretary, who was just dabbing away with a Kleenex the remains of his constitutional eleven o'clock blow-job, "Noone's off, saves me having to get rid of him."

Halstead kindly ordered farewell "drinks and nibbles" for the following Friday, Noone's last day at work, and six people turned up for the free booze, including Trudi and cute, tricksy, little Nina of photocopier fame. Halstead uttered a few public platitudes about how sorry they were to see Noone go, what a great job he had done at Eezigaz, and how well they wished him for the future. In other words, don't come back. Noone in turn thanked them all for their kind wishes, lied about the "great time" he had had working with them and, directly eyeing Nina, said he would be happy to buy drinks in the pub round the corner. Trudi was delighted to accept his offer. Nina vanished from his life forever with a peck on the cheek and a cheeky wink. Much later, Noone, stupefied by the drink required to handle Trudi's outstandingly dull conversation, was delivered home by taxi into the silently unamused custody of his slumbering wife.

Noone commenced his new career optimistically after a week's holiday "to recharge his batteries", during which he exhausted himself felling and disposing of an entire hedge of out-of-control leylandii. Daphne Kinkaid welcomed him haughtily at the door, introduced him briefly to everyone (namely shy Irene and Sharon, for Gordon Sharpe "was out at a meeting") showed him to his own office and pointed out where the sustenance import and export facilities were, warning that "we all make our own coffee here" to emphasise she was nobody's galley-slave. She always liked to tell newcomers what was what right from the start to avoid misunderstandings later. She informed him that Sharon had an hour put aside at 10 o'clock "to bring him up to speed on everything" and quickly returned to her desk.

Noone received a warmer welcome from Sharon, who said she was absolutely delighted to have him onboard and asked him how he intended to "get cracking". He hadn't a clue. Hugo had sort of promised an endless supply of business flowing through the firm from where Noone wasn't quite sure, hadn't he? Sharon leaned forward and engaged him with her encouraging brown eyes and soft, warm voice:

"A word of advice, Adam. It is true that we will help you as much as possible because we want you to succeed and are sure you will. However, it is important for you to become self-sufficient as soon as possible, ideally within a year." Whatever happened to the two years suggested by Bane, Noone wondered? "I suggest you make a list of all the friends and contacts who are now in a position to help you and start ringing them to ask if you can help *them*. And," continued Sharon, before he could voice his unease at selling to friends something intangible which they didn't need, "Don't feel uneasy about selling to friends: it is your best chance of success. After all, they all trust you don't they?"

Noone wasn't sure. He recalled with some embarrassment the time he had imported from France a dozen refurbished pinball tables and sold them as new with a 100% mark-up to friends from his cricket club. Not one of them lasted a year. He had had to sub-contract an electrician with a penchant for pinball, who appreciated the access to free games, to keep them going beyond the so-called warrantee period. He suspected his subsequent demotion to the second eleven was not unconnected to the first eleven captain's malfunctioning Rameses' Revenge.

"But to get you started, you are joining me at a PNB meeting on Thursday. Potential New Business." Sharon elucidated. "I also think it is a good idea for you to shadow Gordon for a month or so, just until you get the hang of things. Although he has only been in our business a while, he is very good on detail, understands all the ins and outs and will be a good role model for you. You should also make sure that one or other of us reviews all the written work you intend to send out. Two pairs of eyes are better than one." She smiled, wished him good luck, told him not to worry about Dragon-lady Daphne Kinkaid, and showed him to her door. Returning to his own office, Noone was grateful for Sharon's concern and advice; she really wanted him to succeed. Sharon returned to a report she was dictating. He was on his own now, she mused, sink or swim.

Gordon Sharpe returned from a highly promising client meeting and decided to size Noone up over a few jars at The Ostler a few doors down. It was a basic spit-and-sawdust, town local of the type with which Sharpe normally wouldn't wish to be associated, populated by yobbish, working-class oiks with hairy, tattooed arms and earrings drinking Carling or Carlsberg, probably the worst lager in the world. As it was a bit of a test of character for this new chap Noone and it was close, it suited his purposes today. For his part, Noone approved of its lack of pretension, with external stimulation simply provided by a dart board and bar-billiards. Although there wasn't any Scruttocks, The Ostler did offer Fullers' London Pride, which usually served up well despite the lack of care perpetrated upon it by temporary barmaids; Sharpe took a medium glass of the house red, which he proceeded to ignore. Seated at a corner table and over execrable cheese baguettes, the two men got to know each other.

Gordon Sharpe was an interesting kettle of worms. His father had been in the Navy (which imbued Sharpe with some appeal for Hugo Reeve-Prior) retiring after a lifetime's solid work in Administration. In short, he sailed a desk and never commanded one of Her Majesty's ships of the line. First son David shone from launch and steamed nicely through a state-assisted place at Charterhouse, pre-clinical medical study at Jesus College, Oxford, complete with rugger Blue, then clinical and surgical study at Guy's. He now cruised serenely on top of his chosen sea, a specialist surgeon of increasing renown in ophthalmology. Regrettably, poor Gordon came a distant second. No athlete, he was bullied at Charterhouse for failing to demonstrate the leadership qualities of his remembered-in-awe, older sibling, ex captain of School and Rugby. Winning the school draughts competition merely served to underline how inferior Gordon was. His father was always on his back, crushing the life out of him, commanding him to improve at frequent intervals, comparing him constantly to his brilliant brother, criticising his every attempt to impress. Gordon's academic successes, perfectly adequate A' levels, which took him off to the University of Reading to study Agriculture and achieve a solid 2:2 degree, allowing passage as a graduate trainee into Spindlers' animal feedstock division, were as dry dust compared to the luxuriant foliage of David's achievements. Gordon remained forlornly in David's shadow.

Then a curious thing began to happen. Spindlers' training programme, unlike so many similar schemes which aimlessly pushed aimless, hopelessly naïve graduates around a succession of uninterested departments, where they were given menial and useless projects to undertake, actually began to work for Gordon. He was allowed six months in the marketing department and found his metier, instinctively understanding marketing mix, the importance of the famous four P's (Product, Pricing, Positioning and Promotion) and how they interrelate. He discovered he could be creative, challenging, persuasive. He blossomed and was confirmed into the permanent position of Marketing Executive. He had made it to the bottom rung.

He didn't stay there long. On the back of a successful campaign which took Spindlers into the mass market for dog food, providing raw, vitamin-enhanced product for a rapidly emerging company called Dogs' Dinners, Gordon was promoted to Marketing Manager. Further promotions followed until, after seven years, he reached the giddy heights of Product Director, Global Petfoods. Still his father remained resolutely unimpressed. If asked over his G & T at the golf club:

"And what is Gordon doing these days?" he would reply dismissively:

"Haven't a clue, old boy. Something terribly hush-hush to do with nutrition. But have you heard about David's latest paper?" The fact was that Gordon's father wasn't terribly interested in his second son. In turn, Gordon had grown a carapace of detached hauteur balanced by occasional manic, self-deprecating stabs at humour.

Collecting a horse-loving wife, Miranda, from good stock along the way, Gordon realised that her fast-developing, high-maintenance habits were unlikely to be satisfied by his steady but unspectacular salary rises and their current shoebox of a house in South Ruislip. He needed to generate large dollops of cash to feed their increasing material desires. If he could achieve a large house with stabling and a paddock or two, a flash car and a private education for his as yet unconceived children, that would show his father! Gordon had joined a gym in an attempt to limit the expansion of his waistline. One evening, whilst vaguely bemoaning his current lot over a post-workout spritzer with a fellow fitness journeyman, Roland Jameson, a solution was presented to him.

"You will never achieve a competitive salary by staying with one employer," Jameson advised. "Look at me, I've moved three times in the seven years you have been at Spindlers and I am earning, what, £15k more than you." Gordon had always looked down on Jameson as a bit of a wide-boy, but he had a point.

"You need to get on the books of Willard Wonks; they are an agency which found me all my jobs. And they specialise in marketing positions," he added. Gordon had never heard of Willard Wonks but he knew what agencies did, needed no further bidding and posted off his CV with a covering letter the next morning. After a month of silence (not unusual, he was to discover) he received a call from someone at Willard Wonks who sounded just like Roland Jameson. It was Roland Jameson.

"Hello old fruit, it's me Rollo. I've just joined WW and I came across your CV on the database. We are fully computerised here, you know. Come in and have a chat; we'll see what we can find for you." Jameson, unlike Gordon, certainly could not be accused of loyalty to his employer. Gordon had duly visited the branch in

Hounslow where Jameson worked, and had been introduced to the Branch Manager, Angus MacTavish, who, to enhance his dour, hard-bitten Scot image, affected a gruff Glaswegian accent, even though he hailed from picturesque Loch Lomond. MacTavish was engaged in a turf war over Windsor with the branch from Bracknell and was hiring staff furiously to boost sales and demonstrate to his bosses in London that he deserved a bigger slice of territory. He knew Gordon was looking for a mainstream marketing role, but he was intrigued by Gordon's detached, confident air, underpinned by a track record of delivering growth for Spindlers. Why not hire him into WW alongside his previous convert Jameson?

As he listened to MacTavish's sales pitch for the business, Gordon was impressed that someone from as tough a background as MacTavish was thriving in this strange but dynamic agency environment. It was a maelstrom of activity, with phones ringing constantly amongst the pack of eager, shirt-sleeved young men with loud ties and women in attractively short skirts, desked in rows in the middle of the office. Occasionally one exclaimed "Yes!" and punched the air, whilst the others crowded round shouting "How much?" Gordon had learned enough about this commission-based environment to surmise correctly that a candidate had been placed and jealous colleagues wanted to calculate where the fee placed the consultant in that month's league table. He was excited, if not slightly intoxicated, by the lure of money and the competitive, testosterone-fuelled atmosphere. If he could make it here, fame, fortune and fellowship would surely follow.

The reality proved different. Successful he was, proving as greedy, cutthroat and dishonourable as the rest, getting into the office early to make the first call, staying late to call that last candidate, developing Jameson's wide-boy persuasive patter (with a touch more refinement, he liked to think) competing amongst his fellow thieves to steal a client here, a candidate there. They all knew the unwritten rules; it was dog-eat-dog and if you survived the first three months and played the game, you began to enjoy it. After working hard, they played hard, easing into tequila-chasing pints of Kronenbourg at the spacious and garish Duke of Wellington on Staines Road before, every Friday, staggering on to overpriced cocktails at Skindles in Maidenhead or Bazooka in Iver. Gordon had more than his share of difficult Saturday mornings as a result, but as he took his marriage vows seriously, he liked to leave before the inevitable drunken couplings at the end of the night and to observe with jealous relish and resultant verbal ribbing the sheepish avoidances or lust-filled glances across the office on a Monday morning.

Gordon won an award for the highest single branch fee and made a baby with Miranda in Venice with the prize money. The next year he outperformed every other branch consultant and made another baby in Acapulco. Five years passed; the bonuses reached five figures, the Saab 900 turbo convertible covered the drive. Gordon enjoyed it, but it wasn't enough. Somehow, there was always another consultant somewhere, usually London, who outperformed him, causing the long-suppressed feelings of inadequacy to resurface at the annual awards ceremonies. Also, by now a veteran recruiter, he realised that in the perceived meritocracy of the trade, search consultants were at the top, shining like stars on a Christmas tree, whilst he was rootling around in the agency sludge at the bottom. He had to escape the "no placement, no fee" contingency world and trade up towards the light. However, he was realistic enough to understand that although he aspired to join a serious search firm, none would touch him until he had made a transitional step upmarket. Additionally, he would have to become attractive to them by offering proven expertise in a specialist market. Fittingly, given this new resolution, at the turn of the year 1990, he had responded to Sharon Ridell's first advertisement, and though underwhelmed by her, had been hugely impressed by Hugo Reeve-Prior's vision for the firm. It had all the pretences of a premier league search firm despite the fact that it was not supposed to offer search, but Gordon could see that changing over time and in any case, Hugo had hinted that there could be a route through to Aspallan, Bane Consultants for those who excelled. He reckoned it would not be too long before he would eclipse Sharon; then Hugo would have to take him very seriously indeed. He joined AB Selection a week after Dragon-lady Kinkaid.

Mrs Kinkaid had by then "taken Sharon under her wing" as she put it to her husband, saw Gordon as an upstart and treated him coldly from day one, firmly implying that he was well behind her in the pecking order of Sharon's favours. Irene didn't count of course, poor little working-class scrap. Gordon despised Daphne Kinkaid's unearned but vicious snobbery, which reminded him of his father, and could only tolerate her presence by ignoring her whenever possible. Now with his own office, the fastidiousness that had kept him slightly aloof from the daily rough and tumble at Willard Wonks was allowed free reign: files were arranged in strict alphabetical order, In and Out-trays placed precisely on the outer corners of his desk, and the usual clutter of paper clips, drawing pins, staples and pens tamed, collected and hidden by a compartmentalised tray which fitted neatly into his desk drawer. That tray was a metaphor for Gordon's life, which he had compartmentalised over time, rarely permitting one aspect to spill over into another. For example, he entertained a secret enjoyment of motorcycling, which Miranda barely tolerated and about which nobody at Willard Wonks knew. He wasn't a "big dog rider", one who rode aggressively at high speeds on public roads without fear of accident, arrest or the receipt of a Fast Riding Award from the Blue Meanies. Nor was he a "canyon carver", who rode the twisties to the extreme astride a high-speed crotch rocket like a Kwacker ZX10 or Gixer Thou'. Gordon was no two-wheeled moron; he owned a sensible, reliable BMW K100RS and rode it sensibly and reliably. He was an ATGATT (All The Gear

All The Time) in possession of a "keep the dirty side down" at all costs attitude which presumes that safety gear should always be worn when riding a motorcycle regardless of temperature, distance to be ridden or peer pressure that might encourage one not to do so. Given his latent tendency towards obsessive compulsion, it was almost inevitable that he would turn into a "chromosexual" in his fifties, carefully adding lots of shiny pieces to his Harley Davidson Chumplugger, which he would fastidiously not take out in the rain, but would polish obsessively on fine Sunday mornings on the drive, before proudly tooling loudly around the village for twenty minutes in a matt black open-face helmet accessorised with Ray-Ban Aviator sunglasses.

On the back of the increased salary and improved prospects following the move to AB Selection, Gordon and Miranda were in the process of moving from South Ruislip to Stokenchurch, the closest four-bedroomed detached house to Uxbridge that they could find for their budget and their growing children, Sole and Loco. Shrewdly, Gordon decided to specialise in telecommunications, as the boom in mobiles, driven initially by commercial applications, was beginning in earnest; the start of the '90s was the time that every serious businessman needed a mobile phone, less for show and more to make dough. The pace of deal-making was accelerating, and being uncontactable was becoming unacceptable. Gordon had become busy very quickly at AB Selection and he reckoned he should be able to palm off some of the unattractive, lower level work to this new chap Noone, providing he shaped up, of course.

That lunchtime in The Ostler, Gordon discovered that Noone seemed to spend all his spare time on cricket, football, golf, squash and real ale and didn't have a clue about recruitment. They had absolutely nothing in common. On the vaguely plus side, Noone had run a business and seemed keen and eager to impress; therefore, he could be malleable and have his uses. Gordon resolved to use him as much as he could.

6. THE PNB

"We aspire to handle the most important jobs for leading organisations in every industry sector and to combine our specialist expertise with thoroughness and speed to provide exceptionally responsive and effective service. We have very talented people – some have been with us for many years, some joined us from other market leaders, others come from the sectors they specialise in. Our consultants are adaptable and approach each assignment with imagination and initiative. They are also very determined – our people make things happen. We dig deep and search widely. We combine precision and attention to detail with creativity and the ability to see the big picture".

ODGERS WEBSITE

Sharon Ridell had asked Noone to prepare for the Potential New Business meeting on his first Thursday at AB Selection. In these pre-internet-for-everyone days, this meant phoning the Head of Research, Millicent Moleshill, in the London office and requesting information on the target company. She would look up the company's annual report, interrogate Hoovers' business information service, run a peer-comparison tool and fax the information over. Voluptuously blessed with two enormous breasts between which men simply wanted to lose themselves, she was affectionately nicknamed "Mountains" for her unwitting but transformational ability in the name-to-mammary department. Although married, as befits one who worked in a "giving environment", Millicent was selflessly sharing her breasts with a well-endowed member of the accounts department, who became the hero of the male fantasists in the London office.

The target company, Potentiality, whose HR Director Sharon was meeting on Thursday, was a training company which liked to think of itself as modern, caring, fast-paced and performing an incredibly important job for its customers. Noone, reading through its self-promoting annual report, soon realised that it was full of shit.

"In an industry with few barriers to entry we simply concentrate on our clients' core business. Utilising top-down, user-centred, bleeding-edge technology, our endgame is to benchmark best practice processes to achieve bottom-line, world-class achievement." he read. "Potentiality identifies mission-critical elements and, developing the game plan envisioned by a blue-sky, results-driven interface, garnered from grass roots level, fast tracks the empowerment of staff. This, linked with a Customer Relations Management model based on metrics, motivates them to think outside the box without fear or favour, providing positive mindsets in an honest, no-blame culture; we guarantee a win-win situation with all the ticks in the right boxes. With synergies in place, all the ducks in a row and the movers and shakers really stirring, it's a no-brainer: let us help you to reach the low-hanging fruit and beyond!"

Noone couldn't believe anyone fell for this rubbish, but then again, he recalled the wife of a friend, who appeared to all reasonable people to be barking mad, yet trained sales-forces using a combination of hypnotism, magic and something called the Power of Positive Persuasion, or the Three Ps. She was about to buy a second house in which to spend more quality time away from her husband and drove a year-old Jaguar Series III XJ saloon.

"I recruited the Marketing Director for Potentiality a couple of years ago," Noone was astounded to hear Sharon reveal, "and it has doubled its turnover since then. It now needs a decent Finance Director." Noone thought it prudent not to point out to Sharon that it also needed a decent Marketing Director.

"I'll lead the discussion since I obviously know the HRD, but feel free to chip in." Sharon continued, leaving Noone in no doubt that he would "chip in" at his peril. "I know enough about the business to wing it but it would help if you have all the latest numbers; you know, revenue, profit, market share, staff count and so on." Noone said he would. "The key is to get him talking first, ask lots of questions and avoid having to talk about fees." Sharon made it sound easy.

"Ah yes, what are our fees?" asked Noone.

"Same basis as search, except that we charge 25% of the remuneration package because the client also has to pay for the advertisement. And they are not cheap: £8,600 for an AB Selection, house-style, standard size Sunday Times 14cm by five columns; The Thursday Telegraph is £8,000. More for a front page position in both papers. We always try to convince the client not to confuse brand advertising with recruitment advertising and therefore to hide their identity under ours. Besides," she continued earnestly, "however powerful they believe their brand to be, there will always be people out there who detest it. Think Rolls Royce. So it is much better to advertise 'blind': the punters are intrigued by an anonymous proposition and consequently reply in greater numbers. Of course, 95% of the responses are rubbish, but the clients don't know that." Noone tried to take this all in.

"How many times does the advertisement appear?" he asked naively.

"Just the once. Although they do repeat it "free of charge" in the following Thursday's edition of The Times." Noone was astounded. He couldn't believe clients would swallow it; they paid nearly nine grand for what amounted to a piece of brand advertising for AB Selection.

"And the clients actually buy this?" he asked incredulously.

"Not always," Sharon replied. "It is our job to sell the proposition to them. And the icing on the cake is that we get a kick-back discount of 20% from the newspaper. Therefore, the more expensive the ad, the more we make. Neat isn't it?" Noone had to admit that it was.

Sharon drove them to the PNB on Thursday afternoon.

She was very proud of her new BMW 5-Series car; shiny, metallic silver, with air-conditioning *and* sunroof, part of the enhanced package granted her by Hugo as a reward for the move to Uxbridge. Dave liked to drive it because it was a "Beemer", the height of his automotive aspirations, Theresa and Daniel loved the electric windows and Sharon luxuriated in the smell of leather upholstery and the feeling of wealth and power it conferred upon her. It was far too big for her for she was at best a poor driver, unable to anticipate road conditions ahead, behind or around her. Consequently, the large machine pitched, yawed and rolled throughout a journey governed by her needlessly heavy pedal-work and over-corrective steering. By the time they arrived at the Potentiality head office in Reading, Noone was feeling decidedly ill.

"You look pale, Adam," Sharon observed as they walked to Reception from the car-park. "The first few PNBs will make you feel nervous. Try to relax but take lots of notes and learn. The old boy is as dull as ditch water, so you have nothing to fear."

Never had the offer of a cup of tea seemed so welcome and Noone felt a rush of gratitude towards the HR Director's secretary as she ushered them into the Boardroom and went off to make the warming beverage. Sharon commanded that they sit together along one side of the table. The tea's restorative properties had begun to take effect after about ten minutes and as his nausea subsided, Noone was relieved to find that he would not disgrace himself by throwing up all over the Boardroom table. Having kept them waiting for a fashionable but annoying twenty minutes, which was meant to imply the client was a very busy and important man, a large, pudgy, grey-haired man entered the room, offered them both a cold, clammy handshake and sat down at the head of the table. They could tell he was neither busy, nor important.

After an early exchange of pleasantries, with both Sharon and the HR Director seemingly delighted to see each other again, Sharon proceeded with an object lesson in how to extract information from a client without offering much in return. She smiled engagingly, offered open questions encouragingly like titbits to a hungry dog, delved into the requirements of the role, the reward package and the likely background of potential candidates and summarised the information confidently and concisely. Sharon left no stone unturned. Noone was mightily impressed and felt no urge "to chip in".

"So in short," she was concluding, "you do not need to go to the expense of search. An advertisement will produce candidates from a range of backgrounds which you would never uncover through search, and," she paused for effect, "we can deliver a shortlist in thirty days." The HR Director, ponderous by nature as well as appearance, turned to Noone for the first time.

"And where would you suggest we advertise?" Sharon's lecture was only too clear in Noone's mind, and brightly he commenced:

"Well, the options are quite straight-forward. The Sunday Times is the most powerful medium for executive positions at this level and has the largest audited readership…"

"But we would recommend Thursday's Financial Times, wouldn't we Adam?" interjected Sharon sweetly but firmly, looking him in the eye and holding his gaze.

"Yes, I think we would." He replied, trying to sound authoritative, but aware he had nearly made a complete fool of himself.

"Good, well that seems fine. We are seeing a couple of other agencies but we'd like to push on as quickly as possible. You will drop me a line with the details and costs involved?" asked the HR Director.

"Of course." Sharon remained in control, despite having mentally shuddered at the employment of the dread word "agency" in relation to AB Selection. "We will send a full proposal covering our understanding of the position, the candidate required, the package, our recommendations, a draft advertisement and our fees, Terms & Conditions;

by Tuesday next week?"

"Splendid." Mr Ponderous stood up to show them out.

"We would handle the assignment together," Sharon said, cleverly bringing Noone into play from the boundary ropes. "As two pairs of eyes are better than one and in case one of us goes under a bus." Crikey, thought Noone, this job is more dangerous than I thought.

"And when you are ready to press the button," continued Sharon coyly to a close, "we will draft a job specification for your agreement, so that we are all singing from the same hymn-sheet." Noone was fascinated that they had metaphorically wound up in church when they were worshippers of Mammon.

On the return journey, besides making Noone queasy again, Sharon had analysed the meeting, concluded it had gone as well as could be expected and tasked Noone with drafting the proposal by Dictaphone, urging him to base it on one from the archives which Daphne or Irene could find for him. On the basis of a package of £65k, she suggested a fee of £16k which represented a decent return. Having neither asked the Dragon-lady for something before, nor used a Dictaphone, Noone felt quite challenged by Sharon's airy instructions. After several hours of struggle, he produced the proposal on audiotape, which Mrs Kinkaid confided to Irene, "sounded like a Dalek". Nevertheless, she created a first draft over which he agonised for another hour and a half before returning it apologetically with corrections for her to produce a second draft. When this too was returned with corrections, the Dragon-lady began to smoke lightly under her collar.

Noone was pretty pleased with draft three and proudly took it in for Sharon "to tweak it". She spent an hour tweaking it and returned it covered in red ink to a crestfallen Noone. He could see now that his style was indecisive and too prolix, choice of words loose and undirective, conclusions and suggestions disjointed and lacking causality. Her suggestions made perfect sense, tightening up the prose, eliminating jargon and clichés and producing altogether a much more purposeful document. He almost smelled the brimstone and sulphur as he sheepishly returned the mangled proposal to Dragon-lady once more. It was hardly her fault that several typographical errors crept in to demand a final, fifth, draft.

"Don't forget the draft advertisement Adam." Called Sharon from her room. Damn, he had forgotten the advertisement.

"Working on it now, Sharon", he replied. The advertisement went through the same process. Noone found it surprisingly difficult to capture in an attractive way the essence of the company, the job and the candidate profile, all within the strictures of the AB Selection house style. The aim was to outdo the previous "new kid on the block", NB Selection, which had pioneered a sparse, punchy, error-free style with an emphasis on "white space", in contrast to the prevailing advertisements of the time; densely-packed, wordy and often grammatically incorrect, as Noone knew only too well from his own candidate experience of sifting through them all. Sharon's review of Noone's ad ruthlessly eliminated pronouns as well as definite and indefinite articles, dramatically changed passive verbs and present participles into active transitives and abruptly eschewed infinitives, anadiplosis, epistrophe, pleonasm, polyptoton, tautology and zeugma. The fifth draft sprang red-hot from Dragon-lady's word processor and was despatched in an envelope along with the other promised documentation to Mr Ponderous, last post on the Monday, as promised.

Silence was the deafening reply. At Sharon's bidding, Noone rang Potentiality the following Friday to check that The Ponderous One had received the proposal and spoke to the gift-giver of tea, by now known as Paula.

"Oh yes, 'e's 'ad it." She confirmed. "It's jus' that we're terrific busy an' 'e 'asn't 'ad a chance to look at it yet. I'll chase 'im on Monday luv." So much for "wanting to push on as quickly as possible" thought Noone bitterly.

"Don't worry Adam," said Sharon, "they are always

like this. We have to produce everything for clients by yesterday and they keep us waiting for everything in return. It's what is called an equal partnership." It was yet another lesson in this weird and wonderful new world.

Finally, on the Wednesday, Paula called to say that Mr Ponderous would be speaking to the CEO on Friday and would call after the meeting. Friday came and went, as did Monday, untroubled by interruption of any sort from Mr Ponderous. By now, Noone was simultaneously frantic and despondent, convinced that "his" proposal had been passed by. The fee was probably too high; he blamed himself for not arguing with Sharon for a lower fee in order to secure the engagement. Rather crestfallen, he busied himself copying out important contacts from his address book for Irene to type up into a list for address labels. Most of his address book, he had to admit, was useless for his new professional pursuit. What could he offer E. Vice-Manky, onetime cartoonist to The Independent? Or "Naf" Stinkor, R.N.? A.N.Venom-Shit, a headmaster? Dr J.F. Avid-Mooney and Dr "Ace" Valve? Ned O'Growler, E.N. Hollowscin, V.E. Gravy-Hod, J.N.L.Goonshine and R. Yewbent, all of them friends from his cricket club? In the past, a reasonably quick partner between the wickets, sure, but sadly they would have no need of a Finance Director at £65k.

Finally, on Tuesday morning, the call came through to Sharon: Mr Ponderous was very happy with the proposal and wanted them to start immediately…providing they could shave a little off the fee. Noone was to realise that this was a ritual game in which most clients, particularly those from the HR community, engaged. Therefore, he was to become quite adept at quoting slightly higher than was necessary in order to draw out this response. He could then knock a couple of thousand off, which allowed the clients to demonstrate to their boss what tough negotiators they were and everyone was happy. Sharon indeed shaved a couple of thousand off the fee and everyone was happy. Not least Noone, who was then set loose on his first assignment with considerable help from Sharon, who proved a surprisingly patient and calm tutor when presented with his barrage of inevitable mistakes. It was real "on-the-job" training.

The advertisement was "set" in AB Selection's house style by an advertising agency belonging to a friend of Hugo Reeve-Prior and "placed" to appear the Thursday after next. Noone fumbled through the five-draft-process with the Job Specification, which became six drafts once Mr Ponderous's minor changes were taken into account. Then he waited impatiently for the advertisement to appear in the FT and the responses to drop through the letterbox thereafter.

In the meantime, he received a call from Reeve-Prior:

"Adam, how's it going?" Noone, failing to sound nonchalant, excitedly told him about the PNB and its successful outcome.

"Splendid. You are off and running; and I have something else for you. An old school chum of mine runs Tantalize, the lingerie company. He needs help." Noone was hardly surprised. A red-blooded male spending his days surrounded by exotic female underclothing: it was a sure-fire recipe for madness. "The business has taken off," Reeve-Prior continued, seemingly blind to his suggestive choice of words, "and he needs our advice about recruiting a strong right hand. Do you think you'd be interested?" Is the Pope a queen? thought Noone; it sounded heavenly, and he understood the need for a strong right hand in the business. "Unfortunately," continued Reeve-Prior, "the business is in Wembley, which is a pretty bloody place to be."

Reeve-Prior "didn't do the Tube" and met Noone at Wembley Stadium, to where he had travelled First Class from Marylebone overland (except for the tunnels under St John's Wood, which didn't count as the Underground). Thankfully, they were able to pick up a Black Cab from the taxi-rank, thus avoiding any contact with minicabs, which Reeve-Prior also didn't do.

The second PNB followed a similar format to the first. Reeve-Prior gave Noone some credibility by introducing him as "a former CEO from industry", but then dominated, asking the questions and giving his opinions freely and firmly with haughty grandeur, while his friend, Humfrey Smallwood, deferred, apologising for "not knowing much about recruitment". However, when it came to the management and structure of the business, it became clear that Humfrey was a control-freak. He was the owner and sole director and everything passed through his hands: sales, marketing, finance, operations. He quite fancied the thought of hiring a Sales Director, but Reeve-Prior decreed that in fact he required an Operations Director "to handle the drudgery" which would free Humfrey to concentrate on sales and marketing, which were his real forte. The meeting finished and proposal promised, Humfrey showed them around the warehouse attached to the back of the office. It was indeed an underwear fetishist's paradise with every conceivable style of bra, panty, corset, suspender belt, stocking and garter in evidence, rich in red, black, pink, cream or white, and in a variety of diaphanous, plush or filigree materials, from nylon through cotton to silk. Not rubber or leather, Noone noted, nothing kinky here. He wondered what the stock losses were like. A strong right hand indeed...

On the cab journey back to the station, Reeve-Prior issued Noone's instructions:

"Adam, Humfrey won't be talking to anyone else so this is what we term 'a pick-up'. Keep the proposal short, but include a Job Specification as well as the advertisement, which we will place in the Daily Telegraph. He doesn't want to pay more than £45k salary, but we can push him to £50k, so offer a fee of £13k and make it clear you will handle the job with me acting in support."

Reeve-Prior proved just as pedantic as Sharon over the written work, which was hardly surprising, since he had taught her everything. This time, little Irene had to endure the drafting process, but unlike Dragon-lady, she didn't have better things to do with her time and didn't seem to mind. Over time, Noone began to appreciate her stoic acceptance of the daily typing drudgery through which she was put.

Reeve-Prior was right. Although it took Humfrey Smallwood two weeks reluctantly to commit to the prospect of allowing another executive into his business and agree to part with money for this privilege (he knocked the fee down to £12k of course) Humfrey didn't talk to anyone else, and gave them the go-ahead. One month into his new career, Noone had won his first two assignments. He was off and running, he proudly told his wife, it was a piece of cake. How little did he know.

7. TRAINING

"Our aim is to provide our clients with a competitive edge through having the best leadership. Although our firm is organised into specific practices with high levels of expertise and experience, at heart, we're one team. Everything we know, we all know. This gives our partners, consultants and researchers access to complete and powerful information that translates into a deep understanding of markets, people and opportunities and enables them to fully engage with both our business and that of our clients, 100% of the time".

WHITEHEAD MANN WEBSITE

Noone was soon plunged into the grind of intensively reviewing CVs, or "shifting the slush-pile" as it was less politely known by the recruitment fraternity. The advertisement highlighting the FD role for Potentiality generated 162 replies. Sharon had told him it was company policy to reply to all correspondents within a week, so, conscientiously, he listed the key criteria for the role on a piece of paper and began to score each application against this list. It took him a morning to read through all the covering letters and judge the CVs. He was pleasantly surprised to find that most appeared relevant. Only 15 had ignored the requirement for one of the three main accountancy qualifications (two of which were self-employed handymen seeking an entree into corporate life, one a taxi-driver, the rest self-styled entrepreneurs who said they were bored, having just successfully sold their businesses). Four replies came from impressively qualified candidates of indeterminate gender from India, and a further two from obvious madmen who threatened to kill him if he didn't give them a job. Noone was a little concerned by this, having only been threatened with his life once before by the (he discovered later) captain of the university boxing team who suddenly found him objectionable at a student party. A dozen applicants were clearly too inexperienced and hardly shaving and a further twenty or so were way too old at fifty or more years. There was even one poor old sod aged sixty-two; virtually fossilised! The rest of the applicants seemed pretty good and it took a second sift during the afternoon to bring the numbers down to a possible thirty, which he took to Sharon, feeling he had done a thorough job.

Sharon was quietly appalled at the time he had wasted, but tried to be gentle:

"Spend a minute on each and ignore the covering letter. Cut out any illiterates, those with spelling mistakes, no dates of birth, gaps in chronology, CVs longer than three pages in length, anyone who includes a photo or written reference, who lives further than an hour away from Potentiality in Reading and anyone who moves every two to three years. Aim for no more than twelve: don't forget you are going to telephone-interview all of them and you don't want to spend time on no-hopers when you could be using that time to develop business."

With this devastating lecture ringing in his ears, Noone went back to his room deeply chastened and spent another hour whittling the thirty down to twelve, feeling guilty and apologetic for the eighteen who didn't make the cut, particularly the chap who had shared a photograph of himself casually leaning on the open bonnet of his E Type Jaguar, that magnificent straight six, 4.2 litre lump gleaming in the captured sunshine. The CVs of the unlucky 150 who had now been meticulously weeded out were passed back to Irene for her to generate and post the AB Selection standard rejection letter to each. The Dear John letter sincerely thanked the applicant for his or her time and trouble but regrettably, on this occasion, there were others who matched the selection criteria slightly more closely. Good luck with your applications elsewhere etc. Noone knew from his own recent experiences as a candidate adrift in a sea of applications how unusual it was to receive any acknowledgement at all. He, at least, was impressed, even if the rejected candidates were not.

Sharon had given him a list of suggested questions to ask the candidates on the phone and advised him that a Sunday evening call on their home numbers was a good time to catch them. Noone metaphorically kissed goodbye to Sunday evenings with friends or neighbours intent on staving off the incoming week with alcoholic "stiffeners" and summer barbecues commencing in the afternoon and finishing hazily and late. They would have to be held on Saturdays from now on. The list of questions developed into a mantra he was to use for the rest of his recruitment life and he soon became adept at anticipating the responses:

"Hello, it's Adam Noone from AB Selection here. You should have received a letter indicating that I would be in touch: is it convenient to talk?" (If not, why not on a Sunday evening, you bastard).

"Thank you for applying to the advertisement I placed in the FT. I just wanted to put 'some flesh on the bones' of your CV; can you spare fifteen minutes or so?" (If not, you are out chum).

"I suppose the obvious start-point is: why are you considering leaving your current role?" (At least half would confess that they had "just left", a further quarter, it would emerge, were in the process of "negotiating their exit", twenty percent knew they were going to be fired and only the remaining five percent were genuinely seeking to move on from a position of relative strength and stability).

"If you could pick the perfect job for yourself now, what would it be?" (Many were looking for "a step up" for nobody ever admitted to having been promoted beyond their competence; or a role in which they could better "express" themselves, "make a difference" and be valued; or perhaps, "a turnaround situation". The truth for most was any job which paid a decent salary and bailed them out of their current predicament).

"What attracted you about the advertisement?" (Usually, "it sounded interesting" and they were convinced that they "ticked all the boxes". Occasionally the location appealed as it would take the candidate well away from his or her ex spouse. Nobody ever admitted that the salary was the main draw. The salary was always the main draw).

"What are your key strengths applicable to the role?" (They were unfailingly great leaders who enjoyed managing a team, highly commercial, change, task, and achievement-orientated, known as "someone who gets the job done").

"What is your current salary?" (The paranoid or those on disproportionately low salaries would stall and flannel-talk about their "package". Noone learned he could discard them immediately, just as he knew that those on equal or higher salaries to that advertised were about to lose their jobs.)

"How does the location suit you?" (Anything commutable in an hour or less was fine. Anyone "happy to relocate or weekly-commute" flagged questions about family situation and motivation).

"Do you have any other irons in the fire?" (Invariably the answer was no. Lying bastards; why else would they be reading the appointments section of a national newspaper? Idle curiosity rarely rang true; they were banging off applications all over the place).

These questions, or similar, would produce the answers (or lack of) which would enable Noone to decide which of these lucky folk he would "invite in for interview". Finally, but not always, particularly if he were in a hurry, Noone would ask:

"Do you have any questions for me?" Those who didn't were axed for lack of interest, along with those who asked too many or demanded an interview "because this job has me written all over it". This, then, became the Noone formula for creating the long-list of candidates whom he would now meet. The very first round of telephone interviews which he undertook on Potentiality's behalf taught him two things; firstly, Finance Directors sounded as dull as hundred year-old farthings; secondly, he was beginning to enjoy the feeling of power that "running an assignment" conferred upon him.

He noted that Gordon Sharpe always rang those he was discarding after telephone interview to explain why he was not progressing their application:

"Aren't you worried that they will start to argue with you?" he asked Sharpe.

"Good God no. They are pathetically grateful that you have called. Remember you are in charge. You can always tell them that the assignment is so confidential that you are not at liberty to explain why they are not suitable." Sharpe invited him to listen in to one of his calls. Noone listened and understood.

"Gordon Sharpe here, we spoke the other day." He announced imperiously. "I wanted to let you know that I won't be asking you to come forward for interview at this stage. I have a number of candidates who look very close to the ideal specification; I am interviewing those now and expect to find the answer. If for some reason this turns out not to be the case and I need to 'widen the net', I may well be in touch again. Goodbye and good luck."

Noone imitated this "best practice" to the letter. Ninety-nine percent of those rejected in this way indeed appeared grateful to be told they were useless, thanked him profusely and hung up acquiescently. The odd one bristled and bridled and demanded to know in what way someone else could possibly be better. The trick was to be able to point to something that the candidate had written in his or her CV and claim that the client was looking for something completely different.

At AB Selection, the secretaries were encouraged to arrange the interviews, borrowing the consultants' desk diaries before telephoning the candidates. The Dragon-lady always sounded as though she were arranging an audience with the Queen, making it clear to the candidates how fortunate they were to be selected to grace the diary of the consultant on whose behalf she was phoning. Candidates took an instant dislike to this underling with ideas "au-dessus de sa gare". Little Irene, on the other hand, was pleasant and down-to-earth with candidates, usually completing the interview schedule rapidly and efficiently, in half the time. Candidates felt she was on their side, a friend.

The next trial for Noone was the interviews. Sharon guided him on how to structure an interview and suggested they conduct a couple together, one with her taking the lead, the next with roles reversed; thereafter, he would be on his own. Noone observed how she used her warm personality to break the ice and set the candidate at ease, commenting on a topic of the day about which to create some light-hearted banter. This was not easy with their first candidate, a stultifyingly boring man from Wigan with no apparent sense of humour, although Noone found his ill-advised dress sense hilarious, matching a dark green suit with a red-checked shirt, yellow tie and Hush Puppies. He had been "welcomed" by Dragon-lady, seated in the Reception area and given a cup of coffee garnished with the Job Specification to read before he was brought before them. Sharon told him that she and Noone were working on the assignment together. Noone hoped he didn't infer, automatically and correctly, that Noone was an assignment virgin and not the seasoned veteran he was attempting to portray. He sucked his biro thoughtfully and kept a dignified silence throughout the proceedings.

Sharon told Green Suit about Potentiality and the need for the new role before kindly asking him about his upbringing (solid working class) and early life (spoiled only child) his hopes and dreams (to become an accountant) his educational achievements and qualifications (he claimed a 2:1 degree in Economics). She then took him through his career, establishing why he had moved jobs (promoted of course or "looking for a new challenge"); where his successes had been (everywhere) and failures (nowhere); the hardest thing he had ever done (work context: firing someone; social context: climbing Snowdon in the fog); what his greatest strength was (processes) and weakness ("didn't suffer fools gladly"); what other people thought of him ("firm but fair"). She noted all the elements of his remuneration and benefits package, including notice period, before asking encouragingly why he felt he should be appointed to this job (being from Wigan apparently made him peerless) and whether he had any questions. Noone by then had begun to realise that far from being the most exciting thing about recruitment, interviewing strangers was actually terribly tedious. He willed him to say no.

"Thank you, just a few," as he reached into his briefcase and brought out a closely-typed list. Noone groaned inwardly, but Sharon never faltered, dealing with each quickly, although he noticed she said several times more than she needed to:

"I'm afraid you would have to address that one to the client." She finished by thanking him again for his interest and for taking the time to visit them, told him they would be in touch when all the interviews were completed and then ushered him out to Dragon-lady to see him off the premises.

"What did you think of him?" asked Sharon slyly. Noone forced himself to overlook the green suit and Hush Puppies.

"Not bad I suppose; he had plenty of relevant experience but he was rather...uh, dull."

"Rather dull?" Sharon was incredulous. "He had the personality of a snail and not a single creative bone in his body. No way would he fit into Potentiality, which is young and buzzy and lacks disciplines and structure. All his companies have been large, well-established regimes where he has just had to turn the handle. He is far too old and staid." The candidate was forty six. Noone had to admit she was right.

"I only gave him the full works for your benefit," continued Sharon. "Normally, I would have had him out the door after half an hour. And Adam, don't ever wear a suit or shoes like that." As if I would, he thought, mentally consigning his rather nice brown M & S suit to the back of the wardrobe.

As agreed, Noone led the second interview. He followed Sharon's patter and pattern religiously. It all went rather well until the end, when he asked the candidate, a sharp, confident Londoner, who had been objectionably arrogant throughout, if he had any questions:

"Have I made the shortlist?" was the blunt reply. This flummoxed Noone.

"Well," he began cautiously, "that's a good question. You are certainly well qualified, and I can see your experience is quite relevant, but..." he tailed off.

"But what? Are you going to put me on the shortlist or not?"

"In all likelihood, all things being equal, in the final analysis, probably..." Noone lapsed into business-babble, turning beseechingly and in panic to Sharon.

"The thing is," interjected Sharon authoritatively, "you are only the second person we have interviewed so it is impossible to say. You are certainly ahead at this stage." She smiled sweetly. "We will be in touch as soon as we can."

"Do you ever tell them immediately?" asked Noone when the Cockney rebel had departed.

"Just occasionally you see someone so good that you need to jump on them at once." She smiled coyly, which reminded Noone that it was fortunate that he didn't fancy her. "Usually though, it is best to hedge your bets. Unless they are complete no-hopers, in which case get rid of them asap." She recounted the story of Hugo's twenty minute encounter with St John Baptiste to underline the point.

Noone was rather disappointed to hear that stars shone infrequently. He had fondly imagined being endlessly entertained by tales of commercial derring-do from thrusting, successful businessmen and, occasionally, businesswomen. Sharon had confirmed what the pruning of the slush-pile had indicated: much of the executive population of Britain was intensely mediocre. This was reinforced over the next couple of years as the recession hit hard. After Nigel Lawson's 1988 budget, hailed by Thatcher as "quite the most brilliant we have seen", it was downhill all the way: interest rates rose as the economy overheated, inflation produced boom-bust excess, the balance of payments became wholly unbalanced and the UK's failure to join the ERM produced the first stress-fractures over membership of the European Economic Community. In businesses all over the country, bonds between employer and employee which promised mutual loyalty for life, were becoming irrevocably shattered. Voluntary redundancies gave way to compulsory redundancies, which became commonplace. Many workers, both blue and white collar, did not enjoy the luxury of Mr Lawson's resignation because of "choosing to spend more time with his family". They were forced to.

For executive selection consultancies, this manifested itself in an increased number of responses, many from so-called managers who had worked in only one company where they had been promoted through longevity to (and usually beyond) the limits of their competence. Forcibly released into a hard and uncaring world, these shattered wretches applied to advertisements in droves, with initially downbeat, then plaintive and anxious and finally desperate covering letters. Almost all were destined to be repeatedly rejected. Especially Gawain Nosworthy, who, over a period of eighteen months, applied promptly and inappropriately to every single advertisement placed by AB Selection Uxbridge. Gordon Sharpe ran a book on which number would be allocated to his CV each time- the quicker he applied, the lower the number. Usually he was in the first twenty. They had to create special, ever-more-inventive Nosworthy rejection letters ("Dear Gawain, mortifyingly, once again it behoves me to shoulder the dolorific burden of conveying to you the infelicitous news that such-and-such position falls tantalisingly just outside your marginally inefficacious skill-set..."). Noone just wanted to tell him to fuck off and die. Then one day he did. Nosworthy was reported as a suicide in the Uxbridge Echo, taking "passenger action" by throwing himself off the platform and under the incoming 0719 from Hillingdon. They never heard from him again.

Noone realised how large this universe of lost souls was as he sifted through the slush-pile for his second assignment, Tantalize. The world and his wife felt qualified to become its Operations Director. Noone had to wade through five hundred and sixty seven CVs. Eager at first, certain that he would spot real stars from such a wealth of response, he emerged the wiser from CV number 567, having brought down his "time spent" to twenty seconds per CV. Applying Sharon's strict elimination criteria plus a few quirks of his own (no garishly coloured paper, no names containing an X or Z, no CVs typed in capitals, no hand-written covering letters) he pruned the 567 to eight possibles, or "Holds" as they were termed. Noone's delight in his improved sifting efficiency ratio of three per minute was tempered by dismay at receiving applications from five hundred and fifty nine no-hopers, or "B's", signifying "Bin". Humfrey Smallwood was delighted to hear that so many people were interested in the job. Noone, advised by Sharon, told him that it was "early days" and too soon to comment on the quality, which after all was the main thing, but that he was confident of finding a shortlist. He also kept Hugo Reeve-Prior in the loop.

"Are you confident of finding a shortlist?" Reeve-Prior asked. Noone didn't really know, but not wanting to appear uncertain quite so early, said he was.

The interviews proved more entertaining than for the FD of Potentiality, and he was able to exclude two male applicants on the basis of their over-enthusiasm for the products; one, he was almost sure, was a transvestite, so lovingly did he describe his desire to be handling, if only metaphorically, female undergarments. In fact, an excellent candidate did appear in the form of Fuchsia Darling, not that Noone was swayed by the name of course. She was a raw-boned, personable, feisty Scottish lass from the glens near Blairgowrie and Noone liked the facts that she was competitive (a single-figure golfer, playing off eight at Alyth) unmarried (therefore unencumbered by husband or children) and had large tits (useful in a tight negotiating position). That she had spent her career to date in Marks & Spencer, including time in Buying within the Womenswear department was an additional bonus. She had also just taken voluntary redundancy, which suggested that she would not be too precious over salary.

Fuchsia Darling was the undoubted jewel in an otherwise ordinary shortlist. Try as he might, Noone couldn't in all honesty add more than two other candidates, one a garrulous chap in a flamboyantly motifed tie and red socks with retail clothing experience from a succession of less than premium brands, the other a staid but forthright fellow from a carpet manufacturer. Within thirty days as decreed by Sharon, he had painstakingly written reports on them (still five drafts, much to Dragon-lady's disgust) and arranged for them to meet Humfrey Smallwood at Tantalize's premises. He then waited in an agony of suspense for Smallwood's verdict. When the phone rang and Irene announced Smallwood on the line, Noone was shaking and his armpits were wet.

"I've seen them all," said Smallwood, "bit disappointing really. Is that the best you can do?" Noone's heart sank. It was just what he feared. He asked Smallwood to elaborate.

"Well, I think the chap in the strange tie is a poof and I can't work with them. Couldn't quite see the other chap fitting in; he has an elderly mother living in Barnsley of all places. And then there is the girl."

"Yes. I thought she was very good and ticked all the boxes," interrupted Noone, trying desperately to impart some enthusiasm.

"But she is of the other gender, so to speak, and I am not sure I saw my second director as a female of the species," returned Smallwood. You stuffed-shirted dinosaur, thought Noone. He screwed up his courage and backed his judgement, in which he had little faith:

"Humfrey, these are the best three, believe me, and I think they could all do the job. If you don't feel there is good, personal chemistry between you and the two men, fine; but Fuchsia has exactly the right experience: don't reject her just because she is a woman. You are not allowed to anyway." Sharon had given him a quick lesson in the "do's and "don'ts" of discrimination and had intimated that the drive towards diversity had begun in some quarters, particularly the Public Sector, which would make their job increasingly difficult. "Invite her back, show her around, take her out to lunch, get to know her."

Reluctantly Smallwood allowed himself to be drawn towards Fuchsia. She in turn had reservations about whether he would be able to "let go of the reins" and allow her to do the job that she could see was crying out to be done. It was a miracle that Tantalize had got to where it was without any real disciplines and controls, other than the whims of Humfrey Smallwood. She confided her concerns to Noone, who understood perfectly. The Four Horsemen of the Apocalypse couldn't have dragged him to work in the fulltime employment of Humfrey Smallwood, but in the meantime, he had to get Fuchsia in there; at least she had indicated she was strongly motivated by the challenge. Grudgingly, Smallwood agreed to make her an offer, ignoring Noone's advice to go £5k more than she had been earning, instead pushing his boat out to a miserly £47k and instructing Noone that he wouldn't be pushed further. Out-of-work Fuchsia could not negotiate from a position of strength, especially as Noone, closely advised by Reeve-Prior, had informed her apologetically that if she played too hard to get, Smallwood would certainly offer it to one or other of her two excellent competitors on the shortlist whom Fuchsia had narrowly beaten *at this stage*. Prudently, again following Reeve-Prior's forcible advice, Noone had "kept warm" the man who was raving good with colours and the carpet-man, now more of an underlay. After some minor discussion about the type of company car she would be allowed and whether it was fully expensed including miles to and from work (it wasn't) she accepted the job at the salary £5k less than her market worth.

Even if Smallwood was damning with faint praise, Reeve-Prior congratulated Noone warmly but warned him the job was not yet over.

"Don't forget the qualifications check and reference taking. Ask her for five referees (two past bosses, one peer, one subordinate and one personal) then ask one of them for another person whom she hasn't volunteered. Spend at least fifteen minutes on the phone with each; and remember, it is a great opportunity to talk about AB Selection and develop business." Thankfully, she had not lied about her degree in Politics from Lancaster University and all the referees spoke adoringly about her. She started work at Tantalize the following week.

"Now we just have to hope she stays put for the duration of our six month guarantee period," said Reeve-Prior. "After that, Humfrey would have to pay us to do the job again." Noone thought this a trifle mercenary, given that Reeve-Prior's and Smallwood's friendship went back some thirty years. In "signing off" the two other hopefuls, Noone made the mistake of apologising to Carpet-man, saying he had been perfectly well qualified for the job and had only missed out because of "the slightly better chemistry of the successful candidate". Noone had thanked him earnestly for his time and told him he felt sure he would soon be successful in his job search. Over the next two years Carpet-man rang him every two months "to see if you have found me a job yet". Noone had learned the hard way never to say he was sorry.

As far as the assignment for Potentiality was

concerned, he was better covered, with four qualified accountants (a competent ACCA, a hands-on ACMA and two rising young ACA's keen to distance themselves from Practice). Mr Ponderous pronounced himself satisfied with the shortlist and the assignment proceeded (far too slowly in anxious Noone's view) to offer. One of the thrusting ACAs was the lucky chap and Noone knew he would accept because he had told Noone that this was "his preferred option". Sharon warned him not to tell Mr Ponderous this, but he was so confident that he did so. When Noone made the candidate the offer, he prevaricated for five days and then rejected it for a better offer elsewhere. Noone was devastated; this bloke had strung him along with blandishments, lied to him and then kicked sand in his face before exiting abruptly stage left waving two fingers. Bastard! Sharon calmed him down. She was sanguine: this sort of thing happened quite regularly, but she stressed the importance of probing the best candidates' motivations thoroughly and not telling the client everything.

"Make them see you as a friend to whom they have unburdened their innermost thoughts. That way, they are more likely to feel guilty about letting you down and less likely to do it."

Fortunately, it had been a close-run decision between The Bastard and the second ACA: Mr Ponderous, although disappointed that Noone had failed to deliver his first choice (having told him he was "in the bag") nevertheless was prepared to consider offering the job to the second candidate. Of course, it took him a week or so to decide (nervous Noone hopping on hot coals the while) for he needed to cover his back by "getting the MD's buy-in" as he put it. This time, all went smoothly and Noone had successfully delivered his second assignment.

The learning curve had been steep. Noone had endured the rollercoaster of emotion that accompanied each assignment, from the exhilaration of winning the engagement, through the uncertainty of wondering whether any decent candidates would materialise and the despair of losing the chosen candidate, to the sense of satisfaction and achievement with the successful conclusion. Overall, he had enjoyed the experience and felt he had found the right niche for himself. Sharon and Hugo, outwardly expressing delight at the completion of both projects, were not so sure. Yes, he had proved he could deliver. But could he develop business of his own? Could he sell?

8. SETTLING IN

"CT Partners is a premier-quality executive search firm that is both results-oriented and nimble. We are a performance driven organisation and strive to exceed client expectations. We do so through searches that feature world-class candidates, supported by industry-best service, intelligence, and proprietary technology and communication tools."

CHRISTIAN AND TIMBERS WEBSITE

It wasn't long before Noone had exhausted his contact list. He had sent out a standard letter revealing to the hundred or so people in business who knew him, the exciting change of career which had brought him to this dynamic, high-quality environment, AB Selection. He had pointed out how he was now trained and qualified to handle on their behalf any executive resourcing needs which they may uncover, now or in the future. Disappointingly, he received only three replies: one said it sounded very interesting and wished him well; the second was from his cricket club Life President who told him he "never used headhunters"; the third wondered if his new company would care for regular deliveries of bottled water. Noone was particularly incensed by this as he couldn't abide the new, continental-holiday-induced desire to pay exorbitant amounts of money for something tasteless that in any case came out of a tap endlessly for free. Spell Evian backwards, he mused maliciously.

Then he had followed up by phone. Some were unavailable and didn't bother to return the call. Some claimed not to have received his letter. Those to whom he did speak all treated him pleasantly enough, but seemed wary, as if he had caught some unspecified contagion. Many told him they didn't have the need for his new services, some said they "would keep his details on file". More hopefully, several agreed to see him, although Noone suspected it was the prospect of a free lunch which he had perhaps injudiciously offered, that attracted them. Nobody expressed undying gratitude because he had called just as the Sales Director had handed in his resignation. Noone wondered what, if he was here to help others, the others were here for? Probably for blaming when things went wrong. Certainly nobody was helping him. He sought solace in a couple of pints of Belters Misfit in the Ostler at lunchtime. Musing into his glass, he felt disgruntled, then wondered whether that word should not more aptly be applied to a pig which had lost its voice.

He went off on a daydream. Talking of pigs, why is a guineapig so called when it is neither from Guinea nor a pig? And presumably, if someone who plays a piano is a pianist, but those who race are not always racists, this proves that racists were invented before racing? In any case noses run and feet smell, although noses can smell that sweetmeats are sweets but sweetbreads are meat. If a priest rather than a woman can be defrocked, then doesn't it follow that electricians can be delighted, musicians denoted, cowboys deranged, models deposed, tree surgeons debarked, and dry cleaners depressed? He marvelled at the sheer lunacy of a language in which a building burns up as it burns down, you play at a recital but recite at a play, fill in a form by filling it out, get up from the table to get down, and turn on an alarm which will go off when it comes on. Why do slim and fat chance mean the same, but wise man and wise guy the opposite? And how can you make amends but not a single amend?

Back in the office, Dragon-lady was fluttering around in an ecstasy of excitement, announcing that Hugo Reeve-Prior had just phoned to arrange a visit to the Uxbridge office at midday that Friday and she was booking time in their diaries for him to meet Sharon, Gordon and Noone individually. Though his pulse quickened nervously at the news, Noone suspected nothing sinister. Gordon, keen to impress Hugo with his epicurean erudition, offered self-importantly to take them all out to lunch to experience "an elegant little place in the country". Come the day, the office having been tidied and told not to step out of place, and Hugo's military-style inspection completed with only one major dust-trap discovered, the four of them squeezed into the Saab. The two secretaries were deemed worthy enough to "hold the fort" until the more important people returned, although Dragon-lady, who had preened and twittered around Hugo, was secretly pleased at the responsibility invested in her.

Avoiding the reverse into Noone's lamppost was a good start but the failure of consumer satellite navigation devices to be invented yet proved Gordon's undoing. He was aiming for The Chequers Inn at Wooburn Common, close to the Thames at Bourne End. "The cosiest 17th century inn imaginable, with beamed ceilings and a modern touch" proved extremely elusive, as Gordon had only visited once before in the dark for dinner. He knew Hugo would appreciate it for it had fine fare and a classy cellar, but after an hour in the car most of which was spent investigating country lanes around the Cliveden estate, Sharon and Noone in the back were distinctly queasy and Hugo was distinctly annoyed. He had assumed they were going to lunch at Cliveden, which although expensive and a trifle indulgent, would have pleased him with its grandeur and sense of history. But they appeared to be heading for some tiny pub which the pompous fool Sharpe couldn't even find.

Gordon's reassurances about the excellence of the menu and winelist had tailed off into a tense, awkward silence. His forehead was damp, his hands clammy on the wheel which was leather, fortunately, and hence slightly absorbent. Hugo had just decreed that they would have to abandon lunch and return to Uxbridge when they rounded a bend and chanced upon a pub called the Walnut Tree on Dorney Wood Road. In desperation Sharon suggested they stop and in desperation Gordon and Hugo agreed. Noone noted the petanque pitch adjacent to the carpark approvingly but judged it prudent not to suggest a game. Inside the smoke-filled interior they received poor service, school-dinnerish, micro-waved ready-meals and a bottle of execrable Chablis (at Gordon's insistence) which would have been best disguised within the fishy entrails of a Marseilles bouillabaisse. Thus, they failed to discover the Chequers's oak posts and beams, and returned circuitously and unhappily to the office, enveloped by Hugo's dudgeon. The afternoon did not bode well.

"Adam, good to see you; how are you getting on?" opened Hugo in his rich, resonating baritone, when they were alone in Noone's office with the door shut.

"Fine, thanks. I'm very happy." It was true. He was immeasurably happier than when he was dabbling in gas bottles.

"And how are they treating you here?"

"Great. Sharon and Gordon have been very helpful; and so have Irene and Daphne." He was feeling magnanimous enough to include Dragon-lady in his praise.

"You've completed two assignments satisfactorily, so you can consider yourself an expert now. In my view, formal training is a waste of time. Either you've got it or you haven't, don't you agree?" Noone thought this sweeping generalisation was a trifle harsh.

"Well, I think there is a time and a place for degrees of training…" He tailed off, skewered by Hugo's gimlet eye.

"And how is the business development coming along?" This was the killer question, not unanticipated by Noone, but perhaps not quite so early and pointedly.

"It's a long job isn't it? I've been in touch with all my contacts and I have several meetings set up. Nobody desperate to throw work at me yet, unfortunately." He said, with a weak attempt at humour.

"That's a pity. It is the business development side which determines how successful you become in this profession." Noone was pleased to hear that he was now in a profession. Nobody could pretend that hawking gas cylinders was a profession. But Hugo's tone was serious as he continued: "Most consultants can transact a half-decent assignment; but developing and winning business yourself, that's the key." Not so much talk about teamwork now, thought Noone wryly.

"How long have you been with us now?" asked Hugo, knowing full well it was five months exactly.

"About five months" said Noone.

"Well I'll give you a little challenge. You have a month to develop your first piece of business." This was a bombshell. Whatever happened to the two years that Giles Bane had promised?

"I see. And what happens if I don't?"

"We will have to look at your terms. If you want to carry on, perhaps we can arrange it on a reduced salary or associate basis. But let's not be negative; I am sure you will rise to the challenge, Adam." Hugo smiled and rose to his feet. "Good luck."

Noone watched him walk back to the main office and say his goodbyes. His taxi was booked for 1600hrs to take him back to London. Honeymoon over, welcome to the real world, he thought bitterly. Hugo's words had a physical effect like a punch in the stomach; there was a large, hollow, contracting feeling, the like of which he had not experienced since his first adult love, Lizzie, had walked out on him. There was also a sense of rising anger and a growing determination to shove those bitter words right back down Hugo's throat, at least figuratively. Noone was not a quitter; he would show the short, self-satisfied sailor what he could do.

Noone applied himself in a forlorn frenzy of phonecalls both to his contacts and those of the firm which were lying dormant and unclaimed, according to Sharon who passed him files containing former, unsuccessful business development approaches. Three cheerless weeks rushed by, during which he cancelled his annual trip to Les Vingt-quatre Heures du Mans to concentrate on safeguarding his income. It was as bad as that.

Finally, there was a bite on one of his lines; a cricketing chum, Mex Knoki (also known as "Flagrant" after his habit of yodelling "Lonely Goat-herd" after eight pints and a vindaloo) worked for a construction services outfit, Bisham Bentley. Mex knew that his firm needed a Project Director to take on a major refurbishment programme behind the façade of a large, listed building in the City, covering over 200,000 square feet of space. He convinced his reluctant MD that it was worth talking to AB Selection and a meeting was arranged. Noone proudly asked Hugo Reeve-Prior to join him.

Bisham Bentley's MD, Lee Stevens, proved obdurate. Painstakingly, they explained that resourcing senior executives requires unique skills, experience, tact and time. By bringing in AB Selection's specialist expertise, Stevens would be able to focus on his core business. Further, they would bring objective analysis, confidentiality, a wide network from the sector, knowledge of the market and a rigorous process that was proven to produce outstanding results. Surely he could see the benefits?

He could see the benefits but naturally he didn't want to pay for them. If Noone and Hugo were so good, so well-connected and confident of finding good people, why should he have to pay for a costly advertisement? Couldn't they produce two or three candidates from their database and agree to being paid a fee only if and when he hired one of them? Noone squirmed: Stevens had a point. He was relieved when Hugo responded eloquently and firmly that it was important to investigate the market thoroughly anew, for each job was unique and this role was so critical to Bisham Bentley's future prosperity that sterile databases should not be relied upon to identify the most appropriate and interested candidates. Stevens was not completely convinced and wondered if there were any guarantees. Noone felt confident enough to assure him that a six month period applied, during which, if the candidate left or was removed for any reason, AB Selection would carry out a fresh assignment free of charge. This seemed to improve Stevens's demeanour, although Noone didn't go on to tell him that there were one or two caveats and he would of course have to pay for a new advertisement; the nasty stuff was all carefully covered in the small print of their Ts & Cs. They agreed on the submission of a proposal being the obvious way forward, shook hands and departed. Hugo was pleased.

"Well done Adam, I knew you could do it. I think he will go for it, don't you?" Noone, desperately hoping he was right, wasn't sure. He sweated over the proposal, and the advertisement, accommodating Hugo's corrections and suggestions into the by now customary five drafts. Irene, contented with her GCE in English, was quite amused by the fuss that was taken over the words and punctuation and regaled her wide-eyed mother with tales of how much stationery was wasted in the office, "I have to put new paper in the printer and photocopier every five minutes, honest; it's like using half a Brazilian rain-forest," she exaggerated for effect. Her mother, bless, wasn't sure how much a brazilian was, but it sounded a lot and she was suitably overawed.

For two weeks, Noone was as jumpy as a shot squirrel, awaiting the call that would seal his fate, conscious that six months was up. Stevens was beginning to validate Noone's inherent distrust of strangers, when Irene finally indicated that the MD of Bisham Bentley was on the line. All the moisture in his body flew to his armpits and his throat went dry.

"The proposal's fine," said Stevens. Noone's heart soared. "Except for the fee." Noone's heart sank. "Overall it is ok." Soared. "But I only want to pay the second tranche if I feel the shortlist is good enough." Sank. "And I'll pay the final tranche when the appointee starts work, not before." Sank further. What would Hugo say?

"Thanks Lee. I'll need to run it by Hugo as what you are suggesting is outside our normal Terms." To Noone's delight, Hugo was happy that the overall fee of £18,000 remained intact; he could live with the delayed cash-flow. A relieved Noone relayed the good news to Stevens; and the noose fell away from Noone's neck.

"YES!" he ran out and shouted to the office, punching the air with both fists, forgetting the state of his armpits. Sharon and Gordon came into his room to congratulate him and even Dragon-lady smiled. The next day a bottle of champagne arrived from Hugo. Noone was over the moon. He had definitely cracked it this time.

Time went by as Noone settled into his new life. The recession decimated the well-established brands such as MSL, Hoggett Bowers and PA that had been at the top of the executive selection tree since the beginning, for they had grown fat and lazy, populated by too many semi-illiterate "travellers" who had forgotten how to sell. The lavish Christmas gifts (£250 John Lewis gift vouchers to every employee) declined to a small box of chocolate-covered peanuts. What had become barren for them ironically proved fertile soil for the sharper, hungrier later arrivals and both NB and AB Selection prospered. Within a couple of years, both had established satellite offices in the major cities- Bristol, Birmingham, Manchester, Leeds, Aberdeen, Glasgow, Edinburgh with London gaining a City office serving Financial Services clients as well as the West End HQ. AB Selection rebranded to the snappier ABS and reached further into the provincial hinterland with offices in Exeter, Basingstoke, Liverpool, Sheffield, Middlesborough, even Norwich, because Hugo had a soft spot for Norfolk, the home county of his maritime hero, Admiral Lord Horatio Nelson.

The Uxbridge office enjoyed more than its share of success and having hired three new consultants and two secretaries, moved to more modern and spacious premises on Harefield Road. Sharon organised a cocktail party for clients to open the office formally and Hugo descended again, reluctantly, to grace the "do" and say a few words. Privately, these words were an incredulous observation to Gordon that several of his IT clients were not wearing proper footwear:

"My God, they seem to be wearing canvas shoes; are they going sailing?" Publically, though, he welcomed all friends of ABS to the new premises, which he hoped would be a powerhouse of continued good fortune for them all, client, candidate and consultant alike. Noone slightly blotted his copybook by enjoying a champagne-fuelled conversation with one of his would-be clients rather too much. It was half an hour after the party was due to end and Hugo pointedly interrupted by seizing the client's hand and, thanking him profusely for attending, walked him to the door.

"I could see you needed rescuing," he said, returning to Noone. "What a ghastly man, overstaying his welcome like that." Hugo then took them for dinner at the Heathrow Radisson Edwardian, where, as far as Noone could recall, the evening passed convivially with more toasts to the new office. Unfortunately, the champagne followed by the wine at dinner, the post-prandial brandy and an ill-advised Grolsch "flusher" took their toll, and he remembered nothing of the drive home.

Noone occasionally felt uncomfortable about the way they were paid to discriminate, but, like an alcohol-induced upset stomach reviving for the next hit, these feelings were receding: he had learned about Hugo's St John Baptiste incident early on, but other stories emerged. One of Gordon's clients refused to interview anyone with a beard, which wouldn't have been much of a problem if Gordon's shortlist had been packed with women. Unfortunately, the job was a particularly nerdy, technical IT role and candidates with beards (and ponytails) outnumbered women lots to nil. As delicately as possible, Gordon advised his shortlist to appear clean-shaven and clean-cut before the client. One hirsute candidate, who had turned up in jeans and a polo shirt, objected to the curtailment of his freedom of choice and told him to "stuff his poxy job". Irene saw him nine months later entering a bank, neatly-trimmed and wearing a suit, which made them all feel better.

Another of Gordon's assignments proved to be the absolute antithesis and tested the client's own commitment to diversity to the limit. It was a US-headquartered IT company that was proud to be pioneering a zero-tolerance stance on any kind of discrimination as well as a positive recruitment policy of appointing normally disadvantaged social minorities such as one-legged lesbian single-mothers of non-Caucasian racial origin. Gordon was pleased to have secured for his Senior Technical Architect shortlist one Leslie Snipkin, an expert specifically in the client company's design format software. Leslie was a Sergeant in the Territorial Army, divorced with no children, and wanted to relocate from Hull to Hampshire, where the company had its UK base. He was the perfect candidate and was offered the job. Only then did he reveal that he was one operation short of becoming Lesley and that operation was booked for the next month. In short, he would be turning up for work as a woman, was that okay? Gordon was hugely embarrassed, having failed to spot Leslie's beautifully manicured hands, powdered chin and budding breasts. He tried to bluff it out:

"Leslie's delighted to accept the offer" he reported to the client's Recruitment Manager with whom he was dealing. "He just asks that you honour two weeks' holiday he has booked next month to complete his sex-change operation." The Recruitment Manager was horrified.

"But the team is expecting a male team-leader. We'll have to withdraw the offer on the grounds of misrepresentation." Gordon pointed out that Leslie hadn't actually misrepresented himself and had notified them in advance of his "changing circumstances".

"In any case," he said, "remember your own diversity policy. It will be quite a coup to have a trans-sexual. Onboard." He completed hurriedly. In the end, they decided to ask Leslie to meet the team and tell the members personally that she would be joining them, memberless. Gordon proved right, the novelty value won them over, with one of the blokes saying it was fine by him as it meant "one less competitor to worry about at the Christmas party".

Noone, himself, had a tricky time with a Japanese company, whose avuncular British Managing Director he had nurtured over several lunches until he conceded a sales director position to Noone.

"And of course," said the MD, concluding the briefing, "you won't give us any females on the shortlist, will you? Mr Nakatake would find that, ah, inappropriate." He nodded in the direction of his Japanese "shadow-director", who had remained unsmiling and mute at the head of the boardroom table throughout. Noone wondered if he spoke English.

"Yes, it would be unfortunate." said Mr Nakatake, in perfect English. Noone started to say that it was his job to provide the best possible shortlist of the three or four most qualified, available candidates for the job, irrespective of age, gender or creed, when Mr Nakatake interrupted coldly:

"If you want to help us with this job, you must do as we say; if not, we will find someone who will." Noone was annoyed and affronted that the gentlemen in front of him were treating him less as an equal, more as a schoolboy. Didn't they understand that he was not just their paid lackey? He was their partner, a *consultant* from whom they were asking specialist advice, not someone over whom they could ride roughshod, to whom they could dictate their terms.

He quashed his qualms and took the job. Luckily, only five women found themselves interested enough in becoming UK Sales Director of a manufacturer of automotive components to apply. Noone felt able to ignore them easily.

The path was not always smooth. One successful candidate, on whom Noone was taking references, turned out to be the subject of a sexual harassment claim from his former firm. It transpired that after a long conference day washed down by a long dinner and even longer tasting session at the hotel bar, the candidate was found on three separate occasions during the course of the night, pounding on a female colleague's bedroom door whilst tired, emotional and naked. When Noone confronted the candidate with the knowledge of this transgression, the candidate protested that "it was all a misunderstanding". Noone wondered how the misunderstanding could have occurred three times and said he would have to report the incident to the client. As he duly relayed the news over the phone, there was a pause followed by an ominous silence filled by the imaginary sound of splintering glass as Noone saw the assignment blowing up in his face. Finally, the client said;

"It's a shame. But the previous incumbent couldn't keep his prick in his trousers either, so I guess we are used to it."

9. "COLONEL" NED R. PORAGE

"Whether our clients need a single visionary leader or an entire company-changing team, Norman Broadbent has the ability to search for and find the very best executive talent. We develop a deep understanding of the organisations we work with, providing them not only with an industry leading executive search offering, but with value added services including interim management, executive assessment and development, and diversity consultancy."

NORMAN BROADBENT WEBSITE

One day, Noone was reflecting on The Culpepper Cattle Company, a reasonably violent Western he had watched selfishly while his wife slept beside him on the sofa the previous evening. There were some memorable lines in it:

"That don't make me nevermind," was one, drawled by a particularly slow-witted cowboy.

"You don't want to put a name on something you might need to eat," was another, by an unsentimental character about his horse.

"Don't let your mouth overload your hardware, cowboy" was his favourite. He wondered if he could work it into a candidate report:

"This candidate possesses the unfortunate ability to allow his mouth to overload his hardware." He carried on extemporising. "With great delusions of adequacy, when he opens his mouth, it seems he does so only to change his feet. A prime candidate for natural de-selection, he has donated his brain selflessly to science before corrupting it with use. Indeed, of his two operating brain cells, one appears to be lost and the other is out looking for it. Some drink from the fount of knowledge, but he only gargled, and if he were marginally more unintelligent, he would have to stand in the corner and be watered twice a week.

This candidate is depriving a village somewhere of an idiot."

The phone rang annoyingly, startling him from his flight of fancy. He thought about pretending to be his recorded answerphone voice: "Hello, I am sorry but I am out of my mind at the moment. Please leave a message at the tone." However, the call was from a real-live cowboy who could be ignored no longer. It was "Colonel" Ned R. Porage.

"Colonel" Ned R.Porage implied he was in the SAS. He never actually said so and if asked straight to his face "Were you in the SAS?" he would merely look pityingly at the person who had had the temerity to ask, raise an eyebrow and allow the corners of his mouth to twitch slightly in a deviously inscrutable way. Years ago, deciding it reflected weakness, he had trained himself not to smile and now he was physically incapable facially of revealing emotion. In fact, it was a moot point as to whether he was capable of emotion, full stop. He was as strange as a hovercraft full of eels.

His parents had been shopkeepers in Buxton, Derbyshire and in retirement, proudly boasted it had been in the days when England was a nation of shopkeepers, rather than a nation of Asian shopkeepers. He never forgave them for being shopkeepers, nor did he forgive them for calling him Ned. As parents do, they had chosen a name close to their hearts, and "Ned" reflected the cosy warmth and rustic charm of the stolidly old-fashioned and soon-to-disappear values of rural England in which they passionately believed: work hard, believe in the community and treat your neighbour as yourself. The adolescent Ned came to hate all of this twee twaddle. He converted his equally homely middle name of Reginald (after his father) to "R." as soon as he was able to write and, convinced of his military destiny early, awarded himself the rank of "Colonel" to counter the weakness of "Ned". He also never forgave his parents for not living in Yorkshire. Whilst Derbyshire seemed to him indeterminate, soft and yielding, of which he could find nothing to be proud, Yorkshire stood for determination, grit and a defiant stare that said "I am what I am, and if you don't like it, you can sod off. And by the way, that spade is a fucking spade."

Saddled with these handicaps from birth, young Ned sought a way out as quickly as possible. After a solitary, lonely childhood seasoned with endless playground fights (he once took exception to and thumped little Albert Dustmote "because he was there") at sixteen he joined the Army and became an early entrant into the Royal Regiment of Fusiliers, formed in 1968 by the amalgamation of four former line infantry regiments and desperate for volunteers. Single-minded, hard-working and utterly driven to make his mark and become a real colonel, Ned rose through the ranks, becoming a non-commissioned officer by the age of twenty eight and subsequently applying for a transfer to Special Forces. He was rejected. He applied every year for the next five years and was rejected every time. Despite not being in one of the more prestigious regiments such as 1 Para, from which the SAS tended to draw its elite, it wasn't that he wasn't capable; he passed all the theory and practical tests with flying colours. It was the psychometrics, or personality tests, which did for him. They uncovered just a little too much missionary zeal for violence. All was not lost for Ned, however.

Since 1964, there had been a continuing separatist revolt in the Dhofar Province of Oman. Aided by communist and leftist governments such as the former South Yemen (People's Democratic Republic of Yemen), the rebels formed the Dhofar Liberation Front, which later merged with the Marxist-dominated Popular Front for the Liberation of Oman and the Arab Gulf (PFLOAG). The PFLOAG's declared intention was to overthrow all traditional Arab Gulf regimes. In mid-1974, realising that its acronym was way too long, PFLOAG shortened its name to the Popular Front for the Liberation of Oman

(PFLO) and embarked on a political rather than a military approach to gain power in the other Gulf states, while continuing the guerrilla war in Dhofar. With the help of British advisors, Sultan Qaboos bin Sa'id assumed power on July 23, 1970, in a palace coup directed against his father, Sa'id bin Taymur, who later died in exile in London. Determined to end the insurgency, Sultan Qaboos re-equipped the armed forces and granted amnesty to all rebels who surrendered. He also obtained direct military support from Britain. The Fusiliers were selected for a tour of duty there. This gave Ned his chance.

Over a two year campaign, Ned and his men waged covert war interspersed with overt firefights across the wadis and wastes of Oman in pursuit of the PFLO. He was in his steel element, finally allowed to impose his violent self legitimately on the illegal enemy of a lawful State; specifically, on several occasions, the Fusiliers acted in support of a sabre squadron of the SAS which had been HALO parachuted into deep battlespace, thus giving Ned's Special Forces aspirations endorsement by association. By early 1975, the guerrillas were confined to a 50-square kilometre area near the Yemen border and shortly thereafter vanished. As the war drew to a close, civil action programmes were instigated throughout Dhofar and helped win the allegiance of the people. Relations improved considerably between South Yemen and Oman over the next few years as the former lessened its subversive activities, and in late 1987, Oman appointed its first resident ambassador to South Yemen, opening an embassy in Aden. Although this was a job which Ned would have coveted, he was long gone by then.

He was promoted to Captain on completion of his tour of duty and return to Blighty. Sadly, the pinnacle of his military career already had been achieved. He never saw active service again and was knocked back for further promotion: his occasional violent rages which had been known to reduce "squaddies" to tears were noted on his service record along with comments about his lack of team orientation and general detachment from fellow man. The phrase "possible loose cannon" was used to devastating effect. Eventually, in 1980, persuaded by the offer of an operations management job in a small manufacturing company belonging to a former Sergeant-Major who had de-mobbed several years before, he resigned his commission. He stayed long enough to "learn the ropes" in civvy street before applying to a much larger firm "with more troops to command", with "Colonel Ned R. Porage" embossed on his italicised, headed, personal stationery. The MD of this maker-of-springs-for-biros company was impressed at the high rank, active service record and relevant manufacturing management experience and hired him immediately, failing to spot his sociopathic tendencies.

In five years, "Colonel" Ned's single-minded, ruthless drive had seen off the MD. It helped that the factory was sited in Pontypridd, which had a large workforce of disenfranchised mining families to sustain and "Colonel" Ned's autocratic, military style of management was tolerated for livelihood purposes. Amazingly, a local woman, Berthog Gedrych, elected to fall for his austere and charmless lack of personality, perhaps mistaking it for masculine mystery but hopeful that, at the very least, he might one day take her away from her drab and meaningless existence, stifled by the area's obsolete pride in its glorious mining history. They married and she bore him three children in four years before shutting up shop with instant migraines. Locally, "Colonel" Ned became known as "The King of the Springs" or just "Zebedee". Then suddenly, Big Business worked its magic and the company was taken over by a biro barrel manufacturer seeking to extend production to other critical component areas in order to secure a stronger market position.

The new owners took one look at "Colonel" Ned R. Porage's autocratic and outdated management style and decided that they could do without it and "let him go". Stunned, he spent the best part of 1989 buying the Sunday

Times and the Thursday Telegraph and applying for MD positions in manufacturing, with predictable results: he was rejected out of hand for 95% of them and where he was offered an interview, the interviewer soon took fright at his detached, slightly menacing and deranged self-confidence. Invariably, "Colonel" Ned was told, the recession was the reason for the client's decision not to hire him. Berthog began to wonder if she had backed a champion horse after all.

The Officers' Association is a charitable institution dedicated to providing residential, financial or employment assistance to officers who have left Her Majesty's Armed Forces. "Colonel" Ned, increasingly bitter and disillusioned at the failure of corporate Britain to cherish his obvious management talents and record of achievement, eventually spotted an advertisement placed by Hugo Reeve-Prior in The OA's monthly magazine. It stated that retired officers would be welcome to apply to AB Selection, an executive selection consultancy, whatever that was. His interest piqued by something that actually seemed to welcome someone like him, "Colonel" Ned sent off a formal letter and his CV, which highlighted his personal involvement in suppressing guerilla warfare, complemented by his subsequent commercial success, hewn, against all odds, from darkest Wales.

Hugo was delighted to receive such a sparkling CV amongst the drizzle of despondency from newly retired sixty year old generals and group captains. (Of course he would always interview naval types, if only to send them on their way, happy with his personal career counselling). He was looking for someone to set up an office in Birmingham, and he thought "Colonel" Ned could easily be that someone, despite not hailing from a top regiment. Calling him into London for interview, Hugo buried this prejudice and actually enjoyed hearing about Ned's Omani exploits and the firm grip on the tiller he had shown with the biro business. He might seem a little fierce and dispassionate, but those qualities would work well for him in AB Selection; he had proved brave in battle, a leader of men and a successful, commercial MD.

"How would you feel about working in Birmingham?" he asked, fearing that it wasn't the most attractive of propositions.

"No problem sir." To "Colonel" Ned, it sounded like Paradise compared to Pontypridd.

"And the family?"

"No problem sir. Where I go, the wife and kids will follow. They know that."

"Good." Obviously a man who kept his wife under control. Hugo liked that. "And you don't have to call me sir."

"Thank you sir."

"Colonel" Ned accepted Hugo's resultant offer with alacrity, spent a month in the London HQ "learning the ropes" and in double-quick time with military precision, relocated his family to Coleshill ("Co's'l") just outside Castle Bromwich, identified an office in Birmingham, took out a five-year lease on the property in Windsor Street, equipped it, had house-style stationery printed, hired a secretary and joined the local Chamber of Commerce. With missionary zeal, he then embarked on a crusade to convert the businesses of Birmingham to the AB Selection cause. Whilst some, particularly women, found his peremptory style rather grating and politely declined to give him work, he met enough like-minded souls of similar vintage and narrow views to furnish himself with an expanding and profitable office, much to Hugo's delight. Three more consultants were hired and two more secretaries.

"Colonel" Ned grew his hair long and kept it black, slicking it back over his forehead and trapping it behind his ears with Brilliantine in the style of the "New Money". He affected a pencil moustache and dark blue, pinstripe, three-piece suits. Subtly, he modulated his voice, such that at first meeting, people assumed he was from the landed gentry with a few hundred acres in the wilds north of

Tamworth. Naturally, he did nothing to dispel this notion. Rightly at last, his star was in the ascendancy and Berthog was delighted with their rise up the social order. She assimilated herself comfortably into the local "coffee and gossip" set, where the talk was of the size of their husbands' company cars and on what domestic enhancement the next bonus would be spent. She and Ned treated the kids to a Beefeater dinner on the first Saturday of every month and on the third Wednesday, the two of them would dine self-importantly and alone at the Grimstock Country House Hotel, which served nice "home-grown English fayre".

Noone had met "Colonel" Ned R. Porage for the first time at a five kilometre charity run in Hyde Park. AB Selection had entered a team and called for volunteers. Noone, still relatively fit despite a slightly gammy knee, the result of an ill-judged off-piste skiing episode, allowed himself to be persuaded. "Colonel" Ned, possessor of a decent physique constantly toned by three sessions a week at David Lloyd Leisure, still keen to impress Hugo and ferociously competitive in any case, needed no persuading. Besides, a leisurely afternoon drive down to London and an overnight stay at the company's expense was due reward for the long hours he had been putting in. Three of the secretaries and an eager young consultant from the London office made up the team.

Noone had heard on the company grapevine that "Colonel" Ned R. Porage was highly driven, ex-SAS and perhaps a trifle strange. He found out for himself that day. Noone was pleased to have finished 1,129th out of around 5,000, ahead of four of his team-mates. "Colonel" Ned left them all for dead at the Starter's gun and came in 15th, annoyed that there were 14 fitter, albeit much younger, runners than he. He drove Noone back to the office to change while the young consultant took the three girls. During the journey, "Colonel" Ned's car-phone rang. It was his wife reminding him of his eldest daughter's sports' day.

"Put her on," he commanded. "Hello dear, how did you get on today?...You won three races and came second in the last one?" Noone was pleased for the child. "Colonel" Ned wasn't.

"That's a shame. Why didn't you win the last race as well? You'll have to take some extra fitness training. Goodbye." Noone couldn't believe someone could be so unfeeling; the poor little kid. He never found out what her name was. "Colonel" Ned never told anyone his children's names.

"That's the trouble these days," said "Colonel" Ned after he had put down the phone. "Youngsters need pushing more. They are spoiled and get too soft." That was Noone's introduction to the real "Colonel" Ned R. Porage and he was hardly impressed. Now, some months later, here he was on the phone, inviting Noone to a PNB in Birmingham. The reason he had called Noone was that the potential client company was an LPG firm and he realised that Noone might be able to "add some value" given his experience in the sector.

What transpired was a lesson in how the recruitment world, despite its attempts to convince the world otherwise, encouraged selfish behaviour. It was also a rude awakening for Noone. Firstly, he was aghast to discover that the LPG firm was one that he had marketed to about a year previously, since he knew the MD at least by sight, having shared an LPG industry dinner table with him, when Noone had been running Eezigaz. They hadn't actually spoken, but Noone had fondly reminded the MD of this connection when writing to him about his move to AB Selection and how ideally Noone was now placed to help. Admittedly, although he had made one follow up call which found the MD "out" and his message had not been returned, Noone had hadn't quite spared the time to pursue him further. Now he was finding out that "Colonel" Ned had been courting the MD on the sly and had set up this meeting to discuss the recruitment of a Sales and Marketing Manager *without involving him first*. This was a flagrant breach of the internal protocol which encouraged all consultants not to dive in on clients without first checking with any colleague who might have relevant specialist expertise or experience.

It was an exceedingly unhappy Noone who attended the meeting and in his view, asked all the right questions and succeeded in winning the assignment. "Colonel" Ned dropped his final bombshell in the car on the way back to his office.

"Of course I will handle the assignment as it is in my patch, but thanks for your assistance. I will credit you with ten percent of the fee." Ten percent! This should have been Noone's assignment; he was far better-equipped to handle it, given his knowledge of the LPG industry, which should mean he would "get" 60% of the fee. And he had identified the target first, so that should be a further 20% for the introduction. And he had definitely won the assignment for a further 10%; which left 10% to go to "Colonel" Ned for setting up the meeting, which seemed fair. Instead, "Colonel" Ned was proposing the exact opposite!

"Well, to be honest, I rather thought that I would be best placed to handle the assignment," he volunteered cautiously.

"No." countered "Colonel" Ned firmly. "I found it, it's in my territory and I have handled plenty of sales and marketing roles before. There's no need for you to bother, but if I need anything I will let you know." Thanks a bunch, thought Noone, but he had detected a dangerous gleam in "Colonel" Ned's eye which he interpreted as a warning not to take on the SAS in head-to-head unarmed combat.

When he complained to Hugo about "Colonel" Ned's cavalier approach, he was disappointed to hear that Hugo, although hugely sympathetic to the moral correctness of Noone's position, felt it was best to let things stand.

"After all," he said, "he has a point and he did make the meeting happen. And you may need his help one day."

Noone, stung by the mild criticism implicit in these words, resolved bitterly never to need "Colonel" Ned's help and to have as little to do with him as possible from now on. The scales were falling from his eyes.

"Colonel" Ned R. Porage continued to build his mini-empire, growing his team to five other consultants and four support staff. He earned respect across ABS for "running a tight ship" as Hugo put it and business certainly flowed through his hands. This was because he was careful to ensure he gained some credit for every piece of work emanating from Birmingham. In any case, he was incapable of delegating. It was much too risky. He developed furtive and paranoid tendencies and operated on a firm "knowledge is power" basis by refusing to share any decisions with his staff. Young, fearful of his SAS reputation and lacking the information or experience to challenge him in any way, his staff followed his commands like silent but resentful sheep.

Hugo Reeve-Prior was mightily pleased with the results that "Colonel" Ned was turning in from the office he was running in Birmingham. He was also mightily pleased with himself for having spotted the talent in the man. He decided that as "Colonel" Ned was such an able leader of men (and therefore of women, it went without saying) it would be stirring and entertaining to have the man share some of his SAS combat experiences with the firm at the annual conference. "Conference" had been too grand a title hitherto for the informal getting-together of the consultants at Christmas-time, usually by way of a morning's session on the year's progress and the year to come, followed by a boozy lunch. In 1992, Hugo decided that there should be a motivational speech from him on the company's success and two outside speakers, one delivering sales training, the other a market study to stimulate a discussion on where ABS might diversify. There would also be "Colonel" Ned R. Porage.

Thus, some fifty consultants gathered for the event at The Randolph Hotel in Oxford. There were knowing, self-congratulatory smiles during Hugo's presentation, which told them all how wonderful they were and how wonderfully well they were doing. Then followed the sales trainer, who was predictably full of jargon that was supposed to keep them energised and focused. Noone found a copy of Bullshit Bingo on his seat, issued surreptitiously and mischievously by Bob Ellis to the more lowly colleagues, who were not too close to Hugo to be seen as "Management". Bullshit Bingo worked like this: a five-by-five box grid was filled with the latest buzz-words which had to be ticked off by the players as the presenter uttered them. The first to complete five boxes horizontally, vertically or diagonally had to stand up and shout "Bingo" or "Bullshit", depending on how brave they were. Thus:

SYNERGY	STRATEGIC FIT	GAP ANALYSIS	BEST PRACTICE	BOTTOM LINE
REVISIT	BANDWIDTH	HELICOPTER VIEW	OUT OF THE LOOP	BENCHMARK
VALUE-ADDED	PROACTIVE	WIN-WIN	THINK OUTSIDE THE BOX	FAST-TRACK
RESULTS-DRIVEN	DUCKS IN A ROW	QUALITY DRIVEN	TOTAL QUALITY	TOUCH BASE
MINDSET	CLIENT-FOCUSED	BALLPARK	GAME-PLAN	ONGOING SITUATION

The game had attracted many testimonials from satisfied players in the past, namely:

"My attention span at meetings has improved dramatically".

"The atmosphere was tense in the last process meeting as fourteen of us waited for the fifth box".

"The speaker was stunned as eight of us screamed 'Bingo' for the third time in two hours".

The sales trainer was an easy target and relentlessly Noone and his collaborators slowly ticked their way towards the "quid in, winner takes the pot" prize-money. Finally, "Fast-track" completed a horizontal row and a brash consultant from London, "Badger" Brock, leapt to his feet ahead of the pack.

"Bullshit!" resounded round the room. The sales trainer stopped, mouth open, in mid sentence. Realising he was now uncomfortably in the spotlight, "Badger" continued before Hugo's disapproving gaze: "That is, there may be a time to fast-track, but there are also times when you need to slow-track." He sat down with a knowing and enigmatic smile to spontaneous applause from the audience. The sales trainer never really recovered his equilibrium and his previously confident delivery faltered away into sentences ending in antipodean interrogative inflections. After the excitement of this presentation, the market study was tame though admittedly more worthy by comparison. Then it was the turn of "Colonel" Ned R. Porage.

In an appalled silence, the audience listened restlessly for two hours as "Colonel" Ned, in a relentless monotone, delivered his self-promoting lecture on guerilla warfare, military tactics, the glories of the Bren gun when cutting down "Fuzzy-wuzzies", the ineptitude of the "Raghead" allies and the relief for the boys available in back-street brothels, all illustrated by grainy and often out-of-focus black-and-white slides. It was hideously misjudged, offending the men through boredom and the women through its casual, cynical treatment of human life and other ethnic groups, even if they were the enemy. Hugo, still piqued by his loss of the Belgrano, thought it was wonderful and inspiring: here was a man who had laid his life on the line for his country (strictly speaking someone else's country, in which we had a keen self-interest) literally shooting from the hip, telling it like it was. That would show these soft civilians what sacrifice was all about! From that day on, everybody bar Hugo thought "Colonel" Ned R. Porage was a complete wanker.

Then, in 1993, AB Selection discovered the Internet and email. Both the company's and "Colonel" Ned R. Porage's modus operandi were transformed forever.

10. EMAIL

"Boyden search professionals are committed to the success of both our clients and our candidates. Experienced and highly trained professionals, people who've worked in the industries we serve, staff our offices. Our senior people proactively manage each client engagement".

BOYDEN WEBSITE

Hugo's decision to equip all staff with desktop PCs was made reluctantly owing to the expense, but driven by necessity. It had been explained to him by an IT consultant brought in by Bob Ellis, the new Administration Manager, that Mr Bill Gates had vowed to equip every single desk in America with a PC and, since he ruled the world, if it was happening there first, as sure as eggs were bacon, it would happen here; it was just a matter of time. Hugo, although one himself, was naturally disinclined to believe the weasel-words of a consultant. However, more practically orientated towards the continued success of his business, he could appreciate that the use of email and the World Wide Web would mean instant access to infinite information sources and this had to be good for ABS; for knowledge, of course, was power. The clincher for Hugo was the revelation that by adding on a database facility, it would be possible to capture every single CV that ABS received. What a stunning thought! Within a couple of years, ABS feasibly could have the CVs of most of the executive population of Britain at its collective fingertips. Hugo, seized anew with pioneering zeal, agreed to the roll-out across the company of Hewlett Packard PCs, equipped with the recently released Windows NT 3.1 operating system, backed by an off-the-shelf database called FLAIRShare, tailored to make it user-friendly for executive resourcing purposes. The investment included an hour's one-on-one tuition for each user and a 24/7 helpline.

In no time at all, ABS employees had become highly effective grumblers about "The System" whilst thoroughly investigating its capability for procuring pornographic pictures. Trans-office flirtations by email became commonplace. The workforce's efficiency was diluted by at least 25% (depending on the level of addiction) as personal business was attended to online.

Like the rest, once he had got the hang of it, Noone was distracted by this new toy, so gratifyingly brought free-of-charge to his desk by the company. One day, Noone was not trying hard enough to "make the phones ring", instead idly flicking through the news pages which he had bookmarked as Favourites on his PC, when an article from his local paper, the Uxbridge Echo, caught his eye. It warned that a specialist marksman was being called in to effect an humane cull of feral domestic geese from the town centre pond and surrounding park to alleviate health concerns. A survey carried out the previous year showed that nearly two-thirds of residents felt that the bird population was too high and created a nuisance, not just because, as large birds, they tended to leave shit as big as dog-turds. There was widespread concern also about their increasingly aggressive behaviour and the possibility of avian flu literally flying in, so Councillors had voted to implement a Waterfowl Management Policy. Noone was fascinated at the thought of a flock of killer geese rampaging unchecked through Uxbridge.

"All waterfowl have a negative effect on the quality of the water and greenspace," said Gerald Jobsworth, town centre manager. He confirmed that gassing and poisoning had been considered, but shooting was more discreet and police permission had been granted for it to be carried out in the early morning. A private pest control contractor had been engaged and the programme would begin sometime in the next month at a cost of £10,000.

"We are also planning to eliminate their food and

prevent park-users from feeding them inadvertently." Mr Jobsworth had stated defiantly. Noone was saddened at this news, but amused by the resultant correspondence into which he was inexorably drawn, generated by Uxbridge's inventive burghers:

Posted by Ivy Bleasdale on 2:08pm Fri 24 April

The geese are part of Uxbridge - they harm no one. The council wastes so much of our taxes with inefficient paving works that are being carried out in the town - which is unsafe - and I can vouch for that as I caught my toe in the pavement and fell over. It has taken ages to get better. Why doesn't the council forget the geese and take action elsewhere when there are so many other things that could be done to improve the town?

Posted by Roger Snoad on 10:56am Wed 29 April

I agree with this action. Geese carry all manner of diseases like AIDS, malaria, rabies and mad cow disease to name but a few. They are also very aggressive and I can vouch for this as I was attacked by a flock and pecked severely while on my way home from origami classes. In fact I would be more than happy to help in the killing of these evil creatures. Well done Uxbridge council keep up the good work.

Posted by: Felicity Pendall on 6:03pm Wed 29 April

Why not just round these flying monsters up in a big net? Surely the council could find some practical use, for example setting up a tasty goose pie stall in the centre of town. I for one would be grateful to see these horrific beasts removed from the borough altogether! They are a nuisance, and also the flying wizards of Satan. There, I've said it.

Posted by: Mr Forsythe on 7:57pm Wed 29 April

I think the correct solution would be to hack the wings off as many geese as possible before joining them together to create one large wing. This could be wafted at the geese by any member of the townsfolk when numbers got too high. Children could also shelter under it at times of heavy rain or possibly loud thunder.

Posted by: Norman Darcy on 8:13pm Wed 29 April

This is preposterous! Geese performed a vital role in assisting communications in both World Wars and should therefore be encouraged to breed in higher numbers in order to remind us that we must never forget. Perhaps the money would be better spent erecting a large memorial of a Goose or perhaps a Swan - I'll leave that decision to the council. I don't think a Duck or Grouse memorial would be particularly appropriate because I don't think they did too much for us during the war. Other than food.

Posted by: Jonathan Swithin on 8:56pm Wed 29 April

I say train the blighters to do an honest day's work and to earn their right to live in Her Royal Majesty's borough. Maybe they could be trained to assist the police as they could spot crime while on high and report back to the station swiftly. The more aggressive ones could become a sort of elite police fighting unit that could intervene in violent incidents that are sadly becoming all too common in our wonderful town.

Posted by: Dave Ranter on 8:59pm Wed 29 April

Kill them with axes.

Posted by: Mrs Doreen Fullerton on 12:05am Thu 30 April

I was once saved from certain death when a pair of geese grasped me by the shoulders and flew me from the path of an oncoming car. Now these feathered heroes follow me everywhere and they often speak to me too. I will be going out tomorrow tooled up to protect this noble race of animals and if I find the marksman then it will be me or him. I say NO to the slaughter of the innocents and am willing to lay down my life in their defence. As for them being the spawn of Satan, well, that is obviously a comment from a very deluded person, get help is all I can say to that, everyone knows they are God's creatures.

Posted by: Ronald Gruntfuttock on 12:29am Thu 30 April

What a lot of fuss over nothing. Everyone knows geese can't be killed, they are immortal and immune to bullets. Where I come from we worship the goose deity and never look them in the eye as this can turn a man to stone. I can only warn the gunman that if he should lift a finger against but one bird he will incur their neverending wrath and more than likely burn in **** for his actions. I would not risk it myself, it's just not worth it. Leave it!!! Many have tried and even the mightiest have failed! The only way that may have some effect is to tie them down and chant incantations while you flay their hides with a stout oaken branch blessed by a high priest of Southen. Mr Jobsworth, the orchestrator of this ill- thought out plan I say unto you beware the consequences of your actions against the blessed ones.

Posted by: Gloria Swansong on 12:57pm Thu 30 April

I'm horrified at the very idea anyone might want to harm these gentle creatures. I myself was raised by geese after being abandoned in Slough as a young nipper. Therefore I know how noble and generous a species they really are. If anyone were to kill a goose in this way, it would be as though they are slaughtering one of my own family. It's murder, I say!

Posted by: Treehugger on 3:24pm Thu 30 April

I know what you mean, reader. I was raised by llamas but I'm sure the experience was similar. How about a council worker cull instead?

Posted by: Rodney Smythe on 4:17pm Thu 30 April.

Geese can be very intelligent creatures. This is because they are actually bred from dolphins and can travel vast lengths underwater as well as through the air. I warn you now Council folk, if you so much as dare remove or cull any goose from Uxbridge or the surrounding locale I shall withhold my council tax! I'm prepared to go to prison to save these beautiful specimens of birds so just forget it ok?

Posted by: Ron Ronson on 4:51pm Thu 30 April

What about cats? Surely these vermin are more of a pest than lovely geese. Any cat seen fouling our beautiful borough should be shot on sight. Great. Tiddly tum te de.

Posted by: Mr Forsythe on 5:06pm Thu 30 April

My elder sister was held captive for nine days by a flock of geese on a small island near Pianosa in 1979 – can't remember exactly where. (Sorry about that). As you might expect she suffers from nightmares and flashbacks but she has also developed a loathing of eiderdown. She is in full support of the cull and, in actual fact, she has already applied for the job and fully intends to carry out her duties as soon as possible - whether she gets the job or not. Be careful around town folks - she's not a good shot.

Posted by: Mrs Forsythe on 5:18pm Thu 30 April

Dear Florence.

As you can see I've finally mastered this email thing! Pru and Pete came to visit today, which was nice, and it was Pru who taught me how to use the email. I shall be writing to you often now that I have figured it out. Please send my love to Philip and the boys.
See you soon Love Mum xxx

Posted by: Mrs Forsythe on 6:27pm Thu 30 April

Dear Mr Kenobi.

Please excuse any email faux pas I may make as this is only the second email I have ever written. Isn't it exciting? I was so sorry to hear about your plight with the Nigerian authorities and the subsequent demise of your mother, it must be a very difficult time for you my dear. My husband was saying only yesterday that the pond needed a new liner and the amount of money you are offering is quite staggering. Those Nigerian authorities have no right to withhold all that money, especially as it belongs to your family. Mr Forsythe has asked that I reply to you and to confirm that the amount you wish to place into our bank account is indeed $850,000? It does seem rather a lot. I look forward to your reply.

Yours sincerely
Mrs D Forsythe.

Posted by: Roger the Dog on 7:04pm Thu 30 April

I myself have never been attacked by a goose, nor indeed defecated upon by such a feathered being, but I feel it is my duty to point out to certain contributors to this discussion that it is no laughing matter to be on the receiving end of pests and vermin. Just the other day, for example, I was held prisoner in my own home by a violent hedgehog which demanded I perform certain "acts" in order to regain my freedom. I was ashamed. But the most shameful thing is, I secretly enjoyed it. How wrong is that?

Posted by: Bernard Killjoy on 8:59pm Thu 30 April

I shat on a goose once.

Posted by: Art Garfunkel on 9:08pm Thu 30 April

This is a subject very dear to my heart. You see, I was a goose in a former life. I know a lot of people don't believe in reincarnation, but it's true. Though I was a different sex as well as species to what I am now. I was a female goose called "Jemima" and definitely not a duck. I'm rather ashamed to admit it but I wasn't a particularly evolved member of the bird family in my past life and I used to **** on people for fun and make loud, squawking noises to gain attention. I'm doing my best to make amends in my current lifetime, but sometimes old habits die hard. The point is, I suppose, that God loves all creatures, great and small and regression therapy might open a few people's eyes to the plight of other species on our planet.

Posted by: Hugh Jarse on 9:46am Fri 1st May

Can I just say that this letter column is rapidly degenerating into a farce, a West End one with bedroom doors opening and closing and men running around with trousers round their ankles and fancy women tottering about in high heels. And what's that got to do with geese? Nothing! That's right! NOTHING! NOTHING! NOTHING!

Posted by: Kylie on 12:15pm Fri 1st May

For me personally, I will not shop in Uxbridge ever again (vote with your money everyone) and I also will be contacting HM The Queen as she is a keen goose fancier and she should know about this.

Posted by: Roger Wabbit on 1:01pm May 1

I for one will be pretty nervous while there's some bloke with a gun shooting at all the wildlife. I mean I'm sure he's a good shot and everything but suppose a bullet goes through the goose - what kind of damage might that cause? Believe me, tree-dwellers will be pretty nervous while this marksman's on the prowl! Don't do anything goose-like, like dressing up as a goose. You could end up getting shot!

Posted by: Regina Hitchcock (Ms) on 1:41pm May 1

Stop, Mr Jobsworth! It has been proven beyond reasonable doubt, that geese are an alien lifeform. Any attempt to kill them will inevitably alert their mothership to this atrocity, and bring fire from the sky upon all our children's heads. I suggest we wrap ourselves up in a family sized pack of tin foil – Have nothing to do with the geese aliens, you know it makes sense.

Noone paused from his scrolling for a moment, a broad grin across his face. Everybody in Uxbridge appeared to be as mad as a box of frogs. Where did all this come from? There was little evidence of this talent amongst the people he passed on the streets or overheard in the shops and pubs. He resumed his study:

Posted by: Billy 'The Kid' Kidd on 1:45pm May 1

Let's just relax here - they're just GEESE, bear that in mind. They're just fluffy little critters who are cute and tickle you with their whiskers ... ah no, that's kittens. Sorry.

Posted by: Harry Handstand on 1:57pm May 1

Gas them like cows!

Posted by: Joe the Taxi on 2:14pm May 1

This story is just a cover up! The real reason they are killing the geese is that they are all genetically created, highly trained, radioactive killing machines. They are bred for the sole purpose of poisoning us all with highly toxic, isotope-laced raw fish. Their sole purpose is to re-ignite the Cold War. You mark my words, the evidence for this will become clear soon enough. The end of the world is night!!!

Posted by Mr Pedant on 2:26pm May 1

Don't you mean badgers, Mr Handstand?

Posted by: Robert Mugabe on 2:53pm May 1

I just hope the council don't get more than they bargained for. I have heard the Goose Liberation Front have been actively sourcing arms from overseas and are preparing for compulsory military goose-step training!

Posted by: Stuart Creed on 2:55pm Fri 1 May

OK, wipe out all the geese. And then what will the squirrels eat?

Posted by: Abby Senior on 2:56pm Fri 1 May

I have heard that this is linked to the poisoning of that Russian spy. These are not your common vermin geese.

These are KGB-trained special forces Putin-style poison geese.

Posted by: The Flying Dutchman on 4:24pm Fri 1 May

Is dit de weg naar Amarillo? Iedere nacht ik heb omhelsd mijn kussen dat dromen van Amarillo droomt waar Marie die mij wacht op

Posted by: Mr Kenobi on 5:20pm Fri 1 May

Dear Mrs D Forsythe,

I have deposited the $850,000 into your account. Your kind offer of 50 viagra tablets would be most welcome.

I am also sorry to hear about the goose problem in your local area. For a small sum, say $10,000, we could arrange to protect these precious creatures.

Humbly yours,
Mr Kenobi

Posted by: Lesley Buttercup on 6:36pm Fri 1 May

I think it's disgraceful, the way that people are abusing the privilege to post replies to this article.

When I was young, my father would have given me a belting with a hairbrush for behaving with so little thought for others. Youngsters nowadays have no manners or respect and cannot see that they are wasting hard working taxpayers' money. I am going to write to the Daily Mail at once. You have been warned.

Posted by: Steve on 6:43pm Fri 1 May

Mrs L Buttercup, Perhaps I can interest you in some Viagra. It will help your husband loosen you up. Yours, Steve

Posted by: Dieter Koblenz on 7:27pm Fri 1 May

Das ist ganz unwarscheinlich. Als sprach before diese goosen von der Britischer schweinhund Tommy Army war ein grosse thornenhausen in mein seid in das krieg! You Britischer pig dogs do not know how to treat your glorious heroes! Ach es machts ein zu schpiten willen!!

Posted by: Mrs Forsythe on 2:52pm Sat 2 May

Dear Mr Kenobi,

I fear a terrible mistake has been made! My bank has informed me that my account is overdrawn to the sum of £425,000. On today's currency exchange that would equate to roughly $850,000, which was the sum you had kindly offered to us.

I'm sure you've just made a silly mistake my dear but I ask that you rectify the problem at the earliest opportunity as I am accruing massive interest charges.

Yours sincerely
Mrs D Forsythe

Posted by: Mrs Forsythe on 3:08pm Sat 2 May

Dear Steve

I am somewhat surprised that you are still sending me offers for Viagra - 17 this week!

As explained earlier I am quite satisfied the with the staying power of Mr Forsythe and therefore I shall (still) not be requiring your product.

Yours sincerely
Mrs D Forsythe

Posted by: Horatia DuMaurier on 3:39pm Sat 2 May

Geese pecked my old Auntie Doris to death at the Vatican in 1952. At first we were very upset but we can all see the funny side when we look back now.

Posted by: Boris on 4:27pm Sat 2 May

Don't worry. We have ways of dealing with geese who have defecated from the KGB. We have booked with BA already.

Posted by: Maurice Ivy on 6:44pm Sat 2 May

Perhaps the council would be justified in killing the ugly ones only.

Posted by: The Scarlet Pimpernel on 10:50pm Sun 3 May

I often linger in the streets of an evening speaking with the geese especially the ones who have those funny little knobs on their beaks which make them leaders of men. They have warned of a mass uprising in the avian population in general should the council go ahead with what amounts to genocide. Be warned Uxbridge Town Council you will be judged .

Posted by: Kylie on 12:15am Mon 4 May

Well firstly these idiots that are posting complete rubbish should have their email addresses deleted.

There are also some very ignorant people out there who just see geese as pests.

A cull will not work - sure for a little while there may be a few less but that void gets filled by the remaining geese who will have more food (people will still feed them believe me) and they will breed and the numbers will just increase again. Catch 22!! Uxbridge Council should have contacted RSPCA who give advice on non-lethal ways of controlling geese. If I should happen on any injured birds that these idiot marksmen have not killed properly, well I shall be contacting the RSPCA to ask them to take the council and their dirty henchmen to court for causing unnecessary suffering to geese as in the 1911 Animals Act.What rights do humans have over other species? - we are destroying the planet anyway so let's stop destroying some of the birds too. It makes me ashamed of my own species sometimes.

Posted by: Mrs Forsythe on 9:18am Mon 4 May

Kylie, sensible comments only please dear. Mrs D Forsythe

Posted by: Roger Wabbit on 9:35am Mon 4 May

The Queen's a goose fancier? Oh dear, what a comical mistake: those are horses, big flightless quadrupeds that she's a fan of. Geese are grey birds who wouldn't get anywhere with Frankie Dettori sitting on them. And there's never been a Dick Francis book about goose racing, at least not to my knowledge. And I'm a wabbit.

Posted by: Mrs Forsythe on 9:45am Mon 4 May

Dear Mr Wabbit

You appear to have made the classic mistake of confusing a horse with a corgi. I do it regularly!

Having said that though I do seem to remember reading a Dick Francis book about corgi's winning the Cheltenham Gold Cup. Perhaps Francesco Dettori would be better suited to riding the corgi than the goose?

Posted by: Secret Santa on 1:10pm Mon 4 May

I find it preposterous that Kylie suggests that we all catch 22 geese each. Why should I do the Council's work ? I fear this proposal is dangerous, difficult and totally unworkable. She should have her email address removed, the silly goose.

Posted by: Mrs Forsythe on 2:02pm Mon 4 May

Unfortunately for Kylie, and possibly several thousand Uxbridge-based geese, there is no provision in the 1911 Animals Act to protect geese. The Act was introduced in order to protect animals and makes no mention of geese. Sorry.

Posted by: Rev Smallpiece on 2:16pm Mon 4 May

Mrs Forsythe you are correct there is no mention of geese in the Animal Rights Act of 1911 and Kylie is sadly mistaken; a case of engaging mouth before brain I fear. I know this because for many years I and several of my flock have been lobbying for a change in this Act so that geese are included as we foresaw that this oversight by the lawmakers would sooner or later rear its ugly head. We continue our struggle and now we will pray for Kylie too who obviously does not know the difference between a goose and an animal!

Posted by: Mrs Forsythe on 2:36pm Mon 4 May

Dear Steve

Enough is enough now! I have already responded to 36 of your emails regarding the cheap viagra and, for the 37th time, I do not wish to take up your kind offer at this moment, thank you very much!

Posted by: Terence Ping Pong Sludgebucket on 2:50pm Mon 4 May

What a pleasant and charming read this debate has been. Maybe a solution to the problem has been overlooked in all this excitement. Would it not be possible for Mrs Forsythe's impressively endowed husband to humanely kill these pestilent geese by clubbing them to death with his Viagra-engorged todger?

Posted by: Mrs Forsythe on 3:10pm Mon 4 May

Dear Mr Ping Pong Sludgebucket,

I wish to make it clear that Mr Forsythe's todger is not, nor has ever been, engorged with Viagra.

This is not the first misunderstanding I have had to put up with lately. In fact it is the 3rd this week!

Only yesterday the bank called to inform Mr Forsythe and I that they would be foreclosing on our mortgage as a consequence of us not being able to keep up with some rather large interest payments.

Thank you
Mrs D Forsythe

Posted by: Mrs Forsythe on 3:23pm Mon 4 May

Dear Steve

Recent events have rather overcome the Forsythe household, to put it mildly, which has led to a straining of relations lately and, as a result, Mr Forsythe appears to be having some difficulty raising his stature sufficiently to meet bedroom expectations. Would you therefore dispatch the 100 Viagra tablets at your earliest convenience.

Many thanks,

Yours sincerely
Mrs D Forsythe

Posted by: The Geese on 6:44pm Mon 4 May

We still be here and we will done aim at de head of de Jobsworth dude. Be warned Mother*****rs!

Posted by: Croc Dundee on 11:53am Tue 5 May

Dear Mr Jobsworth,

Please could you send some of your trained marksmen over to Australia to carry out a "humane cull" of English cricketers? It would be best for everyone, I think. Maybe we could put a few geese in England sweaters and caps instead of the rabble who are over there supposedly representing our great nation, including the Borough of Uxbridge. They would look nice on the outfield with their iridescent plumage, and could provide a more attacking alternative to Monty Panesar.

Posted by: Ross McSquirter on 2:23pm Tue 5 May

If these geese come from Siberia, then perhaps it really is a Russian plot to steal the Crown jewels?

Posted by: sid snott on 3:53pm Tue 5 May

Do pigeons come from Russia? Are you some sort of **** **** or what? They come from **** Greece you stupid **** !!! Now **** off.

Posted by: Cedric Marley on 7:22pm Tue 5 May

Mr Gerald Jobsworth, you are very sick and need to be tied to something stout in the town centre and left there for eight consecutive days, preferably during the months of December or January when it is very cold and wet despite global warming. During this time you need to be subjected to prolonged lashings and taunts from the baying, angry mob that is sure to build up to witness your punishment.

After this time you should be cut down and forced to crawl around Uxbridge making noises like the geese you wish to persecute until your teeth fall from your head. You are not fit to walk the streets of our fair borough; you are worse than vermin and will be further called to account on Judgement Day.

Yours,
C. Marley, high priest of the order of Rastafarians.

Noone couldn't help the yelp of suppressed laughter that escaped at this point and Sharon, who had been passing his door, popped her head round the corner.

"Everything okay, Adam? You seem to be finding something very funny. I hope it is leading to new business."

"Yes… no…yes," he spluttered. "It's just a message from Bob Ellis; you know what he is like." Sharon raised an eyebrow. Bob was a trifle rough and crude for her by now refined tastes.

"Just as long as he is not sending you porn, Adam. That is against company rules." She moved away, allowing Noone to return his full attention to the diversion on his screen:

Posted by: A.N.Other on 7:51pm Tue 5 May

A few years ago, when I was going through a difficult patch, I was convicted on three counts of worrying geese in Uxbridge Park and had another 30 offences taken into consideration. For this I received 100 hours' community service. Now the same people who prosecuted me wish to shoot the geese. Where is the sense in all that? I would like to invite all the geese of Uxbridge to come and live with me, ah what bliss that would be.

Posted by: Kevin Kitchen on 7:57pm Tue 5 May

I recall from my days studying agricultural zoology many years ago that one time-honoured remedy is to lace goose-feed with calcium carbide granules. This compound reacts with the water in their stomachs when they eat the feed to generate acetylene gas which combusts on contact with air and *POW* exit goose. Of course you have to set the doctored feed out on days when it's not likely to rain.

Posted by: Batman on 8:28pm Tue 5 May

When white settlers arrived in Mauritius, there were five million dodos. By 1656 they'd eaten them all and the dodo was extinct. Couldn't McDonalds introduce an Uxbridge goose-burger?

Posted by: Mrs Forsythe on 10:09pm Tue 5 May

I fear they already have Mr Batman; I believe it goes under the name of The Big Whopper (unlike Mr Forsythe).

Posted by: Goosey Goosey Gander on 11:17pm Tue 5 May

Got to be said - killing us geese is plain wrong. End of. Remember that stuff that went down about kids in hoodies hanging out in shopping centres? They never got culled. Yet geese, who aren't into mugging old ladies or nicking electrical goods - not ever - we get it in the neck every time! Nuff said. Your pal GGG

Posted by: Harry Handstand on 11:23pm Tue 5 May

Burn them in cleansing righteous fire

Posted by: Lord Kenobi on 12:13am Wed 6 May

Mrs Forsythe, I am pleased to inform you that my circumstances are now much more agreeable. I donated much of the £425,000 that you so kindly gave me to the Labour Party and now I appear to have gained a life peerage! I was sincerely amazed that in today's increasingly bureaucratic world I didn't even have to fill out any extra forms! The peerage arrived in the post last Monday!

Your Friend,
Lord Kenobi

Posted by: Zebedee on 12:14am Wed 6 May

I love horses. I mean geese, I love geese, not dogs. Not sexually like others seem to of course, that would be insane.

Posted by: Mr Toad on 12:28am Wed 6 May

I'm laughing so much, a little bit of wee just escaped

Posted by: Kite-flyer on 12:42am Wed 6 May

MY NAME IS ABRAHAM IMABANJO, A HIGH COURT JUDGE FROM LAGOS NIGERIA AND I NEED TO TRANSFER 25 MILLION GEESE OUT OF MY COUNTRY

Posted by: Evel Knievel on 12:47am Wed 6 May

I suggest taking off perhaps in a rocket-propelled

motorcycle and nuking the geese from orbit. It's the only way to be sure.

Posted by: Harry Potter's lovechild on 1:06am Wed 6 May

I think Mr Knievel is onto something. Taking the lead from T Blair, couldn't Uxbridge council buy some miniature Trident missiles that could be launched from WW2 Japanese-style mini-subs cruising the Thames and, using the latest global positioning satellite technology, directly target the geese in the Park, or on the boating lake etc? I'm sure the cost could be offset by charging tourists to view the resulting spectacular puff of feathers followed by a visually alluring small mushroom cloud. It might be necessary to require spectators to wear the proper SPF UV-filter sunglasses to avoid health & safety issues etc. PS Aren't you dead Mr Knievel?

Posted by: Mr Kipling Cakes on 1:11am Wed 6 May

Dear Sir,

While serving in Her Majesty's forces in India in the good old days of the Raj in 1947 we encountered a similar problem with tigers. For many months they had been causing a degree of inconvenience by eating the local villagers, although to be fair, there was precious little else to eat that didn't taste of curry. It was my punkawallah Ramjit Singh who, oddly enough, came up with the solution, which was namely to install a number of tiger traps round the local villages. I feel that if a similar tactic were adopted in Uxbridge, then your tiger problem should be greatly assuaged,

Yours sincerely,
Mr K. Cakes, VC

Posted by: Albert Snooks on 1:22am Wed 6 May

I'm sure the geese could be trained to issue parking tickets on the fly, as it were. Why, when I were a lad we used to look forward to munching on goose flippers. Kept us regular, it did. As for that Animal Rights tart, Kylie, get a life, you brazen hussy - we know you love animals and there's quite enough of that perversion around, thank you very much.

Posted by: Brigadier Sir Charles Twisleton Strobes, Mrs. on 1:33am Wed 6 May

Dear Sirs,

I wish to complain in the strongest possible terms about the insinuation that geese are carriers of mad cow disease. Some of my best friends are mad cows, and only a few of them are silly geese.

Yours faithfully,
Brigadier Sir Charles Twisleton Strobes, Mrs.

P.S. I have never kissed the editor of the Daily Telegraph

Posted by: Richard Fitztightly on 1.40am Wed 6 May

The comments posted above are un-called for; we have a serious local issue here being thrown off track by the Forsythes and the other people with their emails. I am going to write a letter of complaint to my local parish meeting about this, it is a shocking waste of taxpayers' time.

PS my wife is quite fond of the little fluffy geese; she likes to feed them, stroke them, and go for luxury cruises with them. She also told me she is particularly fond of me taking her up the OXO tower.

Posted by: Gangsta Rap on 3:27am Wed 6 May

Can I come along and watch the hangings of the geese?

Posted by: BB Woolf on 3:39am Wed 6 May

Dear Editor,

I wish to suggest that rehoming these geese would be a much more humane way to go about things. I personally have access to a large truck which I believe could accommodate several hundred geese. It's warm, dark and damp and more importantly mobile. If I was to visit Uxbridge then perhaps the geese could be lured in with bait; at which point I would be only too happy to shut up shop and transport them elsewhere. I am sure that they would find their new living conditions to be perfectly adequate and would not ever wish to return to Uxbridge,

Regards,
BB Woolf

Posted by: Squadron Leader James Bigglesworth on 5:02am Wed 6 May

Why not use knockout gas on them then put some superglue on the wings of the entire civil aviation fleet of aeroplanes and stick the geese feet on them so that when the geese wake up and fly away they will take the planes with them. Cheap, environmentally friendly fuel and no more geese in Uxbridge!

Posted by: Boy Georgeous on 8:20am Wed 6 May

Why not give them bicarbonate of soda in a sausage so they explode in mid-air?.....or does that only work with seagulls?

Posted by: Lucy Nating on 8:27am Wed 6 May

As this chap is culling a few useless things that contribute little apart from crapping on the general population, could he shoot a few politicians and local councillors as they fit into this category !

Posted by: Mother Superior on 8:42am Wed 6 May

Seavixen, graham@turdburglars, Mrs Forsythe and Kylie all need to take a very long, very hard look at themselves. Geese are evil incarnate.

Posted by: Captain Sensible on 8:45am Wed 6 May

Has anyone yet suggested that we could kill them with love? We could get all the do-gooders and registered nice people such as Kylie, the Pope, Bobby Charlton, Mother Theresa, and that nice young man from Take That who gets everywhere but whose name I can't recall, to stand in a circle holding hands and 'project their love'. Once overpowered, the birds could then be popped in silk-lined bags for transportation to the Megabowl in Maidenhead where they can be used as terrapins.

Posted by: Mr Twitcher on 8:52am Wed 6 May

Geese were invented in 1921- the culmination of a three centuries old cross-breeding programme between emus and greater black-backed gulls. The handling is sublime particularly when cadence-winging. Despite only having a budgie myself I simply know that a goose is far superior to a forklift truck. Why can't I get my ideal job though? I don't understand it. It's not fair. I deserve it. Sod the country we live in.

Posted by: Rt Hon. William Hague MP on 9:04am Wed 6 May

Geese are misunderstood. If only we showed more empathy and understanding these issues would not be such a problem for our society. Give one a nice warm hoodie and hug it today. You know I would.

Posted by: Alex Ferguson on 9:39am Wed 6 May

No! Do not kill our geese friends, instead send them to me. I can then mould them into a top three Premiership side. I am Manchester United's greatest ever manager. They would never have won the double several times were it not for me. And I helped out on that goose film -- you know the one that Dawn French did the voice for. She's funny isn't she and she does look like a goose. And Wallace and Gromit. That was actually based on some geese I loaned Dawn one week when she was feeling down and her career was not taking off. So, you know, geese are responsible for The Vicar of Dibley.

Posted by: Reginald Smart on 9:52am Wed 6 May

References to the 'OXO tower' are frankly disturbing. We're discussing a life and death situation of living creatures, and yobbos on here are talking about taking it up Bourneville Boulevard. Horrific.

Posted by: sid snott on 9:54am Wed 6 Dec 06

mrs forsythe, you are wanted on blasted.com asap please. you are our hero.

Posted by: Wise Old Owl on 10:09am Wed 6 May

Twits to woo

Posted by: Robert Mugabe on 10:10am Wed 6 May

Death to the imperialist running dog capitalist scum of

Uxbridge council! Long live our feathered quantum physics loving friends!

Posted by: HRH Mr Goose Fancier on 10:12am Wed 6 May

Start a goose cull and you will only force them underground. Like flying rats in the sewers ! I should know - I frequent several goose chat rooms. I even once dated a lovely pink-foot from Purley I met on www.goodforgeese.com. She was a model or something, all feather and bone. Never got the chance to take her up the OXO tower, mind. Left me for a rabbit. Bloody typical.

Posted by: General Goosegreen on 10:16am Wed 6 May

Dear Mr. Jobsworth,

You cannot destroy us. We are too much strong.
All your rotten borough are belong to us.

You Will Die!

Posted by: Mrs. Starburgling-Fencepost from Wiltshire, on 10:18am Wed 6 May

For goodness sake I do wish the council would see sense for once. Think of the commercial possibilities. Not only could they encourage tourism but remove the flying monsters once and for all. How to achieve this? Simple. Organised Goose Shooting for those bloodthirsty twelve-bore owners who can't be bothered to shift themselves in their Chelsea tractors down to their thirty-acre estate second home in Wiltshire to slaughter pheasant. I know, what I am talking about, they are my neighbours. Discounts should apply for Children under the age of eight and Senior Citizens.

Posted by: Johnny Rotten on 10:23am Wed 6 May

Surely someone must see the sensible route here: feed the disease-ridden geese to the homeless,
then, once the geese are all eaten, feed the homeless to the poor and then the poor to the elderly then the elderly to the estate agents, the estate agents to the council workers etc etc... it's a far better way of ridding ourselves of the unclean and unvalued parts of our society than the mutant nuclear warfare plan...

Posted by: Mrs Goosegreen on 10:25am Wed 6 May

Removing the food will not deter us ! I did the shopping last week at Costco in Watford and got lots of BOGOF deals on suet and kitchen scraps. General Goosegreen, when you're done saving our species,stop off at the shop for some milk on the way home. The Resistance is having a meeting here later.

Posted by: Sir Stifford Crapps on 10:36am Wed 6 May

On a serious note - I don't consider it acceptable to propose the wholesale slaughter of these geese. Some of them could be quite decent fellows. They should be interviewed individually, put at ease, perhaps given a nice warm glass of flat beer which is the British drink not that fizzy cold gnat's pee that the Aussies drink, although they do seem to have grasped the concept of a decent second innings. What was Collingwood thinking of? Concentrate old man - concentrate. Where was I? Oh yes. If they can't sing Rule Britannia - off with their heads!! I hope this helps.

Posted by: Dermott Mutley on 10:37am Wed 6 May

Why not introduce a colony of feral cats to the town

centre? Fetch a thief to catch a thief. Have you ever seen any geese at the Pyramids?

Posted by: Colonel Kentucky on 10:40am Wed 6 May

Could Mr Jobsworth please contact me asap, as I believe he could prove of great assistance to my latest business venture, a chain of fast food outlets under the banner 'KFG'

Posted by: Tony B'liar on 11:06am Wed 6 May

This website is dangerously close to being shut down as part of our Waugh on Trrrrrr. Most of the geese are peaceful islamic fundamentalists and have flown through 12 neutral countries to claim asylum in England. I say let them all claim benefit and housing, and let them work on our underground system. It's only fair- after all, the true British geese are selfishly flying off to live in Spain.

Posted by: Treehugger on 11:12am Wed 6 May

It is common knowledge that geese and their kind are responsible for climate change. Flying around at all speeds without a care in the world. I say get rid of geese!! This will solve the speed problem in our youngsters and almost halve the methane output. We could also use the droppings to build overflow housing and for fuel. Maybe cars could run on goose poo!? How many BGP(brake-goose-power) could we get per bird?

Posted by: Major Major Major Major on 11:13am Wed 6 May

ave you ever seen geese on the moon? No, I didn't think so! Yet more proof that the so-called moon landing was faked- if you look closely at Neil Armstrong's left shoulder you can see that there are traces of goose fecal matter on it.

It's a conspiracy and the geese are part of it. **** them, **** them all- with shotguns!

Posted by: Harry Handstand on 11:40am Wed 6 May

Gas them like badgers!

Posted by: Kunt Viaduct on 11:57am Wed 6 May

Why not genetically engineer half of them to be tigers, and hey-presto, problem solved.

Posted by: Percy on 12:11pm Wed 6 May

I think you're all being very silly indeed. If I ever meet any of you I will pull the buttons from your coats and eat them, just to show you that you're not allowed to talk about irrelevant things on important local news sites. So there. Yah boo sucks.

Posted by: Alfie Feathers on 12:11pm Wed 6 May

PLEASE DO NOT HURT THE CHICKENS, THEY LAY EGGS.

Posted by: Cyril Trulove on 12:16pm Wed 6 May

Dear Sir,

Please post all the geese to me in a brown envelope and I'll look after them as long as they live.   Yours sincerely C.Trulove, MD The Happy Holiday Home for Geese (Pie Company) Ltd.

Posted by: Jude Law on 12:24pm Wed 6 May

I think it is now time that we adopted a Sarah's Law/Megan's Law for goose identification in the UK. If we are not aware of where these persistent poopers live, how can we protect our children?

Posted by: Dr Torchwood on 12:27pm Wed 6 May

Napalm Uxbridge, job done. :-)

Posted by: Teresa Simpleton on 12:28pm Wed 6 May

Surely hitting them with spades would be cheaper than a marksman? You could get children from the local primary schools to do it, or maybe criminals on community service.

Posted by: Gordon Brown on 12:29pm Wed 6 Nov

Gas them like badgers!

Posted by: Dr Torchwood on 12:31pm Wed 6 May

Gas the whole borough..sorted..

Posted by: Irina Screwfix on 12:42pm Wed 6 May

Plutonium 210 will sort them out. My Dimitri says so

Posted by: Father Benedict on 12:41pm Wed 6 May

We should all calm down and discuss this over some freshly boiled beetroot while listening to obscure punk rock bands from the early 80's.

Father B
Friend of the Feathered

Having reached the end of this wonderful piece of escapism, Noone sat back in his chair and marvelled at the sheer creativity that had gone into these passionate correspondences. There was life after all in Uxbridge. Re-energised, he picked up the phone to tell his best friend Minge about it.

11. CHANGES

"Tyzack's distinction in executive search has been earned over many years. Founded in 1958, no other company can match our continuity and depth of experience. The lessons learned from many years of recruitment at the highest corporate levels are brought to bear on every assignment we are asked to undertake.

Tyzack is proud of its long and pre-eminent role in the industries that it serves. We believe we offer our clients the perfect balance between cutting-edge thinking and tried and tested technique."

TYZACK ASSOCIATES WEBSITE

Early in 1994, Noone was shocked to hear that Sharon Ridell was leaving the Uxbridge office and returning to London HQ. She let it be known that Hugo had asked her to take over the running of "London General" from him as it had become too large for him to manage alongside his strategic responsibilities. Noone wondered what these might be. It was certainly true that Hugo had ceased to transact any recruitment assignments, seemingly content occasionally to introduce a hand-picked consultant to one of his friends in business, either from his social or MBA network. His secretary Beth, who had taken to Noone in a maternal way, and who could always be relied upon to drop a few morsels of indiscreet gossip, revealed that Hugo had been spending time over with Archie Aspallan and Giles Bane in St James's Square. Noone wondered what that meant.

Noone wasn't surprised to hear that Gordon Sharpe was to replace Sharon as Uxbridge Office Manager. However, he completely failed to appreciate that the change had been initiated by Gordon, whose wife Miranda's insatiable appetite for upward mobility, forced her to conclude impatiently that he needed promoting. Sharpe agreed with his wife, as he normally did for a quiet life: Sharon had been useful to him at first, showing him how things were done in ABS, but he had always felt his skills superior to hers and she had become a block on his progress. He arranged an appointment with Hugo and told him that unless he was made Office Manager, he would be leaving for a highly attractive, though illusory, offer from NB Selection. For once, Hugo was momentarily wrong-footed and stalled for time. The memory of the abortive "lunch in the country" was sharp in his mind and Sharpe's vaulting ambition was rather odious. On reflection, however, he would bitterly resent losing one of his consultants to his major rivals. He devised a plan to promote both of them simultaneously and thus alleviate his increasingly burdensome management responsibilities. Since their intimate soiree days were over by tacit mutual consent, he invited Sharon into London for lunch at The Ivy. Beth could always find him a table there.

"Sharon, I wanted to tell you how immensely grateful I am to you for your work in Uxbridge. You proved that satellite locations outside London could work and enhance the brand. I am very proud of you." Sharon smiled sweetly in the warm glow of his praise.

"I think you are ready for the next challenge: how do you feel about running London General?" Sharon's mind's eye immediately transported her back into those Bond Street shops, the fabrics, the styles, the jewellery, the brands. Ralph Lauren, Louis Vuitton, Coco Chanel, Nicole Farhi instead of the Next, H&M, and C & A world of Uxbridge. And a pay-rise to spend there! She silently recalled the Shopper's Prayer to herself:

"Our Marks, which art with Spencer, hallowed be thy foodhall.

Thy kingdom's fun, with all the other ones;

The Gucci, the Asprey and the Garrard.

Give us each day an increase in credit, and forgive us our overdrafts,

As we forgive those who limit our spending.

Lead us not into Topshop, or Dorothy Perkins,
And deliver us from Cashpoints.
For thine is the Visa, or Platinum Mastercard,
For Dior and Prada, Amex."

"Thank you Hugo, I'd be delighted," she purred. And so it came to pass.

Other changes fell into place. Gordon, about to inherit Uxbridge, was determined not to keep Dragon-lady. They had never got on and now he had his opportunity, persuading Sharon that it would be best if she took Daphne to London as he intended to hire someone better and they didn't want to be saddled with Dragon-lady's redundancy costs, did they? Sharon acquiesced, since she knew that Dragon-lady would not undertake a commute to London from the home she shared with Brian Kinkaid in Denham and anyway, Sharon had designs of her own on a more up-to-date, cosmopolitan, modern, confidante type of secretary. Mortified that "her Sharon", whom she had moulded into a decent office manager, was prepared to leave her, Dragon-lady agreed that the commute was beneath her and resigned with great dignity, diverted from an industrial tribunal for constructive dismissal by a handsome farewell bank transfer of £2000 "for everything she had done."

Little Irene, never comfortable with expansion plans, the move to the new office and "Posh Gordon's" airs and graces, realised that, without the cover of Dragon-lady, she would be thrust into the unwelcome spotlight, resigned "to go temping for a while". Gordon hosted a combined farewell lunch preceded by champagne cocktails at the Christopher Hotel, on the bridge at Windsor. With the exception of Gordon, who ruled the serving staff officiously from the head of the table, they all let down their hair a little, professing eternal thanks to, and undying love for, each other. Dragon-lady and Irene promised to come and visit the office from time-to-time. They were never seen again.

Gordon's first two hires in the rebuilding of the office

were not a success. From a supposedly upmarket secretarial agency, he chose as his assistant Victoria, because her name sounded nice, she was well-spoken and wore long, shapely legs beneath a short skirt. He also brought in Felicity, because her name sounded nice, she was well-spoken and complemented Victoria's legs with a pair of perfectly formed knockers. All the things that Noone had considered in his fantasy report about a candidate whose thoughts would get you change from a penny were true about Victoria: she was ignorant, lazy, totally lacking in intuition or self-motivation. She would only produce when cornered like a rat in a trap by close supervision. Even then it was incredible how much rubbish her fool-proof word-processor with spell-and-grammar check could regurgitate. She was "let go" before the end of her three month probationary period.

Felicity was a six-pack of neuroses lacking any kind of plastic thingy to hold herself together. Her boyfriend was a tattooed former weightlifter who pushed drugs from a shady nightclub he co-owned in Park Royal. His machismo both protected and terrified her. He plundered her wages, savings and possessions for funds to sustain his dodgy and ailing enterprise. She bought on credit and was eternally late with these and rent repayments. The bailiffs called twice. She was also anorexic and bulimic, and after a breakfast of boiled egg and toast at home, would eat tuna sandwiches in the Ladies as soon as she reached the office to make her throw up. When she was caught red-handed stealing from the petty cash box, it was clear she was in deep trouble and needed help. Gordon fired her on the spot.

Chastened, Gordon aimed more downmarket and cautiously recruited Elain and Sonya from the local Uxbridge gene pool. They proved to be gems. Elain, equipped only with two A' levels and a budgerigar and recovering from a violent ex-husband, initially hid her light under a series of shapeless sweaters. Despite her self-effacement, she possessed a near-photographic memory, perception and a raw intellect that had been stifled by the lack of any real guidance. Gordon set about providing it, constantly upgrading Elain's use of language and banning her from her own sweaters, advising pointedly that M & S shirts were more in keeping with the image ABS wanted to portray through its female support staff. Elain only needed to be told something once; quietly she adjusted, learned quickly and soon became indispensable and keeper of all the office secrets.

One secret Elain kept was her only major mistake: one day, Gordon had asked her to send a standard "goodbye and good luck" letter to a candidate. With unctuous authority, he had just painstakingly and sympathetically revealed to the candidate that unfortunately the client had decided to appoint someone else. The candidate had been less than happy, despite Gordon's blandishments that "it had been an incredibly close-run thing". Unfortunately, Elain inadvertently sent him a letter which congratulated him on his offer of employment. Understandably, this produced an angry phone-call, which luckily Elain picked up.

"I want to speak to that joker Gordon Sharpe." demanded the candidate.

"I am afraid he is not available right now. I am his secretary; how may I help?"

"Yesterday he told me some other bastard had got the job; today I get a letter offering it to me. What the hell is going on?" Elain quickly realised what was going on.

"Ah yes, I must apologise. We had a problem with the computers yesterday and regrettably, some letters were misplaced. Yours was obviously one. I am really very sorry; it wasn't Mr Sharpe's fault: if anything, it was mine and I *have* given the computer maintenance people a rocket." She said hopefully.

"Yes well, you had better get your system sorted out..." he tailed off, defused if not mollified. With this exchange, Elain had demonstrated two essential qualities required of recruitment consultancy staff; the ability to lie and the ability to pass blame.

Elain only made one other mistake. In producing a batch of acknowledgement letters to send to the respondents to a particular advertisement, she accidentally mis-typed her name as "Alien". Gordon never let her forget it, and referred to her henceforth as Sigormless Weaver. They settled into a love/hate relationship ("Gordon loves himself and I hate him" explained Elain to Sonya) but she enjoyed the work and the security of ABS. Noone appreciated her, especially as she allowed him to call her "Alien".

Sonya also turned out well, although she did not reveal to Gordon and Noone that she was a divorced, recovering alcoholic who was battling to regain custody of her two children. The secretarial agency also did not reveal this, thus betting its success fee on her avowed-but-as-yet-untested, new-found self-discipline. She proved dedicated, particular, malleable, with an excellent attention to detail and she fitted in efficiently, following Elain's self-effacing example whilst attending to Noone's secretarial needs.

Gordon also hired consultants for his little IT empire. First came Peter Serjeant, an ex-army engineer, who had become an expert in the technology side of blowing things up. Indeed, his army career had begun with a bang, when, aged sixteen, he had accidentally burned down his father's garden shed while experimenting with propane as a propellant for a home-made rocket. Father, hideously unamused and keen to show him where his pyrotechnic tendencies would eventually lead, marched him down to the local recruiting office and turned him over to the Army with a metaphorical wash of his hands. Peter couldn't have been happier. The Army allowed him to indulge his passion in a disciplined and informative battlefield-preparation education programme at a time when computer technology was driving the production of more sophisticated guided weapons' systems. Increasingly, from the safety of command posts well away from the battlefront, our Armed Forces could seek out and destroy enemy ordnance with radar and laser-guided weaponry developed by Peter Serjeant and his team.

Then he married and with his first child on the way, was forced to grow up and put away explosive things. His wife, belying her name Bella, was a pacifist. In short order she had Peter out of the army and into a software firm which recognised his IT skills and landed him amongst its programmers. Civilian software development for business applications proved stultifying to one who had been used to seeing instant, spectacular and terminal results. He was lured to ABS by the promise of putting his IT knowledge to wider and more profitable use by becoming a consultant. Ironically for a soldier he was disarming and uncomplaining. He was also hard-working, honest, un-businesslike, affable and transparent: in short, a thoroughly decent guy. Gordon was worried about him. Would he survive the cut-throat commercial environment in which he now found himself? Time would quickly tell.

Gordon's second hire was a deliberate attempt to "soften" the team. Teal Gentian was a stunning blonde, with cascading shoulder-length hair, lovely hazel eyes, an exquisitely upturned nose, pouting lips and a perfectly-proportioned willowy figure. All red-blooded men and not a few female carpet-munchers lusted after her fiercely. Gordon and Noone lusted after her fiercely and agreed her assets would be great assets for ABS to employ. Even her car number-plate, set up to read "S3XY", promised fun and games. Sadly, both their lust and faith in her assets were misplaced, as was the number-plate. She was insipid, vapid, frigid and uninspiring. Of course she appreciated her assets too, and flirted with men girlishly and gigglingly. Once past the opening sequence, however, there was no film in the projector. She understood almost nothing useful for her work as a consultant; not people, not business, not recruitment. She was a shallow, empty vessel. Men soon tired of her puerile behaviour, the initial green "come-on" signal, followed by a stop-sign slammed in the face, and women found her irritating. Nevertheless,

Gordon enjoyed taking her out to meetings for the "eye candy" effect and it bolstered his ego to be seen with, and giving instructions to, such an attractive appendage.

One spring day Gordon drove Teal to a meeting in the Saab with the top down, despite protestations about her resultant wellbeing and likely appearance. Teal arrived shivveringly blue with cold and with her normally immaculate hair blown into an unsalvageable frizzy mess. She felt humiliated and resigned shortly afterwards to become the in-house Recruitment Manager of a London-based accountancy firm, which decided it could provide the intellectual support around Teal to allow her physical attributes to work silently as a subtle attraction mechanism to the firm. At least, that is how the infatuated HR Director put it to the MD.

Other hires proved more enduring: Matthew Coward, a Cambridge graduate with a couple of years in IBM impressed both Hugo and Gordon with his pedigree; and Sally Forth, who was committed, focused, diligent, dowdy and the perfect antidote to Teal. With Elain's help, Gordon also brought in the matronly Doris Moth to act as factotum: receptionist, drinks-maker, keeper of the stationery and inevitably, gossip-mongerer.

Once again, life in ABS Uxbridge settled into a routine as 1994 passed by. Noone continued to plough a generalist furrow, picking up assignments from often unheralded firms, such as the manufacturer of prosthetic limbs, the producer of colostomy bags and the importer of seaweed for Chinese restaurants. He was fascinated to learn about new companies in strange locations, their products and production processes, their obscure yet expanding markets. He enjoyed identifying a candidate from a completely different sector whom he believed would make a real difference to a business in a new environment. He took great satisfaction from introducing such a candidate to a client, knowing that without his "match-making" such a connection would never have been made and the client's business would have been denied the skills and experience of the candidate who was now going to transform the business with the benefit of objectivity and best-practice awareness. He was making companies successful!

Peter Serjeant confounded Gordon's fears and won work through his ability to "talk technical" to clients. Most HR Directors didn't have the first clue about embedding IT to act as a value-added, business-advantage tool. The fact that Peter could "spell it" and impress their IT Directors, greatly impressed them. Sally, true to her name, went forth diligently and multiplied her assignments. Matthew Coward, despite the promise of his pedigree, turned out somewhat louche and disinterested. He spent his weekends with a set of equally louche and uninterested friends in a haze of marijuana smoke and was usually still spaced out on Monday, spending periods fast asleep in the Gents. Nevertheless, he was a competent enough transactor and Gordon was able to pass on lower level work which was of no interest to himself.

Gordon was mining a rich seam of work from mobile communications and other IT-driven companies. Generally, his over-bearing, haughty manner went down well in companies that were emerging from the shock of instant success and rapid growth. They were, accordingly, poorly controlled and appallingly managed by people suddenly elevated in status to gurus but lacking the experience and discipline to hold the business together for the next phase of its development. Gordon was direct, outspoken and told them what they didn't necessarily want to hear or expect. Namely, that they needed professional expertise (his) and this cost money (theirs). His hauteur was less inclined to work with more established, conservative cultures.

For example, Noone asked Gordon to join him at a PNB for a Manufacturing Director at a chewing gum factory in the M4 corridor. After a tour of the facility conducted by a timid, weasel-faced HR Manager, they were interviewed in an oak-panelled boardroom, sat in high-backed, uncomfortable chairs on one side of a huge mahogany table, behind which peered at them an array of grey-haired gentlemen in spectacles. It was the most reactionary and hostile audience ever faced by Noone. The Board didn't want anything to change. The previous incumbent had been in position for 37 years, dying of a heart attack "on the job". Noone refrained from saying "lucky him". Jokes were clearly as extinct as the dodo here.

"We want someone just like Len," said the Chairman, "with old-fashioned values, a sense of loyalty and a passion for our products." Neither Noone nor Gordon could imagine such a person existing. Gordon steamed straight in.

"No you don't. What you really need is someone up to date with the latest Japanese TQM production theories, a track record of improving manufacturing output and experience of modernising an entire facility." Silence followed by much exchanging of sideways glances, harrumphing and clearings of throats. They were unimpressed. The final straw came when Noone and Gordon were each offered a stick of the product to try. Noone occasionally used chewing gum to disguise his bad breath after a heavy night on the Scruttocks and accepted.

"Do you mind terribly if I don't?" Gordon responded, looking the Chairman straight in the eye. The meeting ended as uncomfortably as it had begun, with silent farewell handshakes from the Board and Weasel-face summoned back in to escort them from the premises.

"We're considering five agencies like yourselves and we'll be in touch as soon as we have made up our minds."

"Don't worry" said Gordon sourly as he walked out through the main entrance, "we are extremely busy." He was shaking his head as they made their way to the car.

"My god, can you imagine working with that bunch of old farts; it would be a complete bloody nightmare. The whole place deserves to go down the tubes."

Three weeks later they were unsurprised to be told by a falsely apologetic Weasel-face that on this occasion they had been unluckily pipped by "another agency" which the Board felt had slightly better credentials. He felt sure there would be other opportunities to work together in the future. They were greatly relieved and knew that there wouldn't be. A couple of years later, Noone noticed in the FT that the company, which had failed to adjust to changing consumer demand for sugar-free and innovatively flavoured gum, had been sold to a US confectionery conglomerate which immediately closed down the UK production facility, laying off the entire workforce of some 500 souls. If only they'd listened.

The Christmas lunch party of 1994 passed almost without incident. Gordon had arranged an elaborate murder-mystery event in the gothic confines of the Oakley Court Hotel, near Windsor. During the course of the five course meal Gordon was finally revealed as the murderer of an inebriated Teal, to much mirth and "shock horror". Teal was working her notice-period and, spotting that her defences were weakened by champagne and chardonnay, Gordon made a final attempt to bed her by offering her a lift home after they had all returned to the office in late afternoon by sensible taxi. He was gazumped by Matthew Coward, who whisked her back to her flat in Ealing and mercilessly shagged her almost comatose but perfect form before kindly leaving her to sleep off the booze and awake to her shame and remorse, alone.

Peter Serjeant employed his pyrotechnical expertise to amuse them all by dismantling Party Poppers and filling them with Christmas Pudding before exploding them with impressive, triple-charged results across the ceiling of the private dining room in which they were closeted. The subsequent bill received from the hotel for cleaning ran to £1,500. It seemed money well invested.

Noone made the mistake of inviting "anyone who was still up for it" to early-evening snifters at The Ostler, just to round off the day nicely. Elain and Sonya sensibly declined, Gordon was too miffed at Matthew and Teal's treachery, leaving Peter, Doris and Sally. After a couple of rounds, Peter and Doris fell by the wayside both ordering taxis home. Sally, by now tired and extremely emotional, poured out her sad and lonely heart to Noone, just as she poured herself daily into her work. She was terrified by the contrary twin fears that nobody ever fancied her but that someday somebody might. Noone definitely didn't fancy her and never would and was pleased to escape relatively unscathed with a wet Christmas kiss accompanied by minor tongue activity that could be easily forgotten about during the few days off over the festive season and the advent of the New Year.

But the advent of the New Year brought a new shock. Gordon took Noone to the Green Man in Denham Village one lunchtime and purchased two pints of Flashman's Grandmother and two doorstep ham sandwiches, not in itself shocking. It was what he then announced that jolted Noone's cosy little world of Uxbridge eccentricity.

"Adam, I wanted you to be the first to know that I am leaving ABS". It took a moment for Noone to absorb this.

"What? Are you serious? But it is so sudden...you have only been Office Manager for five minutes..." Noone genuinely couldn't understand why Gordon would wish to go, particularly as things appeared to be going so well for him. Gordon was evasive and told Noone that he wanted to try something on his own. This was a smokescreen designed to cover the six months for which he knew he would have to remain out of the employment of any competitor, per the covenants in his ABS contract. In truth, Gordon now knew that ABS was never going to become the smooth, transitional stepping stone into proper executive search with Aspallan, Bane Consultants. He knew this because he had collared Archie Aspallan at the end of a joint ABS/Aspallan Bane cocktail party for clients held in late summer in the Sackler Wing of the Royal Academy amidst an Impressionist exhibition.

"I hear you are going great guns," drawled Aspallan. Gordon dived in.

"Yes, but a number of my clients are beginning to ask

me to conduct searches. I was rather hoping there might be the chance of a move into ABC from ABS."

"Did you now?" said Aspallan slowly, before repeating "did you now...well, I am not sure that would be practicable. It has never been done before and would require a unanimous agreement from the ABC partners. I think, for the time being, I would stick to what you are doing well and we'll see. And don't forget to refer any searches across to us: you will of course get 20% of the fee." Big deal; this was not what Gordon wanted to hear. He felt the flash-flood of rejection pour over his enthusiastic aspirations. He allowed the cancer of resentment to grow for a while, nurturing it carefully and secretly until he was ready to allow it into the open.

Just before Christmas, he sought out Hugo Reeve-Prior and in relaying to him Aspallan's curt dismissal of his request, complained bitterly that this was no way to incentivise successful ABS consultants. Hugo agreed, but was apologetic that he was powerless to help. In fact, he was engaged in his own struggle with Archie Aspallan on exactly the same subject and had so far received equally adamant rejections. He could see only too plainly that the cream of his consultants would drift away if they were not able to take advantage of the bigger fees to which search allowed access. He told Gordon that he was working on it. Gordon thanked him politely and handed in his resignation.

Hugo tried to talk him out of it, offering a better deal on his bonus percentage, but to no avail. Gordon had already dipped his toes into the market and found his currency pretty high. He was sitting on two offers from search consultancies which were keen to offer the chance denied to him so short-sightedly by Aspallan. After a squabble with Hugo about the timing of his departure and which clients Gordon could approach after he had left ABS, he was now free to tell his team, of which Noone in the Green Man was the first.

"Of course" he said to Noone, amused by his stunned

incomprehension, "I recommended to Hugo that you take over the office. It is good for your career to keep moving forward. You are more than capable of taking it on."

Noone was suffused with righteousness. It was true. He felt more than capable of taking it on. He would be better than Sharpe who was an arrogant twat who really only looked after Number One. There would be a pay-rise, a move into the "top dog" corner office and he might even be able to upgrade the company car. He would also be of equal rank to "Colonel" Ned R. Porage. That prospect gave him great satisfaction.

12. THE MAN WHO SAID EVERYTHING TWICE

"At TMP, everything we do is for the customer. We know our clients have demands on them, and we see it as our essential function to support them in meeting their requirements. This we do by ensuring an excellent customer experience in the short term and working to cement lasting partnerships in the long term. It's about delivering on our promise and exceeding where we can. Our success is founded on Respect, Honesty and Integrity and by taking every opportunity to seek and provide open and constructive feedback in a professional manner, we can continue to build trust."

TMP WORLDWIDE WEBSITE

It took several more days for Hugo Reeve-Prior to broach the subject of Gordon's departure with Noone, for it had not yet been formally announced, even though the news naturally had spread around the company like a computer virus. Hugo descended on the Uxbridge office one morning and after a brief closed-door session with Gordon, he joined Noone.

"I know Gordon has told you he has resigned. It's a pity, but he is rather impetuous and impatient, as you probably know." Hugo drew Noone into nodding his agreement. "I've taken soundings from both him and Sharon" Hugo continued, "and we all agree that you should have the chance to run Uxbridge. What do you think?"

Noone had been thinking of nothing else since Gordon had broken the news to him.

"That's great, Hugo, thanks. I'd love to have a go at it."

"It requires a little more than 'a go'; it's a very important position, since Uxbridge is our oldest office outside London and has always been successful. Do *you* think *you* could get the revenues up to £150,000 a month?" Although this seemed like an innocuous question, the way Hugo emphasised "you" made it clear that this was an expectation, not a hope. It was a tall order, given the current run-rate of around £100,000, but the recession was behind them now, business could be said to be booming and it would be a mistake to appear negative.

"I don't see why not, if I hire several more consultants. Eight consultants achieving £20k each shouldn't be a problem." Noone knew it would be a problem as it would take time for them all to start producing consistently, but the trust that Hugo was investing in him was intoxicating and made him reckless. Besides, if the targets weren't achieved, he felt confident he could find explainable reasons why. He recalled an article in the Economist which highlighted four key skills which kept Chairman Mao in power for so long and could be applied equally to bad managers anywhere: firstly, the ability to justify self-serving actions as being for the good of others; secondly, the art of ruthless media manipulation; thirdly, a conscience which allows the sacrifice of friends and colleagues with impunity; and finally, the ability to disguise activity as achievement. Noone could see all these "attributes" in "Colonel" Ned R. Porage, whom Hugo held in esteem as an office manager. If need be, Noone would follow the same principles, if that was what it took to be successful.

"Excellent," said Hugo, "I will up your salary by £10k and you will join the office managers' bonus scheme, which is based on your team's performance as well as a discretionary element for personal contributions. Good luck, I know you will be a success." Hugo signed off, shaking him warmly by the hand. It was done. Gordon was "allowed to go on garden leave" shortly afterwards and Noone was back in charge of something.

He was gratified to find that everyone in the Uxbridge office seemed pleased that he was taking over. That is what they said, at least. Peter Serjeant coveted the job but knew he was behind Noone in the pecking order; Matthew Coward, Sonya and Doris couldn't give a stuff; Sally Forth was embarrassed by her behaviour after the Christmas party, but was relieved that Noone seemed to have forgotten it and had said he valued her "drive and commitment"; Elain was genuinely pleased to see the back of Gordon, although she grudgingly acknowledged to herself that he had been a positive influence on her. Noone knew that Gordon had only been interested in progressing his own career and was determined to create more of a team environment in the office. He decreed that Friday lunchtimes would be spent together in The Ostler, which had been refurbished under new management, and, in pursuit of more female clientele, even possessed a no-smoking area and served warm food.

These Friday lunchtimes proved to be a successful institution and became envied, if not copied, by other ABS offices. From Noone's perspective, the challenge was to ensure that the cost was not borne by his Uxbridge office profit-and-loss account but passed on to some unsuspecting client via an assignment's expenses claim. At each lunch, he would appoint one of his consultants to pay the bill (either the most or least successful that week, amidst general hilarity) to be claimed back on expenses which could then be allocated to an assignment number. It was a virtuous and motivating circle. Before too long, consultants from London or even further afield would miraculously appear on Friday mornings to participate in this popular Uxbridge ritual. One consultant from Aberdeen visited three Fridays running on the excuse of carrying out candidate interviews. Twice he was delivered by taxi direct from the pub to his return flight at Heathrow's Terminal One, considerably worse for wear. The third time he missed the flight by falling asleep in Departures and had to overnight sheepishly and very quietly at a local hotel. Thrice bitten, he avoided Uxbridge for quite some time.

Bob Ellis, the Administration Manager in London,

entered into the spirit of things by routing all new ABS consultants or researchers through Uxbridge on Fridays "as part of their induction process to visit another office". The poor unfortunate would be plied with drink from The Ostler's bottomless cellar and Noone or one of his team would delight in leaving the bemused and befuddled neophyte on the platform at Uxbridge in the middle of the afternoon. The "newbees" never forgot the Uxbridge initiation, even though they may have been vague as to its exact content.

Next, Noone hired The Man Who Said Everything Twice. At first nobody realised that he said everything twice. He originated as the only son of a Hampshire vicar and his mousey wife, thence a minor public school (Smertins) where he had excelled at precisely nothing. His puny physique, concave chin and almost complete absence of shoulders ruled him out of rugby, football and cricket as well as most of the other minor sports requiring less physical presence but at least some degree of hand/eye coordination, of which he had none. Accordingly, he was bullied mercilessly and developed highly sophisticated defence mechanisms to cope. He made it his mission to find out the most private details of everyone's life- pupils and staff- and as the repository of such knowledge, became powerful. He established a thriving microbusiness, buying and selling information. Blackmail became both a compelling weapon and a highly profitable tool. As he entered the Upper Sixth year, the Headmaster felt obliged to appoint him Head Boy when discreetly shown evidence of his own secret lust for the Art Master. It was an inspired decision widely applauded, for that year was the quietest, most diligent and least prone to schoolboy pranks in living memory.

The Man Who Said Everything Twice built on this success by going straight to work for Twenty-First Century Machines, a computer hardware manufacturer. Fast becoming a major rival to IBM, T-FCM, as it liked to be known, sold both direct to corporate customers and through the retail channel. The Man Who Said Everything Twice made his mark in the retail channel initially, where he found it consummately easy to practise the techniques he had learned at school, for he was dealing with a particularly venal and avaricious set of customers, the retail buying community. They were easily seduced by lunches or dinners at expensive, "in" restaurants, followed by (for the men) a visit to one of the emerging lap-dancing clubs. The Man Who Said Everything Twice had already cultivated the owners of several clubs, ensuring that his guests received the best attention from the best girls, including "extra" services delivered in the private booths or afterwards in the "ex gratia" hotel room. After this, a thoughtful pair of tickets to a Premiership football match or a stylish wristwatch usually procured the required multi-thousand unit order.

For his female customers, a day's pampering at Champneys followed by a subtle piece of jewellery usually did the trick. Within three years he was winning all the T-FCM awards for Best Sales Executive (Retail) and duly promoted to Sales Manager. But he didn't enjoy having a team of people to manage: it wasn't quite the same as manipulating them to do his bidding without the compulsion of them reporting to him and having to do what he said. So, armed with a carefully selected memory from the previous Christmas party, he persuaded his boss to support a transfer to the corporate side.

Where Retail was about "box-shifting", Corporate was a much more sophisticated channel, where "solutions" had to be tailored and delivered, never sold, through multiple layers of the customer's organisation. "Buy-in" had to be obtained from each interested party, each of which would require some special adjunct either to the programme as a whole, or the hardware performance, the intranet communication facility or the software application bundle. The Man Who Said Everything Twice didn't completely discard the tactics that had made him successful to date, but he adapted a more long-range strategy, lightly touching his targets in such a way that they didn't realise they were being assiduously courted. He made friends with people; he found out about their families and always enquired after them. The conversations were mainly convivial and socially-orientated; fleetingly, he would ask only what would make their lives easier, from a business technology point of view, quietly assimilating the moans and groans, complaints and rants about their current system, which never gave the information they wanted in the way they wanted it. Most didn't have a clue what they really wanted, but complained all the same. The Man Who Said Everything Twice would take the problems back to the technical department deep within the bowels of T-FCM and let them work it out.

The Man Who Said Everything Twice also began saying everything twice. It started as a defence reflex, because he didn't have a clue what his potential customers wanted either.

"This system is shit," they would say, "how am I supposed to produce this report when it won't give me the figures I need in the right format?" The Man Who Said Everything Twice didn't have the first idea, but he would look them earnestly in the eye and say flatly:

"You need to get the figures in the right format to produce the report." He would pause, then repeat more slowly: "You need to get the figures in the right format to produce the report."

The potential customers would be deeply impressed that he had taken the time to understand their problems so thoroughly, and since they already knew him to be such a nice guy, would recommend him to colleagues in the organisation as someone who could really get to the heart of a problem. Why not give him a chance to solve all their issues? Over the next seven years, The Man Who Said Everything Twice built a reputation for thoughtful analysis and, thanks to his technical department, for "getting things done". The Corporate sales graph flew upwards, his star was high, but The Man Who Said Everything Twice began to get bored. Sure, the commission money was good but he needed a new challenge for his people manipulation skills.

Archie Aspallan was a parishioner of The Man Who Said Everything Twice's father and he had watched the son's progress in a detached, disinterested way from the safety of vicarage tea-parties until he became aware that The Man Who Said Everything Twice was "doing rather well". He then made a point of engaging him in conversation at any of the parish events at which they coincided. This concatenation produced the news that The Man Who Said Everything Twice was thinking of moving on from T-FCM, and whilst he was far too far down the pecking order to be of fee-generation interest to Apsallan, Bane Consultants, Archie just felt he may be useful to AB Selection as a consultant, given his undoubted selling ability. He introduced him to Hugo who introduced him to Noone who introduced him to Peter Serjeant. The Man Who Said Everything Twice was careful not to say anything twice, for fear of being found out and since Archie had sponsored him, of course they hired him.

He proved a natural from day one. His network of "friends" and contacts spanning retailers, corporate clients, software providers and even former competitors amongst computer hardware vendors was now formidable and he was able to walk in through doors hitherto firmly closed to ABS consultants, even to the little-lamented Gordon Sharpe. His contacts were pleased to receive him as a consultant and could see that his career had taken an excellent natural turn; after all, not only did he understand IT but he also had access to all the stars in this particular firmament, which in turn would allow them access to those stars, when they were needed. The Man Who Said Everything Twice began to say everything twice again. Business flowed in.

"I think we could hire a couple more consultants to help you," suggested Noone one day, uncomfortable that The Man Who Said Everything Twice was running fourteen live assignments.

"A couple more consultants would be good." The Man Who Said Everything Twice reflected further: "a couple more consultants would be good." Noone hired a couple more consultants who came as a set and became known as The Harpies. The first was Stella Coldblood, whom The Man Who Said Everything Twice introduced. He had come across her, purely platonically, as she worked for a software "business partner" of T-FCM. She had greatly impressed The Man Who Said Everything Twice with her single-minded determination to obtain the best possible deals for her company. Actually, since she was paid only on commission, this equated to obtaining the best possible deals for herself. She negotiated fiercely with balls of steel and swore ferociously and passionately like a cockney racehorse owner.

Stella was also in dedicated pursuit of a suitable husband. Given her whirling dervish personality and constant pursuit of designer shopping, there were three criteria: good genes, money and a willingness to play second fiddle to Stella. This circle was proving difficult to square: those with good genes tended not to find her attractive, for she had rather pinched, severe features, a pale, freckly complexion, stringy ginger hair and a figure that could kindly only be described as rangy; those with money didn't want to play second fiddle and could afford something more docile with model-like physical attributes; and those willing to play second fiddle she found weak and unattractive. The Man Who Said Everything Twice persuaded Noone, who had his doubts, to take her on.

She would only join, however, on the condition that she could bring her friend and colleague, Lavanya Tabernacle, with her. Poor "Lavvy" was the antithesis of Stella. Amplitudinous to the point of dumpster, she was warm, hopeless with numbers and devoted to her husband Squiffy and two similarly embonpointed teenage daughters. Disarmingly porcine over food and drink (she ate her corn on the cob with the reckless relish of a wild wart-hog) where Stella was annoyingly calory-conscious and fastidious, calm where Stella was an erupting volcano, fluffily feminine where Stella was macho, they made an unlikely pairing. But just as chalk needs cheese, Lavvy would pick up the pieces after Stella's lightning strikes had left clients speechless, would soothe the ruffled sensibilities of those whose Stella's language had offended, would fill in the holes of Stella's hurried verbal promises with carefully worded contracts. Each recognised her own weaknesses and the compensatory strengths of the other. They were two separate square pegs forming a rounded whole. Again, Noone couldn't see this attractive proposition at first but The Man Who Said Everything Twice persuaded him. Led by Stella's rapacious drive, the Harpies were soon performing well.

The IT team coalesced nicely, with The Man Who Said Everything Twice making senior-level connections, the Harpies chasing any glimmer of business down until it was alive or dead and Peter Serjeant handling anything particularly "techy". Noone turned to the generalist side, where Sally bravely continued to plough her lonely furrow (in more ways than one) and Matthew Coward continued to take things fairly easily. In fact, checking the figures, Coward had been taking things far too easily, sheltering behind assignments referred by the others: in the twelve months since he had been in the business he hadn't generated a single piece of work himself! Noone, now protective of the office P & L, found himself dismissing Giles Bane's "Two Year Principle". If Coward hadn't brought in business after six months it looked dodgy; nil after twelve months was positively scandalous. He would have to go.

Luckily, Coward provided Noone with two other examples of poor performance which made the case against him cast-iron. On one particularly difficult Monday after a speed and drink-fuelled Saturday all-nighter followed by a spliff-induced lost Sunday, Coward had a 5pm candidate interview scheduled. The excesses of the weekend combined with the soporific warmth of the day and the monotone, achromatic performance of the candidate conspired to send him to sleep. Noone, checking that the office equipment had been turned off prior to locking up, found Coward snoring gently in his interview chair. The candidate had thoughtfully exited quietly, leaving a polite note on the table, suggesting that it might be better to complete the interview on another occasion when Coward felt better. To some extent Noone sympathised, for on more than one occasion when faced with a hopelessly dull candidate in that difficult hour after lunch, he had begun a question only to realise that by the time he reached the end of the sentence, he couldn't remember how he had started it. But actually falling asleep? It showed a complete lack of self-discipline. He shook Coward awake, who slunk home crimson with embarrassment.

Secondly, a female candidate, Rowdene Anara, complained about him. Again, in retrospect, Noone sympathised. Rowdene's arrival in the office caused quite a stir, for her CV, containing a photograph, had been widely touted on receipt. It suggested that she had been an erstwhile model of feminine undergarments for a rival to Tantalize and subsequently a marketer for the makers of a female condom. This was too good to be true. Her appearance was eagerly anticipated by the boys; the girls thought them pathetic and were merely jealous. She proved every inch as gorgeous a sex-object as hoped: tall, blonde, flawlessly featured and busted, with the most perfect, stilettoed legs that vanished hauntingly into a scrap of a skirt. Noone himself, seeing that "Leggy" was seated with her back to the glass door of Coward's office, had held up a piece of paper for Coward to see which caricatured her physical attributes and said: "Second interview a must!!!!"

As the interview progressed, Coward became increasingly aware of Rowdene's aggressive use of those long legs: crossing and uncrossing them had elevated the skirt beyond the realms of decency, and he was able to see plainly that she still modelled, quite publicly, glistening, white, wispy, scanty panties. Encouraged by her provocative smile, he asked whether she used the merchandise she was marketing.

"Of course," she breathed, then enigmatically, "you don't eat a cucumber without a test-drive, do you? If you put me on your short-list, we can meet up after work one night and I'll show you how it works."

Coward, slightly concerned about dipping his wick into what amounted to a plastic bag, was up for it nonetheless. After treating Rowdene to an Italian meal, he enjoyed an educational night in her bachelorette flat in Maida Vale. She proved an enthusiastic, uninhibited partner and he surmounted the potentially deflationary experience of entering the female condom with the assistance of her well-lubricated thumb jammed into his anus and agitating his perineum.

"Don't forget me on the short-list," she reminded, as she massaged Coward out of the flat the next morning. He should have realised she was dangerous. He did put her on the short-list, but the female client took an instant dislike to Rowdene because she was so attractive. Gently, Coward attempted to "sign her off", saying he was amazed that the client preferred another candidate. He mistakenly believed that closure of their assignment-orientated relationship could pave the way to a longer-lasting personal lust-fest, enlivened by lashings of finger-licking sex. He was wrong.

Rowdene ordered Coward to get the other candidate to stand down. Realising that he was already sinking in shifting sands, he apologetically refused. The hidden bunny-boiler in Rowdene rose rapidly to the surface as she coldly told him he would regret it. She then rang for the Office Manager and told Noone that Coward had acted improperly by propositioning her during the interview and pressurising her to sleep with him in exchange for a place on the short-list. He expressed his shock and outrage, promising to investigate and take appropriate action. Coward, cornered, crapped himself. Miserably, he explained the true circumstances, acknowledging he had been an unprofessional fool to be duped so easily by this clever but deceitful woman. Noone was sympathetic but clear. He suggested that if Coward resigned with immediate effect, no further action would be taken. Coward gratefully accepted the offer of his own resignation. Noone then called Rowdene back, thanked her again for her brave honesty and told her that he had fired Coward. Satisfied at the destruction she had caused, Rowdene agreed with Noone that in the circumstances, there was no need for her to press charges. Coward packed up his personal belongings and was out of the office within an hour, vanishing from their lives forever.

Relieved, Noone could now concentrate on hiring colleagues to work alongside Sally Forth. An advertisement produced two new consultants: Roger Bachelor-Freebody and Paul Tuttle. The former had become disillusioned with his career in PR and was seeking "something more substantial and worthwhile". Sandy-haired, broad-shouldered, tall and upright, with a purposeful, splayfooted walk, Roger Bachelor-Freebody possessed a rather high-pitched, lispy voice and giggle and wore brightly coloured socks which occasionally flashed beneath his trouser leg turn-ups. Nevertheless, he claimed a girlfriend and scored points by laughing at Noone's attempts at humour and supporting Lincoln City. Noone had never met anyone who supported Lincoln City before. Roger had done his homework on executive resourcing accurately to distinguish ABS from agencies and made a convincing case for being able to transfer his client-orientated skills from PR to this more challenging environment. Noone liked what he heard.

Paul Tuttle was not much to look at, being outwardly of similar uninspiring build to The Man Who Said Everything Twice with the addition of a broken nose. It turned out that he had boxed featherweight for England in the Commonwealth Games and was both a tough and well-connected little cookie. Up to that point, he had made his way by selling corporate hospitality and Noone felt that his skills, too, were transferable, especially as he wanted to specialise in sport and leisure.

Hugo wondered whether Roger travelled frequently up the marmite motorway but gave his blessing to both hires. Two additional secretaries, Sinead and Julie, were added and the office was full. All Noone had to do now was to hit those targets.

13. PARIS

"Sainty, Hird & Partners ltd is synonymous with the highest professional standards in the executive and board search industry. Our highly experienced Partners, Consultants and Researchers combine the greatest level of industry knowledge and a dedication to fulfilling our clients' needs. We are committed to placing the right people into the right role, at the right time."

SAINTY, HIRD & PARTNERS WEBSITE

Noone had set his team a challenge to find the most ridiculous headlines from around the world to lighten up the weekly meeting, which was supposed to concentrate on reviewing fee income. They had had two weeks to prepare for this welcome diversion and when they had settled into the laughingly-named "Boardroom", where three had to remain standing, Noone commenced proceedings:

"Today we are gathered here for some light relief. Did you know that a cocktail lounge in Norway has a sign that reads: LADIES ARE REQUESTED NOT TO HAVE CHILDREN IN THE BAR, a Swedish shop advertises: FUR COATS MADE FOR LADIES FROM THEIR OWN SKIN and a doctor's in Rome is SPECIALIST IN WOMEN AND OTHER DISEASES?"

"No," his secretary Alien replied, "but a laundry in Rome invites: LADIES, LEAVE YOUR CLOTHES HERE AND SPEND THE AFTERNOON HAVING A GOOD TIME, a dry cleaner's in Bangkok suggests men: DROP TROUSERS HERE FOR BEST RESULTS, and a temple there orders: IT IS FORBIDDEN TO ENTER A WOMAN EVEN A FOREIGNER IF DRESSED AS A MAN."

"Ah, but restaurants are also tricky," said Roger Bachelor-Freebody who was keen to offer his contributions. "From Switzerland: OUR WINES LEAVE

YOU NOTHING TO HOPE FOR and SPECIAL TODAY: NO ICE-CREAM but there are: SPECIAL COCKTAILS FOR LADIES WITH NUTS in Tokyo and in Poland you can eat: SALAD A FIRM'S OWN MAKE, LIMPID RED BEETROOT SOUP WITH CHEESY DUMPLINGS IN THE FORM OF A FINGER, ROASTED DUCK LET LOOSES AND BEEF RASHERS BEATEN IN THE COUNTRY PEOPLE'S FASHION."

"And what about hotels," chipped in Paul Tuttle. "GUESTS ARE PROHIBITED NOT TO SMOKE OR DO OTHER DISGUSTING BEHAVIOURS IN BED in Japan but: YOU ARE INVITED TO TAKE ADVANTAGE OF THE CHAMBERMAID, and also Dubrovnik where: THE FLATENNING OF UNDERWEAR WITH PLEASURE IS THE JOB OF THE CHAMBERMAID, whereas in Paris they ask: PLEASE LEAVE YOUR VALUES AT THE FRONT DESK and in Zurich: BECAUSE OF THE IMPROPRIETY OF ENTERTAINING GUESTS OF THE OPPOSITE SEX IN THE BEDROOM, IT IS SUGGESTED THAT THE LOBBY BE USED FOR THIS PURPOSE, but on the same theme in Chiang-Mai: PLEASE DO NOT BRING SOLICITORS INTO THE ROOM."

"I know," said Sally Forth, entering into the spirit, "hotels are fertile ground, especially in Japan: COOLS AND HEATS: IF YOU WANT JUST CONDITION OF WARM AIR IN YOUR ROOM, PLEASE CONTROL YOURSELF. Up and down in Bucharest too: THIS LIFT IS BEING FIXED FOR THE NEXT DAY. DURING THAT TIME WE REGRET THAT YOU WILL BE UNBEARABLE and in the Austrian Alps: NOT TO PERAMBULATE THE CORRIDORS IN THE HOURS OF REPOSE IN THE BOOTS OF ASCENSION."

"Well thanks for that contribution, team," said Noone, "it looks like we are all singing from the same hymn-sheet. Shall we get back to work?"

It was mid 1995 and things were going well for Uxbridge in terms of assignment numbers and the resultant effect on the top and bottom line. Targets were being met, individually and collectively. Of course, each assignment would throw up its little hurdles which had to be overcome. In pursuit of a Project Director for a civil engineering scheme in Ireland, Roger Bachelor-Freebody found himself by accident in a budget hotel in Killarney which had eliminated all frills from its service offering including public meeting areas. He was forced to interview a succession of large, rough-looking, building contractor gentlemen in his room. Noone, after a difficult phone-call, rescued him from the local constabulary, into whose none-too-gentle hands he had been passed by the outraged hotel manager "for committing filthy acts in my premises".

Roger also landed a difficult assignment for an office fit-out company which wanted to take advantage of the collapse of the Soviet Union by expanding into Russia. The advertisement, placed in Izvestia, for a general manager produced a number of handwritten CVs from a collective of disaffected Russian tractor drivers who had obviously decided one vodka-fuelled night that they were ideally equipped to refurbish Moscow's commercial heart. Roger had to disappoint them "on this occasion".

Paul Tuttle had a shaky start. On his first engagement to find a project manager for a housebuilder, he was tricked into interviewing someone whose CV listed numerous residential projects on which the man had worked. He was, in fact, a bricklayer and turned up in dirty hobnail boots, filthy jeans and a torn, grubby green sweatshirt. He was very loud and Noone was privileged to hear the beginning of his conversation through his party-wall to Tuttle's office:

"Fangs fer seenme, mayd. Been a flexiboo bloke oi fanseed an howl newfing wen oi sawed yaw ad. Oim reey mo vayed a smomern intime fer summin diffren, a nowlnyoo boregame." Noone had to go for a walk at that point. Tuttle salvaged some credibility by pointing out that his candidate had been so grateful for the interview that he had offered to carry out any brick-work at their homes "furgoo deel, cashin andlike."

Tuttle also had a slice of bad luck at the end of his next assignment, although it was his dogged due diligence which uncovered the fact that the candidate to whom he had made the offer was not "taking a voluntary sabbatical and considering his options". Already the subject of a sexual harassment claim brought by a temporary secretary, the man had been fired with no options by his former Employer when recorded by the CCTV camera in the company's underground car-park "performing an oral sexual act" on a well-endowed gentleman of Caribbean descent, whose identity was not discovered. Noone was not surprised to hear from a panic-stricken Tuttle that the client had withdrawn the offer. It did leave rather a nasty taste in the mouth. Fortunately, the second candidate on Tuttle's short-list was capable, still available, and a devout Christian, which was a distinct advantage given the sensitive circumstances.

Across in the Technology group, Peter Serjeant had a close escape. A volatile mixture of inexperience and momentary incompetence on the behalf of the new secretary, Julie, allied to Peter's carelessness due to pressure of work led to near disaster. On Peter's instructions but without him checking, Julie arranged a client interview for a candidate called Ian Campbell. Incredibly, for this particular assignment to find a Systems Manager, two separate Ian Campbells had applied and Julie managed to mix them up. The wrong Ian Campbell turned up for the interview with the client IT Director and recounted to Peter Serjeant later what had transpired. Things had gone well through the preliminary small talk and the candidate felt pretty relaxed. Then the questioning began:

"So, a first class honours degree, that's good. I guess it pretty much gave you a choice of employer?"

"Er, I didn't actually get a first class."

"Oh. It says here you did. We'll have to check that. Anyway, why did you choose to go to Oracle?"

"I didn't."

"Ah. It says here you did. You are Ian Campbell, aren't you?

"Yes."

"Of Oracle, IBM and Microsoft?"

"No, of Pace, HP and Digital."

"Ah." They had realised the error and burst out laughing. Since the IT Director had set aside an hour, they carried on talking and got on so well that by the end, the wrong Ian Campbell came out with a different job offer. Julie was forgiven for her brilliant mistake and Peter even managed to place the right Ian Campbell in the right job a couple of weeks later.

Stella Coldblood, still in vigorous pursuit of a husband, had actually test-ridden a candidate for a while until he was rejected at third interview by the client. Clearly, this diminished him in her eyes, and, despite him seeming to meet two of her three marriage criteria, she dropped him like a hot brick.

The Man Who Said Everything Twice continued to do so. Never prolix, he whittled and sharpened his vocabulary until he became a highly effective user of two words which he would employ to devastating effect:

"I see," he would say, and then, more slowly, "I see." This profound statement would be accompanied by a series of slow nods, conveying consummate gravitas. His clients continued to be impressed by how much he said he saw.

Noone tried to read all candidate reports before they were sent out (and, if he was not available, had passed strict instructions that a second consultant should always proof-read any written material heading for clients) for "two pairs of eyes were better than one." Hugo and Sharon had been very particular on the subject. Roger Bachelor-Freebody was developing a nice turn of phrase:

"Do not be alarmed by Mr Smith's initial appearance" was his way of informing the client that a candidate was horrendously ugly, bearded or just generally untidy.

"You may consider that a Donald Duck tie and Mickey Mouse socks are inappropriate attire for an investment banker, but..." was his way of dealing with strangely clothed people.

"The fact that Mr Jones's father was in the RAF is immediately apparent," created just the right degree of positive uncertainty. The client, fearing the appearance of some retro-gung-ho fighter ace, would be pleasantly surprised that the person before him merely wore a handlebar moustache and spoke rather well.

The annual conference that year was a cracker. Hugo Reeve-Prior was delighted that his inspiring leadership had created a market-leading company of over one hundred consultants and an almost equal number of support staff. It was highly profitable and had accrued a reputation for quality at least the equal of bitter rivals NB Selection, which had shortened itself to NBS in an attempt to keep up. The runaway success of ABS continued to cause some friction between Hugo and Archie Aspallan, for Hugo understood only too well the dilemma his star consultants were facing; increasingly, they were being asked by their clients to advise on senior appointments where executive search was the more appropriate methodology than advertising-led selection. It was humiliating for them to have to tell the clients that they were not allowed personally to handle such assignments, but they would have to introduce a colleague from Aspallan, Bane Consultants who could. Gordon Sharpe was not the only one who had walked off to a search firm.

"It is contrary to the message we have always preached," he complained to Archie. "Instead of respecting and servicing the client's demands, we are compromising ourselves for the sake of our ABC/ABS internal hierarchy. It's just not on."

"Oh yes it is," retorted Archie, unbending. "We cannot have an inferior search product sold on the cheap. *That* would be the real compromise. ABS must stick to advertising and leave search to ABC."

In fact, Hugo knew that the main cause of his consultants' disgruntlement was not the inability to serve their clients personally but the fact that they were only credited 20% of the vast (to them) fee charged by their ABC colleague for such an introduction. They would be prepared to concede the moral high-ground in exchange for a larger slice of the pie. Eventually, he and Archie reached an uneasy compromise whereby the intro percentage was raised to 25% and ABS were allowed to offer a "hybrid product" which included something called "targeted search". This meant they could offer their clients an advertising-led engagement backed up by a limited search into "no more than six named organisations" for a fee of 30% of the remuneration package. Pointedly, Hugo did not invite Archie to his conference, instead asking Giles Bane to represent ABC in glad-handing Hugo's troops.

Hugo decided to hold the conference in Paris in early October. That way, the weather should still be clement, yet it would be far enough through the year to be able to talk about the probable financial outcome as well as the budget and objectives for next year. He devised a programme of events with Bob Ellis and tasked him with identifying a suitable tour operator and hotel. Bob quietly and efficiently put everything together. The group of consultants and researchers (the latter numbering six) would travel late morning on a Thursday by Eurostar from Waterloo, stay two nights at the Saint-James & Albany Hotel on Rue de Rivoli, near the Tuileries Gardens and return via Eurostar to their loved ones or spouses on Saturday morning. There would be a trip up the *La Tour Eiffel* late Thursday afternoon, followed by a *Bateaux Mouches* dinner cruise on the Seine. Friday would see a full conference programme, including a talk by Sir John Harvey-Jones (accompanied by his epithet, "the man who saved ICI") whom Hugo had secured, thanks to his and Sir John's common submariner pasts. There would be a Gala black-tie dinner on Friday evening in the hotel.

Hugo probably underestimated how much the hard-working guys and gals of ABS liked to party. In hindsight, it was a mistake for the outward Eurostar trip to include lunch. By the entrance to the Tunnel at Folkestone, ABS had drunk the train dry of champagne and beer. Even reserves of the execrable Carlsberg had been emptied. At least the wine lasted as far as Lille; thereafter, they survived on shorts.

As a small concession to cost-management, Hugo had decreed that rooms (which were all twin-bedded) should be shared by same-sex colleagues. Noone checked into his hotel room and was taking a well-earned nap after the alcoholic rigours of the day and prior to the departure for the Eiffel Tower. His room-mate, Nevis Undertow, the Manchester Office Manager, had gone for a walk to clear his head. The rattle of a key in the door followed by a sharp, angry-sounding knock awoke Noone from his shallow sleep. Blearily he opened it, expecting to harangue Nevis for disturbing him. Hugo stood at the door, suitcase in hand. Noone was clad only in M & S boxer shorts.

"You seem to have my room," Hugo said in his superior way. For one ghastly moment, Noone thought Hugo intended to share with him.

"I don't think so Hugo; this was allocated to me and Nevis. What key have you got?"

"212."

"Ah," said Noone, gratitude and a small measure of triumph sweeping over him. "This is 312. You've climbed too high and should be a floor down." It wasn't every day you could say that to your boss. "Who are you sharing with?" He enquired innocently.

"Nobody." Hugo turned abruptly and stamped back to the lift. Of course not. The leader couldn't be expected to bed down in the trenches with his troops, thought Noone. C'est la vie, as the English say.

It was a pleasant, clear evening and the observation deck of the Eiffel Tower afforded its customary glorious views over the famous boulevards and landmarks of Paris.

The ABS crowd, minus a few who decided that vertigo mixed with the liquid lunch might prove a tad volatile, chattered excitedly, pointing out the views to each other, before descending en masse to catch the *Bateau Mouche* close by at the Port de la Bordonnais. Noone was seated on a table between a kilted Scot from the Glasgow office and a flirty blonde from Basingstoke with a flashing smile and ice-blue eyes to die for. Opposite him sat Sharon Ridell and someone from Middlesborough, whose job offer from Hugo had been contingent on him shaving off his beard.

Over the starter, smoked salmon steak with taramasalata and an olive oil and herb dressing, Noone caught up with Sharon, she clad in a Donna Karan cocktail dress accessorised with an Hermés silk scarf. She was clearly delighted to be working and shopping back in London, not necessarily in that order, and waxed lyrical about the vibrancy of it all, compared with staid old Uxbridge. As salmon was becoming rather too ubiquitous, Noone would have preferred the simmered frogs' legs with morel mushrooms and he noted there was a ratio of one bottle of wine between three people. That was nowhere near enough.

He turned his attention to the Scot, Jim McDougal, during the main course of "Roast chicken supreme, barigoule-style vegetables, with basil and garlic and Espelette pepper jus". Jim confirmed that he never wore underpants under his kilt because it was fresher that way and gave him easy access, when required, to all things genital. Noone was not surprised to hear this; he had recently received an email picture from Minge which showed the Queen sitting for a formal photograph in the middle of a Scottish regiment of which she was Patron. Stretching from either side of her was a seated line of bekilted officers all with serious expressions, legs together and kilts primly tucked tightly around their thighs. Except one. On Her Majesty's immediate right sat a Jock with his legs wide apart, a matching wide smile and his manhood in full view. At least he hadn't been standing to attention.

Jim managed to filch another bottle of the average Fronsac and recounted a recent "summer jolly" whereby he had organised for a group of Scottish clients and consultants to play golf on the west coast at Machrihanish, staying at the Ugadale Arms Hotel. Arriving late afternoon, they had enjoyed a splendidly gamey dinner of grouse, hare and venison (with fresh sea trout for the wimps) washed down with plenty of beer and claret. Repairing to the bar, they had traversed the lower shelf of Scottish Single Malts, paying particular attention to snare all seven distilleries from their offshore island neighbour, Islay. Suitably fortified, they went out to watch one of the famed late Machrihanish sunsets sinking slowly into the sea. Then someone suggested "skinnydipping".

"Aye, that's when it got interestin'," said Jim. "There we all were, clients and consultants, male and female, frolickin' in the buff. Bear cold, mind. In the rush back up the beach fer our clothes, one of the clients put 'is foot down a rabbit hole and broke 'is ankle. Aye, we forced a few more malts down him to deaden the pain, put him in bed and called for the ambulance in the mornin'. He never did get to play golf. Aye, t'was hilarious."

"And how were things between you all, so to speak, as you had all been naked together?" asked Noone, curious for any salacious details for possible future fantasy material.

"Grand. Three shags and two new assignments. Aye, it more than paid fer i'ssel'." Clearly, they had more interesting ways of doing business in Scotland. Noone briefly considered the possibility of a transfer.

The boat turned round at the *Ile de la Cité*, where the brilliantly floodlit *Cathédrale de Notre Dame* looked down upon them, the dinner guests pausing their animated conversations to admire its soaring gothic superstructure, the solid square towers and the great, black, hunched back of the nave.

For the dessert of iced juice of strawberries and raspberries, fromage blanc sorbet and sweet, crispy pastry,

Noone turned to Miss Basingstoke, Nerissa Wadsworth. She had a lovely, bouncy personality twinned with a pair of equally described front-facing assets enhanced by a low top. Noone liked her immediately. They found they had plenty in common as Nerissa was a sporty type who liked cars, cricket and golf. She had even played cricket in a ladies' league. Given her all-round attributes, Noone was prepared to overlook that she supported Arsenal. At least it wasn't the Überfilth, Manchester United (or Moan U, as every non-Moan U fan knew them). The other thing they had in common was that they were both married, which was disappointing.

On disembarkation, the group was coached back to the hotel where the sensible ones drifted off to their rooms for the night. A decent hardcore of revellers, including Noone, all his Uxbridge consultants, Jim and Nerissa, went out in search of more liquid and fun, landing a short walk away in a bar on the corner of Rue du 29 Juilliet and Rue Saint-Honoré. There was a long-haired, four-piece band playing French thrash metal and after a couple of drinks Noone and Nerissa joined a few others on the floor-space in front of the band, undertaking Status Quo shoulder gyrations and head throws. After that, Noone's memory departed for the night, leaving a dim recollection of an exploratory fumble with Nerissa in the lift and a slight, 3 a.m. altercation with Nevis after he had crashed into Nevis's bed by mistake.

Nevis awoke him at 8 o'clock for breakfast which Noone, feeling gillish and glurred, was quite happy to miss. He did, however, arrive in the conference room downstairs smiling, scrubbed and clean-shaven five minutes before the start. His brave face lasted until mid-morning, when during the coffee-break, Peter Serjeant asked him whether he had eaten a dodgy piece of salmon the night before, so green was his pallor. Coffee Noone could not face, so he drank water, which he never drank. He was gratified to see that Nerissa gave him a coy smile and held eye contact. Good, nothing irreparable there, then. Giles's stirring talk, congratulating them all on creating in ABS, under Hugo's brilliant guidance, a real jewel in ABC's crown, largely passed Noone by. So did Hugo's speech, which thanked Giles for his thanks and his supporting Consultants and staff for their support, before launching into his vision for the future. Continue to grow, aim for higher fees, never compromise on quality, and work more closely with ABC seemed to be the gist. He did, however, warn them of the hideous canker of "political correctness" which was invading their jealously guarded privacy.

"Apparently," said Hugo, "impending anti-discrimination legislation is conspiring to make our job hugely more difficult. To start with, we have been advised to stop putting the required age ranges on our advertisements. This means we are supposed to consider all the over-fifty has-beens for every job, instead of just dismissing them out-of-hand as we usually do. It's a real bore and it makes me angry: after all our job *is* to discriminate. It's what we are paid to do."

Noone, still feeling deeply gangrenous, tackled the group buffet lunch in the hotel's Restaurant Le Noailles (named after the Duc de Noailles, who had commissioned the building in 1672) with a high degree of circumspection, avoiding alcohol and managing a small bowl of *soupe des poissons* and a *salade mixte*. He remained attentive as Sir John Harvey-Jones (introduced by Hugo as "the man who saved ICI" and complete with trademark ill-fitting, garish, multicoloured tie) congratulated ABS on its eighth birthday but warned that ninety percent of firms which reached ten, would not reach twenty years old. He advocated the need to embrace change and to seek continuous evolution, for those which tread water for a moment, taking the time to look around and admire their achievements, are surely doomed. The audience was chastened but its defiant murmuration suggested that this would never happen to ABS.

After Sir John's politely applauded exit ("interesting

but probably past it" said Nevis) there was a session on next year's budget and objectives followed by the now traditional awards ceremony, both serious and not so serious. Noone was pleased to receive a plaque for Uxbridge being the highest billing office outside London in 1995, and not quite so pleased to be identified as the consultant who lost his briefcase most often, even if it was probably true. This occurred usually when he visited London for a function and inadvertently ended up in a dive like the Dover Street Wine Bar, forgetting his briefcase during a difficult, stumbling, late-night exit. In his defence, Alien had only had to rescue it three times from oblivion.

By the time the conference broke up at 6pm, Noone felt quite human again, certainly strong enough for a sociable snifter in the bar before a shower and change into black-tie rig for the Gala Dinner, which was preceded by the customary ABS champagne cocktails. The ladies glittered and shone like so many birds of paradise, the Scotsmen paraded (rather absurdly in Noone's view, despite Jim's enthusiasm) in their dress kilts, whilst the Englishmen could only inject colour through their choice of ties and matching cummerbunds, which were mainly not black. Noone managed to engage briefly "the man who saved ICI", who was joining them for dinner.

"Sir John, I believe you were in Naval Intelligence after the war and prior to ICI. What was it like?"

"Top secret, next question." Noone, as an old car enthusiast, had one ready:

"For your TV series Troubleshooter, why did you get Morgan so wrong?"

"I didn't," came the retort. "If they fail to modernise their working practice they will soon follow all our great automotive marques to the grave." Noone wasn't so sure: Morgan's cachet was precisely that it took so long to build each car by outdated, labour-intensive methods, that it built up a long waiting list. It was almost a badge of honour amongst 40-something-year-old businessmen with no taste "to be on the waiting list for a Morgan". Mind you, the cars were a complete anachronism and he would rather own a real classic car with a personal history and patina than a brand-new, old-style Morgan. Hugo arrived to steer Sir John to his guest-of-honour seat on the top table.

A stroke of ill-fortune (at least, Noone presumed it wasn't enemy action) seated him on a table of eight next to "Colonel" Ned R. Porage who dominated dinner with opinionated, provocative pronouncements on each topic of conversation. He was especially keen to let it be known that he was on the waiting list for a Morgan, despite Sir John's ill-founded criticism of the company. Typical, thought Noone, his enjoyment of *Foie gras au naturel légumes et fruits croquants, émulsion du verger* accompanied by a fresh, shy village Chablis from the Domaine William Fèvre, quite spoiled. Even the gentle fruitiness of the following '88 Graves from Château Rahoul to go with *Carré d'agneau rôti au Romarin, Soissons et Figatelli en fin ragoût* somewhat passed him by. Just as they were finishing dessert, *Moelleux au chocolat, infusion Vanille et tuile à l'orange,* something extraordinary happened: "Colonel" Ned R. Porage began to pick apart and eat the floral decoration in the centre of the table. Perhaps this was as a result of an SAS-type challenge from one of the Scotsmen on the other side of "Colonel" Ned; perhaps he was still hungry. Noone, having observed him knocking back the drink steadily, reckoned it was because he was plain pissed. And mad.

Hugo rose to say a few more words of thanks to them all and to "the man who saved ICI" before raising a toast to ABS, heartily echoed by all present, conjoined in the belief that it would last forever. Sir John then exited with a rambunctious wave and a general milling around ensued while drinks were finished. Bob Ellis appeared. Bob was an ex-Met.copper who had been born and raised on a council estate in Stoke Newington. He joined the Force in 1974 and was posted to Notting Hill as a probationer, where, after four years of increasing boredom, he applied for, and won a place in, the Special Patrol Group. He underwent firearms training, and, by avoiding mishap, became the unit Officer Safety and Physical Training Instructor. When the SPG was disbanded in 1983, Bob took promotion to Sergeant and, by now knowing a thing or two, applied to the Flying Squad as a detective sergeant. He was selected and posted to Barnes. There, during a surveillance operation, he became detached from his team and was given a royal kicking by his "Targets", several nasty armed robbers intent on reliving the glory days of the Kray twins. He recovered from injuries sustained, but thereafter walked with a pronounced limp (L-I-M-P, pronounced "limp") and as a result, was moved from "Ops" to "Office Manager", acquiring a bitter cynicism enroute. His final move was a secondment to Paddington Green as Security Suite Manager, ordered by the management, which had recognised that his multi-skills experience and world-weary knowledge of "The System" would serve him well in dealing with suspected terrorist scum.

Bob had retired at fifty with no great expectations but had signed on at an agency which had led him to Hugo. Hugo recognised that Bob's qualities and laconic but aggressive attitude would equip him for a twilight career dealing with unpredictable consultants and hired him as Administration Manager on the spot. Noone knew that anyone who had regularly handled this country's finest terrorist enemies and coped with the aftermath of an IRA bomb planted in a telephone kiosk next to the building in 1992, wasn't all bad.

"Bloody good show, Bob, well organised," said Noone, genuinely.

"I had to control Hugo pretty closely, I can tell you. Do you know he wanted to take everyone to Folies Bergères? Can you imagine how that would have gone down with some of our sensitive young female consultants?" Noone, surveying the room, wouldn't have minded going down with some of the younger female consultants himself, especially the promising Nerissa, but he knew what Bob meant.

"Yes, they can be fiercely politically correct and they don't like to be seen as natural objects of our desire any more. Pity really, spoils it for the rest of us. We won't be allowed to tell dirty jokes soon."

At that moment, Noone watched in horror as "Colonel" Ned R. Porage circled around to land both his hands on Bob's shoulders, and proceeded inexplicably to plant a kiss on Bob's forehead. Bob, short, shaven-headed and built like a barrel was understandably unamused. He grabbed the taller "Colonel" Ned's throat with his left hand and made to punch him with his right. Noone and the Scotsman intervened and after a short, unseemly scuffle to separate the two, walked Bob away from trouble.

"Don't let him anywhere near me in future," he fumed. "I don't care if he was in the SAS, I'll punch his fucking lights out." Noone would have liked to have seen "Colonel" Ned's fucking lights punched out but knew Bob would have been sacked on the spot by Hugo.

The ABS throng, led by some young thrusters from London, descended to the basement Night-club and the inevitable decline in professional behavioural standards continued. In the dark corners, the young shoots of liaisons both legitimate (between consenting adults of single status) and illicit (between consenting adults married not to each other) were growing, watered well by large quantities of alcohol. Nerissa and her friend Jade Summerflower, from Exeter, joined Noone and Nevis at a table and their chatter became increasingly risqué. Nerissa flashed one of her gorgeous smiles:

"You seem up for it tonight, Adam."

"Up for what?" he enquired with a leery grin.

"A little bit of what you fancy, maybe," she replied and nudged Jade. "What *do* you fancy, Adam?" With that she leaned forward and licked her lips. "A dance?"

It was a start. Nerissa entered into the spirit by dancing

in a suitably abandoned fashion, arms alternately raised, pointing, beckoning and mussing her hair while Noone tied himself in knots trying to impress with his fancy footwork. He discovered yet again that thin line between manageable, alcohol-fired, inhibitions-receding, synchronous Travolta-worship and unmanageable, alcohol-ruined, inhibitions-gone, uncoordinated lurching. Then Noone's recollection of the rest of the evening formed an increasingly sporadic patchwork. He remembered professing undying love, in a strictly platonic sense, to Sharon Ridell, avoiding Sally Forth who seemed to have revived her Christmas spirit, bumping into "Colonel" Ned R. Porage on the way back from a trip to the Gents, who looked at him glassily and said his life was effectively over, and weaving arm-in-arm with Nerissa, Jade and Nevis as the men chivalrously escorted the girls back to their room.

The unpleasant, harsh intrusion of the wake-up call brought everything and everyone sharply into focus. Noone and Nevis hastened back to their room and missed breakfast again. ABS assembled itself groggily in the hotel lobby for the coaches to take them to *Gare du Nord* and the return journey on Eurostar was more subdued, although, as it was a Saturday morning, they still managed to clear the train out of beer by Calais. Noone was gratified to catch Nerissa's eye as the group said collective farewells at Waterloo. She didn't seem to be regretting anything that might or might not have happened. Luckily, Sunday imposed itself as a day of recovery and back in the office on Monday, everybody agreed it had been a first-class conference.

14. CANDIDATES

"At Garner International, our team has in-depth search experience. Just as importantly, we have had extensive experience out there in the workplace across a range of industry sectors. This means we understand the problems and pressures of operating within a client business. Our consulting experience is complemented by the quality of our research. Using the latest tools and technology available, our research team ensures that all information about candidates and clients is accurate, reliable and relevant. This provides a solid basis for successful search. Remember, however, we focus on real research – we don't merely trawl through databases. Executive search really does mean search!"

GARNER INTERNATIONAL WEBSITE

It took a week or so for the firm to settle down after the conference. The airwaves were atwitter with rumours about who did what to whom, when and where. Noone heard with relish about a naked threesome in the hotel swimming pool, a secretary and a consultant caught in the middle of an energetic bout of Ugandan Relations in the Spa changing rooms, at least two passionate embraces recorded in the Night-club, an unfortunately-female, Glasgow-based researcher seen leaving the room of "Colonel" Ned R. Porage, two London Consultants spotted swapping tongues and a young chap from Basingstoke found asleep under the hotel's grand-piano by the night-porter. Thankfully, there was no apparent record of Nevis's liaison with Jade, nor his own dalliance with Nerissa: Friday night's sleeping arrangements remained a deeply covert, instantly deniable, black operation.

Noone kept his head down for a while, winning and transacting a reasonable amount of business himself and enjoying the growth in collective fee revenue which his

Uxbridge teammates were providing. This reflected well on his leadership. Of course, he liked to be diverted from work, such as when he amused himself with a history essay written by his seven year old nephew, Toby, which his sister had sent to him, thinking it would tickle his fancy. It did:

"Ancient Egypt was very old. It was owned by gypsies and mummies who wrote in higher airfix and lived in the Sarah Dessert. Moses led the Hebrew slaves to the Red Sea which he opened while they exited on unleftover bread without any ingredients. Moses went up on Mount Cyanide to get the ten commandos. Solomon had three hundred wives and seven hundred porcupines and was a actual hysterical figure as well as being in the Bible. The Greeks were a highly crafted people who created history with Myths. A myth is a female moth. Socrates was a famous old Greek lecher who died from an overdose of wedlock, which is poisonous; after his death his career suffered a dramatic decline. In the first Olympic Games, Greeks ran races, jumped, hurled discos and threw up broccoli spears. It was messier than they show on TV now. Julius Caesar extinguished himself on the battlefield. The Ides of March murdered him because he wanted to be king. Dying, he gasped: 'Same to you Brutus'."

Noone could follow they logic in all of this, even though the vocabulary was ill-chosen and facts somewhat distorted. Even more up-to-date events were no less misshapen;

"Joan of Ark was burnt to a steak. Gutenburg invented removable type and the Bible; another important invention was the circulation of blood. Sir Walter Raleigh is famous because he invented smoking and ate potatoes. Sir Francis Drake circumcised the world with his 100 foot clipper which was very dangerous to all his men. Shakespeare was born in 1564, supposedly on his birthday; he is famous only because of his plays and wrote tragedies, comedies and hysterectomies all in Islamic pentameter. Writing at the same time was Miguel Cervantes who wrote Donkey

Hote. The next great author was John Milton who wrote Paradise Lost. Since then no-one has ever found it."

Music also went the way of literature: "Johann Bach wrote a great many musical compositions as well as a large number of children. In between, he practised on an old spinster which he kept in the attic. He died from 1750 to the present. Bach was the most famous composer in the world and so was Handel, who was half German, half Italian and half English. He was very large. Beethoven was so deaf he wrote loud music and became the father of rock and roll. He expired in 1827 and later died for this".

Finally, science got the treatment: "In the nineteenth century, there were many thoughts and inventions. People stopped reproducing by hand and started reproducing by machine. The invention of the steamboat caused a network of rivers to spring up and the McCormick raper did the work of a hundred men. Louis Pasteur invented a cure for rabbits and Madman Curie discovered radio. She was the first woman to do what she did. Other women have become scientists but they didn't get to find the radios because they were already taken. Charles Darwin was a great naturist who wrote the Organ of the Species. It was very long and people got upset and had trials on it. He sort of said God's days were not just 24 hours from Tulsa but without watches who knew anyway? I don't get it".

Noone could tell that his little nephew was unlikely to get anything other than a clip round the ear on this sort of form, but the rich tapestry of his selective historical knowledge brightened up Noone's day at least. He rang his half-sister, Amelia. She wasn't really his half-sister. She was his real sister but she was a lot shorter than Noone:

"Tobes certainly has a unique grasp of history, hasn't he?"

"Yes, I thought you might be amused by his perspective."

"Probably best to steer him away from it for GCSE, then?"

"Oh no, it's his best subject and he loves it. As he gets

older he will straighten out the facts and dates." Noone wasn't so sure; it all seemed so slapdash these days.

"Well, it's probably not necessary. He could walk into Alastair Campbell's job right now with that ability to spin reality…anyway, thanks for the light relief, must go, got a business to run," he said to impress her. "Cheers Half-Sis."

Later that day, "Badger" Brock rang. He was the youngish consultant from the London office and winner of the first "Bullshit Bingo" game, with whom Noone had struck up a reasonable rapport in Paris:

"I say Adam, have you heard the news about Sharon?" Noone hadn't heard the news about Sharon.

"She's off. Fleeing the coop. Says she's setting up her own business. Seems odd, don't you think?" Noone agreed it seemed odd. He knew Sharon's thirst for designer-wear did not come cheap and that she was determined to see Theresa and Daniel through an equally costly public school education. She needed significant regular income and good old Dave wasn't in a position to provide it. He called Sharon immediately.

"Hi Sharon, what's all this about you leaving?"

"God, word travels fast in this place: I only told Hugo this morning."

"He must be devastated," said Noone, increasingly intrigued, for he knew all the rumours about the sexual frisson between Hugo and Sharon.

"Yes, he wasn't too happy at first, but he understands my need to move on." This wasn't true: Hugo didn't understand it at all. Old St Trisstram'sians stuck together for life like musketeers, friends through thick and thin and he was dismayed at Sharon's betrayal. His initial shock and disbelief, during which he had offered her more money and tried to dissuade her, had given way to irritation and then anger. He had *made* her and now she was abandoning him. All his previous pride in her success and the enduring warmth he held for her began to evaporate. He dismissed her rather coldly, saying that Personnel would handle the exit details on his behalf.

Sharon was relieved that the end was in sight. She knew she owed Hugo her career to date but she hated feeling beholden and tried to keep at bay the gratitude he expected her to show him for shaping her career so satisfactorily. She had outgrown him and resented his "ownership" of her. Cynics jealous of her position as Office Manager for London General still occasionally whispered that she was "horizontally indebted" to him. She had grown into a strong and independently minded woman and she needed to break free from the claustrophobic hold that Hugo held over her at ABS. Besides, like Baldric, she had a cunning plan.

Candidates continued to disappoint Noone and his team with their cavalier attitude to the career assistance they were receiving free from ABS. Noone would have thought that they would at least be mindful of the fact that ABS had a fee resting on the candidates' ability: their actual ability to do the job as well as their ability to tell the truth and deal straight. Too often, it seemed like a game to them: they would pretend that they were genuinely grateful to appear on a short-list and assure their consultant that he or she had become a real confidant(e), with whom they would discuss everything before taking a decision. Then at the last minute, an offer having been made, they would unfurl their true colours like a pirate ship, reveal they had received a superior offer from another direction and sail away without so much as a "Gor bless you Guv". Ungrateful bastards. The Man Who Said Everything Twice had just received one of these "virtual" kicks in the teeth.

He had safely completed an assignment to find a Head of Sales for a communications business. There had been only one hiccup at short-list, when the qualification check on one of the candidates revealed a 2:2 Honours degree instead of the 2:1 that appeared proudly on his CV. The Man Who Said Everything Twice called him up and because it was an awkward moment, became positively garrulous:

"Hello Jim, hello Jim; we have just been checking your

degree; yes, checking your degree. It seems that your 2:1 wasn't a 2:1 but a 2:2. A 2:2 not a 2:1 Jim; a 2:2 Jim, what do you say, what do you say?"

Jim, faced with the facts so succinctly put to him, was a salesperson after all:

"Gosh, was it really? Yes, you may be right. Do you know, I can never remember which one it is. I mean, it was such a long time ago and it's not very relevant, is it?" The Man Who Said Everything Twice knew that for some clients, particularly the swashbuckling, aggressive, pioneering, "new media", American types, bent on world domination, it wouldn't matter. They were less interested in integrity and more in "getting the job done" by whatever means. They would become the Enrons of tomorrow. For others, particularly the evangelical, God-respecting, zealous, politically-correct, American types, bent on world salvation, integrity was all. If a man cheated in his CV, what could he be doing to his wife and employer? The Man Who Said Everything Twice advised Jim to stop lying and dropped him from the short-list.

This hiccup over, the job was offered to a candidate called Jonson Frost, whose impeccable credentials all checked out. He resigned from his current employer and was placed on "gardening leave" for the three month duration of his notice period. It was highly unusual for companies to want people in the highly sensitive sales function to work their notice periods. They might allow resignees in less important functions such as finance or HR to "finish what they were working on and tidy their desks", but they couldn't have salespeople whose minds were elsewhere talking to customers, oh no. The Man Who Said Everything Twice sent in his final invoice (once) and moved on to concentrate on his other assignments. He was therefore somewhat surprised to read a headline in "Wireless Week" two months later ("Frost bites!") informing him that his successful candidate was about to join another firm, not his client. He was on the phone immediately to Jonson Frost, whose voicemail answered and asked for a message to be left. The Man Who Said Everything Twice, said everything once:

"Jonson, I've just seen the headline in 'Wireless Week' and I'm a little confused. It suggests you have signed up for a job elsewhere and are not taking up the role with my client. Please call me and tell me it isn't true."

Frost never called back and did as predicted by "Wireless Week". It was back to square one for The Man Who Said Everything Twice. Noone commiserated by sharing one of his own qualification-check disaster experiences. He had worked for a FTSE 100 retail client to find a Human Resources Director for its Asian subsidiary business. Noone had managed the assignment successfully through to the offer and the chosen candidate had accepted and resigned his current position. Unfortunately, there had been a delay in sending off the qualification-check request to the appointee's alma mater, a university in the north of England. The university failed to respond initially. By the time that the offer had gone through and there was still no confirmation from the university about the candidate's degree, the alarm bells had moved insistently to the front of Noone's conscience: he needed to complete the due diligence. He telephoned the university record office and found Miss Prim-and-Guarded on the end of the line. Noone played Mr Tact-and-Diplomacy, gently explaining the reason for his call:

"Hello, I am a Director with ABS; you know, the leading executive resourcing business? The thing is, we always check qualifications to safeguard the reputations of our candidates, ourselves, and of course the establishments from which qualifications are claimed. Our faxes don't seem to have reached you and I'd be so grateful if you could confirm my successful candidate's degree."

"I don't need to be patronised, Mr Noone," came the sharp reply, "and yes we received your faxes. We don't deal with agencies." She said the word "agencies" as if she had bitten into an apple and found a slug inside. Noone felt her unseen grimace.

"However, if you would care to give me your clients' details, I will speak to them directly." Grey hair tied in a bun, tweed skirt, glasses, sensible shoes, never married, thought Noone.

"Fine, but could you please just confirm that my candidate attended your university?"

"No. Goodbye Mr Noone." At least he knew where he stood, he thought wryly. Stupid bitch.

He telephoned the client to explain the situation. The next day the client phoned him back to explain the subsequent situation. Miss Prim-and-Guarded had confirmed that the candidate had indeed attended the university and embarked on the Business Studies course as stated. She also confirmed that he had been rusticated, sent down after a rather unsavoury incident involving a serving girl from the refectory who had been found (by the police after a tip-off) naked, bound and screaming in his room late one night. Miss Prim-and-Guarded hadn't gone into full detail, but in hushed tones she had mentioned the final incriminating discovery of a honey-covered cucumber. The candidate had not completed his degree, despite the claim on his CV. The client, from the virtuous side of the fence, had no alternative but to withdraw the offer.

Noone contacted the candidate and relayed the damning information. The candidate was defensive and unapologetic: he *would* have achieved at least the second class honours mentioned in his CV, had he been allowed to finish the course. The university had prevented him from reaching his potential. His unabashed parting shot to Noone was:

"Incidentally, I'd had second thoughts about moving to the Far East and was going to pull out anyway. Thanks for saving me the call. Cheers." With that, he rang off, leaving Noone with a broken assignment back at square one, thus able to empathise now with The Man Who Said Everything Twice.

Some months after the incident, with the assignment finally put to bed, Noone was interviewing someone coincidentally in the same company from which his by-now-infamous candidate had previously resigned. Noone couldn't resist mischievously mentioning that he knew the former HR Director and wondered where he had gone.

"Didn't you hear?" asked the interviewee, "it was terribly sad. He only resigned to look after his wife who was dying of cancer. He didn't want to tell people the truth and make a fuss. After she died, he contacted the MD and of course the whole story came out. The MD kept his job open until he had come to terms with her death and felt ready to return to work. He has borne up marvellously and is more highly regarded than ever." Bloody nerve, thought Noone, recalling that the candidate's CV had said he was unmarried, which was why he had been able to relocate to the Far East. It was a strange world in which he worked: the real truth is often buried under layers of obfuscation; half-truths and lies become the commodities and "facts" in which people deal.

Noone was by now experienced enough to realise that candidates were very rarely in the wrong and nobody was actually fired any more. It wasn't true of course, but it was very unusual to hear a candidate admit that he or she had been "relieved of duties". Occasionally, one would admit that the relationship with the boss had broken down over the boss's unrealistic demands, or the relationship with a new boss hadn't worked out because "they didn't see eye-to-eye". Even so, there would have been the ceremonial drawing up of a Compromise Agreement, confirming "termination by mutual consent", protecting both parties from any allocation of blame. Candidates euphemistically said of such cases that "we agreed to part company". There would be a bland reference attached for the departing employee to brandish at future interviews: Noone now knew that written references quite literally were not worth the paper on which they were written, particularly those which were self-penned. One of these was unforgettable:

"My CEO said in my last appraisal that I will go far; the Chairman ditto. My Mum says I am a lovely boy."

This had been the literary self-destruct equivalent of enclosing the picture of oneself draped over the company car. It betrayed a fearsome lack of touch and earmarked the individual as bargepole material.

This was not to say that references were a waste of time. On the contrary, it was very important to take verbal references from current or former colleagues, superiors and subordinates, not least, as Hugo, Sharon and Gordon had drummed into him, because referees were an important source of business. He would never forget the candidate with the sexual harassment case, evidence of which had slipped out during a conversation with a referee, and he had heard of other revelations that had brought down a candidate at the last. Indeed, it was a good job that Noone could cope with ambiguity, for there was a clear conflict of interest involved in taking verbal references. On the one hand, ABS's proud boast was that its consultants carried out the most rigorous of qualification and due diligence checks (pointing out in self-righteous shock that many competitors couldn't be bothered). On the other hand, its consultants were desperately afraid that the checks might throw up an anomaly and thereby wreck an assignment right at the end. Further, they would have to call a Chairman, CEO or an MD to take a reference on an employee whom, if he or she hadn't "been let go", the referee was understandably disgruntled to be losing. More than a few tended to be a little stilted, and Noone had been quite scarred by one telephonic encounter.

"Hello, Adam Noone from ABS here. Thank you for taking the call. I am calling you to take a reference on John Snipe. Is it convenient to talk?"

"No it bloody isn't. Are you the bastard who headhunted him?" Not a promising start: a gruff northern accent.

"No, not at all. He responded to an advertisement."

"Which you bastards had put in the paper. So you did headhunt him." Noone sensed the situation was sliding out of his control and now was not the time to enlighten this Chairman with Hugo's precise dividing line between the semantics of search versus selection.

"Um, not exactly; he was clearly unhappy and looking for a job and the client has made him an offer. We are just carrying out the due diligence."

"Bollocks. He wouldn't have been unhappy if you bastards hadn't offered him more money." This guy was clearly in denial.

"Well, that's not strictly true, but anyway, what can you tell me about him, please?"

"Nothing. He worked for me and now you bastards have taken him, that's all."

"OK, fine, I understand why you might be upset; I just wondered whether you could verify a few things he has told us?"

"No. If you are so damned clever you can find it out for yourself." Noone now realised that the business development part of the call was going to go down like a collapsing skyscraper.

"Ah, ok, I respect your position," and then he said it anyway, "if we can ever be of any help to you, please don't hesitate to get in touch…you know, you might not have anyone lined up to take his place…" he trailed off weakly. There was an explosive cyclogenesis on the other end of the line:

"Fuck off, you cunt." Noone fucked off and still warmed with embarrassment at the memory.

Reference-taking threw up astonishing revelations the equal of the sexual harassment case from time-to-time. Noone was aware of the husband who hadn't lived at his registered address for years, preferring the more intimate surroundings of his mistress's flat; the female executive who had been kindly given HIV by her husband who in turn had contracted it from his homosexual lover (he wasn't gay himself, he just happened to sleep with a bloke who was); the bigamist who, for two years, had undertaken a weekly commute "for work" away from one wife and two children in Newcastle-on-Tyne, staying Sunday to Thursday with his other wife in Harlow, Essex; the man whose three year career break, explained on his CV as time spent studying for a degree at Kingston University, turned out to be a spell in detention at Her Majesty's pleasure, for GBH, whilst defending Tottenham Hotspur FC's honour against some Arsenal scum one Saturday afternoon outside White Hart Lane; even the woman whose entire life turned out to be a lie: she did not possess the PhD from Cambridge and MBA from Harvard and had used seven different names during a life of deceit, moving on to the next name each time she was unmasked as an imposter (owing to most employers' slack, un-ABS-like due diligence procedures, this could take several years). The more audacious the lie, the longer it endured.

Noone mused that this was why Americans who had failed in America could prosper in the UK: their natural brash ebullience overwhelmed the British tendency towards self-effacement and their brazen confidence made close scrutiny seem pitifully small-minded. After all, if they were going to do such great things for your company, it would be churlish to attempt to undermine them at the start, wouldn't it?

Noone reflected ruefully that the proud, standard-bearing edifice of executive resourcing, where the self-burnishing ABS shone like a bright new coin in the muddy shallows, was constructed almost entirely of these lies and half-truths. Strip them away and only a few upright steel girders of absolute truth remained firmly cemented in the foundation of reality, around which the cladding of deceit was hung.

Another nest-lining technique which candidates liked to employ in attempting to slide seamlessly between employers was the "redundancy pay-off versus new job acquisition" power play. This was a precarious balancing act whereby the candidate would attempt to engineer a redundancy pay-out from the current employer whilst simultaneously agreeing to a new job offer elsewhere.

"So why do you want to move from your current position?" Noone would ask during the interview, to check whether the story had changed since the telephone interview.

"Well, as I said," (implying "you can't catch me out with that old trick") "I've achieved all I set out to achieve here and it is time to move on to the next challenge." This was standard patter and Noone knew it was almost certainly untrue. It wasn't often that companies "ran out of things to do" for their executives.

"Have you discussed the situation with your boss?" He would enquire, innocently.

"Yes. He agreed that I have worked myself out of a job. They don't want to lose me and he offered me an alternative role, but it would be a backward step, to be honest." Usually this was enough to terminate the candidate's prospects as far as Noone was concerned. After all, how likely was it that a dynamic, effective, well regarded manager would run into a cul de sac at work, where there was suddenly nothing to do? Where the candidate was about be let go by an employer eternally grateful to have benefited from his or her dynamic, effective, well regarded services for a while, whilst wistfully acknowledging that there was nothing else to be done? Just occasionally, however, the candidate did have a more lively personality than the rest which suggested possible short-list material. He would push back gently.

"Surely there must be a role there for a man of your achievements and talents?"

"Well, there is a role in India and one in Uzbekistan, but I wouldn't relocate there for the family's sake." The alternative positions always seemed to be in the most inhospitable, culturally different or unattractive of places. Then, slyly and slowly, the truth would slip out. "The company is offering voluntary redundancy, so I am considering taking that option."

There we have it, thought Noone. When he set out on his business career the stigma of retrenchment hung like a poison cloud over the land. His first company had proudly boasted that it had never had to make anyone redundant. To be made redundant was the worst thing bar death that could happen to a man; worse even than his wife running off with somebody else. At the breakdown of a marriage, at least there were extenuating personal circumstances which were understandable and allowed people to take sides. But redundancy was a big, looming, impersonal monster. It just happened. Notices and papers were served. It was beyond any individual's control. If you were made redundant, there was something of the leper about you; people would lower their gaze as you walked by, desperate not to be drawn into conversation. What conversations that were had studiously steered clear of any talk about redundancy, for fear of the infection spreading. A false, strained bonhomie resulted and another lie that all was well was lived.

Now, it had become part of both business and personal strategy. Organisations used it as a regular and perfectly valid cost-cutting tool. It was usually the first action imposed by an incoming Chief Executive: a quick review of staff numbers, ask each department for a ten percent reduction and, bang, away you go, thousands, if not millions of pounds of operating costs saved. Candidates, meanwhile, were no longer carriers of an obscene disease; they were even admired if they could wangle their way through several redundancy packages. So, a candidate might progress onto the long-list, the short-list, the even-shorter-list of the last two and finally to the offer. The candidate might want to accept but:

"The thing is, to get my redundancy pay-out, I mustn't be seen to have lined up another job already. Can the start date be put back for a couple of months?" Noone found the overt greed of "wanting to have your cake and eat it" vaguely distasteful, but he understood the candidate's desire to make as much out of the situation as possible, and usually the request could be accommodated. The deal done, Noone would ask to speak to the candidate's referees, at which point his own integrity would be compromised.

"Ah, well of course you can talk to them, except for my current boss. He mustn't know that I have a new job until I have left the company under the redundancy terms. Could you leave it for a week or so and when you do talk to him, make out that it is at the beginning of the process and not that I have already accepted a job." What could Noone do? He had to play along with the charade or else he risked the offer collapsing if the candidate's boss withdrew the redundancy offer which would upset the candidate and might send him off in a sulk. Worse still, lawyers might be invoked (like an old-fashioned duel, "I slap your face with my lawyer and he will meet your lawyer at dawn") in which case his client might get cold feet and withdraw the job offer. Noone was damned either way, but the candidate always expected the consultant to prostitute him or herself in this way on their behalf. Such were the joys of "coping with ambiguity".

Despite the vagaries of candidates, Noone and his Uxbridge team remained close-knit (not least because of the Friday lunchtime ritual) happy and successful. Until the call from Head Office which removed Noone from this cosy little world.

15. LONDON CALLING

"The philosophy of the Firm is to win repeat business from a restricted client base. This enables us to minimise our off-limits issues and maximise our ability to approach the best candidates for our clients. This freedom to access candidates from the widest possible universe becomes increasingly important in specialist areas and when recruiting for the most senior positions, where there are often only a limited number of qualified people. The team at the Miles Partnership is stable, experienced and focused. We deliver exceptional work for our clients by insisting that a partner of the Firm lead and execute each and every one of our assignments."

THE MILES PARTNERSHIP WEBSITE

It was the Summer of 1996. Undertaking some preparation and analysis before a meeting with a newspaper publisher, Noone was reviewing a selection of that week's world headlines sent to him by Minge. Minge was in strategy consulting and the internet had transformed the way he and his fellows communicated and worked. It enabled them instantly to deploy their irreverent humour on topical news items, launching "funnies" as virulent, viral epidemics via intensive email traffic. More often than not, a celebrity scandal or unanticipated death in suspicious circumstances, especially where strange sexual proclivities were hinted at, provided the ammunition with which they would bombard the world, mercilessly flaying a reputation in a remorseless onslaught of scurrilous innuendo and jokes in hugely poor taste, which Noone greatly enjoyed. Occasionally, a collection of headlines provided the fun and currently, The Far East had more than its share of strange incidents, often reported in unintended double-entendres:

"Flooded car parks keep firemen busy" came from

Johore Baru and in Kuala Lumpur, "a Chinese herbal medicine used as a male aphrodisiac has been found to come from a drug which causes impotency." From Semarang "Women beat up male referee" while in Pulau Tekong, where "Woman fell into sea from bum boat... Government doctors who carried out a post-mortem ruled that the cause was drowning soon after death."

The Bangkok Times offered "Thai cabinet reshuffle on the cards". From Jakarta, "Peanut wrapper shock" revealed that important government papers were being used to wrap peanuts. "Snatch thief grabs cashier's" and on the same theme "All the victims came forward to say they had been grabbed from behind and fondled for several minutes." Also, bizarrely, "Crackers: special police teams on prowl. Set-up for a perfect bust." A film review noted "The fighting scenes are stereotyped and the climax is hard to come by."

Singapore's Straits Times reported ambiguously "Foot rot hits plant" and "Boy wonder Wang admits: I directed attack on plant." It had also announced the winner of the Most Meaningful New Year Greeting Contest: "Madam Lim of Singapore 0315 wins first prize for her effort which literally means *The golden rooster brings us great happiness; this year will be even more prosperous.*" Stunning stuff. Continuing a bird theme: "Turkey admits torture" but also "Turkey sets up office in Singapore." It highlighted "PR body asks members to donate deposit to library" and ruminated quizzically: "Are there more than one bogus fortune-teller?"

Over in America, the Washington Post recorded "Motorists may have to accept new curbs" and that in the Middle-East, "Hostages allowed to see old Reagan movies" which must have been more painful than any other form of torture. Worryingly, "About 1,000 shells from WWII, containing gases designed to burn or paralyse the victim on contact, have been found to be leaking at an army depot in Alabama, a spokesman for the base said today. He added the potentially lethal leak of poisonous gas was of no danger to the public." More from Alabama, where an eyewitness was quoted: "They could have been reading the Bible together, but I don't think so. He had his trousers down and was on top of her."

Closer to home, Noone was pleased to note: "Hungary devours Yugoslavia to confirm berth" related to football, "Sweden finds car in search for mysterious subs" and "Two oil nations have Swede missiles." "Life-jackets designed to save people from drowning by keeping their heads above water have one major flaw: they fail to work." A regional Dutch paper confirmed that "The Beatles, especially now with John Lennon gone, will never play together again."

The English Press found some gems of its own: "Authoress admitted to 346-year male preserve" and reported that an uncle of an arrested man had complained about police harassment of his nephew: "They couldn't leave him alone. The police couldn't handle the fact that Colin was the best ram-raid driver in North Shields and they couldn't catch him." Sexual predilections had not gone unnoticed. A man was undergoing therapy to change his sexual preoccupation from cars to women which had been partially successful, said his doctor: "George developed a greater interest in women, helped by social skills training. However, he retained a strong desire for Austin Metros which we have not yet been able to modify." Noone's mind boggled. Finally, he was returned to the present by a note in The Daily Telegraph: "At the same time, employers were able to get the best out of their workers. They made substantial savings by using machines wherever possible." Very motivational, thought Noone.

The fun over for the day, Noone returned to the important task of trimming his email inbox down from over 1,000 read messages. He was very conscientious about opening new emails and responding promptly, but then he let them lie fallow in his inbox, keeping them there "just in case" he needed to refer to them in the future. Once a month, however, he knew he had to undertake a pruning exercise, for the Head of IT had exhorted everyone to delete emails assiduously and regularly, otherwise the server would grind to a halt. The phone rang. It was Hugo Reeve-Prior.

"Hello Adam. How are things in Uxbridge?" Hugo's cut-glass voice didn't really "go" with the word "Uxbridge". He made it sound like a leper colony.

"Fine thanks Hugo," said Noone. "The team are all firing on full cylinders, even Roger Bachelor-Freebody, about whom you were a little worried."

"Ah yes, the possibly gay cavalier. Well, your numbers are very good and it looks like you will be in for another record year if you keep on going the way you are. By the way, who do you see in your team as potential office manager material?" Unsuspecting, Noone said he felt The Man Who Said Everything Twice was shaping up well and seemed to be managing his Technology mini-team competently.

Then Hugo dropped his bombshell. "The thing is, how do you feel about a change?"

This took Noone quite by surprise. His immediate thought was that somehow his dalliance with Nerissa Wadsworth had leaked out. He was only too keenly aware of Hugo's memo issued a few days after the Paris conference, which revealed that spies were about and Hugo was not as ignorant about life in the trenches as people thought. The memo pontificated sternly:

"Relationships commenced at work are possible, if not probable, and can lead to marriage, but affairs cannot be allowed to damage the business. They are particularly discouraged between people of very different seniority and if someone is conducting an affair with someone over whom they have managerial responsibility, the senior person will probably be invited to leave the company." The memo went on to list three reasons why such behaviour was unacceptable: firstly, the junior person may feel obliged to cooperate to avoid giving offence or to gain career advancement; secondly, possible compromise of confidentiality and exposure to accusations of favouritism may result; thirdly (and rather bleakly in Noone's view) Hugo suggested "most relationships end, normally leaving at least one unhappy person. This can negatively disrupt team dynamics. In any case, the company's legal duty is to prevent behaviour which can constitute sexual harassment."

The message was clear: do not dip your wick in the office ink, shag your colleagues at your peril. Noone wondered whether rumours of "Colonel" Ned R. Porage's Glasgow-researcher conquest in Paris and his predilection for attractive temps had partly inspired Hugo's memo. Or perhaps the unfortunate dose of the clap to which Jim McDougal had admitted after a lost night in a "Hostess Inn" had had further legs and ramifications than he had thought. Noone noted that Hugo hadn't covered people who were married and worked together. Perhaps this was a hot potato too far. Noone knew of companies where, if intra-office marriages did occur, one of the spouses would have to resign. Presumably such companies feared marital pillow-talk as the highest and most potent form of industrial espionage.

For a moment, a hot flush drove the sweat to his armpits. He hedged for time:

"A change, Hugo? What sort of a change?" Was his career hanging in the balance?

"I was wondering if you would care to take over London General?" Noone was truly astonished. He had not been expecting this.

"What, you mean, take over London General? Me? Take over London General?" he stammered.

"Yes, that's what I said," said Hugo. "Now that Sharon is going, we need a good pair of hands there. In my view, either you or "Colonel" Ned could do the job, but it would mean a domestic upheaval for him, so I wanted to sound you out first."

Noone was instantly accosted by conflicting emotions: on one hand, he was reluctant to relinquish the relative security of Uxbridge, not to mention the ease of the journey to-and-from work. He had never envied The Crumble, as he called the London-bound commuters, wrapped in sullen silence, heads buried in newspapers or eyes closed, attempting an uncomfortable nap, sardined on seats or forced to stand, having paid a small ransom for a season ticket for the privilege of enduring cattle-class daily torment. He had never coveted the cachet of working in the West End ahead of a morning drive in the cocooned bubble of his car accompanied by the reassuring tones of Humphrys, MacGregor and Naughtie on the Today programme. Mind you, the former two angered him with their limp style of questioning and why did they always have to end a story just when it was getting interesting with: "I am sorry but that's all we have time for and we will have to leave it there." A triumph of form over substance. How tedious and time-wasting it would be to become one of The Crumble.

On the other hand, here was a chance to get one over on "Colonel" Ned R. Porage, to leap-frog him in the ABS pecking order. If Noone didn't reply affirmatively to Hugo's suggestion, "Colonel" Ned would sweep down from Birmingham and install himself on Hugo's right hand. He would be seen clearly as Hugo's protégé and Noone would remain in the backwater of Uxbridge whilst "Colonel" Ned hoovered up all the best clients and resultant accolades. He would become insufferably superior. Noone couldn't allow this to happen, even if it meant sacrificing Radio Four and losing half-an-hour's sleep in the morning in order to catch the fast train into town. Perhaps he could soften the blow.

"It's very kind of you, Hugo, and I appreciate your faith in me. The thing is, it will mean quite an upheaval for me too, what with leaving earlier and getting back later. It's not much fun on the train and Tube."

"No one said life was always a bowl of cherries, Adam," Hugo retorted sharply. "Sacrifices have to be made in order to move one's career forward. I only ever see my children at weekends." Exactly, thought Noone, that's the point. What sort of a family and social life does that leave? However, astutely realising that some sort of a sweetener was called for, Hugo then softened.

"We may be able to help out on the cost of travel; perhaps, go halves on a season ticket, that sort of thing. There will be a pay-rise as well to reflect the increased management responsibilities. London General is, after all, our flagship." Noone enjoyed a flush of pride. He was going to be in charge of the flagship. Still, best to tread cautiously and keep his powder dry.

"It is a great honour, but I feel very responsible for Uxbridge and reluctant to let it go. I'll also need to clear it with my wife." This was not true, but he wanted to play a little hard to get. "And what about my bonus situation, which is predicated on Uxbridge's performance for the year?" Noone was conscious that the performance of London General had flattened out, no doubt as a consequence of Sharon's heart not being in it and the fact that a couple of other consultants had also left recently.

"As to Uxbridge," said Hugo, "that was why I wanted to know whether you had a clear successor. Pro tem, you can continue to keep an eye on it and I will base your bonus calculation on the Uxbridge outturn at the year-end. Longer term, you should have the potential for a bigger bonus operating from London. It should produce the most revenue and the highest profit." The pound signs lit up in Noone's eyes. Yes, that was true and a clear argument in favour.

"Of course you need time to think it over. Give me a call with your decision by close of play tomorrow."

Noone realised that he had no option but to agree to the move and told his wife that evening. She paid little heed, a trifle distracted by how to broach the subject of the new dent in the rear bumper of her car, caused by an errant concrete bollard placed illogically in the line of her reverse out of a Sainsbury parking space. They settled down in front of the television, each preoccupied with unspoken thoughts. Noone considered a new car which his enhanced financial situation might allow, his wife considered the old car she had just made older. Both settled on silence as the correct course of action. As the reality of the move to London began to sink in, Noone realised his primary emotion was nervousness. London was big, daunting and full of strange new consultants who would eat him for breakfast, wouldn't they?

The next day, Noone duly rang Hugo and agreed the deal. Salary up to £70k, discretionary gratitude bonus this year for the change-of-circumstance embuggeration factor, Second-Class season ticket allowance which Noone could top up to First-Class, and an improved car allowance when due for change next year. They settled on a timetable: Noone could tell his Uxbridge team immediately, Hugo would reveal Noone's promotion to the London General team at five o'clock and email the news around the rest of the company thereafter. He would then formally offer the Uxbridge Office Manager position to The Man Who Said Everything Twice. Noone would take over in London after the impending August holiday season, on Monday September 5th, committing to the tyranny of the very early morning alarm clock.

Noone was gratified that the Uxbridge team seemed genuinely disappointed. Sally Forth's eyes were decidedly moist and Doris Moth in her quiet way went even quieter. Alien told him after the meeting that she would leave to spend more time with her family. The Man Who Said Everything Twice said;

"Deserting us for the bright lights, eh? Deserting us for the bright lights." He sensed the opportunity arising for himself. After all, it was his Technology team that was providing the lion's share of the fees for Uxbridge, not Noone.

"Hardly deserting, no option really. Following in Sharon's footsteps. Hugo must see Uxbridge as an ideal training ground" joked Noone. "Besides, it gives you the chance to take over here and make your own mark."

"Yes, yes, I suppose so; I suppose so," said the Man Who Said Everything Twice. He was already planning an office shake up.

The summer holiday coincided with Noone's 40th birthday. With his sister (replete with husband, son and daughter) and Minge (wife, son and daughter) he (wife and two sons) had hired a villa in the Algarve for the last two weeks in August. Villa Fábrica da Salsicha sat some way back from the coast at Vale De Parra, beyond Galé, secluded, although the offensive high-rise apartment blocks of Albufeira could be glimpsed in the distance. Classically whitewashed with red-tiled roofs, it was spacious enough for three families and came with large garden lined with small rosemary hedges, tennis-court, swimming pool and resident chameleon. The six children, ranging in age from two to eight, were horrified and fascinated by the beast's zygodactylic toes and independently rotational hooded eyes. Cuddly, friendly teddy-bears had not prepared them for life in the wild. They discovered it couldn't swim very well and Noone had to rescue it from the pool and hide it, black with shock, in a far corner under a hedge.

For a holiday designed around relaxation and sunbathing, it was an action-packed. One child caught sunstroke and was sick on day one, another was found to be allergic to Factor 30 suncream and developed an all-over itchy rash; excess swimming pool water ingestion caused diarrhoea for two others; one caught her finger in the gate, another fell over on the gravel drive and gashed his knee badly, necessitating a trip to the hospital in Albufeira. The three hire cars were raced by the men in time-trials on a section of single-track road behind the villa. The Renault Twingo proved most agile, the Fiat Panda ended up in a ditch and had to be lifted out (thank god for the collision-damage waiver). The men played golf at San Lourenco, Penina and twice at Salgados, a little-known fiendish gem of a course which claimed six of Noone's balls. The wives went shopping in Portimão and returned high on sangria for the loss of one handbag. There were collective family outings to The Big One waterpark (no drownings, one child lost for half an hour) to the hilltop village of Silves an hour's drive away (the stark, square beauty and calm of the red fort ruined by children bored, grizzly and hot) the beach near Armação de Pêra (where gaily coloured sun umbrellas concealed the lack of facilities on land and raw sewage in the sea) and a visit to one of the ubiquitously named O! Littoral restaurants (two down with food-poisoning). The adults hired a baby-sitter one night and dined expansively at the Hotel Alamansor, near Carvoeiro, which offered the meaningless, rear-terrace experience of watching a cliff face suffused reflected red by the hidden, dying sun. After several bottles of Douro, Noone left his never-to-be-seen-again camera hanging on the back of his chair. Self-catering culminated in Noone ruining barbecued sardines by failing to dilute the piri-piri sauce; his liberal dousing of the fish set lips, tongues and mouths afire and rendered the fish inedible.

Finally, there was a five hour delay at Faro airport for the flight home. Noone found himself talking alone to his history-savant nephew, Toby, and asked him whether he had had a good time. Apparently he had, except when Minge's daughter had held his head underwater until he started choking. Noone asked what the boy had done to her to cause this reaction.

"Nothing," he replied, "'cept I only put sand in her knickers."

"Well that's not very nice, is it?" said Noone, "you won't get any girl to kiss you if you go around doing that."

"Don't wanna kiss her. You have to marry 'n' have kids then. An' you gotta be eighteen."

"Well, that's not true, Toby. You have to get to know each other first by going out with each other."

"Yes, then you can leave Mum an' Dad at home, an' tell stories or lies to each other to get interested." Toby was catching on fast.

"Sometimes, though, it doesn't work out first time," said Noone. "What would you do then?"

"I'd run home and pretend I was dead. Then I'd call the newspapers and make sure they wrote about me bein' dead in all the dead columns."

"I see," said Noone, intrigued by Toby's simple death-wish strategy for survival in a complex world, "do you want to get married?" Toby frowned and was silent for a while. Then he said quietly:

"I s'pose so. Otherwise nobody will look after the kids. An' boys need someone to clear up." Ignoring Toby's emerging gender role assumptions, Noone asked:

"What do you think your Mum and Dad have in common?" Again a moment's thought and a pensive reply:

"Um…well, they don' want any more kids."

"I see," said Noone, "and how do you think you can tell if two people are married?" Toby responded more quickly this time:

"If they are not holding hands, you can guess; if they are shouting at the same kids." Yup, that would be one way. What else did a seven year old think about marriage?

"Toby, when do you think you might get married?" Toby looked up at the sky as if for divine patience.

"Prob'ly when I'm 'bout twenny, 'cos you know someone forever by then, an' wevver it's safe to kiss an' stuff." This was interesting.

"What sort of stuff, Toby?" The boy smiled coyly and looked away as he answered.

"You know. When they suck tongues an' blow each other up. That's grossed." He giggled.

"That's just Mum and Dad's way of saying they love each other," said Noone.

"Yuk," said Toby, pulling a face.

"Well how else would you keep the marriage going, Toby?" Toby pondered again.

"S'pose you tell your wife she's pretty even if she is fat like Mummy." Amelia appeared as if on cue.

"You two are having a long chat, aren't you? And

what's that about Mummy?"

"Oh, nothing Half-Sis," said Noone hurriedly, "Toby was just giving me his philosophy on love and marriage."

"How nice to see a meeting of minds of equal intellectual depth," she said archly, and in Noone's view, a trifle unkindly, "and I wish you would stop calling me that ridiculous name. Come on Toby, let's go and get a drink; and don't believe everything Uncle Adam says. In fact, don't believe *anything* he says." She whisked Toby off efficiently, leaving Noone to deal with the current and pressing lickerish demands of his own children. His conversation with Toby had revealed how out of touch he was with the world seen through the eyes of those under ten. Their fetching childish innocence was vanishing so fast. He really must spend some time with his wife and children. But right now, all he wanted to do was get home and go to sleep. Eventually their flight was called, and seated onboard with a calming alcoholic beverage, the adults agreed it had been an eventful and not-to-be-repeated-soon holiday.

The following Monday, Noone's alarm rang at 0600 precisely and having shaved, showered, dressed and made a cup of tea with equal precision, he drove fifteen minutes to Beaconsfield station, parked his car for the ridiculous price of £3.00 and awaited the late-running 0659 Chiltern Rail cattle-truck to Marylebone. Thence, Underground, one stop on the Bakerloo to change at Baker Street for the Jubilee southbound. He alighted two stops later at Green Park and walked apprehensively to the beating heart of ABS and his new office in Berkeley Street. A new era had dawned. Ironically, it was the high noon of Noone's recruitment career in ABS.

16. LONDON GENERAL

"At Hanson Green, we believe that strong boards make better companies. In conducting searches, we do not simply look for 'a name' but for candidates with the right experience and relevant skills to add real value to a board. We have established a reputation, built up over nearly 20 years, of carrying out stringent research and drawing on an extensive network of talented candidates known to us as well as "rising stars". Our track-record also makes us familiar with the specific and often sensitive challenges involved in appointing non-executive directors and chairmen with the right personal chemistry and cultural fit. The result is an ability to generate challenging and diverse shortlists and to consistently find successful candidates who will help your board and company to perform at its peak."

HANSON GREEN WEBSITE

Noone had barely sat down at his new office desk, recently vacated by Sharon Ridell, when the phone rang. It was "Colonel" Ned R. Porage.

"Congratulations on taking the poisoned chalice," he said brightly.

"Well, thanks, but I don't see it like that," Noone replied evenly, his confident retort masking the qualms he had been feeling since being briefed by Sharon on the task he would face.

"Oh don't you? You will, dear boy. Always in the HQ spotlight, too close to the meddling bigwigs, must grow revenue and profit, managing a crowd of primadonnas: no thank you." Noone didn't like being called "dear boy" by wanker Porage and he resented his cynical analysis.

"That's a bit harsh, Ned. London General should be the jewel in the crown and I intend to make sure it is."

"Well good luck. Give me Birmingham any day: I

prefer the safety of the sticks. More autonomy, less interference. That's why I turned the London job down," he dropped in casually. Noone was stunned by this revelation. Surely Porage hadn't been offered the job ahead of him? Hugo had said he was offering it to Noone first, hadn't he? Again his faith in Hugo was shaken. He recalled his very first meeting with Hugo, at which Hugo had set him straight about principles, conscience and "coping with ambiguity". There could be no doubt that Hugo practised what he preached when it came to ambiguity, the bastard. Still, he couldn't let "Colonel" Ned go one-nil up.

"Yes, Hugo said that on reflection he was worried about a culture clash and he felt it best not to move you from your comfort zone. Thanks for the call, 'bye." That would stir the porage nicely! He put down the phone quickly, no sense in talking further to the ghastly man. Noone wondered whether Bob Ellis would ever get the chance privately to deck "Colonel" Ned, as he had threatened to do. He sincerely hoped so.

He wanted to have a weekly meeting of all consultants to review assignments, PNBs and billing information but experience had taught him that everyone resented one held at 0900 on a Monday morning. The pleasures of the weekend were too fresh, the disheartening tasks of the week ahead too incipient and the hangovers too real. He decided to hold them on Tuesdays instead. He also knew it would be important to "walk the floor" on a daily basis, so at 0930, he set off on a tour of the office. 0930 was time enough for stragglers to have turned up for work; anyone arriving after this time was either away at a legitimate client or candidate meeting, or guilty of "pulling a sickie". Sharon had briefed him on some of the characters (or primadonnas, as "Colonel" Ned would have it) which he had inherited.

"Firstly, there is Rodney Shakeshaft. Old school and complete old goat. On his fifth marriage to the au pair of his last wife, nine children but will shag anything that shows signs of life. He is well connected with the ageing Boardrooms of UK plc and therefore a good source of business, so keep on the right side of him. "Badger" Brock I think you know: he is trying to emulate Rodney, but if he keeps out of the girls' knickers long enough, he could go far".

"Yes," said Noone, unthinkingly "I thought he showed a lot of spunk in Paris."

"As I said," continued Sharon, "sometimes too much and in too many directions. There are two other young blades like him: Darth Gwent and Caspian Cordell. The three of them compete for the secretaries and researchers." Noone was pleased to hear that Hugo's memo about intra-office liaisons was being taken seriously.

"Then there is Remy Aquarone. We are not quite sure how she ended up here: American, married to a Brit, ex Russell Reynolds and Diamond Chance where she had a reputation for hot air rather than real action. She is very status conscious so I don't know why she has stepped back from search into selection; rumours are that Archie Aspallan shagged her and pressurised Hugo to give her a home."

"I remember her being not very well on the way back from Paris," said Noone, "some sort of mystery virus?"

"Virus? Says she. Per-lease." Sharon rolled her eyes. "Monumental hangover. She was throwing up in the toilet all the way home and has bitterly regretted it ever since. Apart from that, she has yet to deliver anything substantial." Noone recalled the thin, wild-eyed blonde with the pallor of light avocado. She definitely talked a good car-park, but perhaps it was devoid of cars, as Sharon was suggesting.

"Watch out for the Politically Correct Brigade. Visa Maunfeld is the worst. She doesn't believe anything in our lives before the age of eighteen is relevant and refuses to ask candidates about anything other than work."

"Bloody hell," exclaimed Noone, "her candidate reports must be as dry as a bull's bum going up a hill backwards...um, sorry Sharon."

"That's just the point: any remarks like that and she will have you up before a tribunal for persistent use of foul and abusive language in the workplace." Noone remembered a willowy and rather attractive raven-haired girl who resolutely refused to dance in Paris, remaining steadfastly engaged in earnest conversation with a couple of other women. The "Keep Out" signs were writ large there, alright.

"Nevertheless," continued Sharon, "she is highly committed and conscientious. Clients like her. Similarly with Sara Sternhold. She could be Visa's twin: same age, outlook, style, clothes and they both live in Wimbledon. Could even be married to the same bloke." She giggled. "Whoops, that's not very politically correct, is it?" There was something refreshingly straightforward about Sharon which these new generation females clearly didn't possess. They sounded highly complicated and not a little dangerous: Noone could see a rival force to The Harpies, the dynamic duo of Stella Coldblood and Lavanya Tabernacle, whom he had left behind in Uxbridge, here. Sharon went on:

"The final member of the trio is Attracta Mann. Her name is a false premise: she is an ex City lawyer; you know, Berwins, Freshfields, ferociously bright, considers everyone beneath her and terrifies all men. She is what you mustn't call a "ballbreaker".

"She sounds perfectly ghastly," said Noone.

"She is. Square peg in a round hole, but Hugo liked her pukka background; you know how he is." Noone knew how he was: a snob. Hugo's own pukka background seemed to give him easy access to smooth lies and economy with the truth. Or "coping with ambiguity" as he would put it.

"Next we have a mad Italian woman who is quite exhausting, Sabra Termignioni, all lipstick and mascara, who works for luxury goods clients and always asks her clients for samples so she 'can really get to understand the soul of a product'. She's an antidote to the PC Brigade: not afraid to open her mouth before engaging brain, very flamboyant and 'in your face'. You might like that Adam." Sharon smirked. Did she know something else she wasn't telling?

"Another strange individual is The Hedgehog. I couldn't fathom him out. He is terribly quiet, creeps in and out unnoticed, keeps himself to himself, stays late and doesn't join in anything. I am not actually sure what he does all day; he is supposed to be developing the legal market, but he hasn't brought in any work yet so you will need to get tough with him soon." Noone was glad to hear that The Hedgehog might be an obvious target for some bicep-clenching, *pour encourager les autres.*

"I think the only other ones to keep an eye on are the three in the FMCG team; very close-knit they are, and it is an esoteric world full of Shop-floors, Industrial Relations, TQM, Kanbans, Supply-Chains, Procurement specialists and 'time-served engineers'. Sounds wonderfully exciting, don't you think?"

"Deathly dull, more like," replied Noone unenthusiastically.

"That's as may be, but they seem to enjoy it and have a nice little business going there. The danger is that they keep everyone else out of their silo so you won't know what on earth they are up to in there."

"Nothing like having team players around, eh?" Noone joked.

"Yes, and they are nothing like having team players, rather like all the others." As he reflected on Sharon's words now, Noone suspected that "Colonel" Ned's term "poisoned chalice" was fairly near to the mark.

"One final thing," warned Sharon, "you are at the epicentre here and it is very easy to be distracted and frustrated by the company politics. On one level you have Aspallan and Bane, who hate each other's guts and resent Hugo. They are utterly opposed to ABS offering search whereas Hugo is adamant that our clients and consultants increasingly require it. Hugo and Archie Aspallan have regular arguments about this. And then you have Hugo, who wants to know everything that is going on and can't resist giving you advice all the time. And finally you will have turf wars with all the office managers; you will even find consultants from Scotland popping up in London from time-to-time. You can forget the image of ABS as one big, united, happy family: everyone is out for what they can get and will guard every client jealously. I got fed up with it all in the end." Noone was a little shaken by Sharon's stark portrayal of life in the flagship and reasoned that much of it probably demonstrated the jaundiced view of a demob happy sailor.

"Don't think I am spreading poison just because I am leaving. It's a friendly warning, that's all. You will see it for yourself soon enough. But, having got to London, you won't want to go back to the sticks in Uxbridge. London is for the grown-ups. Good luck, Adam." Sharon had smiled and departed on a waft of White Linen, the "in" perfume from Estée Lauder.

Sharon had refused to tell Noone what her plans for the future were, other than she was planning on a rest for a couple of months "to recharge the batteries" before deciding what to do. He didn't believe her and was sure she had something worked out. He was sorry to see Sharon go even if he still didn't fancy her. She had been a good mentor in Uxbridge although her move to London hadn't been wildly successful. He fleetingly wondered whether she was still shagging Hugo, but assumed not since she was leaving. But then again, perhaps Hugo was taking his own memo to heart; of course he couldn't leave, so perhaps Sharon had had to go? Mmm, interesting speculation: he must check it out with Bob Ellis.

So on his first Monday morning in London, Noone "did the rounds" noting that Rodney Shakeshaft and The Hedgehog were missing. All the secretaries and even most of the consultants smiled at him, if a trifle warily. The Politically Correct Brigade were as predicted: chilly and correct. The FMCG team hardly said a word, Sabra Termignioni gushingly showed him her new Louis Vuitton handbag. She had long, perfect legs, Noone noted. He discovered a couple of new consultants whom Sharon hadn't told him about as they had been in the company for less than a month. The Personnel Manager was busy as Personnel Managers always were: there was hiring and firing going on, policies to write up, courses to attend, empires to build, guarded secrets to reveal confidentially and other mischief to make. This one, Linnet Trilby, was a particularly ingratiating and pudgy little number. Her nickname was "Toenails" as she was said to be so far up Hugo's arse that that was all that was showing. Noone planned to avoid her as much as possible.

Hugo dropped in on him after lunch, which was unfortunate as Noone had asked "Badger" Brock, Darth Gwent and Caspian Cordell to show him the best pub nearby. Being young, beer-illiterate and lager-drinkers their idea of a good pub was not Noone's idea of a good pub. They took him to Mulligans in Cork Street, a perfectly foul, mock Irish, full-of-itself, bar-restaurant pushing overpriced Guinness down the throats of unsuspecting and gullible American tourists and slightly loud young men, such as Noone's colleagues. It did not sell real ale. Noone discovered that "Badger" Brock was extremely proud of his BMW 3 Series (which lowered him in Noone's estimation) and that he lusted after one of the research girls. Turning to Gwent he asked:

"I suppose your parents had a sense of humour to give you the name of the universe's most feared and hated criminal mastermind?"

"No, my Dad was pissed," came the reply. "He was down the Registry and couldn't write straight. I was supposed to be Garth." Noone wasn't sure that was much better but he sympathised all the same.

"Oh it doesn't matter; I'm used to it. It was a bit of a pain at school where I was always billed as an evil genius, but now it is quite a good opener with the ladies."

"My name is Gwent: Darth Gwent," said Noone, Bond-style, trying it for size. He couldn't quite see it as a huge turn-on, but then again, it wasn't his name. Perhaps Darth Gwent licked his eyebrows at the same time…

Caspian Cordell was a real pretty boy. Long flowing blond locks, light blue eyes, slim build; he could have been a film-star. He joked about competing with "Badger" for the affections of the aforementioned researcher and Noone didn't think there would be much of a contest if Caspian set his mind to it. He intimated at intimacy with Sabra Termignioni as well. And Remy Aquarone. And Attracta Mann. And several secretaries. What it was to be young, free and single: lucky bastard, thought Noone. He didn't mention Hugo's edict about fraternisation but made a mental note to keep a wary eye open for any obvious overstepping of the mark by Caspian. All three young tyros were keen to develop beyond selection into the bigger ticket of search. He began to appreciate how much of a problem this could become and why Hugo may be having problems with Archie Aspallan and Giles Bane. If ABS consultants were not allowed "to grow up" into search, they would surely leave. Why should ABS become a nursery from where other search consultancies would cherry-pick their stars of tomorrow? Surely Aspallan and Bane could see this?

Noone suffered three pints of Guinness which lay heavy on his breath and stomach; he resolved never to return to Mulligans. He was concerned that Hugo might have noticed his Guinness affliction, but luckily, Hugo had lunched well at Langan's and was seeing things pretty rosily from behind a bottle of claret. He betrayed none of his annoyance at losing Sharon's services.

"What do you make of your troops then, Adam?"

"Seem to be an interesting and diverse lot, Hugo," replied Noone cagily.

"Yes. Well, there is a fair bit of underperformance in there so I hope you will be able to de-diversify them a little and get them pulling together in the same direction,"

Hugo replied, his choice of metaphor subconsciously betraying his coxing and nautical training. "It is absolutely critical that London General is super-fit. If they don't shape up, ship them out, eh?"

"I certainly will, Hugo." Hugo vanished as quickly as he had appeared. He was steeling himself for another difficult discussion with Archie Aspallan about search versus selection.

The Tuesday meeting was Noone's chance to see how the consultants shaped up in open forum. He had asked them all to make a five minute presentation on their current assignments and concurrent business development activity. Rodney Shakeshaft and The Hedgehog both blessed him with their presence and Noone could see immediately that he would have problems with them. The old goat Rodney already seemed to have his eyes on one of the new, young consultants, Rebecca Knightley and pointedly invited her to join him for his admittedly impressive "programme of lunches". The Hedgehog didn't seem to have a programme for anything and mumbled and stammered through his pathetic presentation. His pipeline appeared to consist solely of a client who was willing to pay him £10,000 to make a single phone-call to offer a position to a candidate coveted by the client organisation. Noone mentally gave him a month. The others were competent enough in various degrees. Both Sara Sternhold and the FMCG team mentioned the thorny issue of clients wanting them to undertake search assignments and Noone had to remind them of the referral procedure for search to Aspallan, Bane Consultants. He could see they were unimpressed by his evocation of the party line.

Overall he felt that his team was basically sound, but individually, rather than collectively, motivated and in need of some common goals. Knowing that drink was a powerful tool, he instigated bottles of champagne for new client wins and planned the communal Friday lunch that had proved so effective in Uxbridge, just as soon as he could find a decent pub. He also told them that there would be a daily "Quiet Hour" when business development calls would have to be made, and a quarterly prize for the most team-orientated action, to be awarded during a group night out. On the whole, he felt pleased that his initiatives were received in acquiescence, although he did note a few furtive glances, smirks and raised eyebrows.

Under "Any Other Business", there were a couple of complaints about consultants from other offices encroaching on London territory without any courtesy calls. Noone diplomatically refrained from pointing out that London consultants had historically trampled all over Uxbridge when they felt like it. There were always two sides to every story, both of them right and both of them wrong. He said he would look into it and sent them back to work with an encouraging smile, asking Rebecca Knightley to stay behind after the meeting. He wanted to find out what made her tick.

It turned out that whilst outwardly a "good time girl" of the Sloane Ranger type, Rebecca was in fact deeply insecure and emotionally damaged. Her parents were as surprised as everyone else when she was conceived, as they already had two sons in their twenties. Father was a successful stockbroker and the family had wanted for nothing: a large house near Godalming, Jaguar XJ 12 in the drive, exotic overseas holidays in five-star hotels, the boys public-schooled with an open door to Daddy's business when they needed it. What they didn't need in their comfortable fifties was a daughter. Of course Rebecca enjoyed the best of educations, the local Prior's Field School eschewed for the social cachet of Cheltenham Ladies' College where she boarded from eleven years' old. This allowed Mummy and Daddy to carry on with their self-important adult lives more-or-less unhindered by Rebecca's unnecessary childhood. Shunned at home, Rebecca compensated by becoming easily led and something of a party-animal. She started smoking at fourteen. At fifteen she was found drunk on cider in the returning coach after an away hockey fixture, which necessitated a warning letter home. Luckily, the school authorities did not discover the circumstances surrounding the loss of her virginity at sixteen, by now pert, blonde and petite: having eyed up one of the assistant groundsmen over the summer term, she "chanced" upon him in the tractor shed one hot June day and gloried in her power over him. She watched his hardening agitation as she undid her school tie and shirt, commanded him to drop his shorts and pants, and as he bobbed dramatically to attention, pushed him down to the ground before straddling his chest. She inflamed him further with the dusky scent of her damp gusset before sliding her non regulation skimpy panties off behind her and lowering her liquid warmth onto his engorged member. She rode him to her rhythm, using him as she did the handle of her hairbrush in the secret self-intimacy of the shower. Of course he exploded too soon, but not before she had glimpsed the exciting possibilities of having sex with a more accomplished partner. Satisfied with her new-found experience, she ignored the assistant groundsman completely thereafter and pursued a policy of one-night stands on through university and beyond, seeking the one who would fulfil her totally. She had not found him yet, arriving at ABS via a graduate trainee job with an advertising agency which left her equally unfulfilled.

Rebecca kept all of this from Noone, but he recognised a "poor little rich girl" when he saw one. Even the sanitised life story she had fed him revealed an unhappy childhood bereft of warmth and love. Beneath her tidily-framed exterior and behind her classically enunciating voice lay a lost soul. He wondered who would find it.

"Well it's been good to catch up with you, Rebecca, and I do hope this all works out for you. It looks as though Rodney will be introducing you to some useful contacts so stay close to him and …watch him carefully." He meant this as advice but hoped she would also take it as a warning.

"Oh I will," she replied, "he is quite an old sweetie isn't

he?"

"Yes and no," said Noone, keen to make it perfectly clear. "You will have heard that he is on his fifth marriage? Apparently he still managed to proposition eight of the women here last year. I mean it, watch him carefully and let me know if you need any help." He watched sadly as she nodded and left the room, her vulnerability wrapped around her like a cloak. Noone suddenly realised he was getting old. Having sensed Rebecca's rootless existence, there would have been a time when he would have made a play for her himself, but now he just felt protective towards her. At least, he didn't think he was jealous of Rodney, the randy old goat, for eyeing her up. Just rather appalled and desirous of saving her from his rabid clutches.

To regain some of his lost youth, Noone rang Nerissa's mobile and was pleased that she seemed pleased to hear from him. Noone observed wryly that Basingstoke was out of his territory but they agreed to have a drink when she was next in London; consultants could always find an excuse for visiting London, even if it was just a private audience with Toenails on some personnel matter.

Noone took stock of what he had discovered about London General: the bad news was that it lacked team orientation, a sense of humour and one or two of the consultants appeared cold and defensive. The good news was that nobody had openly laughed at him for having the temerity to descend on London and he had inherited a number of consultants who seemed to possess the right qualities. They were ambitious but needed leadership to mould them into a team. One or two might not make it, but in general he felt optimistic. Perhaps he could pull this off after all.

17. "HUFF"

"Clients have stated that Alexander Hughes delivers: a comprehensive assessment of each assignment with the expertise to present innovative solutions. A genuinely personal service, with experienced consultants closely involved in all aspects of the assignment. A thorough and highly professional search process clearly communicated, with informed research, extensive evaluation, reference checking and detailed reports on short-listed candidates. A very high success rate including completion of assignments where other search firms have failed."

ALEXANDER HUGHES WEBSITE

Noone bedded himself in, not with Nerissa, about which he continued to fantasise, but in London General, keeping abreast of news items which had little to do with his work but which amused him. A competition to unearth the world's most boring postcard certainly made him smile. It had already produced an exciting image of the first footbridge over the M1 and a caravan site spoiling an idyllic corner of the Lake District. The thrilling first prize was a weekend for two in Wigan. (Yes, thought Noone, and the second prize will be a week for two in Wigan). The event organiser was quoted as saying enthusiastically:

"There are many postcards from the late Fifties to the early seventies of some spectacularly dull aspects of post-war reconstruction, such as modernist office blocks, shopping centres, the M1 and the Croydon underpass. I don't think people necessarily want to go on holiday there; it is just the 'dull thud of civic pride and second-rate photography landing on your mat'. My own favourite is a prized snap of Brent Cross shopping centre on the North Circular Road in London."

Noone remembered unfondly a childhood holiday spent

in a caravan park in Skegness and how bored he and Amelia had been, watching from the unheated windows as the rain drowned everything in an atmosphere of defeat.

"However," continued the organiser proudly, "we may have to create a sub-section for kitsch. Like you see romantic postcards in Spain and Portugal of very well dressed lovers on mountain tops looking meaningfully into each other's eyes." Noone knew what he meant. "We are grateful to Wigan Borough Council for offering the holiday prize," ended the organiser, "which will include as a highlight a trip to Granada television studios, probably the most interesting place in Wigan." How very apt, thought Noone. He immediately photocopied the article and sent it through the internal mail system to his counterpart in the other, Financial Services, London office, Henry Ughyngton-Fitzhardynge, whom he knew would find the absurdity of a boring postcard competition hilarious.

Noone had enjoyed Huff's company over time at the various ABS formal and informal gatherings and marked him as a good if slightly eccentric egg. Since his move to London, he and Huff had agreed to get their teams together once a quarter in a wine bar to foster fellowship and bonhomie. Also, they had begun to pass increasingly filthy email jokes to each other.

Huff, as his double-barrelled surname suggested, came from two long lines of English aristocrats. In 1344, Sir Thomas Ughyngton was granted a licence to crenellate his Leicestershire property, previously a large baronial house with more emphasis on style and comfort than defence. He built a quadrangular castle with four large corner towers and four lesser, intermediary hollow towers sitting across the connecting curtain wall which was thirteen metres high and 2.5 metres thick. By any standards, the castle is an imposing edifice and the construction team and materials used were on a similar scale. A workforce of 350 men working day and night were employed over the first ten years of construction, and in the first eighteen months

6,000 tons of building stone, 22,000 tons of mortar and 800 tons of wood were used. Sir Thomas called his enlarged seat Sandyland on account of the prevailing subsoil thrown up by the foundation excavation. He pronounced himself satisfied with his creation, and expired contentedly shortly afterwards.

The castle saw action in 1536 during the "Pilgrimage of Grace" rebellion and again during the Civil War. The Ughyngtons were loyal to the King and in 1643, the castle was attacked by Sir Edward Wickham, a fierce Parliamentarian commander, and after a siege, the defenders surrendered to him. He put to death Sir Oswald Ughyngton and several of his loyal retainers, whose ghosts are said still to stalk mournfully the castle's walls and galleries. Later in the year, Sir Oswald's son Richard led a successful Royalist counter-siege, culminating in the collapse of part of the south face of the castle when gunpowder mines laid in a drainage ditch exploded to great effect. Richard was rewarded handsomely by Charles II with land, coin and the hand of one of the King's illegitimate daughters, Catherine FitzCharles. After Richard's premature death (he broke his neck and that of his horse in a fall while hunting) she proved an able and energetic "lady of the manor", restoring the castle, constructing stables, an ornamental lake, outbuildings and alms houses in the village of Skirton. Further rebuilding was carried out in the 18th century, turning the castle into a comfortable stately home with landscaped gardens.

At the turn of the 19th century, Sir Henry Ughyngton made a judicious marriage to the daughter of the Lord Chancellor, Lionel Fitzhardynge, agreeing to share names and accept an Earldom. The size and splendour of an estate were clear indications of the standing and fortunes of any family and investment continued to be made to enhance the grand seat as befitting a family destined to reside amongst the ruling classes for future generations. Sir Henry presided self-importantly over the apogee of Sandyland's local influence.

Until the 1870s, the family fortunes flourished and the estates covered some 15,000 acres, the zenith of prosperity. Then, disaster struck: enter the agricultural depression which deeply affected all landed gentry such as the Ughyngton-Fitzhardynges, who lacked revenue from coal or increasingly valuable urban commercial and residential property. The last Lord Ughyngton-Fitzhardynge inherited the estate in 1925, by which time many acres and much of the art collection had been sold. The following year, he was appointed a provincial governor in India and took his family with him, leaving Sandyland unoccupied. They returned in 1932, but India had ravaged Lord Ughyngton-Fitzhardynge's constitution, and, greatly weakened by dysentery and disappointment, he succumbed to pneumonia shortly afterwards, leaving his widow with enormous death duties. She closed the house during the Second World War and lived out the rest of her days in impoverished circumstances in the servants' quarters with only a smattering of retainers.

Sandyland's rehabilitation commenced in 1961, when Huff's parents Saunton and Dorothea moved back into the castle and set about repairing the decay caused by centuries of wetting, drying, heating, cooling, freezing, thawing and subsequent years of neglect. Leaking roofs, oak beams attacked by insect infestation, white-rot and brown-rot fungi, frost-damaged walls covered in pollution-derived calcium sulphate crusting, mortar shrinkage and general mineralogical conversion: the scale of the renovation required was enormous. Saunton's job in investment banking provided seven figure bonuses which helped. The income from the estate was ploughed into the castle and further finance raised as necessary by selling off pieces from the art and artifacts collection.

Meanwhile, Huff was born, and enjoyed an idyllic early childhood roaming unchecked around the estate. He learned how to set traps, collected wild birds' eggs, made bows and arrows and built tree houses with the help of the Estate Manager's son. None of these things prepared him in any way for the reality of life outside the environs of Sandyland Castle. Abruptly, his idyll ended when he was sent to St Trisstram's aged eight, although, perversely, his solitary childhood at least conveyed a degree of independence which enabled him to survive. Tall and muscular, in due course he excelled at rowing and helped the St Trisstram's First VIII, coxed by his now-friend Hugo Reeve-Prior, win the British National Schools' Championship. Despite his obviously superior pedigree, he was less of a snob than Hugo, although he preferred it that people knew their place and he didn't have to engage too much with the hoi polloi. Naturally, he went to Cambridge where he knocked around with Hugo and achieved similar things, including his first female-induced orgasm on Midsummer Common, during time out from a Summer Ball, with a well-bred ex maiden from Clare, whom he had met at a Boathouse jazz party. He rowed for Goldie in the Reserves Boat Race for two years, gaining a "Blue" in his final year at the expense of his degree, in which he only managed what was called "A Gentleman's Third" in Philosophy. Oxford won by a record margin.

Huff emerged blinking into the world aged twenty two and was directed to his father's investment bank where he plodded along in the middle of the road. In the style of a louche aristocrat with "old money", he wore suits that were never quite cutting edge, shirts frayed at collar and cuffs, shoes scuffed and down at heel and his ties carried animal or vegetable matter more often than not. His intuitive and enquiring mind unfortunately tended to become diluted by the intellectual abstraction which had lured him towards philosophy at university. He was never quite decisive or quick enough to conjure the really big deals which would have ranked him with the legends in the City's lunchtimes. He dabbled around in certain comfort in small and mid cap deals until being converted into a headhunter by the Americans at Diamond Chance in 1983. He married Arabella Purkiss-Smythe and they moved into Sandyland Castle at the request of his mother when Saunton passed away in 1985.

During the Great Storm of 15th October 1987 ("a lady has just rung in to ask if there is going to be a hurricane tonight...there is not." Michael Fish) the battlements of the four corner towers were badly damaged and Huff successfully applied for his first government grant for their repair. This new avenue of funding enabled the acceleration of the internal and external restoration of the castle, but even grants of several hundred thousand pounds from English Heritage are easily absorbed when the cost of brocaded curtains for a bedroom cost £15,000. After some challenging discussions with the Estate Manager, who preferred an easier life of wood and heathland maintenance, Huff diversified into tourism in partnership with English Heritage, pheasant rearing and shooting, corporate conferences and black-tie dinners, wedding receptions, and activity days.

Huff fared reasonably well at Diamond Chance. He was not a natural business developer or "salesman", a word he detested for its "new money" connotations; but his status in "proper" society and the links he had made at St Trisstram's and Cambridge enabled him to progress. The Yanks delighted that they had a "jen-u-wine" member of the aristocracy in their midst, about whom they publicly boasted and privately thought lived on another planet. Sometimes there were misunderstandings, as when Huff and one of the Senior Partners visited Lord Weinstock, at the height of his powers and busy with building the juggernaut that GEC became. Aware that their time would be short with the Great Man, Huff had quickly described the search technique. Unfortunately, the Senior Partner foolishly could not resist adding a colourful metaphor:

"We believe in using a rifle-shot approach when we undertake a search for you."

"I want my candidates alive, not dead," replied the famously dour doyen of post-war British industrialists.

On another occasion, Huff had his British sensibilities outraged by the President of a US bank, who, before commencing the meeting with Huff and his colleague, ostentatiously pulled out a tape recorder and turned it on.

"We want to ensure that we all know exactly what has been said so that there are no misunderstandings later on. We cannot be too careful now, can we?" Huff, brought up on an Englishman's word being his bond and conscious that the conversation was supposed to be held confidentially between them, was appalled that the man was suggesting that the tape could held "as a safeguard" against them. How could he possibly trust someone who established mistrust as a basis for doing business from the outset? Surely, since they had not given consent to the recording, the client was acting illegally anyway?

"That's fine," he heard his colleague say, "jolly good idea. Shall we proceed?" After the briefing, still suffused with resentment, Huff rapidly offered the job to his colleague.

"You handle it, old chap; you got on so well with the client and he is not really my type." His colleague, accustomed to the "grab-what-you-can-for-yourself" mentality, thought this was incredibly gracious and altruistic. Huff knew it was self-preservation. Sure enough, the client proved to be the nightmare from hell, refusing two shortlists and finally threatening legal action over Diamond Chance's failure to deliver against his specification "which had been articulated very clearly". Huff's poor colleague went mad and had to be destroyed. At any rate, he left the firm under a cloud.

One autumn, the US management board arranged a Partners' meeting in the UK and Huff hosted a night at Sandyland Castle. The Septics just loved the suits of armour, the fact he had servants (to Huff they were merely employees) and the sheer age and size of the place. Huff took them to the top of the West Tower to watch the sunset adding to the fiery colour of the outer wall clad in Parthenocissus Veitchi and, knowing their penchant for aggrandisement, casually remarked:

"It's quite satisfying to stand here and know that

everything as far as the eye can see in every direction belongs to me." They loved it. Several exclaimed: "Way to go, fella." One nudged another and drawled churlishly, if half in jest:

"We must be paying him way too much if he can afford a house like this." The other, a Brit, pointed out that the house had been in Huff's family for a couple of centuries before Myles Standish and the Pilgrim Fathers set sail from Plymouth to found "modern" America and he hardly thought that Huff was funding a mortgage off the back of Diamond Chance…

In fact, the obligation conferred by Huff's heritage to renovate and maintain a "pile" such as Sandyland "for the nation" was worse than a mortgage. At least with a mortgage on normal freehold residential property you could trade on, up or down, with the objective of decreasing the mortgage percentage of the value of your asset in the hope that one day, the mortgage finally paid, you could release a lot of the cash with one final sale, the embarrassment of the downsize to a bungalow assuaged by the money to spend on cruises, healthcare and eventually nursing homes, should you be lucky to survive as long as the onset of Alzheimer's. Huff was trapped, in debt to the inheritance which cost him dearly, daily.

Still, if you were in possession of the right job at the right time (as search consultants are always telling their candidates they are) headhunting for City clients occasionally brought unexpected rewards which other sectors could never sustain. Once, Huff had been briefed to find a Head of Private Banking for a firm whose performance in this area had been slipping and generating millions of pounds less revenue than its competitors. Huff hit the jackpot when his preferred candidate intimated that he might be able to encourage his team to defect en masse with him. Negotiations were long, delicate and quivering, like an acupuncturist's needles, but eventually Huff had soothed and smoothed a way to a satisfactory deal between his client and the team. The five of them resigned on the same day and their employers, caught unawares, realised they had been regally shafted: although the employment contracts specifically "outlawed" such mass conspiracy against the employer, it was impossible to police and pointless to hire lawyers to enforce. Once hearts and minds had been lost, it was best to let them go immediately, invoking garden leave if necessary to keep the defectors out of the market for a period, whilst surreptitiously employing different headhunters to launch a tit-for-tat counter-strike. Huff didn't care: he was paid five fees instead of one, all at one third of each team-member's package. That paid for the new roofing of the Great Hall.

As the diversified activities built up around the castle, more of Huff's time was required "for Sandyland business", such that international or even City assignments for Diamond Chance became wearisome rather than entertaining. Hugo had suddenly decamped to Aspallan and Bane with Sharon Ridell on some hare-brained adventure to establish a new selection business which sounded both high-risk and down-market. Huff's disenchantment with Diamond Chance grew over an incident involving his boss and his secretary. The Wellington-educated UK Managing Partner of Diamond Chance, Tudor Stuart, had begun to believe too much in the high life. Often, he would rather sample London's alternative carnal delights than return to the bosom of the woman who was bringing up his children. He found his wife increasingly bland and unattractive and was disappointed in himself for marrying her. On the other hand, his status in the City conferred on him an aura of power and mystique, which the chattering secretarial classes found alluring, dangerous and exciting, and he was exploiting this rich vein of available females. Huff was unaware of this. He had arranged a two-day visit to several growing, financial services businesses headquartered in Birmingham. Tudor Stuart and he were to impress these provincial upstarts with their smooth presentation of Diamond Chance, its impeccable track record amongst

Fortune 500 and FTSE 100 firms, and its firm transatlantic foundations, allowing it to tap into "happening geographies" about which less fortunate competitors could only dream impotently. The night before the trip, Tudor Stuart had called Huff and told him "something had come up which needed attending to urgently". Huff endured a miserable and solitary thirty six hours amongst the Brummigans and their distasteful, droning dialect. They in turn thanked him for troubling to visit, marvelled at his cut-glass, aristocratic tones, said they were very pleased to have met him and inwardly doubted they would have anything further to do with him. His misery was compounded by the discovery that his secretary, Carol, was "off sick" and therefore the reports he had left her to type up would remain unattended, threatening their successful delivery to the client before the deadline. Tomorrow would be manic.

Back in the office the next day, Huff found his secretary miraculously restored to health and his boss extremely evasive about the exact reason for his failure to experience the delights of Birmingham alongside Huff. All day he drafted and redrafted the reports with Carol. At six o'clock, he overheard one of the homeward-bound support staff comment to his secretary with a giggle:

"Not working late with the boss again, Carol?"

When they had finally finished at 7.30pm, he thanked Carol for staying late and casually enquired:

"What did Shiraz mean about you 'working late with the boss again' Carol?" She blushed and stammered that she didn't know what she was talking about. Then, the penny dropped with a resounding thud. He could now see what had "suddenly come up" two days ago and he didn't like the look of it at all. He pressed on:

"She didn't mean me though, did she Carol, because this is the first time I have asked you to stay late for months? She meant staying late with Tudor, last night, when you were supposedly off sick. Didn't she, Carol?"

Carol broke down and admitted the deception

miserably. Huff told her to pack up her personal belongings and not return. The following day Tudor Stuart was waiting for Huff in his office.

"Um, about Carol, I wouldn't wish you to act precipitously," he said. Confounded cheek, thought Huff, it wasn't him who had acted precipitously.

"Too late, job done," he retorted, "if you want to carry on seeing her, it'll have to be out-of-hours. By the way," he continued, "I didn't appreciate being deceived by both of you like that," and as an afterthought, "especially as I was in Birmingham."

Huff was still peevish and smarting when Hugo called him and demanded that they have a decent fish lunch at Wiltons. He avoided the Beluga caviar at a reasonable £99 and tucked into wild Scottish salmon and scrambled egg, while Hugo, being slighter of frame, sampled the lobster bisque. These starters they washed down with a fresh but complex Muscadet from Le Clos du Château L'Oiselinière before turning to a more serious Domaine Pierre Morey Meursault to accompany Hugo's poached turbot and Huff's grilled Dover sole. Huff was intrigued but not immediately persuaded by Hugo's vision for domination of the executive selection marketplace.

"It's a little, you know, mass-market, needing a lot of investment in offices and people. And no serious search consultant will step down to it, will they?"

"You're missing the point, Huff. We are creating a new up-market selection model, and we don't need search consultants. We will grow our own from successful agency folk who have proved they can develop business, or from sector specialists who can talk the lingo of their audience." He paused, then looked at Huff slyly. "Mind you, search consultants should find it a piece of cake. How are you doing, anyway?"

Hugo knew about Sandyland's constant thirst for essential spend, Huff's diversification projects and the time they demanded. He was surprised, however, to hear about Huff being shafted by his secretary and buggered by his boss.

"Tudor Stuart, milking away from home, that's disgraceful. What sort of example does that set?" Hugo was always able to separate one rule for himself and one for the rest.

"Yes, well, it's left me without a secretary and rather irked," said Huff.

"I should say so," sympathised Hugo. "Look, let me get straight to the point: I need someone to set up and run a City office for us. Come and join me Huff; it will be like old times, you know, rowing against the spring tide but knowing we are better than the rest."

Suddenly it began to make sense: selection couldn't be as demanding as search, could it? He could bring in a team to do the donkey work whilst he made the introductions, pull a few wires here and there and have more time to spend on Sandyland's business. What about money?

"It's an interesting thought, I grant you," he told Hugo, "but I couldn't afford a drop in remuneration; you know, castle outgoings and all that."

"Don't worry," said Hugo, "what are you on now? £125k base? I'll raise it to £150k plus a bonus based on your office's contribution. You shouldn't be worse off. And if you need to spend a day or so a week 'working from home', so be it." That was the clincher for Huff: the relentless drive of a full five-day week plus the hours spent commuting allowed precious little time for the husbandry of the castle and he valued the flexibility which Hugo was offering greatly.

So he had taken Hugo's silver shilling, signed up to AB Selection, found an office near Bank tube station and started to recruit young consultants to his team. A few of his former clients expressed surprise at his perceived move downmarket and told him that, regrettably, their search work would have to remain with Diamond Chance. Most didn't understand the differences between the two businesses, but a more-enlightened few realised that AB Selection operated a different methodology and began to give Huff work, much of which he passed on to his burgeoning team of eager beavers. Over the years, Huff watched other offices start, saw Sharon Ridell (whom he knew of course) come and go in London and welcomed Noone in a collegial way, soon finding in him, despite their different backgrounds, a kindred spirit who shared the same schoolboy, smutty sense of humour. This was just as well, since Hugo was greatly preoccupied with growing the overall business and distracted by increasingly bitter discussions with Archie Aspallan.

By mid 1996, ABS was at the peak of its power. In a relatively short space of time, thanks to Hugo's drive and determination, it had become a confident, mature business with excellent support and administration systems which conformed to ISO 9000 standards. It vied with NBS for market leadership, had developed an excellent reputation for quality and, because of this, was an attractive and sought-after place for aspiring recruitment consultants, who were proud to say that they worked for ABS, the UK market leader. It seemed that nothing could go wrong; and then it did.

18. ARCHIE ASPALLAN

"We are highly selective in the choice of our consultants and researchers. They have the knowledge, experience and ability to deal with complex and sensitive issues at board level; to understand all elements of corporate culture: values, strategies, systems, organisation and accountabilities; and, critically, to make judgements about people. We operate internationally and work with a relatively small number of clients in any one sector, thereby ensuring the greatest possible choice of management talent."

CORPORATE CONSULTING GROUP WEBSITE

Overcrowding on an inhuman scale, standing, sweating people crammed together tightly and unable to move, minimal ventilation, temperature in the muggy 80s, Noone reflected that the Black Hole of Calcutta must have had similar conditions to the Bakerloo Line on a sweltering summer day. Certainly cattle, on their occasional rides from the auction ring and to the slaughterhouse would not be allowed to travel in the way that London commuters were expected to, daily. Noone had read of a study by the Department of Forensics at University College London, which had removed a row of passenger seats from a Central Line tube carriage for analysis into cleanliness. Despite the London Underground's claim that the interior of their trains are cleaned on a regular basis, the scientists made some frightening discoveries.

On the surface of the seats, they found: four types of hair (human, mouse, rat, dog), seven types of insect (mostly fleas, mostly alive), vomit belonging to nine separate donors, human urine from four people, human and rodent excrement and of course, the ubiquitous traces of human semen (Noone was thankful it wasn't from a lion or something dangerous).

When the seats were dismantled, they yielded up: six dead mice, two dead rats (no dead parrots, amazingly) and a previously undiscovered fungus. The scientists also detected the bodily fluids of around 400 people in a single armrest. Whilst noting that more "sick-days" are taken because of diseases picked up while travelling on the Underground than for any other reason (including hangovers), they estimated that it is probably healthier to smoke five cigarettes a day than travel for an hour on the Tube. Finally, the scientists concluded that it was more hygienic to wipe your hand on the inside of a recently flushed lavatory bowl before eating, than to wipe it on a London Underground seat before eating.

Noone couldn't take much comfort from those statistics. He looked at the man standing next to him: 60-70 years old, dressed in tweed jacket and tie, over which was a buttoned-up fawn mackintosh. His trousers were filthy and had he been seated, he would have undoubtedly have contributed greatly to the UCL scientists' study. Surreally, on his feet was a pair of black Wellington boots. He was clearly mad or a Queen's gardener.

As he toiled into work that morning, arriving flushed and greasy at his desk, Noone wondered how long he would be able to endure the senseless trail in and out of London, he and 5.2 million other rats blindly following a non-existent Pied Piper. He had heard an interesting thing on the grapevine: the word was that Gordon Sharpe had set up a new business with three partners, one of whom was *Sharon Ridell!* He could hardly believe it, knowing that Gordon had engineered her ousting from Uxbridge. It was beginning to dawn on him just how mercenary recruitment consultants were; everyone had a price, the most successful would happily stab anyone in the back to protect their territory and further their own advancement and there was very little sense of loyalty to anyone and anything. But Sharon, setting up shop with Gordon? It seemed an improbable scenario. Just how much pride did she have to swallow, if that was all she was swallowing?

Not for the first time, Noone was grateful for his good fortune in landing on his feet in the rock that ABS had become. Despite his loathing of the commute, things were really going very well indeed: reporting directly to Hugo, he was now on the management board of ABS, an Executive Director no less, along with five other senior office managers including Huff and, annoyingly, "Colonel" Ned R. Porage. The London consultants seemed to be responding to his leadership (though he was still a little worried by Rodney Shakeshaft's designs on Rebecca Knightley) he was billing well and finding work to pass on to others and for the first time since taking on the disastrous bridging loan when he moved house, he was generating some disposable income, which he was disposing on golf, holidays and fine food and wine. After the demands of his wife and children, of course.

Recently, on the pretext to his wife of "entertaining a client and staying in town for the night because it would hardly be worth coming home just to go back into town the next morning", he had set up a tryst with Nerissa Wadsworth. They had dallied over pasta and veal in a forgettable little Italian restaurant in Albemarle Street, the two bottles of nondescript chianti classico driving their conversation ever-more risqué and salacious. Aflame with passion, they repaired to Nerissa's hotel room where, after some desultory foreplay, the two bottles robbed Noone of his performance and they fell asleep rather pathetically. This was Noone on top of his game, but failing to rise to the occasion. It could only go downhill from there. First there was the next morning's guilt and awkwardness, with which Noone dealt by quickly exiting the hotel and busying himself in the office. Then came external interference, in the form of Archie Aspallan's avarice.

Some people develop gently through their lives, generally maintaining an even keel and forward momentum, and about whom it is said: "what you see is what you get". Others experience an abrupt change of direction at some point, either imposed on them, sometimes with unfavourable consequences, or because they suddenly find their metier and prosper. Some scheme and worry their lives away; others, like Noone, seem content to float down through the streams, eddies and pools of their lives, just so long as their heads are above water. There are also those for whom everything is not enough, who develop darkening, complex, impenetrable personalities. They lose perspective and their own self-knowledge, following a thirst for power that becomes both all-consuming and destined to remain unslaked. Archimedes Aspallan was one such as this.

Of less than humble origins, Aspallan was a distant cousin of the Duke of Edinburgh. His great-great-grandmother had been one of four sisters born to Grand Duke Louis of Hesse and Princess Alice of Saxe-Coburg, daughter of Queen Victoria and brother of Edward VIII. His father's line could be traced back to the Isle of Man in the late fifteenth century, where Aspallan in gaelic meant "steps of the gods". The Aspallans moved across the water during the seventeenth century, settling in a large manor house in the Cotswolds, with a considerable arable estate where they farmed sheep and procreated vigorously. The wool trade took them into City commodity trading and they mixed in ever-more exalted circles, collecting a minor heiress of the diluted Saxe-Coburg-Hesse line along the way in the shape of Archie's mother.

She was a tiny but indomitable woman with an obsessive compulsion for tidiness who ruled the household with military precision. Children were not allowed to run and shout indoors and under sufferance were permitted toys only in the playroom, except for one teddy-bear in each bedroom. If a plaything was inadvertently liberated and left forgotten in a "public place", it was confiscated for a month. A nanny had been "let go" for allowing a wooden train belonging to Archie to surface in the library. Archie's mother ate scrambled eggs every morning at eight o'clock, accompanied by two slices of lightly toasted bread spread with thick-cut marmalade procured from Fortnum & Mason. Afternoon tea was served in the drawing-room on the dot of four o'clock and a cook had been summarily dismissed for once failing this aspect of his job description.

There was a nanny for Archie and his three sisters, a cook, a cleaning/serving wench and several gardeners to tend the house's formal three acres, swimming pool and grass tennis court. By the time of Archie's father, the farming side was run by a Farm Manager and his staff. Archie's father, having survived the horrors of the First World War, ensured he was passed unfit for military service in the Second by leaning gently on the family doctor and after the war, took refuge in the City from the sterile life of his home; he lunched at Boodles and frequently stayed over at the East India Club. He had inherited the stockbroking firm established by Archie's grandfather and which he passed on subsequently to Archie. But first Archie had to be made ready.

Archimedes Aspallan was launched literally, if inadvertently, as a baby into the bathwater in 1940. This was before home births and birthing pools became fashionable and was entirely accidental, his mother being caught short, as it were, during her nightly bathing experience. Archie being a son after three daughters was seen by his father as a "Eureka" moment, and he felt inspired enough to christen him accordingly. As a child, he led a solitary existence, watched over by Nanny and Mummy and tolerated barely by his sisters, who treated him as a creature from a different planet. With tales of the recently ended War ringing in his ears, he made up his own games with toy soldiers and roamed around outside whenever possible, doing what little boys do: getting muddy, catching whatever wildlife possible, bird-nesting, squashing slugs and snails to see what colour guts they had, finding water to fish and launch boats in, making bows and arrows. All of which his mother was largely unaware, apart from the getting wet and muddy part. In due course, he was packed off to St Trisstram's, where his self-absorbed nature fitted in pretty well from the start. There, he learned new skills, including how to masturbate, from the boy in the next door bed, who would flip his willy out every night and whip it to a frenzy before expiring in a tortured sigh. Archie grew into a strapping adolescent, becoming good at rowing, racquet sports and Fives and representing the school for all of these things. Academically, he proved shrewd at analytical subjects, less good at the Arts and could have gone on to university, but his father ruled against it as a waste of time.

"No sense in wasting time, m'boy," he said gruffly, "the firm is yours to run one day, so the sooner you come in and learn how to do it, the better."

"But Father," protested the eighteen-year-old Archie, "what if I don't want to run the firm?"

"Don't be so stupid, boy," retorted his father, "it's what you were born for. You'll start as a junior broking assistant in September, take the exams to become an Authorised Person and learn from the bottom up."

"But Father," Archie said again, a trifle foolishly given his father's obvious intransigence, "suppose I'd rather go to university and then choose a career in sport? I am quite good at tennis and squash..." His father exploded.

"Sport? That is for fun, not for making money. If you want to namby-pamby off to university and then daydream about a career elsewhere, fine. Just don't expect me to support you; as of today, you will be out on your ear. There will be no slackers in this household, d'you hear?"

Archie heard loud and clear. He left school with a ridiculous number of O'levels and three redundant A' levels which he imported uselessly into the family firm after a three week holiday in Roddy Tooting-Curveball's family villa in Tuscany. Roddy had been Archie's tennis doubles partner at St Trisstram's. During the holiday, Archie fell in love with Roddy's stunningly-formed, older sister, Honeysuckle, who would lay out in a white bikini by the pool, tanning her already creamy-chocolate skin darker by the day, the sun and the chemically-treated water bleaching her hair ever blonder. At twenty one, she was like a luscious, ripe peach, her flesh firm and lightly furred, her proportions perfect. With nothing better to do, she toyed with Archie, bending down provocatively to pick up a towel, stretching her delectable cleavage over him as she reached for fruit at lunch, going bra-less in the evenings, her pert nipples always alert against the chiffon of her short dress. She became Archie's agony and ecstasy; his heart contracted with a sharp thrill each time he saw or thought of her; the sound of her voice uplifted him; he fantasised madly about her; he was running out of handkerchiefs. Roddy could see that Archie was increasingly distracted and pulverised him mercilessly at tennis while taunting him about the object of his increasing affections.

"She's only a bloody girl, for god's sake; she doesn't even play tennis. All she does is lounge around all day and read books."

"Exactly," said Archie, who had never seen anything like her before.

Finally, miraculously, one night Honeysuckle took him all the way, first allowing him a kiss as they sat on a couch in the bougainvillea-entwined loggia, overlooking the dusky Tuscan hills and then, impressed by his growing agitation, leading him to her room. There, she liberated him from his shorts, stroked him gently to full attention, laid him back on the bed, straddled him and gently lowered her moist, golden-framed love-tunnel down onto him. Archie didn't last long of course, but she hushed his apologies, told him they had all night and languorously brought him back to life by showing him how she pleasured herself. By the fourth time, Archie got it right, and with a shudder, she dug her nails into his back sighed "Yes!" into his ear and subsided into slumber. They made love again before breakfast and continuously for the two remaining nights of Archie's holiday. He returned home physically and emotionally drained, in no state for starting work. She returned separately to her job in corporate hospitality and her London friends and got on with the frenetic social whirl that was her life.

But Archie was a competitor, so he lived with his pining for Honeysuckle and wrote her long, complicated love-letters to which she never replied, whilst learning his trade under the eagle-eye of his father. He knew from Roddy that Honeysuckle had a succession of feckless and sometimes titled boyfriends, each a new shard piercing his heart, and he saw that she was often snapped by "Paps" at celebrity parties as she led her active nightlife about town. He gritted his teeth, passed his exams, was made a director of the firm, started broking in earnest and vented his frustration by playing plenty of competitive squash and tennis. Suddenly, when Archie was twenty nine, his father died of a heart-attack in the middle of breakfast during an apoplectic pronouncement on the declining Wilson government of 1969. Fuelled by an article in the Times opened on the table beside him, he thundered:

"Enoch Powell is right. We are letting far too many wogs into this country. They don't speak English, they eat strange food, have strange habits and worship strange gods. In any case, there's no room," he harrumphed. "If I had my way..." Archie never gained the benefit of his father's blueprint for immigration, for at that point he exhaled sharply, keeled forward slowly into his kippers and expired. Father and kippers, both wasted. The former was buried with due pomp and ceremony, the latter tipped into the kitchen waste bin.

Although there were some misgivings amongst the three elder statesmen in the firm, it was clear that Aspallan Senior had wanted Archie to take over the business on his demise, not least because his Will said so. In any case, Archie had proved "a chip off the old block" and really quite capable, so they smiled indulgently and stood aside as Archie claimed his father's office. Within two weeks he had put two of them out to pasture, retaining one as a figurehead Chairman. He then recruited fresh, dynamic young blood and before the year was out, had doubled revenue and profit. At that point, sufficiently in charge of and confident about his destiny and future security, he asked Honeysuckle out to dinner and proposed to her during coffee. She giggled enchantingly:

"Oh Archie, don't be silly, you're not serious!"

"I have never been more serious about anything in my life," he replied seriously. "I fell in love with you the first time I saw you, have remained in love with you, and will always love you."

"Come on Archie, that was just a holiday fling. We've gone our separate ways."

"So far," he replied, "but I intend change that. I am now in a position to look after you properly for the rest of your life. And if you want to carry on with your job and all those parties, fine." Honeysuckle became more interested. This could be a decent deal and Archie was actually quite handsome in an outdoor, manly sort of way. Appearing more intrigued, she elicited from him that he had banked a million pounds this year and wanted to triple that over the next five years. Yes, he really was proving much more interesting than she had previously given him credit for. However, she knew how to play her cards slowly, and left him alone that night, promising she would think about it.

Slowly, Honeysuckle allowed herself to be comprehensively wooed, not least by Archie's assiduous deployment of diamond jewellery, until she finally accepted his hand in marriage after a public showing of togetherness at Glyndebourne. The wedding was a sumptuous affair and one of the great events of 1971, along with decimalisation, the launch of Intel's first microchip, Evel Knievel jumping over nineteen cars and the birth of Bangladesh; only the former of these immediately affected the happy couple and their Best Man, Roddy.

Archie was true to his word and lofty ambition, and the success of his business allowed him to accumulate expensive possessions in addition to Honeysuckle, including a Porsche 911 Carrera, a Bentley Continental and three children to put through private education. He was blissfully proud to be seen with Honeysuckle on his arm and she surprised herself by reducing her time on the London scene as she accepted and settled into her new life of wife and mother (though not yet mistress of the manor while Archie's mother remained alive). Archie continued to play competitive squash and, through the firm, sponsored the UK Closed Championship for several years to 1980. Passing the age of forty, however, caused Archie to reassess his direction: although he wouldn't belittle himself by saying he had been born with a silver spoon in his mouth, apart from Honeysuckle, everything in his life had more or less been laid on a plate. Yes, he had everything he wanted, but he had a sneaking feeling that the churlish might say that he had only got to where he was because of the advantages of his birth, rather than through his own efforts. In short, that he had underachieved. Of course this wasn't true in his view, but the suspicion rankled and niggled away. Now, if he were to start something very different from scratch, that would silence the imaginary voices in his head, wouldn't it?

He had opened his door recently to a pair of consultants from Diamond Chance, the firm of US headhunters, who had pitched for his business. He listened with genuine interest and had been intrigued by the glorious simplicity of their proposition. It seemed that they expected him to pay them a full third of the presumed remuneration package over a ninety day period in the vague hope that they might find someone to fill a vacancy which he might not even realise he had. There were no guarantees: even if they didn't find someone, he would still have paid them in full with no prospect of a refund for failure. The arrogance of it took his breath away but the low-risk, high-margin Diamond Chance business model appealed greatly to the entrepreneurial itch which he felt an increasing need to scratch. This then led to the post-prandial discussion with Giles Bane in Boodles and the resultant forming of

Aspallan, Bane Consultants. Its immediate success was immensely gratifying for Archie and when they moved premises to the opulence of St James's Square, he took the luxury flat on the top floor as his London pied à terre and passed it through the business's books. He was particularly pleased with the million pound fee he won which took him to Paris to celebrate at Giles's expense even though their "friendly rivalry" ceased thereafter because Giles became so bitter and twisted about it. It really was rather tedious the way he wanted to build a class-war mountain out of the molehill of his jealousy.

Hugo Reeve-Prior approached them and appalled Archie with his idea for a selection business, but he had acquiesced, more to mollify Giles, who seemed quite keen on the scheme, than because he saw any great value in it. Amazingly, Reeve-Prior had confounded them and in no time seemed to have created an unstoppable force which had reached market-leadership and was repaying them handsomely. With hindsight, he should have realised that Reeve-Prior was an arrogant, avaricious, self-serving little shit who, like Oliver, would only ever want more. How could you really trust a chap who coxed rather than rowed and who had lived happily below, rather than above, the waves, even if he was from St Trisstram's?

Sure enough, trouble brewed. It began over the fifty percent of AB Selection's annual profit which was appropriated by Apsallan, Bane. This sum grew year-on-year and by 1995 had reached five million pounds. Reeve-Prior had begun to argue that the percentage should be halved, to twenty-five percent, allowing him to re-invest more into ABS to maintain its growth strategy. Then he started complaining that ABS consultants should be allowed to offer search as well as selection. Preposterous. The whole point was to keep them separate and "sell" search up to the "bespoke tailors" of Aspallan, Bane, rather than down to the less elite, "off-the-peg" ABS. Then came a further bone of contention brought directly about by Archie.

Archie, of course, was not without ambition himself and when one of his City contacts told him that a specialist Technology search firm was about to be put up for sale by its two owners, a plan began to form in his mind. What if he created a holding company and bought up several high quality boutique search businesses, each with a different sector expertise, to place alongside ABC and ABS? He could create an entity that was greater than the sum of its parts, preside over it as Chairman, and at some point realise its value with a high profile sale and retire to the country with both reputation and fortune considerably enhanced. Of course, they may have to take the company public to generate the investment required for acquisitions, but that would look even better: Chairman of a FTSE firm! Father hadn't even come close to that. In fact, his father's tenure at the helm of the family firm seemed positively limp-wristed compared to Archie's grandiose new objective. He set to work on a business plan.

Although by now he considered Giles Bane boorish, uncultured and unnecessarily bloody-minded (a typical Northerner in his view) and whom he resented for having negotiated a fifty percent share in the business, he grudgingly recognised his consistency and value; operationally, Giles had a far better eye for the detail than did Archie. He also needed Giles "onside" with regard to his ideas for expansion and he developed the business plan into a presentation which would impress him. Predictably, Giles was unimpressed.

"I don't see the point in expanding for the bloody sake of it. We'll only end up with a number of businesses all competing with themselves."

"No Giles," remonstrated Archie, "each will operate in a different sector in which they are specialists. There will be no treading on toes, but they will need to toe the corporate line laid down by you and me. I thought you might like to be Group CEO," he finished craftily, "it plays to your management strengths."

"Leaving you swanning around as Chairman, of

course." Giles was no fool.

"Hardly swanning. My job will be to seek out and evaluate M & A targets. The whole point, Giles, is that we create a group that is not reliant on the two of us, so that when we want to retire and buy the second home in Tuscany, the yacht on the Med or the castle in Northumbria, we can." Giles could see the logic and he quite fancied a castle in Northumbria rather than a poncy yacht or villa in Chiantishire where all the toffs like Archie lived. So he acquiesced slowly, forcing Archie to engage him several times in earnest conversation, something he hadn't done since before the wretched one million pound fee episode, after which Giles had cut him dead. Giles enjoyed the experience of watching Archie grovel to him, although Archie saw it as the art of gentle persuasion.

Finally, it was agreed and Archie took off on the great adventure. It was a time when the City was going through one of its periodic frenzies, when a particular sector had become hyped up and overheated by investment analysts still in short trousers. The early-to-mid-Nineties was the time of recruitment companies, typified by Michael Page, which was sold publicly by its eponymous owner in 1994 for an extremely high multiple and was then taken private again three years later by Interim Services Inc, one of the USA's largest recruitment agencies, which paid a ridiculously high £346 million for Michael Page's hand in a subsequently turbulent marriage. At first, this worked in Aspallan, Bane's favour, for willing buyers were found for its shares issued by Initial Public Offering, raising a "war chest" of nearly ten million pounds. Roles were reversed, however, when Archie went shopping. The banking advisors of the Technology firm about which he had been tipped off felt emboldened by the mood in the market to price the company at a multiple of twenty-five times earnings. It was wildly optimistic, but it succeeded in forcing Archie to bid higher than he had wanted, just to get the negotiations rolling. They settled at fifteen, still probably a third overpriced in Archie's view, at the end of

February 1996. The celebrations were muted in the Boardroom, which now contained two Non-Executive Directors, as befitted a public company, and a press-release was drafted. Only now did Archie get round to calling Hugo Reeve-Prior to his office to tell him that he was about to be encroached upon by a new, selection-offering sister company. Hugo reacted as if a roman candle had been lit and forced, burning end upwards, into his fundament.

"How could you do this behind my back?" he fizzed and popped, "haven't I done enough for you? Why bring in another company which will directly rival ABS in the technology area? Can you imagine how my consultants will feel about this?" Archie couldn't very well tell Hugo that it was the first piece in his grand jigsaw, which on completion would allow Archie self-satisfied, enriched retirement, so he tried charm, flattery and bribery:

"Come on Hugo, it won't be that bad for you. ABS has been a brilliant success thanks to your vision and able leadership and it has shown us the way. If we can add a few more businesses like ABS, we will be in an immensely powerful position in the market. What's more, we would like all the selection business to come under your command, so your own bonus will be substantially enhanced." It sounded lame and Hugo wasn't in the mood to be lamely charmed, flattered or bribed.

"I don't like it at all, Archie. You wouldn't allow ABS the bigger fees from search, you kept your high percentage for introductions, you take half my profit and refuse me more money to invest further in ABS. I feel betrayed and I must consider my position." Well bugger him, thought Archie, the jumped up little prig. We invested in him, we created him, we can do without him.

"Well I am sorry if that's how you feel, Hugo. I had hoped you would see the wisdom of our strategy and work with us to achieve it. But you must do what you must do. Now, please excuse me, I must get on." With that withering dismissal, he turned to the papers on his desk which told of another recruitment business for sale.

Hugo immediately telephoned both the NEDs to ask for their opinion. They had been brought into the company expressly by Archie to support his growth scheme and indeed stood to earn substantial amounts from their gifted share options in the event of a successful sale of the business further down the line. Thus, while they unctuously sympathised with Hugo's predicament, clucked and tutted at the way he had been presented with a fait accompli, and agreed to broker his concerns back to Archie, there was no way that they would prevent Archie from following his chosen course. However, such was the brilliance of their false support for Hugo that he felt emboldened to ask for an Extraordinary General Meeting of the Board with him in attendance to debate the issue. A little cornered by the zeal of their duplicity, they agreed to recommend it to Archie.

Archie was even more annoyed with Hugo when he received their solicitations. The little shit was going behind his back to drum up support for what amounted to a vote of no confidence in him, Archie, the Chairman of the company. It was outrageous and no way for a Trisstram'sian to behave towards a fellow Trisstram'sian! He put the NEDs in their place in no uncertain terms, appraised Giles of the situation and agreed to the EGM, knowing that Hugo faced certain humiliation. Come the day, despite protesting his position eloquently and cogently and appealing to the better judgement of those who had seemingly promised to support him, Hugo was duly humiliated.

"So we have heard Hugo's views, and you all have in your possession my strategy for growth," said Archie, keen to bring proceedings to a speedy conclusion, "all those in favour of remaining as we are with no policy for acquisitions, raise your hands." Nobody moved. The two NEDs studiously avoided Hugo's plaintive stare.

"There we have it. I am sorry it had to come to this, Hugo." He wasn't at all. Hugo had been utterly defeated.

Hugo consulted Field Fisher Waterhouse, employment lawyers, which submitted his claim for constructive dismissal. He then retired to the farm on "gardening leave" while the lawyers for both sides made tens of thousands of pounds battling out a final, out-of-court settlement. Hugo walked away with half a million pounds "for loss of office", but they had stolen "his baby" away from him.

19. BETRAYAL

"Our business is the identification, attraction, assessment and retention of senior executives. Backed by our in-depth expertise, we offer our clients strategic advice on the market, the talent pool, remuneration and best search practice.

The Curzon Partnership provides a valued search capability to clients in a number of <u>key sectors</u> where we enjoy deep <u>specialist expertise</u>.

We adhere to three fundamental principles: hands on involvement of the partners at all stages of the search process; speed and professionalism in all we do; creativity in our approach

The measure of our success is the ability to close deals with candidates who are better than our clients could have expected and who quickly and demonstrably contribute to our clients' businesses."

CURZON PARTNERSHIP WEBSITE

When Noone heard the whisperings that Hugo was engaged in a mortal battle with Archie Aspallan, he was still quite preoccupied with his management tasks, getting to know the idiosyncrasies of his team, their strengths and weaknesses. So much so that he'd only briefly been able to review his nephew's latest test results. He learned that: a turbine was something an Arab wore on his head; that Nelson's column is the highest award for wartime valour; that the four seasons are salt, pepper, mustard and vinegar; steroids keep the carpet on the stairs; Christians go on pilgrimage to Lords; mushrooms look like umbrellas because they grow in damp places; rhubarb is a kind of celery gone bloodshot; and, hysterically, that the equator is a menagerie lion running round the earth but mainly through Africa!

"He's coming on, half-sis," Noone reassured a worried

Amelia. "His spelling is really very good. It is just some of the meanings that are confusing him. I am sure he will get there before too long."

On the other hand, back at work, The Hedgehog didn't last long at all. It wasn't so much that he wasn't billing anything, although that meant inherently that he was a leprous drain on the bottom line; nor that a woman claiming to be his wife kept calling the receptionist and asking her to tell The Hedgehog to come home as she hadn't seen him for weeks; not even that he seemed a compulsive user of online porn, as witnessed by "Badger" Brock, who had breezed into his office one day, only to find The Hedgehog actively engaged in "manly relief" as he watched images of an "actress" with a fanny as big as a clown's pocket being seen to by an excited male pony. No, the clincher was him taking off for a few days of "business development"; when he tried to pass his expenses through Accounts, Noone found out what this euphemism meant: The Hedgehog had taken off, literally, to Amsterdam, where he had apparently spent three days and nights in various whorehouses (nevertheless dining at a trail of fine restaurants, including De Vijff Flieghen and De Waaghals) before apportioning all these expenses to an assignment belonging to Rodney Shakeshaft. As pass-offs went, it wasn't a bad try and he almost got away with it, but Accounts queried one item with Rodney, the purchase of three videos, which The Hedgehog had optimistically described in his expenses narrative as "Lunch with client." Rodney, of course, retorted that although he might be getting on, he wasn't senile and hadn't had lunch with a client in Amsterdam since 1968. From that moment on, The Hedgehog's fabrication unravelled rapidly and Noone had no choice but to fire him on the spot.

Unfortunately, although he regained The Hedgehog's mobile phone and office keys, Noone forgot to ask him for the keys to the company car and The Hedgehog took it round Britain for several weeks before abandoning it with four flat tyres, a petrol tank full of water and a dead fox in the driving seat which rendered it an insurance write-off. The Hedgehog then vanished without trace.

Noone's next problem was Rodney himself. True to form, he had been pursuing Rebecca Knightley with unseemly ardour. Whilst she was grateful for the high-level contacts to whom he introduced her and from whom emanated a steady stream of assignments, they were all hoary, hairy old goats like him, who leered at her cleavage and called her "Dear". Rodney took her out to lunch relentlessly ("intra-office communication enhancement" as he put it in his expenses claim) and capped it all by appearing outside her flat on the evening of her birthday with a bottle of Krug, demanding to be allowed to share it with her. Exactly what he wanted to share became clear after she had allowed him inside.

"Rebecca, my dear, it cannot have escaped your attention that I find you extremely, ah, invigorating."

"Oh don't be silly, Rodney," she simpered, but she knew where this was going.

"No, it's true. You are a dashed attractive young woman of very fine stock and I very much enjoy working with you. So much so that I, ah, wondered whether you would care to, ah, go a little further?"

"Whatever do you mean, Rodney?" She knew exactly what he meant, but she wanted him to say it.

"Well, you know, it might be nice to, ah, consummate our working relationship; raise it to a different level, so to speak." He really was a randy old sod.

"Don't beat about my bush, Rodney: you want to fuck me don't you?"

Rodney admired the way these modern gels got straight to the point. He thought of the wasted days of his youth, when protocols dictated that one had to spend so much time endlessly wooing the object of one's desire in a formal pattern, usually with marriage the only guarantee that one would get to the holy grail. Today's females were so much more, ah, accommodating.

"Well, if that's how you want to put it, yes." Rebecca

was now in a quandary. She knew that if she refused, the likelihood was that Rodney would turn cold, transfer his attentions elsewhere and her flow of business would dry up. But could she face the prospect of having sex with someone old enough to be her father? He was hardly attractive, but unlike her father, at least he was showing an interest and he was certainly experienced; think of all those wives he had had, and he was still up for more! But she definitely didn't want him rampant in her flat; she told Rodney firmly that she had to think about his proposition and sent him home semi-tumescent and a little crestfallen; the next day she confided in the HR Manager, Linnet Trilby and relayed the conversation to her. No harm in getting things on record.

"Well for a start, we can bring a charge of sexual harassment." Linnet said smugly. She may have been mousey and unsought-after herself, but she knew employment rights alright.

"No, I don't want to do that. He is a sweetie really and he's been very kind to me. I want to preserve our working relationship." Linnet was rather disappointed; bringing a legal action would have brightened up her drab existence no end. Rebecca was one stupid bitch and quite frankly deserved all she had coming to her.

"Well in that case, you have a simple choice: say 'no', and find something else to do; or agree to his suggestion and no doubt your career will blossom accordingly," she spelt out, rather sourly.

"I don't feel like leaving, I enjoy it here. So I guess I will stay. Thanks for your help." She left Linnet with rather a hard stare. In truth, Rebecca had known all along what to do. Given her so far fruitless pursuit of sexual fulfilment, Rodney had become a fascination, a target, part of her quest.

Pausing only to remove her panties in the Ladies, she went to Rodney's office, shut the door behind her and unfastened the buttons on her blouse as she walked slowly towards Rodney. He smiled broadly and spun his swivel chair to welcome her onto his lap.

"My dear girl," he said, "welcome home." She unzipped him, releasing his turgid, red and veiny member, which, she was delighted to see, was almost as big as her Satisfaction Guaranteed Black Mambo dildo, on which she usually relied. Hitching up her skirt, she fed the huge tool slowly into her melting cleft, momentarily appreciating why Rodney had been able to attract five wives, and rode him up and down to her pace. Amazingly, he stayed with her, only driving back into her when Rebecca's eyes began to roll and she began to pant "yes, yes, yes" with each downward thrust. As she crashed upon the shore of her climax she screamed "Daddy!"

The noise alerted "Badger" Brock, who had been passing by and he cautiously peered through the window in Rodney's door, delighting in the scene of post-coital collapse that greeted his eyes. To cause maximum mischief, he felt duty-bound to report his serendipitous sighting to Noone, who listened incredulously.

"I don't believe you! Here in the office? No!"

"I can assure you he did, and what is more, she seemed to be enjoying it."

"Bloody hell. The old bastard. Strange kind of on-the-job training. Well thanks for telling me, but keep it to yourself, eh?"

"Sure thing." Brock immediately told Darth Gwent and Caspian Cordell. All of them were peeved that they had been beaten to Rebecca's ABS cherry by someone more than twice their age.

"It's disgusting, to think of that old goat ploughing away in a luscious fox like her," said Caspian, who was seriously disappointed.

"Technically, she's a vixen. Not sure how she can bring herself to shag him but you have to hand it to the guy. He must have a gargantuan todger."

"Yuck, that's appalling," groaned Darth, "still, one in Kate's Bush is worth two in Mia's Furrow, as I always say." They fell about laughing.

Noone was also quietly informed by Linnet Trilby that "there may be a problem with Rodney and Rebecca". She delivered her insight into likely sexual harassment with malice. Her news had been surpassed by "Badger's", of course, though Noone didn't enlighten her as to the rapid development of Rodney's amorous antics.

"Thanks, Linnet, you were right to tell me," he said, making a mental note never to trust the conniving little meanie. "Leave it to me: I will proceed with caution, tact and diplomacy." Noone decided to do nothing. Reflecting on Hugo's infamous and ignored memo on fraternisation, he was quite sure that Rodney, a senior consultant, had put undue pressure on Rebecca, a junior consultant. However, he didn't fancy asking Rodney point blank whether he was bonking her. Not when Rodney was such a major source of business. Not yet anyway.

Noone had just about left Uxbridge behind him. Whilst he missed the easy commute and intimacy of the office life there, it was one dimensional compared to the complex spice of life offered by London. It had taken him a while not to feel responsible for it and to stop ringing Bachelor-Freebody and The Man Who Said Everything Twice "to see how things were": it seemed that they were managing quite well without him. He had hardly given a thought to the fate of Uxbridge's geese, whether the council had proceeded with the proposed cull. He had to admit that he was no longer one of the provincial set but a fully-fledged Londoner (even if real Londoners wouldn't recognise him as such). Although he didn't feel entirely in control, Noone tentatively allowed himself the satisfaction of believing he had made a positive contribution in London: the Friday lunches in The Guinea (Young's Bitter, no Scruttocks, sadly) were melting the barriers, encouraging the consultants to get to know each other and begin to share experiences and even clients. The champagne prizes also contributed to a sense of pride and purpose amongst them all. His termination of The Hedgehog had been well received, for nobody liked a loser and a slacker.

Although the FMCG squad remained a little aloof, Noone had developed a good relationship with the young, male consultants, for in them, he recognised the earlier version of himself: ambitious, self-centred, testosterone-driven and hedonistic. The more extrovert females had also taken to him and both Sabra Termignioni and Remy Aquarone had raised their respective games by concentrating their charms on their would-be clients, and had started billing well.

The Politically Correct Brigade proved to be one of those irritating, supermarket, ready-meal packages which are impossible to open without burning one's fingers. Several times, Noone had to intervene in petty squabbles between Attracta Mann and other consultants over fee splits. She also ate up secretaries and was on her third since Noone's arrival. Her unpopularity knew no bounds. Visa Maunfield and Sara Sternhold sailed steadfastly selfish courses of their own setting, jealously guarding their clients, refusing to take other consultants to client meetings.

Noone had tried to change this habit to no avail. Their relationship with their clients was unique in their view and nobody should intervene or question their judgement. Noone was put firmly and frostily in his place with the implied threat that if he continued to interfere, they would take their services elsewhere. Noone wouldn't have been at all surprised to find such a resignation accompanied by legal action for constructive dismissal or the dreaded sexual harassment charge, even though he couldn't see anything remotely sexual in either of them. So he was forced to back off and leave them to their own devices, which was why he didn't feel entirely in control, even though Hugo had belied Sharon's warning and been very hands off. Then he found out why.

The memo from Archie Aspallan informing all employees of Hugo's departure sent shockwaves through ABS. Noone felt it particularly keenly. At first, he found it difficult to comprehend. He knew that Hugo was battling

Archie and Giles over some aspect of policy, but that it could lead to his removal or dismissal, whichever it was, was surely madness. He may have been pompous, arrogant, snobbish and interested only in his own opinion, but he had been tremendously successful. He had created something of real value, a highly successful and respected market-leading business, from nothing. His drive, his vision, his self-belief, his management had contributed greatly to the rich lining of Archie Aspallan's and Giles Bane's pockets. And his own of course, but Noone didn't begrudge him that. Hugo had believed in Noone and offered him a chance and for that he would be eternally grateful, even though he had come down hard after those early months and shaken Noone out of any misperceptions he may have had about ABS being a cosy nest; the rude awakening had led Noone to apply himself properly and become a fully-rounded, business-developing consultant. With Hugo's passing, Noone had lost the last of the mentors who had unpeeled all the vagaries and trickeries of the arcane world which he had willingly, if somewhat blindly, entered: Graham Sharpe, Sharon Riddell and now Hugo, all gone. Naively, Noone had believed that they were all here for the long-term, intent on building upwards from Hugo's firm foundations, taking ABS to ever-greater heights before retiring to the comfort of a well-provided-for house in the country next to a golf-course and a pub. That was what he envisaged, but he was beginning to wonder if it was achievable. Sharon had been discarded, Sharpe frustrated, now Hugo gone. Noone's belief system had been shaken, as psychologists would say.

If Hugo's departure was the stone dropped into the pond of ABS, the ripples spread relentlessly across its surface, gathering momentum to crash over its banks to disturb the opaque equanimity of the Group. Archie Aspallan's next problem was what to do about replacing Hugo. At first he considered not appointing anyone: Hugo had developed ideas above his station in the position and by eliminating both the man and the position, Archie wondered whether he could eliminate the problem as well. Surely he could get Giles to watch over ABS?

"You must be joking," was Giles's swift reply. "I am already tied up with all these other businesses you are buying. I don't want to be responsible for another 200 people, thank you very much."

"Well I am sorry you don't feel up to it, Giles. What do you suggest then?" Giles ignored Archie's sneering tone.

"Feeling up to it isn't the point. It's not what I signed up for and structurally it doesn't make sense. You need to put someone in charge there and get him to report to me as Group CEO." Archie knew he was right and so to assuage his previous acidity, he asked for Giles's opinion as to whom the person might be. They debated whether to move in one of the MDs that had been inherited from Archie's acquisition trail but were concerned that might prove divisive; then they wondered whether the best solution might not be to appoint from within. This would send positive signals to ABS through its endorsement of aspirational and loyal behaviour while at the same time ensure that they would have more of a beholden puppet in place to do their bidding. Unfortunately, there didn't seem to be an obvious choice. In terms of seniority, there was Henry Ughyngton-Fitzhardynge, but although he was head of the Financial Services practice, in reality he presided over a number of self-governing mini-fiefdoms, each specialising in some discrete, esoteric niche of finance: Archie wondered whether anyone really understood what credit default swaps were? Given Ughyngton-Fitzhardynge's aristocratic pedigree and second job of castle maintenance, they doubted both his "across all levels" people skills and his commitment to their cause. Besides, his friendship with Hugo Reeve-Prior made him deeply suspect.

They ruled out all the other practice and office heads for mainly parochial reasons based on geography or personality, Noone because he was adjudged "still getting to grips with London". Despite Giles Bane never having played cricket, they were stumped. Finally, Archie decreed that the only option was to bring someone in from outside; Giles, still fearful of being lumbered with ABS, agreed, and as with doctors who sniffily refuse to see a doctor, they naturally chose not to practise what they preached: this would have entailed commissioning a full, independently-managed search for the position. That would have been the correct, transparent and optimal solution. But no, they could "use their contacts" to identify and appoint some blessed soul to become MD of ABS. One or two discreet enquiries revealed an ex Hoggett Bowers general manager, now working as a sole trader. Hoggett Bowers had been a major selection player before the recession, so they reasoned that someone who had managed a couple of hundred troops there could do the same for ABS. They paused not to wonder why that firm had faded away to almost nothing and whether this individual, Bly Huxford, had played any culpable part in its demise. They had convinced themselves that if they offered enough money to tempt him away from his own business, he would be the answer to their problems. He was flattered to be called by so prestigious a person as Archie Aspallan; of course he would be delighted to meet him and Giles to discuss "future possibilities". They treated him to lunch at Conran's new and immensely popular Quaglino's, although Archie found it a noisy barn of a place which took itself far too seriously and priced accordingly. He deliberately chose understatement by way of six oysters followed by fillet steak Rossini with truffles and foie gras. Giles, always a more down-to-earth trencherman, piled in with potted shrimps and haddock and chips. Huxford, rather vulgarly in Archie's view, took steak tartare as a starter and the hamburger and chips as a main. Archie ordered a crisp Felix Meyer Alsatian pinot blanc for his companions' consumption, and for himself and his steak, an overpriced Château Certan Giraud Pomerol '88. He was annoyed that both the others wanted to sample it as well: a Pomerol with hamburger just wasn't done, and didn't Giles know that Sean Connery's Bond had realised that there was something fishy about Robert Shaw's Krassno Granitski masquerading as Captain Norman Nash because he had red wine with his fish? After the usual pleasantries about the poor state of government, the increasing personal and business tax burden the state of the recruitment market and how brilliantly Huxford had been performing in it, Archie came to the point.

"How much did you pull in through your business last year?" Huxford had had rather a lean time since being thrown out of the boutique search firm he had joined after being thrown out of Hoggett Bowers and had barely managed to bill £65,000 in 1996 as Huxford Associates. He knew he was "good with people" and his presentations were brilliantly crafted, delivered with erudition, loquacity and style and couldn't fail to impress those lucky enough to receive the benefit of his considerable experience. Discerning folk realised he was a total wanker and made a point of ignoring him thereafter. He really wasn't very good at consultancy.

"Oh, let me see, good question, I think it was about £250k," he lied. Giles, the self-made man, had taken an instant dislike to Huxford, with his boring, flat, monotonous Londoner's voice, crinkled gingery hair and stupid, pencil moustache; however, he wasn't going to rock Archie's boat if Huxford was going to save him from the management of ABS. Allowing for Huxford's undoubted exaggeration of the figures (the fact that he didn't know the exact amount was a clear giveaway) they might be able to tempt him over for less than £200k. He let Archie make the running.

"Always a little precarious, though," mused Archie, "and not for the faint-hearted, working on your own. Overstretched one minute, underemployed the next; constant worry of income and the need to keep looking for the next job while you are delivering. Can't be easy."

"No," agreed Huxford, allowing himself to be reeled in, and for once keeping it brief, "it's not."

"Not the sort of thing a man wants to do forever," continued Archie. In fact it was just the sort of thing that many businessmen wanted to do when they became completely disillusioned with the daily grind of corporate life. However, there were an equal number like Huxford, who took the option as "a distressed career move" and were always hoping to find a gullible new employer to take for a ride for as long as their luck lasted.

"We can offer you stability, the prestige of our brand, a decent salary with bonus linked to ABS's profitability and the usual perks," announced Archie.

"What sort of, you know, numbers are we talking in terms of, if I may be so bold," the garrulous Huxford asked cautiously.

"Base of £175k plus hundred percent bonus for achieving budgeted profit." Archie was nothing if not direct, thought Giles, keeping his own counsel. Huxford could hardly believe his luck. The salary was nearly three times his current income and he could double it on the bonus! What was more, he could operate by the old adage: "if at first you don't succeed, try management": this was purely a management role, so he wouldn't have to be busting his balls, as he was currently doing unsuccessfully, to generate new business. The plebs would be doing that. All he had to do was crack the whip to make sure they did it. He would re-embrace the team ethic which meant that he would not have to take all the blame himself if things went wrong; he would smile in the face of any adversity, knowing he would be able to find a scapegoat. It was a dream job.

"Mmm," he pondered, "it is quite an attractive offer, which I appreciate and for which I thank you. However, in absolute terms it represents a step down from my current earnings." Lying came easily to a man who had built his life on false foundations.

"We could offer equity in the business, if that would interest you?" Archie saw the flicker of greed in Huxford's eyes and knew he had landed his fish.

"That certainly helps," said Huxford, with unwarranted pomposity. "May I think about it for a day or so and get back to you printemps?"

"Of course," said Archie, magnanimously mishearing "pronto", as he waved the waiter for the bill with a flourish.

Archie and Giles spoke briefly afterwards, agreeing that they had got their man, even though he "was not really their type". He was long-winded, dull and limited, lacking in vision and backbone. In short, he would be a perfect stooge for them at the helm of ABS. Huxford accepted the job two days later, spent a month receiving instructions alternately from Archie and Giles on how to manage ABS and was launched amidst a blaze of apathy at the beginning of May 1997. Archie walked him round the London office, after which he benefited his grudgingly assembled new troops with a few words marked by consummate gauche triteness:

"I am tremendously excited by the opportunity Archie and Giles have offered me to become your leader. I guess some of you might hold an allegiance to my predecessor, but the sun has set on that era and a new one has dawned." Noone could see "Badger" Brock and Caspian Cordell putting their fingers down their throats.

"I aim to build on the foundations of this great company and with your help, take it on to even greater heights. I will offer you a constant flow of effective information and performance criteria to maximise your assignment successes and minimise cost and time required, based on system engineering concepts." Rebecca Knightley had gone glassy-eyed.

"Our product configuration baseline will be exponentially improved by evolving our specifications over a given time period. As you know, any associated supporting development will present extremely interesting challenges to the philosophy of commonality and standardisation which we all espouse." The FMCG squad all had mouths open in horror.

"For example," Huxford continued inexorably, "the incorporation of additional mission-critical constraints recognises the necessity for greater fight-worthiness concepts and must not allow independent functional principles to affect a significant implementation on any discrete configuration mode." Rodney Shakeshaft was inching towards the door.

"With respect to the specific, individual and collective goals which I will set, the primary interface between our systems technology and personal performance will be paramount in the final analysis, at this moment in time, as I see it, without putting too fine a point upon it." Darth Gwent was now eye-rolling with Sabra Termignioni, who wouldn't have had a clue what Huxford had been saying.

"Anyway, the thing is, what I really mean…is onwards and upwards and I very much look forward to working with you and getting to know you all." He stopped at last and looked around as if anticipating a smattering of applause after this uplifting message. Applause was there none. Only the Politically Correct brigade looked vaguely interested. Huxford had lost the rest before he had begun.

20. HUXFORD

"Stanton Chase International is committed to building world-class management teams for clients competing in a global market. We provide exceptional leaders and organizational solutions to enhance your competitive advantage. We do so through long-term client relationships built on experience, insight and teamwork. We are a disciplined team of professionals who accept the challenge that each search assignment brings. We stay the course until an assignment is successfully concluded and commit the appropriate resources of as many offices as necessary to ensure project completion. Our consultants invest significant time to gain a thorough understanding of our client's culture, industry, competitors, strategy and value proposition. Our industry practice leads have extensive backgrounds combined with an intimate knowledge of their own local, regional and national markets. They exceed client expectations with their global perspective and local insight by following globally adopted quality assurance standards and procedures."

STANTON CHASE WEBSITE

Noone knew that one should never underestimate the power of stupid people inside large organisations and that this made Huxford extremely dangerous. Therefore, he needed quickly to render himself harmless, a non-threat, to Huxford's eyes. He found it quite easy to adopt Huxford's clichéd style of address. At his initial "one-to-one", when Huxford asked:

"So in the general scheme of things, all things being equal, how are things going?" Noone felt able to reply:

"Things are pretty adjacent at the moment, thanks Bly. As we say in the trade, we have plenty of strength in depth and have had go-confirmation on a number of new engagements lately. I think we are asking all the right questions in the market place, are usually there or thereabouts as favourites to get there first despite it being a dog-eat-dog situation. Several of our main rivals are in all sorts of trouble and are absolutely nowhere at the moment while we remain in and counting across the board."

"Excellent, excellent, just what I expected to hear. It's not a bad position in the ongoing situation in which we find ourselves in," Huxford replied, tautologically. "The build-up sounds good but can you make the finish even better; can you keep turning our territorial advantage into goals, so to speak?"

"Well, that's the sixty-four thousand dollar question, isn't it? Things are definitely beginning to gel at the coalface and that's about the measure of it. Mind you, questions still have to be asked about the performance of one or two of the consultants and the odd change may be on the cards, but generally speaking, when all is said and done, things are panning out well. This is what we find and you can't say much fairer than that, can you?"

"In the sort of terms you are talking in terms of, no, but I have seen things go umpty-fiddle before now in similar situations, as so often happens in this game of cricket," said Huxford, with cosmic irrelevance. "Perhaps I may clarify, very briefly and very, very simply, but I hope fairly: the thing is to keep their noses to the grindstone, always go the extra mile and continue the beatings until morale improves, eh!" He chuckled. "Remember, when the going gets tough, the tough don't take a coffee break."

Fuck my old boots, thought Noone as he returned to his office, exhausted by this exchange. He knew from David Coleman that you couldn't "afford to give that sort of time to that sort of player in that sort of a situation and hope to get away with it". Huxford was going to prove very hard work indeed.

Sure enough, as a man who had made a success out of being unsuccessful, Huxford knew how to make his presence felt. His first three months were a whirlwind of useless activity. He rushed round the country (by plane and first class train carriage "to save time") visiting all the offices and depressing all he met. Duly inspired, he had then: voided the one page "T's and C's" which had served ABS perfectly satisfactorily on the grounds it was "too loose and vague" and replaced the simple sheet with two more complex documents constructed with unseemly relish by the company's expensive lawyers, grandly named "General Terms of Business" and "Specific Conditions of Trade"; constructed a complex, needless and ignored-by-all Venn Diagram showing "workflow parameters" to improve the quality of adherence to ISO 9000; produced an organisation chart showing each person's position in the company which demotivated all the secretaries when they saw how un-influential Huxford believed them to be; exchanged the soothing classical landscape scenes which adorned the ABS office walls around the country with over-priced, garish and universally derided examples of abstract modern art, which "better reflected the forward-looking, dynamic atmosphere in which we are working"; commissioned a psychological assessment programme of all consultants to see whether common traits for success could be identified; and changed what had been a simple bonus policy (dividing the credit for fees between introducer and handler only) into a convoluted scheme involving four different percentage splits and a stern warning: "Ultimately all bonuses are discretionary, may be more or less than these guidelines indicate, and will not form part of any contractual entitlement."

Noone knew that these last two actions would be extremely unpopular with the consultants and so it proved. They began to walk. For The Man Who said Everything Twice, the tinkering with the bonus scheme was the final straw; he had already seen his technology team swamped by Archie's acquisition which had brought in some twenty five consultants acting in direct competition under a different brand. How foolish was it to turn up at a client only to find you had been preceded by "colleagues" from your sister company who were pitching for the same business? Hugo had been right and The Man Who Said Everything Twice had had enough. He contacted a boutique firm that lacked a technology presence, offered his services and those of The Harpies if required, promised to bring over a complete list of technology contacts filched surreptitiously from the ABS computer database, and, offer in hand, resigned.

Countrywide, the defections grew: the head of the Glasgow office left to set up his own business, taking two other consultants, including Jim McDougall, and three secretaries. Aberdeen had its prime "Oily" poached by Spencer Stuart. Manchester, Leeds and Birmingham lost a couple of consultants each and there were a sprinkling of departures amongst the smaller regional offices. Huff mislaid specialists in asset management and structured finance to City search firms and the Head of Research, Millicent Moleshill, converted her maternity leave into full-time retirement, taking her Mountains with her. In Noone's team, a couple of the FMCG squad walked to NBS. The ABS Management Board tasked Bob Ellis to maintain a permanent hiring programme through widespread use of "Recruitment-to-Recruitment" agencies (hitherto avoided like lepers) Sunday Times and Daily Telegraph advertisements and direct targeting of promising young consultants in Michael Page and Willard Wonks. Huxford thought it was only natural that the "old guard" should want to leave and that it was "only to be expected" and actually quite healthy to have a high turnover of staff "early on" in his new regime. He didn't seem bothered that intellectual capital and important client relationships were walking away from ABS. Then again, thought Noone, if he could remain so calm amid the growing turbulence, he probably didn't understand the seriousness of the situation.

"Colonel" Ned R. Porage definitely understood the seriousness of the situation and advocated suing all of the defectors for breach of contract and tracking the movements of each for twelve months after his or her leaving date to ensure that they did not "solicit, approach or offer services to any person, firm or company who was a client of the Company (ABS) on the Departure Date or who was a client of the Company during the twelve months prior to this date, nor solicit, approach and work with any employee of the Company for a period of twelve months from the Departure date", as written in the covenants of their contracts. Huxford, in a rare foray into practical management, deemed this "impractical and a waste of valuable company resources", namely Bob Ellis, who was now "far too busy filling the incoming hopper with fodder to worry about outgoing chaff".

It was a time when ABS, from the apogee of its development, like a fierce and proud lion looking down from its position as lord of the jungle, began to feel its age. Wearied by battle and the chase, it was bleeding from numerous cuts and open sores were beginning to fester. Hugo, its heart, had gone, and its body was twitching and convulsing in shock. Disillusionment had crept in and like a cancer, grew and spread.

The sense of pride which had driven people to work in the mornings was ebbing away, replaced by insidious lethargy and cynicism. Huxford was the embodiment of what "they" were doing to ABS, "they" being the faceless Board in the ivory tower in St James's Square who clearly didn't understand how ABS worked.

Noone met Huff for a quiet commiseratory lunchtime drink in the Goat in Stafford Street, a small, cosy pub which occasionally sold Marston's Pedigree. Today, it didn't, and they had to make do with the rather insipid and tasteless bitter that was Greene King IPA, only good really for determined session drinking, in Noone's view, even though they were not in for a session.

"It's all got rather bloody, don't you think?" asked Noone. It was always difficult to know exactly what Huff was thinking as he tended to affect a disinterested, faraway look when tasked with an awkward question.

"Certainly disappointing. With Hugo gone, we seem to have lost a sense of purpose. And I am afraid I do not see our new leader delivering one."

"Too right," said Noone, "the bloke is not even just an affable wanker or a friendly tosser; he is a complete prick. I haven't heard one good word said about him. Why on earth did they hire him?"

"He was an easy pick up, I suppose: one of Archie's or Giles's chums recommended him, he was available, so corners cut, job done."

"Well it's pathetic. We are supposed to pay rigorous attention to detail on behalf of our clients so why can't we do it for ourselves?"

"Good question. Expediency and thrift are the twin mothers of mediocrity, I suppose."

"Well he is a mediocre bastard son, alright. He is so fatuous, it is impossible to defend him and it puts us in a very difficult position."

"Yes. Tarred with his basil brush, I'm afraid. I think we should bide our time awhile: he is bound to make some god-awful cock-up soon that we can take to the plc Board as evidence of his incompetence. Now did I tell you about this new secretary we had..?" He proceeded to titillate Noone with the juicy tale of the forthright temp who had landed on the doorstep of the City office one day. Taking an immediate fancy to one of Huff's handsome young male members, she had marched into his office and in eloquent silence announced her intentions by slowly pulling up the front of her extremely short skirt to reveal the commando nature of her orienteering. His eyes had lit up, and in an unspoken pact, they remained in the office until all the others had gone home. Then, she had calmly walked to his desk and bent over it, legs splayed invitingly. He had taken full advantage in a delirious few minutes of fantasy-fulfilment.

Huff had been told this by the cleaner who had entered the main office just as the rhythmic thuds from the aforementioned desk accelerated to an obvious crescendo.

Shocked and embarrassed as a result of her repressed Catholic upbringing, she backed out and wrote Huff a note advising him to investigate the "after-hours goings-on" which she had unwittingly discovered in the corner office. There was also a hint that the trauma she had suffered might be actionable if *he* didn't take action. Huff had carpeted his consultant who admitted the offence then called in the temp who had told Huff not to be such an old fogey and that he should call in on her flat to join her and a girlfriend in a threesome, as he "obviously needed perking up himself."

"I ask you," Huff concluded to Noone, "the brazen hussy!"

"I don't know, sounds like every schoolboy's dream. So what did you do, take her up on the offer?" asked Noone, agog.

"No, I had to fire her. Shame though, she had wonderful legs." They had consumed two pints of IPA each and a chunky ham Ploughman's enlivened only by homemade English mustard.

The annual ABS conference in September was, for the first time, a downbeat affair. The country was reeling, vicariously and strangely, from the tragic death of Lady Diana, whom everybody seemed to have known personally. Tony Blair, for once appearing out of character not as the grinning fool, delivered his sickening and sycophantic eulogy, iridescent with false emotion, revealing his true colours as a self-publicising actor. Huxford had chosen Cliveden as the conference venue, justifying its expense on the grounds that he wanted to make a statement that ABS remained a class act, and in any case, it was cheaper and "more time-effective" than misguidedly taking everybody to some European capital such as Paris or even further afield. Certainly, Cliveden's bold strapline struck a chord: "Dedicated to the pursuit of pleasure, power and politics for over 300 years." The order of the nouns interested Noone, especially as its most notorious guest had been the prostitute Christine Keeler (pleasure first) who had corrupted (power) the MP, John Profumo (politics). Other guests apparently had included every British monarch since George I as well as Charlie Chaplin, Winston Churchill, Harold Macmillan, President Roosevelt and George Bernard Shaw. The house itself, a grand Italianate mansion, has been home to some of the most famous names in English and American history, including three Dukes, the Prince of Wales and, of course, the Astors. ABS would be mixing with distinguished company. As its advertising blurb modestly announced: "Cliveden is unique. One of the world's finest luxury hotels, this grand stately home is set in the heart of the Berkshire countryside, surrounded by magnificent formal gardens and parkland. It is arguably the finest of luxury hotels near London and Heathrow Airport." Noone thought it odd that one of the world's finest luxury hotels should be only "arguably" the finest near Heathrow Airport.

"From the moment you are ushered into the beautiful Great Hall with its grand fireplace, oak panelling and priceless artworks, our aim is to ensure you feel like a treasured, personal guest," the blurb continued with restrained understatement. "You'll be treated to the very highest standards of quality, with excellence in every detail. Where else can you be surrounded by such extraordinary extravagance and remarkable refinement, but at the same time feel so welcomed and at ease? Cliveden is, at heart, a charming country house hotel where you can come away to escape, relax and be indulged at every opportunity." Noone wasn't sure he had ever been "indulged at" before. Honestly, what a load of bollocks. The writer of the blurb had conveniently overlooked, if indeed he or she had ever known, that the Duke of Buckingham, who conceived the first house on the site in 1666, was a notorious rake and schemer, looking for somewhere discreet temporarily to house his mistresses.

ABS arrived late morning Friday in time for a buffet lunch in the Terrace Dining room, where six sets of massive French windows overlook the Parterre formal garden and the expansive estate of mature trees beyond. As the hotel only had 37 bedrooms, Huxford decreed that these would be given out in order of seniority/longevity in the firm, with the more junior consultants and researchers being coached in from lodgings nearby, namely the Burnham Beeches Hotel for the consultants, and the Thames Riviera in Maidenhead for the researchers and assorted support staff such as Bob Ellis. Noone was allotted the Joyce Grenfell room and found himself saying "George, don't do that" as he unpacked his washing kit.

There is nothing like creating a sense of unity and identity, and this was nothing like it. The mood, as the crowd congregated for lunch, was muted, with small groups gathering discontentedly to discuss in hushed tones the changes which had occurred, commencing with Hugo's shock departure. Huxford, seemingly oblivious to the unpromising undercurrents, decreed that only soft drinks should be served and bounded hither and thither like an excited Tigger, scattering blandishments and meaningless exhortations.

"Good to see you, looking good, wonderful location isn't it? Hope you're as up for this as I am! Looking forward to your contribution in the break-out sessions: let it rip eh? Do try the asparagus tips, absolutely first-class." As he moved on from each group, eyes were raised and people quickly turned their backs on him. It didn't bode well and sure enough, the afternoon session, led by a long and dull review from Huxford, did little to bring any excitement or even lighten the palpable sense of disappointment that hung over the proceedings. In his long-winded way, he noted that revenues were down, attributed this to the departure of "one or two big-hitters", and urged everyone "to get on your bikes and ride, for the glory of this great firm and of course, your own bonuses, heh heh!" Silence was the loud response. Noone marvelled at Huxford's fatuous attempts to motivate this sullen gathering. The words just didn't really follow the music.

Not that there was any music.

On a brighter note, at lunch Noone had caught up with his old team from Uxbridge and discovered that the goose cull had been aborted. He had also made contact with Nerissa, who seemed pleased to see him, but to his chagrin they were seated far apart at the Gala Dinner. Sadly, there were too many of them to experience the intimate fine French dining experience in Waldo's, so they were packed into the Terrace once more in tables of twelve, which made meaningful conversation impossible. The lasagne of Scottish langoustine with petits pois fraises, broad beans, cos lettuce and truffle cream sauce produced the news that the young female consultant on his left had become allergic to lettuce since becoming pregnant. Noone then upset the buxom lady on his right during the roasted cannon of Cornish lamb, "from farm and field" with braised shoulder, buttered spinach and Vichy carrots. Momentarily musing whether the lamb had earned its name by being snuffed out in an artillery barrage, he had introduced himself with a dazzling smile. On learning that she was from Scotland and her name was Mary Brazil, he undid all his initial good work:

"Ah ha. So you must be a tartan nut," he said and laughed. She looked at him as though he was a necrosis-ridden wound and sneered:

"Plainly, bein' a complete twat, you couldna carry the tartan yoursel'." Noone realised he may have overstepped the mark and that there would be no pleasantries emanating from Mary's direction. He sought solace in the Pinot Grigio, which seemed distinctly bottom-of-the-range, before moving on to a similarly average Corbières. Hugo would not have been so skinflint; Huxford really did lack any class or substance. Bob Ellis had tried to persuade him that the hard-working, hard-partying crew of ABS would be thirsty after dinner and in need of further entertainment and had wondered about Cliveden's ability to absorb the high-spirits of around 150 well-lubricated folk desirous of fun. Despite Bob's advice that this might suggest a single location in an hotel large enough to accommodate the entire company and in possession of a night-club attached, Huxford had doggedly stuck to his course for the refinement of Cliveden and decreed that the coaches would leave for the other two hotels at midnight.

Most of them repaired to the Club Room and overwhelmed the two hard-pressed staff who had to call for reinforcements. It was still mayhem. Noone observed that whispered-about, inter-office relationships began to emerge from the shadows into open view. A couple here, a couple there, looking deep into each other's eyes, smiling readily, talking intimately then disappearing together. Even the rumours about a specific male-on-male liaison appeared to be true and Visa Maunfield seemed very wrapped up with a female consultant from the City office. It didn't take Noone long to zero in on Nerissa who had been snared by "Colonel" Ned R. Porage. He appeared entranced, in a deeply unseemly way in Noone's view, by Nerissa's cleavage, and it took at least ten minutes for Noone to convince him that he should toddle off to the bar and procure a round of drinks.

"Thanks for rescuing me," cooed Nerissa, "he was telling me how hard, red and shiny his new motorbike was."

"I didn't know he was a biker. That's a pity, I thought they were all decent cool dudes like Peter Fonda. Now talking of things, hard, red and shiny..." She giggled as they slipped furtively outside. Turning right, they headed behind the huge greenhouse complex and found a convenient bench under the shelter of a huge oak. They sucked each other's tongues urgently, with increasing abandon. Nerissa felt for Noone's lust-filled member, rubbed it, released it and lowered her lips around it. Noone found it difficult to reciprocate in any satisfactory way for her from his seated position, but the commitment she was showing rendered him helpless. The luxuriant swirl of her tongue, the warm wet caresses of her lips took him all-too quickly to his peak. Being a gentleman, he sought to give her options as he neared climax and told her breathlessly that he was about to come; but, game girl that she was, she refused to withdraw and took his full force into her mouth with apparent relish. Noone could never understand how women could get any pleasure from swallowing semen. The thought of it made him quite queasy and he was quite reluctant to kiss Nerissa again even though he felt obliged to offer her a similar service. It was a tricky moment luckily interrupted by a blast from a coach horn. Nerissa glanced at her watch. She was staying in the Burnham Beeches Hotel.

"God it's midnight. I need to get on one of the coaches." She stood up, smoothed her dress and ran her fingers through her hair."

"What a bugger," said Noone, relieved, "I'm sorry we can't, you know, carry on."

"Don't worry," she breathed, as they made their way cunningly down the side path to the Terrace, to avoid being seen emerging from the undergrowth, "you owe me one."

The next morning it was clear that Huxford must have had an early night, for his enthusiasm remained undimmed in the face of a giant, collective hangover. He continued to smile encouragingly at everyone and even slapped the back of a number of male consultants as he welcomed them all to another exciting day of, as he put it, "discussion on teambuilding and how to maximise our hit-rate scenarios, distilling and marketing our brand essence as we accelerate towards, and power through, the year 2000". They filed reluctantly into the conference room. Noone caught Nerissa's eye, winked and found himself sitting next to Bob Ellis as Huxford began his turgid address.

"He wouldn't know if someone was up him sideways with an armful of deckchairs," muttered Bob Ellis to Noone, sotto voce. "He couldn't team-build if there were only three people and a cow left on earth."

"He'd make the cow team leader!" Noone nudged Bob

and they chuckled aloud, attracting a sharp glance from Huxford behind the lectern.

"He looks as sour as a cat licking shit off a thistle," continued Bob graphically, causing Noone to splutter and hide himself behind the person in front. It was the highlight of the morning as Huxford bored them all senseless, with the help of meticulously constructed Powerpoint slides. Never before in the field of human conferencing had the coffee-break been anticipated so eagerly by so many, the concluding session by so few. Never before had a conference, designed to stabilise, energise, motivate and collectivise, succeeded so thoroughly in upsetting, enervating, discouraging and fragmenting its audience. Even a cameo from Archie Aspallan, who had deigned to visit the conference for an hour via his chauffeur-driven Bentley, did nothing to raise the spirits. Concerned that post-Hugo, things might be getting a little slack at ABS, he also urged renewed vigour, ending with an ominous bon mot:

"When you've time to talk about taking time off to have fun, the business is healthy; when you have time to have fun, it isn't." Well thanks a bunch, thought Noone, as Archie exited stage left with a grand wave. Huxford beamed down on them all as he received the desultory clap he so richly failed to deserve after his closing address, urging everyone to "strive onwards and upwards to make this great firm great again, if not greater". How very grating, thought Noone.

Ironically, a "fun" lunch had been arranged onboard a large Thames cruiser, The Moby Dick, as an entertaining replacement for the gym, spa, swimming pool, squash, tennis and other amenities which the group had had no time to enjoy. To avoid the locks downriver, coaches took them to Marlow, where they embarked. As it was the last act of a diseased project, Huxford had graciously allowed alcohol to be served. The beer was fizz or lager, the wine strictly gulp-plonk and the food mass-catering pap, namely frozen prawn cocktail followed by overcooked breadcrumbed chicken breast in a stodgy sauce styled as cordon bleu. They sailed upriver to Henley-on-Thames and turned round outside The Angel at the Bridge. Those with a strong constitution like Noone bravely imbibed to numb the combined pain of last night's hangover and the knowledge that ABS, like the now returning Moby Dick, was heading downstream towards the weirs. As boat trips went, it was uneventful: nobody was sick, nobody fell in, and in the words of Stanley Holloway "there was no wrecks and nobody drownded; 'fact nothing to laugh at, at all."

Back on dry land at Marlow, the coaches took them back to their respective hotels and reunited them with their cars. Farewells were said a little wistfully, though in some cases fondly; Noone told Nerissa he looked forward to repaying the compliment soon. As he drove away through a beautifully autumnal Burnham Beeches, Noone reflected that it might be a metaphor for ABS. Yes, winter might just be round the corner.

21. BIX NAPIER

"We offer the personal attention of a Director on each assignment and work for only a small number of clients in any one sector - ensuring as much access to candidates and as few off-limits conflicts as possible. The firm was founded in 2000 in the belief that, even in an overcrowded recruitment marketplace, there would be room for a firm with a philosophy based on quality, professionalism and personal service. We work in partnership with our clients and each assignment has the direct involvement of one or more Directors from initiation through to conclusion. We engage with our clients to challenge their thinking to deliver the best possible result."
OXYGEN WEBSITE

Noone received a call from his sister Amelia which necessitated all his patience and diplomacy. She had recently bought a computer and required a man at the end of the phone from the help-desk to make it work properly. She told Noone:

"I was ringing 0800-1900 for two days and couldn't get through so I asked Directory Enquiries to put me through. When they did I told them about the 0800-1900 number and they asked where I had got the number from. I told them it was on the box and then they told me those were their opening hours!"

"Easy mistake, half-sis," said Noone sympathetically.

"So I then asked for Jack's telephone number and they asked what I was talking about. I told them that on Page 1, Section 5 of the User Guide, it says to plug the PC into the wall socket and telephone Jack before switching on, so I asked again for Jack's number."

"And what did they say then?" asked Noone, knowing the answer but not wanting to appear too clever.

"They told me that it meant the telephone socket.

Honestly, these Americans, why can't they speak English? Anyway, then I asked whether the UK Guarantee would cover me if I happened to take it to Europe or somewhere else and they got sarcastic and asked if I thought there was a clue in the wording 'UK Guarantee'. These people get very jumped up, don't you think?"

Noone could feel the Call Centre operative's frustration, but he played forward defensive down the wicket for his sister's sake: "Yes, the customer is always wrong. So then what happened? Did you get it working?"

"Well, the man told me how to switch it on and told me to right-click on the Open Desktop icon. So I did and he asked if I had a Pop-up Menu and I said no, I have Weetabix and he laughed and said 'Jesus', explained what a Pop-up Menu was, and asked me to right-click again and look for the Pop-up Menu. I told him I still didn't have one so he asked me exactly what I had done in response to his commands. I said that he had told me to write 'click' so I wrote 'click', twice in fact, and still nothing had happened."

"Ah, I think I can see the problem," said Noone.

"That was just it; he then asked: 'in the bottom left-hand side of the screen, can you see the OK button displayed?' I was amazed Adam, so I told him I thought it was incredible that he could see my screen from where he was."

Noone was having trouble maintaining an even tone. "And what did he say to that?"

"I think he said something about abroad, but it didn't make any sense. Anyway, eventually he was able to show me how to get words on the screen, and it was going really well, then suddenly, there was nothing. I told him I was typing away and all of a sudden the words went away, disappeared. He asked what my screen looked like, and apart from being dusty, I told him it was blank and none of my typing showed up.

He asked if I was 'still in Word or did I get out?' so I said I was trying to type words in, not out, and he got quite short. He asked if I could see the C:prompt on the screen, so I asked what a sea-prompt was. He said 'never mind' quite curtly and asked if I could move my cursor around the screen. By now, I knew what a cursor was but he didn't seem to be really listening so I told him quite sharply that there wasn't a cursor, there were no words, nothing." The experience of re-living the experience was clearly distressing for Amelia.

"You poor thing," sympathised Noone, "it's not pleasant to lose your words and your cursor."

"It jolly well isn't; then he asked if my monitor had a power indicator. I thought monitors were big lizards and so I told him I didn't have reptiles in my lounge, thank you very much, and he explained it was actually a TV screen; I mean, why do they have to invent a new name for it? Anyway, he asked whether it had a light showing to tell me it was switched on, so I said I didn't know." Noone was beginning to marvel at his sister's relentless stupidity, which he suspected of being a little wilful.

"So he said to look at the back of the lizard-TV thingy," continued Amelia, "and find where the power cord went into it."

"And did you?" asked Noone, leading her on."

"Oh yes, that was easy," said Amelia, airily. "Then he asked me to follow the cord to the plug and check whether it was plugged into the wall-socket and switched on."

"I can see his logic," conceded Noone.

"Duh, of course it was, I was using it wasn't I?"

"It might have become accidentally detached for some reason, someone tripping over it, for example," volunteered Noone, searching for closure.

"Well it wasn't. So then he asked whether I had noticed that there were two cables plugged into the back of the TV-lizard and I had, so he asked me to see if the other one was plugged securely into the back of the computer and I told him I couldn't."

"Yes, they are always a bugger to trace," said Noone knowingly, but Amelia was reaching a crescendo of indignation and wasn't to be side-tracked by her brother's mollification.

"He asked whether I could see if it was plugged in and I said 'No', so he asked me to find a better angle by leaning on something closer. So I told him it wasn't because I wasn't close enough or anything: it was because it was dark. He got all aggressive again and positively snarled 'what do you mean, dark'? So I explained that because the lights were off, the only light was coming in through the window from a street-light. He asked me to turn on the light and that was when I was able to tell him I couldn't."

"Why couldn't you?" asked Noone.

"Because of the power-cut," replied Amelia, sweetly.

"Aha," said Noone, who hadn't seen that one coming, "I hadn't seen that one coming."

"Exactly," said Amelia, "that's just what I was telling the man all along; that I couldn't see anything, but he kept on asking these silly questions about TV-lizards."

"So what did the man say then?" Noone was now curious to know how this strange dialogue had concluded.

"At first he was fine and said he understood the problem fully now and not to worry, he felt sure he could solve it. He asked whether I still had the boxes and manuals and packing stuff that the whole lot came in, and I told him they were up in the loft. So he said 'Good, wait until the power-cut has ended, then get them all down, unplug the system and repack into the boxes just like when you got it. Then take it all back to the shop you bought it from.' I said 'Really, is it that bad?' and he said he was afraid it was."

"And then what?" asked Noone in an agony of anticipation.

"I said 'alright then, but what do I tell them in the shop?' and that's when he got very nasty, which is why I called you to do something about this rude man."

"And what did he say, Amelia?" asked Noone.

"He said to tell them that I was too fucking stupid to

own a computer!" Noone had to try extremely hard not to burst into laughter at this point. Whilst sympathising utterly with the hapless IT drone, it was his sister who needed his support after her confidence-draining encounter with home technology. She whimpered that she had only bought the thing to help Toby keep up to speed with his friends, all of whom had home PCs, in many cases their own. Gently, he explained that the incident was best forgotten, that he would help her to set up a PC for Toby, who would be a natural on it from day one, because 'kids just are' and offered her a nice lunch in town to revive her shattered spirits. She was easily bought.

Back at the day-job, Noone was concerned about the ennui that had gripped the firm, spread like an infection from Huxford; it was the antithesis of Hugo's drive and passion for ABS. Noone's own time was spent increasingly on "management" and less on transacting business. Sure, he would receive calls from his contacts and former clients which might lead to assignments, but invariably, he found that he lacked the time and hence inclination to take them on. Certainly, the lower the level, the quicker he passed them on to one of his team. Standards were slipping: Huxford hired someone whose entire career turned out to be a fabrication: born Vera Scutbuttle, to a single-mother housewife from Stockport, she had started off in the accounts department of a local haulage company where she learned how to misappropriate cash. Discovered and fired, she wrote her own glowing reference with which she impressed a large regional retailer which duly hired her, offering the anonymity, which she embraced, for her safely to hone her embezzling skills.

She might still have been there now, "creaming off the top" of those poor suckers to supplement her meagre salary, were it not for an unusually sharp auditor who dug further than usual into the invoicing and discovered several dozen fictional suppliers all with the same bank account, which turned out to belong to Vera. She was sent to prison for two years, but, unfazed, viewed this as a career opportunity. First, she conducted a mercenary affair with a female warder which gained her surreptitious privileges. Then, becoming a denizen of the Prison Library, she studied and learned all she could about Accounting. Finally, utilising the Library's internet facility, she researched the names of Harvard's imminent MBA graduands and duly emerged, as from a chrysalis, as "Olivia Renfield", replete with summa cum laude from one of America's finest.

She dispensed with her first husband and moved south, having secured a new job as Finance Manager for a mid-tier London firm of Solicitors delighted to have scooped such a rising star fresh from a Harvard degree. This was merely a stepping stone, however, and in rapid succession she became Head of Finance for one of the Big Five consultancies and then Head of Operations for another, which regrettably fired her for incompetence after a year. Amazingly, one of the London search firms thought she would make a decent headhunter, persuaded by her fictitious connections in exalted circles, and hired her into its Board Practice. There she failed for six months before her name was passed to Bob Ellis as "someone not quite at home and looking for a move". His police instincts told him there was something fishy about Olivia's CV, but Huxford was extremely keen and overruled Bob, announcing her appointment with considerable fanfare as another coup for ABS in hiring an ex Tier One headhunter.

It became clear after a couple of months that despite her clever charm and ability to name-drop, Olivia was actually useless. As a "finance specialist" she had been mistakenly placed under Huff in Financial Services and only impressed him with her ability to achieve nothing. He wondered aloud to Noone how she had managed to attract the blue-chip names onto her CV and what she had achieved for them: he suspected that her current form which he was witnessing was an indicator of past performance.

"Do we know whether Huxford took references on her?" he asked Noone. Noone assumed so but wasn't sure. They checked with Bob Ellis. Bob certainly hadn't and didn't think Huxford had either.

"This is outrageous," conferred Noone to Huff. "We are not even practising what we preach with regard to a key differentiator anymore. What would our clients say if they found out?"

"I shudder to think," said Huff. "We would be revealed as charlatans."

"Perhaps we are charlatans," mused Noone dejectedly. When he tackled Huxford on the subject, in general terms of course, Huxford assured Noone that references were taken religiously on all new hires; after all, they had to practise what they preached, didn't they? Noone asked nonchalantly who was taking them, as, making the point firmly so that it might register in Huxford's dull brain, he hadn't been asked to take any recently.

"Usually me myself, goes straight in the person's personal Personnel file. Sometimes I delegate to Bob Ellis," Huxford assured him airily.

"So, specifically," said Noone pointedly, "who took La Renfield's references?"

"No need to worry old chap," enthused Huxford, "had a word with a few of my chums in the Big Five who had come across her - not literally of course!" Noone didn't laugh. "Absolutely clean bill of health, 20/20, A*, Alpha Plus all the way through. No need to worry on that score. Why do you ask?"

"Because she is completely useless and if I didn't believe in the rigorous nature of your referencing, I would say someone is taking the piss, big-time."

"Well she is not your responsibility, so I suggest you back off and mind your own business; like anyone else, she needs some time to establish herself in her new environment; I am sure even you needed time," Huxford finished loftily.

Within six months, Olivia Renfield had gone. She

breezed into Huxford's office one Friday and informed him that she had received an offer she couldn't refuse "back in the real world". Recruitment consulting was ok as a stop-gap, but it was a strange, twilight world, wasn't it, and she needed to head back towards the light. She had been offered the job of Head of New Media for the BBC and was delighted to accept. Thanks for everything, no need to bother with her notice period, they wanted her to start at once etc etc…

Except that she didn't. For the BBC, unlike the "professionals" elsewhere along "Olivia's" obscure and winding path of a career, did take thorough references and only then did the whole fabricated edifice come tumbling down, revealing Vera Scutbuttle in her naked shame without the cloak of Olivia Renfield. Huxford avoided Noone and Huff for weeks, fervently hoping that the oblivion into which Vera/Olivia had passed would act retrospectively on her tenure at ABS.

The Old Guard such as Noone and Huff figuratively began to huddle furtively on street corners, whispering to each other that "it wasn't like this in the old days" and bemoaning Huxford's latest crass act; what right he sought to do was immediately tarred, feathered and paraded with ridicule by the Old Guard as yet another example of his stupefying incompetence. He "just didn't understand the culture of ABS" and as a result he was ruining it. They may have had a point, but there were events happening outside ABS which would nevertheless affect it in just as profound a way as the departure of Hugo Reeve-Prior and the interference of Huxford.

The occasion of Giles Bane's sixty-fifth birthday was initially a source of pride and celebration to himself. On a Saturday in late July, he hosted a lavish party at his "country seat" for family and friends (even, grudgingly, Archie Aspallan) with a giant marquee on the lawn, and entertainment by way of a recital by the Northern Chamber Orchestra and dance music by Humphrey Lyttleton's Jazz Band (nothing so vulgar as a discotheque). Food was specially prepared and delivered by Henri LeFou, a top London chef reputed to have invented several dishes at The Ivy, to the hungry hordes, who couldn't have cared less where the food came from as long as it was filling. There was cold-running Bollinger and cider for the teetotal. The day was warm and conducive, Bane thanked them all briefly for being important parts of his self-made life and only those husbands and wives who had quarrelled during the afternoon went home disappointed.

The following Monday, Archie dropped into Giles's office and casually asked him what he would be doing with his retirement.

"Retirement? Who said anything about retirement? Over my dead body," he said with unwitting irony. The fact was that he had established a pleasant enough way of life, living out of his Kensington flat during the week, where he had made a mistress of a saucy and pneumatic Portuguese maid, who allowed him to do things to her body which his straight-laced and frigid wife would never permit, particularly at his age. At weekends he would return home and play the loving husband and father, sailing his Hans Christian 38T, for which he had a berth at Canvey Island, and enduring the odd infuriating round of golf for business purposes. Unfortunately he had reckoned without Archie Aspallan's ego and cunning. In anticipation of Giles's great event, Archie had been working quietly but diligently on his fellow Board members, dropping honeyed words laced with poison:

"Good old Giles, made it through to retirement age; he deserves a long and happy one, don't you think?" And "He's been invaluable and we will all miss him, but the signs have been there for a while that he's ready for a rest. Time for some new blood, don't you think?" The "New Blood" he had in mind was a Managing Director whom they had inherited through one of Archie's acquisitions. Bix Napier was a dashing, debonair, youthful forty-five, the antithesis of Giles Bane. Where Bane, white-haired, portly and faintly regal in bearing, represented sound northern stock and inherited wealth built up from generations of honest commodity manufacturing, Napier, with flowing blond locks and a lean six feet two physique, had the suspicion of an Eastern European immigrant mother and a part-time minor actor and full-time pimp of a father, who despite no claim to a family tie with the Napier-Railton automotive engineering racing heritage, claimed it constantly. Father had "taken up" with one of his string of girlfriends, Bix's mother, although they were never formally married, and after kindly passing on the clap which he had caught from another of his girls, was stabbed to death in a Whitechapel alley by an angry punter who had also caught a dose.

Bix's mother fell back into prostitution and then drugs to assuage the awful, relentless monotony of being poked about by foul-smelling strangers, leaving Bix to fashion his own life unaided. He was nothing if not determined and unscrupulous; from running errands for the local drug-dealers he graduated to handling and dealing (even generously supplying his mother "at cost") eventually building up a powerful local regime which required a legitimate "front". So he established a second-hand car business, dealing mainly in cash for drug-money laundering purposes, and proved that his gift-of-the-gab was a valuable and transferable skill by becoming equally successful in this alternative career. Although viewed as "a bit of a chancer", he was respected for his readiness to "flash the cash" and his easy charm and charisma. Increasingly rarely did he need to resort to violence. By now he had acquired a number of legitimate business associates, that is, men who ran legitimate businesses, and from them he gleaned enough information to diversify further into legitimacy himself.

Business training seemed to be the hot topic, so Bix looked around and found a privately-owned sales training company with a turnover of around £1.5 million. The owner considered himself to be doing quite nicely, thank you, and rebuffed Bix's first attempt to buy him out. Bix suggested it might be better for the man's health if he reconsidered and had him tailed night and day by one of his less legitimate friends. After two weeks of being followed by the same accusing, malevolent glare belonging to a barrel-chested, broken-nosed, toothless former bare-knuckle prize-fighter (illegitimate) in every public place he chose to visit, materialising on his street as soon as he walked through the front door of his house in the morning and vanishing into the shadows last thing at night as he fumbled for his key on the doorstep, the man changed his mind and agreed to Bix's not ungenerous offer.

Bix grew the business with great gusto, diversifying from the core sales area into training for marketing, accounting, software, hardware, systems and management. He even trained trainers of all these specialisations and in the world of mediocrity that is training, his firm stood out as being less mediocre than all the others. Eventually, Archie Aspallan's City firm of M & A advisors listed it as a potential acquisition, for it was "human resources based" and might complement the recruitment businesses in the Aspallan, Bane Group. Archie thought so too. A meeting was arranged over lunch at the Savoy. By now, Bix had thoroughly cleansed himself of his less-than-salubrious past and what was presented to Archie was a charming, handsome, confident, sharp, entrepreneurial fellow, who, despite a lack of any obvious breeding, reminded Archie very much of his younger self. He liked the cut of Bix's jib and Bix ensured that the two men hit it off immediately. Bix sensed great opportunity in the cultivation of this posh, complacent, vain, arrogant megalomaniac, whose established, birth-ordained position in society and lifelong easy access to wealth represented everything Bix hated.

Further meetings were arranged, advisors put in touch with advisors, accountants with accountants, bankers with bankers and a deal was struck. Bix's business, with Bix remaining firmly at its helm, was absorbed into the Aspallan, Bane empire, which was renamed Aspallan,

Bane Resources plc better to reflect its now broader offering. Bix gained a seat on the plc Board and bided his time while he studied the internal relationships, frictions, rivalries and planned the way forward for his future career.

He relished the demise of Reeve-Prior, noting that nobody was indispensable. He saw that Giles Bane, although nominally Group CEO, was really only interested in his headhunting business and had become isolated on the Board. Archie made the decisions that drove the Group and the NEDs, who were his cronies, rubber-stamped them. Therefore, Bix made sure that he always responded with sycophantic enthusiasm to any of Archie's suggestions and Archie knew he could count on Bix's support. Archie, who had long wished to be free of Giles's surly and uncooperative presence, soon came to appreciate that Bix might make a perfect CEO in the event of Giles's departure. He was open to Archie's ideas and, being slightly common, both impressionable and keen to impress. Indeed, not only was he malleable but he could be used as a lever, an instrument to effect such a change.

So Archie cultivated Bix assiduously and one day, whilst lunching him at Boodles, casually brought up the subject of Giles.

"I expect you won't know this, but he is soon to turn sixty-five. He's had a pretty good innings, I'd say," said Archie, lining him up for a fall.

"Yes," agreed Bix, "what is he going to do then, retire?"

"Well that's just it," said Archie thoughtfully, "it seems like he wants to soldier on, instead of sailing off into the sunset with the appreciation and congratulations of all smoothing the waters ahead."

"I see," said Bix, who was beginning to see. "And you don't want him to continue?"

"Well, he is really only interested in the headhunting business and he can be a little cantankerous. I do feel that if I had a, ah, younger man alongside me as CEO, we'd get things done rather more quickly and easily."

"I see," said Bix again, who now definitely saw, although he thought this was a bit rich coming from one who, he estimated, was barely five years Giles's junior. "But if he doesn't want to retire, how are you going to make him?" He asked, innocently, while mentally drawing up a list of the kneecappers he might have used in one of his earlier lives.

This was the question for which Archie had been planning. "It needs a Board resolution, which is where you come in." Archie turned to face Bix squarely, and looked him forcefully in the eye. "Suppose I were to offer you the CEO role in return for your support in the, ah, encouragement of Giles's retirement?"

"Could you do that? Would the Board agree?" asked Bix, enthralled at this example of ruthless plc power-politics.

"Oh I think so," replied Archie loftily, "with some careful feeding and watering and a gentle talking to, I am sure my plants will face in the right direction."

Their pact sealed over two glasses of Jean Fillioux cognac (the blended: Napier wasn't worth pushing the boat out for La Pouyade) Archie had set about refining his plan, attentively cultivating "his plants" with whispered words about Giles's frailties, which were "now becoming all too apparent" and the need for development and change. Encouraged and armed by their expected encouragement, he had dropped into Giles's office the Monday after the party to confront him with the requirement for retirement.

"Retirement? Who said anything about retirement? Over my dead body." Giles had said.

"We don't want your dead body, old boy," Archie responded, then pointedly, "but now you are sixty-five, we do want you seriously to consider retiring, per contract. Consider it for, say, a week, then resign, 'to spend more time with your family', so to speak. We think that would be best."

"What do you mean *we*?" exploded Giles. "*You* think, *you* want. Bloody nerve. Nobody else is expecting me to retire."

"Ah. That's where you are wrong. I think you will find that they are expecting an announcement imminently," countered Archie, smoothly.

"You bastard. You've been talking to the Board behind my back, haven't you?" The seriousness and weakness of his position began to dawn on Giles for the first time. Unlike Archie, he hadn't bothered to court his fellow Board members, believing that his status as a founder of the company and, despite one or two high profile but dispensable departures, the continued success of the original headhunting business, which he headed, spoke for itself and rendered him inviolable. He was Group Chief Executive, for Chrissake! He realised that this was deeply personal; Archie had always resented giving him fifty percent of the original company, notwithstanding the fact that Giles had been a consistent and diligent fee-earner over the years. He recalled wryly the little competitions they used to have until Archie had fluked that million pound fee one year, after which Archie had rather wound down his fee-earning activity to develop his ambitious and costly plans for growth. They should have kept it simple and stuck with ABC alone and not wasted time on all these other trashy businesses which diluted the purity of the original search model and cost time, effort and money, particularly his time and effort.

There could be no doubt that Archie wanted him out, and from the looks of it, he had already been preparing the ground well. Still, Giles could not believe that the Board was prepared to discard him and his fee-earning capability after all he had done over the years; he was a proud man and he would make his case passionately to the Board and show that rat Archie. His famed persuasive powers, that over the years had convinced many a Chairman and Chief Executive in many a boardroom that his rigour, probity, diligence and tenacity were the qualities to deliver a successful search, would be rolled out to convince his own Board of his enduring efficacy and Aspallan's crass misjudgement.

"Alright then Aspallan," he snarled, "we will debate your ill-advised suggestion at the next Board meeting; and I'm warning you, I won't go without a fight."

He was wrong. It was his misjudgement of Aspallan's ruthlessness and Giles's failure to grasp the extent to which Aspallan held the Board in his pocket that were cruelly exposed. Stony faces did not respond to his impassioned entreaties, sullen silence greeted his fervent eloquence and the list of impressive achievements he laid before them was dismissed as yesterday's news. Keenly, he felt the knives being sunk between his shoulder-blades. It grated when Aspallan said he wanted to "throw off the sheet-anchor of the past and take a breath of fresh air into the sails to carry the ship strongly into the twenty-first century." How dare such a spoon-fed landlubber use a nautical analogy?

The final straw was when Aspallan unveiled that slimy upstart Napier as the "breath of fresh air" to be the potential new CEO *in his place*. The heads around the table nodded sagely in agreement and Napier smiled cruelly at him. That smug cunt had the self-serving morals of a cornered rat; Giles felt sure there was the whiff of the second-hand car dealer about him. He half-expected him to say 'no hard feelings'.

"No hard feelings, Giles," said Napier, "you've earned your retirement. Enjoy it." Giles looked round the table at the people he had admittedly never called friends and realised he had not a single friend amongst them. That was it then; no use kicking against these pricks. He stood up and, maintaining his dignity, went quietly.

The press release concerning Giles Bane's retirement paid tribute to his prowess as a headhunter, his foresight and vision in helping to found, then build, Aspallan, Bane Consultants, and his skills as a CEO in leading and shaping the highly successful group it had now become. It also introduced Bix Napier as "an experienced and astute businessman with vision, charisma and the dynamic approach ideally suited to leading the Group through the next stage of its development in becoming a truly twenty-first century, client-centric business."

As he read through the flattery and flannel, Noone recalled his first meeting with Giles Bane, a man then not only utterly in command of his vast empty desk but seemingly of much of the world outside. Now he too had exited the stage. Noone had had one encounter with Napier when the latter had been invited by Huxford to a meeting of the ABS Office Managers in order to share his secret for successful selling. They were to incorporate Napier's techniques into their consultants' training in the vain hope that this would increase their collective pitch-winning ratio. Noone had thought Napier a little too eager, a tad flashy, a touch arrogant, whose rather spivvy methods might work in the mass markets in which *he* had dwelt, but had no real connection with the relationship-led world of executive recruitment. He feared even more for the future of ABS with people like Napier and Huxford in charge. Perhaps, he mused, thinking the unthinkable, even the future of ABC was imperilled?

22. THE BITER BIT

"Search can take place at a time of great corporate stress. A satisfactory result is not enough. You need assurance of progress. To deliver this, each search is managed by one consultant throughout. Your constant point of contact. It is this consultant's responsibility to keep you informed. At all times. By telephone, in person, and in writing. The nature and scope of our written progress reports is unprecedented in search. You need detailed and timely communication. We consider it a failure if you have to call us for information. Our experience enables us to understand your strategic aims. It also helps us match candidates to cultures, not merely to job descriptions. Our knowledge and reputation earn the respect and cooperation of the best people. We give you the opportunity to choose from a range of excellent candidates."

STCP WEBSITE

It was a reflective Noone who studied the group photograph on his office wall taken at the Paris conference. Was it only five years ago? Of those smiling faces, seemingly united in their joy of the job and their belief in the brand, at least half had disappeared, dissatisfied. How proud they had been of ABS and their part in its success. How quickly that sense of identity and purpose had dissipated. Noone had lost "Badger" Brock and Attracta Mann; recently, Sally Forth and Peter Serjeant had left Uxbridge. All of them had been snaffled up by well established search firms, which, like piranhas scenting blood, had darted amongst the ailing body of ABS and bitten off tasty morsels of its flesh. It was ironic that an organisation which had miraculously survived the non-existent apocalypse promised by the Millenium Bug was intent on destroying itself.

Information Technology was partly to blame of course. People were now continuously plugged into email, which had rendered everyone instantly accessible to everyone else, overloaded them with useless and often misleading information and led to constant distractions. Noone himself no longer licked envelopes because of the rat-shit used in the glue, nor drank Coca Cola because of its toilet-stain-removing properties, nor used deodorant because it undoubtedly led to ineffable cancers. If he smelled like a rutting skunk, so be it, at least he would die healthy. He had diverted some of his meagre savings to poor, sick, eight-year-old Donna Love, who was dying in hospital for the 1,467,801st time, but he was about to be compensated by some $20,000 donated by Bill Gates personally in thanks for Noone participating in a special Microsoft survey and that would surely be augmented by the ten percent of the $27m, which a senior government official in Nigeria had promised to send him for the temporary use of his bank account. He had learned that if he didn't forward emails immediately to at least seven people, an eagle would crap on his head at precisely midday following, and the resultant parasite infestation would cause all his hair to fall out and a large lipoid lump to grow from his neck. He knew this because it had actually happened to a friend of his next-door neighbour's cousin's ex-wife's mother-in-law's beautician's doctor's patient. Apparently. Now, his prayers only got answered if he forwarded emails to ten of his friends and made a wish within five minutes, but as a result of doing this, his soul was being cared for by 514,279 angels.

There was no point in taking chances, however, and he was wary of being drugged and robbed by someone proffering perfume samples, of serial killers crawling into the back seat of his car when he had stopped for petrol, and of using public lavatories for defecation in case one of the hordes of deadly African or Australian spiders or snakes that live under seat-rim might crawl out and bite him in the yarblokkoes, causing his instant and agonising demise. Even answering the phone was a problem, on account of the probability of having his number cloned, leading to the receipt of a telephone bill for £3,846 for hour-long calls he didn't make to New Zealand, Botswana and Tajikistan.

He comforted himself with the cornucopia of conflicting insights and knowledge he had gained directly from the Dalai Lama via email: that great achievements involve great risk, that not getting what he wanted was really what he wanted, that learning rules meant that he was better placed to break them properly, that silence was often the best answer, that he would become immortal by sharing knowledge, that he should be gentle with the earth, that success can only be judged by what was lost to achieve it, that the lesson from loss must not be lost, that love should exceed need but that love and cooking should be approached with reckless abandon. What a load of platitudinous, sanctimonious twaddle. Noone resolved never to forward another email that demanded to be forwarded, as soon as he had forwarded the one he was about to forward.

He took lunch with Huff in a small, unassuming Italian restaurant on Albemarle Street run with clinical efficiency by Mama Rossetti, whose waitresses greatly appealed to the two men who routinely lusted impotently after forbidden and untouchable fruit.

"First we get lumbered with the wretched Huxford, now wide-boy Napier," moaned Noone. "I don't understand what Archie Aspallan is playing at."

"It's all part of a Grand Game in which we are mere prawns," replied Huff, matter-of-factly. "Archie always wanted Giles out, but he couldn't do it on his own; he bribed Napier with the CEO job and thinks he can control him. I wouldn't be too sure though: he is a very slippery fish." He poured some more of the rustic Chianti Classico, which was adequate for lunchtime quaffing alongside a bowl of pasta.

"I agree," said Noone, gloomily. "He's also a 'pile-it-high-sell-it-cheap' merchant and he doesn't understand our quality-driven approach. He told me the other day that he expected all our consultants to be making at least twenty business development calls a day; I ask you! We shouldn't be asked to cold-call or ambulance-chase like that."

"He said the same to me. Like it or not, ABS has changed and will continue to change."

"Well I *don't* like it!" Noone exclaimed. "I wouldn't mind so much if I felt I could trust him. But he seems so shallow and glib and I am not sure that he really likes ABS and ABC. Call me old-fashioned…"

"You are old-fashioned. But you are right that he doesn't like us. He thinks we are arrogant, vain and don't want to learn anything new."

Meanwhile, Bix Napier, who despised the culture of superiority which he had found amongst both ABC and ABS consultants, all of whom he found arrogant, vain and resistant to change, was working on the next stage of his Grand Game, which differed markedly from Archie Aspallan's, in that it was about to exclude Archie. Since becoming Chief Executive by twisting the knife in Bane's back he had set about charming the old fogeys on the Board, quietly displacing Archie in their affections. The Non-Execs appreciated this young, virile, ambitious, fearless leader which their bold foresight and perspicacity had placed in executive charge of the Group. His energy and decisiveness reminded them all of the younger selves they fondly imagined they had been and placed even Archie in the shade. They began to see what he meant about Archie's single-minded pursuit of growth and acquisitions; it was rather self-serving and reckless. Some of the acquisitions had proved overly expensive and delivered little by way of incremental returns and business synergy. The share price, far from rising constantly towards the five pound mark he had promised, had faltered at two pounds fifty and had even begun to fall back. This was not good, for they had all invested in the company as shareholders. And in retrospect, Archie's almost hysterical desire to remove poor old Giles from the business could now be judged hasty and verging on megalomaniac in intent.

The next Board meeting, in June 2000, was a highly charged affair. Concern over the share price led to discussions regarding the wisdom of Archie's strategy, during which Bix appeared to show reservations at continuing to chase acquisitions. Archie was astonished to find his protégé apparently questioning his judgement. He was rendered speechless when Bix, with considerable regret, mentioned to the Board the existence of an extremely obscure company bank account from which Archie had traditionally paid the costs of his London flat as well as his entertainment expenses. Apologetically, he pointed out that such misappropriation of the Group's money for the private use of the Chairman without the knowledge of the Board was at best unseemly and at worst illegal; would the Chairman care to comment?

"No," Archie thundered, "I set up that account when I set up the company. It's none of your business."

"Unfortunately it is," countered Bix smoothly, "you may have used the company accounts as your personal fiefdom in the past, but you cannot do so now." Bix, of course, had first-hand experience of such opaque financial engineering techniques from his own past on which to draw. "Given your cavalier approach to the financial assets of the company, I am afraid I must table a motion of no confidence in your Chairmanship of this plc." He sat back, his eyes locked on Archie. It instantly dawned on Archie how Giles must have felt when he found himself isolated in front of this very audience. Bix Napier, his creation, had set him up for execution. The show of hands expressing no confidence in his tireless and, in his view, impeccable leadership, was unanimous. The lily-livered lap-dogs had listened to Napier's lies and turned on him. The full impact of this "danse macabre" hit him like a Mike Tyson punch to the solar plexus. *They were removing him from his own company.* He had always been confident and in control, his demeanour complementing his tall and well-dressed image. Now he felt small, sick and helpless. How could he face his still fragrant Honeysuckle and tell her that he had been ousted and, gallingly, would have to leave his name behind on the business? His shame and bitterness obscured the objective revelation that this bleak harvest was the just and inevitable reward for his own betrayal of Giles Bane. He returned Bix Napier's look:

"So this is the thanks I get for dragging you out of the gutter. I knew you were sly but I didn't realise you were quite so shamelessly amoral. And as for the rest of you," he looked intently round the boardroom table, "you should all be ashamed of yourselves. You have sat there feeding off the fat of my endeavours for years and overnight you switch horses to this jumped-up barrow-boy. Well, good riddance to the lot of you: I will do everything in my power to make sure you and Napier fail."

He wasn't sure what he could do to make sure they would fail, but an empty threat was better than no threat at all. "My lawyers will be in touch to agree my settlement. You can all fuck off to hell." And with that eloquent farewell, like Giles before him, in high dudgeon he collected his papers into his briefcase and exited without another word.

The shock news that Archie Aspallan was to leave the firm that he started and which bore his name rippled out in widening circles from the Group, through the headhunting fraternity to the wider business community. Coming within a year of Giles Banes's equally shock departure, tongues were soon wagging knowledgeably that the ABC Group had hit the rocks and was sinking fast. Some sagely shook their heads and confirmed that it was inevitable, given the too-rapid expansion, the focus on growth at all costs, the paying over the odds for marginal acquisitions and the consequent diminution of focus and quality within an organisation which had lost sight of its core business and values. The more cynical within the Group, such as Noone, quoted from the Book of Corporate Life, Chapter

11, Verses 1-15, which went like this:

1. In the beginning was the Plan.

2. Then came the Assumptions.

3. And the Assumptions were without form.

4. And the Plan was without Substance.

5. And darkness was upon the faces of the Workers.

6. And the Workers spake amongst themselves crying, 'It is a crock of shit and it stinks.'

7. And the Workers went unto their Supervisors and said, 'It is a basin full of dung and we cannot live with the smell.'

8. And the Supervisors went unto their Managers, saying, 'It is a container of organic waste, and it is very strong, such that none may abide by it.'

9. And the Managers went unto their Directors, saying, 'It is a vessel of fertilizer, and none may abide its strength.'

10. And the Directors spake amongst themselves, saying verily one to another, 'It contains that which aids plant growth and it is very strong.'

11. And the Directors went to the Vice Presidents, saying unto them, 'It promotes growth, and it is very powerful.'

12. And the Vice Presidents went to the President, saying unto him, 'It has very powerful effects.'

13. And the President looked upon the Plan and saw that it was good.

14. And the Plan became Policy.

15. And that's how shit happens.

Naturally, the Press Release steered a different course, acknowledging gratefully Archie's tremendous contribution in building such a powerful force in the provision of human capital and a name synonymous with quality. He was leaving the Group in great shape and capable of embracing the challenges of the new century with Bix Napier at the executive helm, ready to drive it forward with his refreshing vision and dynamic leadership. Indeed, the Release quoted him: "We all owe Archie a huge vote of thanks for what he has achieved here and for recognising that it was time for change. I eagerly accept the responsibility for the care of the Group which he bequeaths to me and look forward to the support of our shareholders and employees as we jointly build an even greater company than it is today."

"Conniving, lying, cheating bastards," said Archie to the newspaper on his breakfast table, only marginally mollified by his £1.5m pay-off agreed by the lawyers two days previously, about which his lips were sealed by way of the Compromise Agreement which both parties had signed, and which therefore was carefully ignored in the Press Release.

"Sounds ominous," said Noone on the phone to Huff, as they digested the news and tried to make sense of the immediate present and the likely future without Hugo, Giles and Archie, dancing to the tune of Napier and Huxford.

"Yes," said Huff, "one hesitates to say that the lunatics have taken over the asylum, but they certainly are in the Governor's office. I'm not exactly sure where we go from here."

They soon found out. The day after the Press Release, Bix Napier called a meeting of the Group's senior management to outline his strategy. Huxford sat nodding beside him. Firstly, he reaffirmed the aim of driving the share-price from its current low of £1.52p to £5.00 over the next five years. This would be achieved through organic growth and diversification into non-recruitment-orientated HR products, so that the Group would be able to offer a much broader platform of services to clients, a 'one-stop-shop' if you like. Consultants would be encouraged and incentivised to 'cross-sell'. Importantly, Bix was keen to harness the burgeoning use of the internet. He had seen the future of recruitment and it was online. He wanted to be at the 'bleeding edge', as he put it, of technological development and create a web-based business which would become a conduit for candidates to post their CVs and act as a lightning interface between them and the clients' requirements. No more 'thirty days to shortlist': it would take hours at most. It would be brilliant, simple and unique. The Old Guard were horrified. Clearly, Napier wanted to work with blunt tools in "the mass market" and didn't understand all the subtleties of senior level recruitment. Following this less-than-inspiring vision of the future, another raft of ABC consultants and researchers quietly departed, leaving only a small rump of average performers. Whilst small rumps are admired in many quarters, they ill behove a formerly stellar search consultancy.

Equally, the drive had gone out of ABS, as evidenced by the number of disciplinary issues with which Linnet Trilby had to deal. Fanning the rumours of their affair, Rebecca Knightley organised a cocktail party at Balls Brothers' wine-bar for Rodney Shakeshaft's sixty-fifth birthday. So carried away was she by the adulatory event that the cost of both the present which she adoringly presented to him (a silver-topped cane costing £650 from Aspreys) and the £3,500 worth of champagne into which delighted London ABS employees piled with abandon, she unwisely tried to pass through her company credit card expenses as "client entertainment". Huxford withdrew the company credit card scheme shortly afterwards in an effort to curb "unnecessary or frivolous expenditure". At the same event, a male and female researcher were discovered *in flagrante delicto* in one of the ladies' lavatories. After they had emerged, tousled and wide-eyed, to loud cheers, the next visitor to the lavatory excitedly reported vestiges of white powder on the marble sink-surrounds.

One of the secretaries dissolved in tears at her desk and revealed between sobs over a cup of tea in Linnet's office that her husband had just walked out, saying that her supposed best friend "gave much better head than her". The news that she had "recently become single" unfortunately prompted Caspian Cordell to wage an unhealthy campaign of unrequited ardour for her favours. It started innocently enough with a drink after work, progressed more worryingly through roses delivered to her desk, and culminated scarily in him phoning her on his mobile from outside her flat before she went to work in the morning, to tell her what she was wearing even down to her underwear. Encouraged to mend his ways or face a police restraining order, Cordell found a job at one of the other large UK search firms where he was soon reprimanded for bonking one of the female partners who had become besotted with his blond, playboy good looks and dazzling smile and had made her intentions clear by reaching for his manhood while he was driving her to a client meeting.

One of Noone's FMCG team also had to be carpeted. This individual was renowned for his ability not to be able to hold his drink, as demonstrated by the domestic incident which had led directly to his divorce, involving Sunday lunch fortified by a bottle of claret followed by his narcolepsy at the wheel of a ride-on mower and the subsequent demolition of the garden shed, patio French windows, and, the final resting-place of the mower, the pond. Having invited his secretary out for a convivial, morale-boosting dinner, the drink unfortunately took hold and he unwisely revealed to her that she was the most hated person in the office. The next morning, he couldn't remember having said this, was surprised to find his secretary had phoned in sick and was even more surprised to be told why by Linnet, who once more was coping with a staff member in mental meltdown. He was not alone in having secretary trouble.

Another member of the FMCG team had gained a reputation for (figuratively) riding secretaries hard and running through them too quickly. At a small farewell drinks gathering in Walkers Wine Bar for his latest failure, he was accosted by the poor girl's boyfriend, who angrily accused him of ruining their lives and, before he had a chance to reply, bopped him on the nose before exiting triumphantly, dragging the girl behind him. The consultant then threatened to resign twice: firstly when he was forced to share a secretary (a hard-bitten, highly competent "stayer", who was the only one prepared to work for him); and secondly, when as a cost-cutting measure, Huxford decided to downgrade the biros which vanished at an alarming rate from the stationery cupboard to be scattered liberally on and around every single desk in the office. Because his fee revenues were high and valuable, the consultant was prevented from leaving "on this resignation issue" by being allowed to buy his own biros through "expenses".

The troubles weren't confined to London. Linnet had to deal with a Regional office where sex toys had been discovered in an air-conditioning duct in the office of the female Office Manager. Under questioning, the staff there mentioned her penchant for leather and rubber and complained of her overly tactile management style: breasts and thighs had been touched appreciatively and lingeringly. They also confessed to feeling intimidated by the late night meetings she held with "customers" behind closed blinds in her office, during which sounds usually associated with mutually satisfactory sexual congress would emanate. She had to go.

Elsewhere, three male consultants were reported for

pretending to be doctors on a night out, during which they held a competition to see who could proposition the most women and gather the most phone numbers. It only came to light because one of their targets turned out to be an off-duty policewoman from the Fraud Squad. The ringleader was asked to leave immediately, but was then discovered that night trying to break back into his office to remove a collection of porn videos that he had stashed in his filing cabinet there.

And then there was "Colonel" Ned R. Porage. His increasingly bizarre behaviour, possibly originating from the stress of combat from his army days, became a full-blown mid-life crisis. First he bought a Yamaha YZF-R1 motorcycle, "a 150bhp track bike to demolish rivals and wring the rider's adrenal glands dry" as Motorcycle News put it, and would tell the Birmingham office on a Monday morning what speed record he had broken over the weekend. Then he was heard to remark about the long-suffering Berthog, his formerly beloved wife, that she "was no good for sex after the age of forty". This preceded the appearance of a string of attractive young ladies from an escort agency who would arrive at the office door, "to take the Colonel out to lunch". Later, after he had brought a more mature model to the Birmingham office Christmas bash and introduced her as his girlfriend, the office Receptionist was accosted one day by an irate woman of substantial embonpoint and coiffured hair, seeking "Bob Jenkins".

"I am afraid we do not have a Bob Jenkins working here," she answered politely.

"Oh yes you do; he's my fiancé and I know he works here. I followed him here today," came the perplexing reply. At that moment "Colonel" Ned inadvertently popped his head round the door.

"There you are!" squealed the woman triumphantly. "That's him. I told you he was here you daft bitch. Now tell him I want to see him right now." Nobody was privy to the ensuing conversation, but the woman was never seen again.

Finally, "Colonel" Ned upset the schoolgirl who was spending a week in the office on work-experience. She breezed into his office to ask a question only to find him waxing his dolphin with considerable hand-speed to the accompaniment of the pornographic website "Big, black and bouncy". Her shriek and attendant faint necessitated the calling of an ambulance which sped her to A & E where she remained in deep shock and unable to talk of her trauma for seventy-two hours. This was one affront to human dignity too many and Huxford traveled to Birmingham, accompanied by Bob Ellis in case of trouble, to relieve "Colonel" Ned of his command, keys and computer passwords. Copped fairly, he went quietly. The clearing out of "Colonel" Ned's office revealed a cornucopia of pornographic literature, a hard drive stuffed full of hard porn, condoms and, rather unpleasantly, a bottom drawer of tissues containing dried "gentlemen's spendings". He had certainly been busy. When the gory details were leaked out by Bob Ellis to Noone, he took some satisfaction that Porage had at last been exposed as a total wanker.

"I always said the bloke was a nutter," Noone confided to Bob over a pint of Scruttocks.

"Proper East Ham," confirmed Bob, "one stop short of Barking. The whole office up there was terrified of him."

"Not surprised. We've lost the plot somewhere and I feel very uncomfortable," said Noone.

"Have I ever told you about the four ages of policing?" asked Bob.

"No, I don't believe you have," said Noone.

"Well," said Bob, "it goes like this: when you first join up, there is the Idealistic Stage. For most officers, this is their first time outside the comfort zone. They have never seen a dead body, never seen life-threatening injuries, never dealt with a family disturbance, never witnessed the shit some people call 'home life', and never really understood the phrase 'Man's Inhumanity To Man', until now. Everything is new to them. You can identify them by the amount of fancy new equipment they carry: a ten-billion-candlelight-power torch, pens that write in the rain, ballistic vest rated to stop Tomahawk missiles with lots of external pockets and straps, and an equipment bag large enough to house a squad of marines. They love it and can't get enough of it. They show up early for their shift; they work way past the end of it without considering an overtime slip. They believe rank within the job is based solely on ability and those in the upper ranks got there by knowledge and skill in police work alone. They believe everyone is competent, is on the same page and working towards the same high-minded goals. When they finally go home to their significant other, they tell them everything they did and saw. The ultra-keen ones even purchase a police scanner so they can hear the radio calls while at home."

"Yes," interrupted Noone, "that's exactly how I used to feel in the early days about ABS. Although I didn't purchase a police scanner, obviously."

"Next is the complete opposite, the Hostile Stage," continued Bob. "They now show up for work two minutes before their shift, and are hiding 30 minutes before its end, writing reports so they can chuck them in the Sergeant's in-box and leave ASAP. Their spouse is no longer interested in hearing about all the gore, heartache and 'real life stories'. They get the 'you spend more time with the cops than you do with me' speech. Often, this leads to the need for a second job to earn money to pay for the impending divorce from their insignificant other. They gripe about everything, drink excessively, chase women, and hate the public, politicians, media, all the people they are supposed to be protecting. They feel they have more in common with hookers, thieves, druggies, but hate them too. Those pens that write in the rain are no longer needed: writing traffic tickets can be a lot more trouble than they are worth, even on a nice day. To write one, or to write anything while standing in the rain, is a sure sign of madness."

"Ah," said Noone, "I recognise this too. It's when you learn how to work smarter because you've done it all before."

"Exactly," said Bob, "and the logical extension of this is the Superiority Stage.

This is when cops are at their best. They have survived the continuous changes in administration. They know how the political game is played, both inside and outside the job. They know whom they can trust and whom they can't. They have select friends within the job, and stay away, as best they can, from the nuts and boot-lickers. They know the legal system, the judges, prosecutors, defence solicitors, clerks of court. They know how to put a good case together and to stand in the dock and testify convincingly. They are usually the ones that the gaffers turn to when there is some clandestine request or sensitive operation that needs to be 'done right'. These cops are still relatively physically fit and can handle themselves on the street. They will stay around the station when needed, but have other commitments, such as a second spouse, a second girlfriend or both, and most of their friends are non-job."

"Yes, yes, just like us in the Old Guard here," said Noone proudly.

"But beware," warned Bob with a wag of his finger, "the fourth and final stage will surely follow and again it is a 180° turn. This is the Fearful Stage. Now the cops have a single objective: retirement and pension. Nothing is going to come between them and their monthly payslip. The boss, the Force, the idiots around the station, and the creeps on the street are all to be avoided, because they could prevent them 'sitting on the beach'. There is no topic of discussion that doesn't somehow lead back to retirement issues. These guys are usually sergeants, detectives, scenes-of-crime or community officers, or some other post where they will not be endangered. They have seen and done it all and especially don't want some young, stupid cop getting them sued, fired, killed, or anything else likely to lose their 'beach time'. They spend a lot of time having coffee, hanging around the station, and looking at brochures of things they want to do in retirement. But do you know the funniest thing?" asked Bob.

"No, tell me," said Noone.

"Most retired cops die within five years."

"Bloody hell," said Noone, "that's a bit of a chiller. And your point is?"

"If you don't want to go through the Four Stages yourself, bearing in mind you are already quite far down the line, you'd better do something about it. Shake it up or leave would be my advice."

"Good old Bob," said Noone admiringly. "As blunt as ever. Still, you have a point. By the way: you retired over five years ago and you are not dead."

"No," acknowledged Bob, "that's because I joined this madhouse!"

23. TRANSITION

"We bring a professional approach, and the confidence which comes from having worked with hundreds of organisations to find just the right person for a critical appointment – often at times of change and uncertainty. We have developed a unique process for executive search and selection, which we review and improve all the time. Every project is bespoke, and our search capability is renowned within the industry. And every project begins with original research. In fact, we typically call 100-150 potential candidates, as well as searching our existing database. (This also helps to keep our database as current, and far-reaching, as any you will find.)"

VEREDUS WEBSITE

Again, it was a reflective Noone who looked into the mirror one morning in early December 2000. He had dwelt on his conversation with Bob Ellis many times and was forced to conclude that Bob was right. No matter how much one might wish it, change was inevitable; the only variable was to what extent each individual was active or passive about it. Until now, Noone had passively accepted the changes in ABS, perhaps naively believing that the things that had deteriorated or that he didn't like would somehow self-correct and the cosy, glory days would return. He could now accept that Hugo Reeve-Prior's legacy of the most dynamic, confident and quality-driven selection business in the UK was being reshaped comprehensively and irrevocably by the dead hands of the outsiders Huxford and Napier. His malaise could be down to the onset of middle-age, which he felt he was still only approaching in his late forties, but he also had to accept that certain things were beginning to suggest otherwise.

Radio Two now played more songs he knew than Radio

One and had some really relevant and topical guests who spoke cogently about the decline of morals, standards and manners in society. He had stopped going to pop concerts because all pop music now sounded the same and even when he did, he would leave before the end to 'beat the rush'. Tribute Bands, however, were brilliant, and he had seen four different "The Beatles". He could now get more excited about having a Sunday roast than going partying the night before and rather than go clubbing, he quite fancied fancy restaurants and admired hanging baskets outside pubs. But before going anywhere, he always checked if there was anywhere to park.

He knew he would never play football or cricket for England, but he dreamed that his son might. Before instinctively throwing the local paper away, he now tended to look through the property section. Rather than throw a knackered pair of trainers out, he kept them because they were useful for DIY or 'in the garden'. A growing number of his T-shirts had nothing written on them and his oldest ones were too tight around the arms. In fact, although he had more disposable income than ever before, everything he wanted to buy cost between £200 and £500, but instead of laughing at the Innovations catalogue that falls out of the newspaper, he could see both the benefit and money-saving properties of many of the things in it.

He enjoyed building a garden shed and filling it with clutter, particularly all those things he was 'saving for a rainy day'. There was always enough milk in the house and the benefits of a pension scheme had become all too clear. Instead of tutting at old people who take ages to get off the bus, he would now tut at rowdy school children or young lads driving faster than himself. He had even caught himself saying: 'They don't make them like that anymore', 'Not in my day', 'Do you remember when beer was 11p a pint', and 'Is it just me or is it cold in here?' Finally and perhaps most damningly, he had started worrying about his health and appreciated that it was the most important thing to maintain as he got older.

He had to make a change before he vegetated. If he chose to go, to where would he go? He couldn't possibly contemplate another selection firm after having tasted the fruits of heaven with ABS, although he felt sure that his years of experience and executive director status with ABS would prove good currency in the market, as others had demonstrated. The Man Who Said Everything Twice was now running the selection business of a search boutique and Peter Serjeant was setting one up for a large US-based search firm seeking to expand its presence in the UK, to name but two. Noone had never been able to understand the snobbery that existed in search firms towards "lesser brethren" in selection. To his mind, the quality of service was identical and only the method of attracting candidates differed. He felt that search was too often offered as the resourcing methodology just because it was perceived as a more expensive product, rather than because it was the best tool for the job. Search consultants were no better qualified or more intelligent than selection consultants; indeed you could argue that much of their work was done for them by the researchers. Good researchers, who could uncover the hidden gem of a candidate, engage the individual through a random phone call and interest him or her in the job, were as valuable as Fabergé eggs. Largely unsung stars as far as Noone could make out.

Search consultants would take the credit for the placements however, inferring that they did all the hard work, whilst concealing the existence of researchers from naïve clients. In the Group, search and selection had been kept religiously apart and ABS consultants were told they had to aspire to search. Even then, they weren't exactly encouraged into Aspallan Bane, which is why so many had stepped onto the search ladder with other search firms outside the company. When Noone considered his "colleagues" at Aspallan Bane, he saw that they were more arrogant, more highly paid, but unquestionably no brighter than he. Whereas the average ABS assignment fee had crept up to around £17,000, he knew that the minimum

ABC fee was £30,000. The bonuses were said to be amazing, *possibly even up to seven figures.* Given that they had been haemorrhaging talent like ABS, perhaps it was time for Old Guard chaps like him to move across? The more he thought about it, the more the prospect appealed. His people management burden had taken increasing amounts of his time and this meant he spent less and less of it actually handling engagements. When his clients contacted him about a job, he tended to introduce them to one of his team who would handle the assignment. Unless, of course, there was a particularly attractive, high level role or a juicy fee. He was in danger of becoming a supernumerary supervisor and paper-pusher like Huxford.

"I'm thinking of asking for a transfer to ABC," he told his unassuming wife.

"Why?" she asked. He had not married her for her brains. He explained why and asked what she thought.

"I don't know. It's up to you." Emboldened by the endorsement he had anticipated, at first he considered confiding in Huff to see his reaction. So far, following Gordon Sharpe's abortive attempt, only one ABS consultant had been allowed to transfer across to ABC, and she had been so ostracised and criticised there that she had left, her nerves in shreds, after only six months. It hadn't helped that she chanced across her husband and their next-door neighbour's wife enjoying a mistletoe moment rather too lingeringly and subsequently discovering that they had been having an affair for seven years. She was found by the au pair, cradling an empty bottle of Bols Cherry Brandy in the family pooch's basket, whimpering that only the dog understood her misery, it having been killed by a hit-and-run driver two days previously. She had been carted off to The Priory to be straightened out and by all reports was now as mad as tea-party full of hatters. The omens were not good.

Perhaps he might persuade Huff to do the same and they could present a strong case as a team? After all, Huff had been a genuine headhunter once. But then again, if they were competing for a place, Huff would surely be chosen because of this experience. He decided it was best not to mention it. On one thing he was clear. He needed to bypass Huxford and go straight to Napier. He felt sure that Huxford would wish to stymie any such defections.

"Bix Napier's office, how may I help?" The soothing tones of Napier's throughbred Personal Assistant reassured Noone as he commenced his subterfuge.

"Adam Noone here," he replied. "Could I drop in on Bix one day soon?" he asked nonchalantly.

"Certainly. How about next Wednesday at 1030? May I tell him what it is about?" Noone was ready for this.

"Wednesday's fine. I have a business project which I would like to raise with him to ask his advice." He knew that with such weasel-words, many a researcher had been able to get past gatekeeper-secretaries and speak to their targets.

"Can you be more specific?" came the warm and silky reply, "just so he can be prepared." Uh-oh, she had obviously been trained heavily in the use of defensive counter measures.

"It's rather confidential and I think Bix would want it kept that way for the time being."

"Very well." Warm and silky had been replaced by haughty and frosty. "But he doesn't like me putting new things in his diary without knowing what they are about." She apparently saw no contradiction in what she had just said. Noone was discovering that Napier was a man who didn't like surprises.

"Just tell him it's a small matter of the future of ABS and ABC," Noone conceded wearily and patronisingly and put the phone down. Although he had always tried to establish open and honest relationships with his secretaries, Noone often found it difficult to be open and honest. At the start of their employment with him, they would be eager to please and stay late to complete tasks. When they made mistakes, Noone would lightly mention the way he liked things done and tell them not to worry.

Then came the critical stage. If they began to show initiative and an attention to detail, the relationship would flower: they could almost behave as equals could joke and even laugh at the odd mistake; his relationship with Alien had been like this. The bond would remain strong and friendly even beyond the time when the secretary would desert Noone for a husband and to have children. If, however, the mistakes persisted and no evidence of initiative was shown, a strained silence would descend. Noone would return drafts covered in red ink with little comment and the secretary would attend to the re-typing in hostile acceptance. It became a battle of wills: Noone would will the girl to resign while she would sullenly will him to sack her. Eventually, relations would deteriorate to the point when Linnet Trilby would tell Noone that she had been visited by his unhappy secretary and that he had to do something about it. Then he would sack her gently, suggesting that she might be happier working for another consultant, which he would ask Trilby to arrange, or indeed in another, less demanding business. Noone's ABS record of keeping three and losing three was in the upper quartile.

On Wednesday 21st February 2001, Notts County played Halifax Town Reserves, the Tayside Health Board agreed an overspend of £8m for its University Hospitals' NHS Trust, the Leyland Accordion Club opened its concert with Tulips From Amsterdam, and Spelthorne Council met and minuted grave concern at the increasing problem of youths congregating on street corners in the Borough and the implications for Fear of Crime and Youth Crime. How prescient it was. On the same day at 1030 precisely, Noone strode purposefully to the antechamber of Bix Napier's office, where the secretary whom he had offended glared at him.

"Mr Napier has somebody with him; I am afraid you'll have to wait," she said with considerable venom. Noone sat down and mentally rehearsed some of the lines he felt like practising on her:

'I can see your point, but I still think you're full of shit'; or 'You like never, don't you? Is never your middle name'? Or a sarcastic 'I see you've set aside time to humiliate yourself' and 'Nice perfume, but must you marinate in it'? Perhaps a more sweetly delivered 'I'm really easy to get along with once you learn to see it my way'; or more pointedly 'I don't know what your problem is, but I bet it is hard to pronounce'; then finally 'By the way, who lit the fuse on your tampon?' Yes, that one would certainly get her riled. But he resisted and merely smiled sweetly at her.

After an interminable ten minutes, Napier's door opened and Huxford came out. He looked at Noone pointedly and nodded as he went by. Noone was happy not to engage him in conversation and stood up as Napier beckoned him inside. He noted that Napier had inherited Giles Bane's furniture and aircraft-carrier-sized desk and fleetingly wondered what the old boy was doing now.

"Letitia tells me you were very coy about the nature of this meeting," Napier began with a disapproving look, "other than that it was a matter of life and death." What a cow, thought Noone; she was trying to make him look foolish.

"I didn't exactly say that Bix; just that it was a confidential matter, although I am sure she is very discreet."

"Of course she is discreet: she tells me everything," said Napier with a degree of menace. "She wondered whether you shouldn't be talking to Bly first?" So she was poisonous *and* dangerous, thought Noone. "Anyway, let's cut the crap. What do you want?" This exchange had hardly been a friendly and encouraging start to what Noone hoped would be a friendly and encouraging discussion about how he could enhance his contribution to the business.

"Well Bix," he began, "we are all worried about the state of the business. We have lost some good people in ABS and I know the same is true in ABC. Bly Huxford and Bob Ellis are busy trying to fill the hopper with new recruits but I wanted to suggest an additional measure."

"I see," said Napier slowly, "and what did you have in mind?" He did indeed think that all recruitment consultants were arrogant bastards who needed taking down a peg or two.

"Well. I'd like to volunteer for a move across to ABC," said Noone cautiously.

Napier paused for a second. "And why on earth would you want to do that?" he asked.

"I've been in ABS for over ten years now and to be honest, I'm ready for a change. I am worried that my network is getting rusty; I spend so much time managing people that there is hardly any time to develop business and even less to transact it. And that is not good for a recruitment consultant."

"No," said Napier, "that's not good for a recruitment consultant, not to be earning any fees." Noone hoped he detected some sympathy there but was equally concerned that he did not. He needed to generate some for sure.

"I could have just worked selfishly on my fee income, but I took on the management tasks because that is what the firm required. It's the eternal dilemma: either you stick to pure recruiting, become a primadonna and earn lots of money for yourself, or you try and contribute for the greater good and end up managing a whole load of people, which prevents you from recruiting. I have always been a team-player and therefore happy to do the latter, but I need to get back to my recruitment roots. And I'd like the chance to work as a headhunter in ABC." Noone couldn't put it more plainly than that. He hoped Napier wouldn't be too surprised.

Napier wasn't surprised. He had heard this before. In fact, a few days previously, that toffee-nosed Ughyngton-Fitzhardynge had visited him to suggest exactly the same thing. And he hadn't been the first. Napier wasn't sure which metaphor was the most appropriate: rats attempting to leave a sinking ship or flies gathering on a stinking shit.

Ever the entrepreneur, however, a plan was beginning to form in his mind, driven by his, and now apparently others', desire to see changes. There was only one thing worse than an arrogant, supercilious recruitment consultant and that was an arrogant, supercilious recruitment consultant who wasn't making the Group any money. If people like Noone and Ughyngton-Fitzhardynge were prepared to expose themselves to the rigours of business development and delivery on the grander stage of Aspallan, Bane Consultants, he would not stand in their way. If they proved successful, and were able to generate fees in excess of half a million pounds a year, then under the less favourable (to them) new remuneration terms he was about to introduce, they would be making more money for the company. If they failed, he would terminate them. He didn't care either way.

Besides, he was already working on his internet-based Masterplan and had briefed three sets of web-designers to put forward their ideas for the world-spanning, CV-capturing, client-delighting website with which he would steal global domination and dispense with expensive, arrogant, supercilious recruitment consultants. Bix was convinced that by using this new business channel, recruitment could be speeded up using technology, made more cost effective through the saving in time and more efficient as an overall consequence while removing the dependence on consultants to transact the business. He would revolutionise the way recruitment worked and be hailed as a fearless "dot.com" pioneer. That would show them. Reluctantly, he returned his mind from these exciting musings on impending greatness and glory to this fool in front of him. Let him stick his neck out if he wanted to: all consultants were expendable.

"So you want to play in the big league, do you? Bit of a high-risk strategy, don't you think, leaving your comfort zone for the sake of a more lonely existence as a Search Consultant? Especially if, as you say, your network is rusty."

"Not really," replied Noone, flushed with naïve eagerness. "I feel I have been training for it all my life in Selection and I am definitely ready to make the transition. ABC has a great name and some great clients, so there is plenty to work with."

If it were that simple, thought Napier, why have the "big hitters" of yore left ABC? Several went out of allegiance to Giles Bane, and one or two similarly followed Aspallan out. Some had gone to other major consultancies, a few had set up new "boutique" businesses. None of those who had left were prepared to tolerate any attempt to modify their bonuses. Come to think of it, the few that were left were distinctly average billers. The brand needed all the help it could get and even then, Napier doubted its future once his internet business had taken wing. Best shore it up in the short term with willing fools like Noone until he, Napier, decided what to do with it.

"Well you are not the first one to ask for a transfer and I suppose you have been a loyal servant," he said, in a more conciliatory tone, "and deserve a promotion. But," he warned, "we will have to find someone for your role in London for ABS: there will be no going back, you understand." Noone understood. He was interested to hear that he was not alone in seeking ABC and he asked Napier who his fellow travellers might be.

"Sabra Termigniogni, Rodney Shakeshaft and Ughyngton-Fitzhardynge. I am going to move you all over and I am changing the employment terms in ABC to accommodate you. Working there will not be a licence to print money like it was in the cosy old days, but you will be able to earn up to 40% of your billings. Linnet Trilby will issue your new contract." So there it was, fait accompli, easier than expected. Noone was to be a real headhunter.

"One more thing," said Napier, standing up as he did so, "I have made Barry Bargewell MD. You will report to him." Napier ushered Noone through his door and into the disapproving gaze of Letitia, which Noone avoided, instead allowing a small, superior smile to play across his face as he walked to the lift lobby.

Barry Bargewell, eh? That was a bit of a setback. Of all the gloriously revered consultants from the golden days of ABC, Barry Bargewell was the least glorious and least revered. In fact, he was neither glorious nor revered. He had been brought into the business in the late Eighties as "a runner" by Giles Bane, having been masquerading as Marketing Director for the experimental pre-alcopop alcopop division of Universal Beverages. Bargewell, a big, bluff fellow, had made the most of his limited talents by allowing his father to buy him a scholarship to his father's Cambridge College, St Crispins, where he resolutely pursued women and champagne in equal measure and avoided libraries and lectures so successfully that, anonymous and unrecognised by his tutors, he was able to pay a stand-in to take his Final exams, emerging with a creditable 2nd. Thus armed and accepted by the Universal Beverages graduate management training scheme, he had specialised in marketing, where the key requirements had been an ebullient personality, loud voice, penchant for vacuous ideas and the ability to spend lots of money. Bargewell possessed all these attributes.

He had progressed by default rather than diligence or drive and when the Marketing Director of a minor brand, Vodkatinski, was fired for being drunk and disorderly at his desk, Bargewell was offered the position with an attendant caution not to over-sample the product. The vodka base for Vodkatinski was mass-produced in a large, bland distillery in Newbury, with twice fermented wheat "for that authentic Russian flavour". Into it was mixed dry vermouth (one part vermouth to ten parts vodka) and just enough angostura bitter to render it vaguely pink. It was packaged into clear glass 75cl bottles shaped like Marilyn Monroe's torso, onto which were stamped random Cyrillic letters and sent out into the world as "a delicious European fusion of the new, zestful, Eastern pioneering spirit and the mature, sophisticated Western taste, designed to electrify both young and old." It was revolting, but had achieved minor cult status in northern towns where, in mid-winter, bare-chested youths and micro-skirted girls chose it as a badge of defiance, if not honour, to neck down whilst teetering or tottering from club to club.

Having been dealt this limited hand, Bargewell's own limited abilities ensured that Vodkatinski remained bypassed by mainstream marketing budgets and meandered up and down a few percentage points each year to languish in the long grass marked "profitable but unexciting". Then, out of the blue, he had been called by a young researcher working for Aspallan, Bane, Consultants who was undertaking "desk research" on behalf of Giles Bane for a FTSE 100 FMCG Head of Marketing role. On the phone, Bargewell had made much of the illusory tremendous success he had created for Vodkatinski and impressed the researcher enough to be summoned in to meet the great man, Giles Bane. Within five minutes of meeting him, Bane knew that Bargewell was too lightweight for the job, a rough and ready, mass-produced Ford Escort instead of the smoothly purring, limited edition, hand-built Ferrari he sought.

However, he recognised in Bargewell the qualities of obedience, lack of imagination, and an eagerness to please, allied to some experience "in the field" of business, which suggested that he could be the raw material for a search consultant. With consummate ease, Bane "turned" Bargewell, pointing out kindly in his avuncular fashion that he was not quite right for the client's role, and whilst time would obviously count in his favour, had he considered making a career change, perhaps into the exciting and well rewarded world of headhunting? Of course Bargewell, to whom the idea of "thinking outside the box" was way outside his box, hadn't, though he was predictably flattered to be asked about it, as Bane had surmised.

Thus he had become Bane's "bag-carrier", initially just

fetching-and-carrying at the whim of Giles Bane. Over time, he was passed a couple of clients "to play with" as his own and thanks mainly to the brilliance of the bright, young graduates and seasoned matrons who made up the research team, succeeded in completing more assignments than not. He learned the gift of the search consultant's gab and was able to win a few FMCG clients of his own, which kept him fed and watered, even if his light shone dimly compared with the brilliance of some of the megastars around him in ABC. Finally, after Bane and Aspallan had quarrelled terminally, Napier had taken control and seen off Aspallan, and all those stars had departed in high dudgeon to shine in new or alternative firmaments, Bargewell doggedly remained as almost the last of the ABC Old Guard, basically because no other search firm wanted him.

Bix Napier conceived his plan for ABC around the thought that as Bargewell had so far failed to shine, he might as well try management. He breezed into Bargewell's office one day and came straight to the point:

"Barry, I am deeply concerned about ABC." He wasn't, but he didn't want Bargewell to know it. "We have lost critical mass and all the highest billers, revenues are a pale shadow and it will probably lose money this year for the first time in its history. It is fast disappearing up its own arsehole, not to put too fine a point on it. Something must be done and I want you to do it: Barry, I am making you Managing Director of ABC. I want you to rebuild it and recover its former pre-eminent position in the league of global headhunters. Are you up for it?"

"Up for it? I sure am," replied Bargewell, affecting a strange, mid-Atlantic twang which he felt enhanced his image as a macho go-getter, for whom the bigger the challenge, the better he rose to it. "Fantastic, great, just what I have been waiting for. We need to repackage and relaunch the brand pronto," he said, lapsing into the marketing jargon that he often used as a substitute for action.

"You need to get some bodies in there quickly; there may be one or two in ABS we can transfer in," said Napier, already ahead of the game.

"Don't worry Bix, I am on the case and I won't let you down."

"I know you won't," said Napier, knowing he would. If a bumbling fool like Bargewell could resurrect ABC, he would eat his hat, not that he ever wore one. "Good luck and let's review progress regularly." Napier bustled out, leaving Bargewell bathing in projected glory.

Bargewell smiled to himself. He had outlasted all those flash bastards, even Aspallan and Bane themselves, and made it to the top. In his view, his triumph had been entirely based on merit, diligence and loyalty. He completely lacked the self-awareness which would have enabled him to see himself as others saw him. He had smiled in the face of ABC's recent adversity and chaos and remained calm, largely because he failed to understand the seriousness of the situation. For Bargewell, indecision was the key to flexibility and he never put off until tomorrow that which he could avoid altogether. He knew that plagiarism saved time and that teamwork meant never having to take all the blame himself when things went wrong; when the going got tough, he would be tough enough to take a coffee-break. Unfortunately, his secretary would undermine him by noting to her girlfriends that his ineptitude with technology proved that artificial intelligence was no match for natural stupidity.

This, then, was the man-mountain in whom Napier had invested the resurrection of the once-pioneering institution of Aspallan, Bane Consultants. Noone had every right to be deeply concerned.

24. ABC REBORN

"Since we started in 1986, we've adhered to one passionate belief: excellent executive search depends on doing your own original, rigorous research. We've grown into one of the UK's leading executive search firms by combining that focus on research with real insight into the dynamics and leadership requirements of organisations across the globe. Our involvement is long term, intimate, analytical. Our search consultants work closely with our psychological assessment specialists. By assessing the top team and abstracting their core values, we can help clients build those values into the way they recruit - not just at the top, but at all levels."

SAXTON BAMPFYLDE WEBSITE

By the time Noone attended his first "management" meeting at ABC one Monday early in 2001, Napier-encouraged changes had already occurred. The lease had been relinquished on the 5,000 square feet of self-contained magnificence that had been the office of Aspallan, Bane Consultants for so many years and its remaining denizens had grudgingly and with dragging heels moved across to Berkeley Street to "slum it" with ABS, albeit on another floor of the building. For the Aspallan, Bane secretaries, or "PAs" as they now universally called themselves, it was particularly hard. Well-bred, haughty but confident and efficient in their roles as business partners for the consultants, for whom they worked "one-on-one", they had been accustomed to being treated with respect by clients, deference by candidates, courtesy by their consultants and fear by any other personages that dared to engage them, particularly the oiks from ABS. Now, heavens above, they were forced to mix with those oiks on a daily basis! And the ABS secretaries! They were plainly mindless, gossipy schoolgirls, easily distracted from the job and endlessly chattering about the qualities or deficiencies of current and aspirant boyfriends and the venue and duration of last night's shag.

Worst of all, they now had to "look after" two consultants apiece, signalling an end to the cosy "one-on-one" relationships that had been such a strength in the past. (Except, of course, for the newly-promoted Barry Bargewell's PA, Deidre Fettle. His management tasks required complete confidentiality and neither he nor she could be compromised by having to share with others). It was shocking: how were they supposed to cope? Two resigned immediately on principle and the rest formed a seething, toxic residue hardly beneficial to the relaunch of ABC. Bargewell seemed blithely unaware as he set about building his empire. Certainly, Deidre Fettle was unlikely to enlighten him; he had acquired her several years back after she had been laid financially and reputationally low by a court-case she had brought against her former employer, a supermodel. Their relationship had been stormy ("Well, we all have our Epsom Downs" Deidre had quipped to a girlfriend) with both parties frequently verbally abusing the other. Deidre would react to the more volcanic eruptions of her employer ("You stupid bitch, where did I leave my Filofax?") with icily measured ripostes ("If madam would care to use her eyes before opening the sewer that masquerades as her mouth, she would find the Filofax on the sideboard.") until the day when the supermodel lost it completely and flung her mobile phone at Deidre for stupidly arranging two interviews in one day with different fashion magazines.

"Bitch, bitch, fucking stupid bitch," she howled, as the phone disintegrated against the wall above Deidre's head. "You know I cannot possibly prepare properly for two in one day." Deidre knew alright, but had decided to risk it. The diatribe which followed the launching of the phone was the last straw, and Deidre sued for assault. In court, her employer's smarmy lawyer had painted her as a scheming, money-grabbing lesbian, obsessed with the supermodel, so jealous of her employer's contact with other people that she had deliberately sabotaged her diary. The idiot, mainly male jury, overawed by being in the same room as the glamorous and sexy supermodel, decided that poor, frumpy Deidre was indeed an ungrateful subordinate with psychotic tendencies and found against her. The ruined Deidre had retreated into herself, only speaking when spoken to and avoiding eye-contact whenever possible. An agency had sent her along in response to Barry's request to interview a quiet, efficient Personal Assistant. Barry thought she was perfect, especially as she called him "Mr Bargewell" throughout the interview. They had settled into a relationship like a platonic married couple, Deidre coping uncomplainingly with Barry's permanent state of frenzied disorganisation. She managed him well and kept intruders at bay, whilst hiding him from any malicious gossip that she might have heard around the office.

Noone had spent what remained of December after his tête à tête with Napier busily tidying up and closing down his affairs at ABS. One affair which he felt didn't require termination was his dalliance with Nerissa Wadsworth. She had been on client business in town on the day of the much-reduced London Office Christmas lunch in late December: no more the grand all-company gesture in Paris, or even Cliveden, with consultants flying in from all over the country. This time, Huxford had encouraged the regional offices to hold their own Christmas bash locally and urged them to keep to a budget of £20 per head. Apart from one or two of the Scottish offices, they all ignored the budget ceiling, with the Office Managers intending to lose any overspend in "client expenses". As she was already in town, Noone had suggested that Nerissa gate-crash the London party and stay in town for the night. He had already informed his wife that he would spend the night at his club in town, for the Christmas lunch was bound to be taxing and would inevitably carry on into the evening as the alcohol consumed drove ever-raging thirsts, the slaking of which would be bound to lead to pubs (and inevitably clubs later on, although this latter piece of information he elected not to pass on to his wife).

In the spirit of thrift, Noone had directed the London Christmas party to The Chopper Lump in Hanover Square- not an obviously festive choice of venue as it was subterranean, gloomy and sprinkled with token sawdust across its mock-wooden floor. It was perfectly adequate as far as Noone was concerned, making a passable fist at "Olde English" vittles, which stretched to roast turkey with all the trimmings at Christmas: overcooked, crumbly breast, pre-formed and sliced into neat, uniform ovals, bizarre stuffing with pasty chestnuts concealed within it, bullet-hard roast potatoes, soggy, drowned sprouts, limp "caramelised" carrot slivers, stodgy cranberry jelly from a jar and a triumph of solidified bread sauce to top it all off. However, Noone knew that this could all be washed down successfully by pints of Davey's Old Wallop real ale and bottles of perfectly quaffable House sauvignon blanc and claret.

Come the day, Thursday 14th December, at the very moment that Barnsley Metropolitan Borough Council was united in congratulating itself on receiving a letter from Superintendent Price of the South Yorkshire Police congratulating the Council on its stand against racial harassment and simultaneously informing the Council of the award of a commendation to P.C. Jane Rees, the Community Constable for the South West Area, in recognition of her efforts to combat and eradicate racial harassment in the course of her duties, ABS London trooped out of Berkeley Street and descended into the bowels of The Chopper Lump. The secretaries were already bedecked in strings of tinsel, foam reindeer horns and red plastic noses or floppy, Father Christmas hats. Darth Gwent had acquired a tie which depicted Rudolf with a battery-powered, flashing red nose. Snapping crackers soon afforded everyone else suitable coloured-paper headgear. Noone eyed Nerissa's bust covetously, silently appreciating the properties of Wonderbra, so uplifting for the boys.

At first the jollity was forced, the conversation stilted and embarrassed, as the male Consultants impressed the secretaries with their wit and worldliness while the female Consultants talked fashion and au pairs amongst themselves. Gradually, the alcohol began its inevitable and insidious inhibition interference. Synapses fired up, laughter loosened the awkwardness and the lunch party hit full swing by the arrival of the Christmas pud. Rebecca Knightley and Rodney Shakeshaft were whispering to each other on the corner of one of the tables, Darth Gwent was impressing a couple of doe-eyed researchers with the measurements of his brand-new BMW Z3 sportscar (hairdresser's car, in Noone's view) and Caspian Cordell, who was working his notice period with gay abandon, seemed to have a couple of the secretaries in hand as well. Only Visa Maunfeld and Sara Sternhold were soberly drinking orange juice and commenting disapprovingly on the noise level. Noone did not notice a shadow emerging from one of the dark recesses of the basement to the side of the ABS party area until it was too late. A wet kiss was planted from behind on his balding pate and in shock, he looked up to see the leering face of "Colonel" Ned R. Porage looming above him.

"Hello Noone, old boy, thought you'd got rid of me?" He looked flushed and pissed. Noone rapidly took stock: he could tell Porage to fuck off, or he could be falsely polite. He chose the safe option.

"Ned, old chap, how good to see you," he lied effortlessly, "I was wondering what you were up to? What brings you down to London?"

"Set up m'yown business. S'great. Nobody interferes. Can do what I like for my clients and go wherever I shoes." Added to his slurred words, there was a manic gleam in his eyes. Noone was amazed that any client would choose to work with Porage. One or two of the consultants who had known him and relished the prurient rumours surrounding his demise came up to engage in a little banter.

"Still getting good service from the Jodrell 0900 numbers Ned?" asked Darth Gwent playfully, as Caspian Cordell leaned across to slip a spoon filled with cranberry jelly surreptitiously into one of "Colonel" Ned R. Porage's inviting jacket pockets. "How is Miss Whiplash these days?" Porage's face turned even more puce and Noone wondered whether there was going to be an indoor rerun of his famous battle in Oman. But Porage's judgement had not become totally impaired by drink and he recognised that in a fight, the strength and size of the consultants in front of him were a different prospect to the fuzzy-wuzzies of his glorious yesteryear.

"Jus' fuck off, the lod of you," he said, with all the dignity he could muster, before turning on his heel and marching unsteadily back to a dim corner of the room where he disappeared once more into the shadows.

"There always was something of the night about him," mused Noone aloud.

"Something every night, I heard," chortled Caspian, as he turned back to the adoring researchers.

Noone began to concentrate on Nerissa, who had been talking a little too animatedly to a sharp-suited male researcher. By now the formal lunch proceedings had finished and the tables had broken up, with people standing and moving around, smaller groups forming, the chatter increasing in volume, punctuated by shrieks or brays of laughter. Noone beckoned Nerissa to join him and she complied with a wink. As she slid into the seat beside him, she reached for his hand under the table and gave it a squeeze. He roamed his hand under her skirt to the upper reaches of her thigh, where he discovered, joy of joys, the soft flesh between her stocking tops and her panties. His growing erection was cut short prematurely by Caspian shouting that as the sun was now past the yardarm (it was 4.30) they should all go forth into the night and party on at a great place he knew. Noone encouraged everyone to follow Caspian and graciously accepted the apologies of Visa Maunfeld and Sara Sternhold, the Ungrateful Dead as he thought of them. He wouldn't have been surprised if they were going home for a bit of mutual carpet-munching. He ushered Nerissa ahead of him, watching her pneumatic posterior every inch of the way up the stairs into the crisp December air.

Caspian's "great place" turned out to be Digress in Beak Street, a long narrow bar of shiny new wood, coloured chairs and stools. Quirkily, there was an electronic "scoreboard" which counted people in and out, so that you knew how many people were inside at any one time. The twenty or so from ABS doubled the tally substantially. Inevitably, since it was popular with the younger Soho drinkers, it did not sell "proper" beer, but you could get bottles of foreign muck with lime stuck in the neck to inhibit the gassy taste. However, on the plus side, they landed just as Happy Hour commenced. Noone sought refuge from the fizz in gin-and-tonics and his sense of time began to disappear along with his self-control. He vaguely remembered exchanging meaningful glances with Nerissa as the drinks went down, vaguely remembered the walk to Dover Street Wine Bar, vaguely remembered dancing with Nerissa and several secretaries, vaguely remembered escorting her to her hotel, vaguely remembered giggling drunkenly in the lift as they groped and snogged their way to the fifth floor and vaguely remembered collapsing into bed with her warm and voluptuous breasts pressed to his lips. He vaguely remembered attempting to commence cunnilingus to repay the Cliveden blow-job, but somehow Nerissa had fallen asleep and shortly afterwards so did he. Despite this and the inevitable hangover difficulties in the office the next day (thank god it was Friday and nobody had to try too hard) Noone judged the "budget Christmas party", his last as the ABS Old Guard, to have been a qualified success.

The retail frenzy which masqueraded as Christmas

loomed ever-larger, swallowing all in its path. Prospecting for business in December was almost pointless because of festive distractions, approaching year-ends, and collective anticipation of sun-, snow- or sex-based holidays. Clients and prospective clients were, however, unusually receptive to invitations to lunch, and most consultants put on weight in the lead-in to their own family Christmas food-binges, during which they would put on more weight. It was a tired, jaded, bloated cadre of consultants which returned to work in January. Noone effected his transfer to ABC by briefing his successor, the lawn-mower crasher now deemed a safe pair of management hands, on how appalling Huxford was as MD, and removing his belongings to his new office one floor below. Greeting his arrival, thoughtfully printed and positioned in the middle of his desk by his (shared) secretary, was a haughty memo from Bix Napier.

"You may have seen the piece in the Sunday Times, commenting on people who have left ABC". Indeed Noone had; the news that a pointedly accurate article had appeared spread like wildfire and the Sunday Times had become required reading the previous weekend.

"Like so many such scurrilous, speculative and muck-raking articles," continued Napier's memo suavely, "it is important to keep it in perspective. We are reshaping the business so it is fit-for-purpose and capable of going forward. This does not mean we will replicate inferior structures and practices which may have worked in the past but will not serve us effectively in the future. We will not, in the future, worship the cult of a small number of primadonna individuals, but instead be a robust, integrated organisation supported by strong systems and offering varied careers to those who work with us. We are building a customer-focused recruitment and training business which includes the contracting and contingency areas."

Those last few words "contracting and contingency" tolled heavily. Noone could feel Napier's hatred of the highly successful former ABC consultants, who had absconded with Giles Bane, burning through the page of the memo. Napier resented the past successes, power and reputation of "former" ABC and was determined not to depend on their ilk again. Noone could understand that, since Napier didn't understand the intricate subtleties of executive search and selection, but "contracting and contingency" definitely set alarm bells ringing; Giles Bane and Archie Aspallan would be turning in their graves if they were here to hear those words uttered in the context of the once-glorious tradition and ideals of the business which bore their name. And what would Hugo Reeve-Prior have made of the word "recruitment" so recklessly positioned at the beginning of a statement about strategy? Noone could see Hugo's face puckering up in distaste, as if he had taken a swig of malt vinegar instead of malt whisky. There seemed little doubt that Napier intended to cheapen and coarsen the output of both ABC and ABS, aiming for volume rather than style. Not for the first time, Noone felt the frisson of a cold wind of change running down his back. However, for the time being, he had no option but to wait and see where this ill wind might blow him. He was ready for his first consultants' meeting in ABC.

He surveyed his new colleagues with initial interest followed by increasing concern. The known quantities were his fellow travellers from ABS, hand-picked by Bix Napier to re-seed Aspallan, Bane Consultants: Huff, of course, he both liked and appreciated, amused by his aristocratic eccentricities; Rodney Shakeshaft had been diplomatically "bumped upstairs" to create some distance between himself and Rebecca Knightley. At least he still had cronies on the boards of plcs who would give him work. Amazingly, and against Noone's advice, Sabra Termignioni had also been promoted on the back of the £500k of business she had written in 2000 with one large fashion house, La Femme Qui Chant. He watched her ostentatiously filing her blood-red nails and shivered at the wayward thought that had her raking his back with those talons as he rode her to an explosion of ecstasy. She looked up, caught his eye, winked and resumed her filing.

Sat next to Sabra was Stephen Addergoole, the only other remaining ABC search consultant. He was a dull, grey, ingratiating little man, who, like Barry Bargewell, had been left behind in the mass exodus of talent because he was deemed talentless. This was a tad harsh, as he had deliberately cultivated boring personnel directors in the automotive sector, whence he had materialised, having reached the dizzy heights of Production Manager for a line of nearly obsolete cars which represented the dying throes of the once-great British car industry. Addergoole found favour with the personnel departments of the automotive community who were easily impressed by unimpressive people like Addergoole who "talked the talk" and they passed him work: dull, mundane, manufacturing and production assignments for a dull, mundane man. Noone could perfectly understand why Addergoole had been left behind in the stampede for the exit: he may indeed "talk the talk" but he didn't "walk the walk".

Next to Addergoole, and looking somewhat nervous and apprehensive, came the first of the new recruits, Henchley Longbad. Longbad had apparently made a name for himself in a search "boutique" where he had specialised in anything that had come his way, working ridiculous hours and generating more business than he could handle satisfactorily. It was the need for a greater support infrastructure that drove him towards ABC. This was the first time Noone had met him and he thought Longbad looked out of place: he wore a brown suit and shoes (both of which were absolute style crimes, in Noone's view) a pale blue shirt and what looked suspiciously like a polyester tie, with broad dark and light blue stripes, also style suicide. Perhaps worst of all was his short, wiry black hair, which appeared to have been worked into a quiff at the front *with gel.* He became aware of Noone's visual appraisal, nodded and said "alright, mate" in a West Country burr. Shocking.

Seated on Longbad's left was the second newcomer, Amber Reddie. Again, Noone had not met her, but he had seen her CV, and she came well recommended by Bargewell; a retail specialist, she had joined Marks & Spencer as a graduate trainee, progressed steadily through the buying and merchandising ranks in Ladieswear and left before she became institutionalised. She joined Dolce & Gabbana, being promoted as far as Head of UK Operations before being headhunted to a niche fashion house, Katz, as Commercial Director. There she fell out with the owner over whether to extend Katz's line of elegant satin lingerie into "thongs for the discerning woman"- not something, thought Noone, which would appear on a Frank Sinatra album. A mutual friend introduced her to Barry Bargewell, who had been overwhelmed by her ability to name-drop and persuaded her that this talent would stand her in great stead as a prospective headhunter. And here she was, small, wiry, skittish as a sparrow, with dark, darting eyes and hands fluttering constantly, touching her hair, playing with the pen on the leather-clad personal organiser before her. Noone decided she would be fairly high maintenance: how right he proved to be.

Finally, seated next to Barry Bargewell at the head of the Boardroom table, was Dexter Macdangle, the third of the new faces. Yet another seemingly unimpressive individual, his career had been spent in the Personnel (subsequently renamed Human Resources) departments of large FMCG companies. His last role had been as HR Director of a frozen food producer and when Barry had appeared in response to his call to discuss the appointment of a new Sales Director, the two of them had hit it off immediately. They felt unthreatened by (and safe in) each other's mediocrity and they laughed conservatively at the brilliant little jokes each made at someone else's expense. Uncertain of themselves amongst powerful peers, they revelled in their common bond of superior, management-speak catch-phrases and in-jokes. Macdangle was tall and broad, running to fat, with thinning hair and a louche, diffident air. Noone thought he looked extremely satisfied with himself for no discernible reason, sitting there with an unnecessary smirk on his face. Well, he would soon find out what it took to become a successful search consultant!

Noone reflected on that thought for a moment. Did he himself know what it took to become a successful search consultant? From his perspective as a successful selection consultant, it was only mildly daunting. After all, Reeve-Prior had drummed into everyone at ABS that the only difference between the selection work that ABS consultants carried out and the search work in Aspallan, Bane was the methodology of attracting candidates; selection spread the net as wide as possible by throwing an advertisement out into the ether, search "rifle-shotted" those where the requirement was narrow and therefore the universe of potential candidates was small, discrete and readily identifiable. Noone now acknowledged that Reeve-Prior had cleverly reduced the differentiation to this simple formula to boost NBS's self-esteem: they could all believe that they were real search consultants, it was just that only the "front end" was different. Everything else was the same, including the all-important focus on quality. Indeed, when ABS consultants had rubbed shoulders occasionally with their colleagues in Aspallan, Bane, almost always they had reported being completely underwhelmed by their snooty and surprisingly shallow approach to clients.

As Noone now realised, Reeve-Prior had carefully protected them from the scorn of their lofty brethren; it was actually all about *level*. The Aspallan, Bane folk looked down on ABS because there was a gulf in assignment salary levels, and therefore fee levels, separating them. They were mostly older (therefore wiser) with better-established "old boy" networks; their chums from school or university were more highly placed in industry, banking or commerce, where they were earning a minimum of a quarter of a million. This produced invitations to talk about FTSE 100 or 250 roles at that level, not the fiddling little sub-£100k stuff in which ABS swam. As he was about to take the step up to that level, Noone could now appreciate the subtleties of difference which Hugo had blithely glossed over. He felt apprehensive and hoped, without much confidence as he surveyed his new colleagues, that Barry and Addergoole, the remnants of Old ABC, together with Shakeshaft, would provide the introductions to the Great and the Good which he undoubtedly needed to survive. For the first time, he regretted his rash decision to cast away the comfort of the well-worn cardigan of ABS.

"Welcome everyone," Barry interrupted Noone's disconcertion, "to our brave new world!" Noone wondered whether Barry was another one who spoke only in clichés; he was.

"It's great to have you all on board at a very exciting time in our development and thanks to you all for standing up and being counted." Noone felt it was perhaps too early in his relationship with Barry to point out that they were all seated.

"I don't want to rake over lost coals," continued Barry, "or beat around the bush. Aspallan, Bane is a pale shadow of its foremost self. The fact is we have a lot of hard work ahead to rebuild this place and turn the ship about, but we can do it if we all pool together and fly the flag. Irregardless of what our enemies may say, the brand still has excellent recognition in the market and that will help us bring in work over the transom. The proof is in the pudding, as they say, and it's up to us guys…let's do it."

Barry sat back, flushed with the effort of his inspiring speech. Noone was appalled: this lunatic was to be his boss? God help them. Noone wondered whether Barry really believed that he could lead his troops to success or whether the rhetoric was the instinctive, convulsive twitch of the dedicated marketer who couldn't help but talk in platitudes, malapropisms and sound-bites.

The round-table conversation which followed greatly inspired Noone even less. Amber Reddie, who seemed to have an opinion on everything, featured prominently, dropping the names of all her dear friends in high places, who would undoubtedly give her oceans of business. For one who was new to the trade, Dexter Macdangle seemed to have an equally firm set of opinions on how they should go about things and Sabra was as vociferous as always, in that delicately deranged, Italian way of hers. Barry warned that current global trends, the UK economy and ABC's own business performance "were all tightening". There was no doubt in his mind that the focus had to be on "sales, sales and more sales". Everyone must be "a keen business hunter" and responsible for generating a surplus of fee-income, enough to more than cover their costs. Noone's heart sank still further: this was just the sort of gung-ho, positive, fighting talk that had such a negative effect on consultants.

"So what exactly is our fee target, Barry?" he enquired, with a mounting sense of dread.

"We haven't quite finalised that yet, Adam, but we should have all our pigeons in a row by the end of the week." Barry replied. Noone wondered who the royal "we" was; he supposed Barry and Napier.

"Do we get any input into the figures?" chipped in Huff.

"Not really as such," said Barry, "you see, we have fixed costs to cover and cover them we must, so that's the bottom line. I am sure you all know the score and the formulas, so it won't be a surprise to anyone." Charming, thought Noone, they were to be given arbitrary targets over which there was to be no discussion. This was truly inspirational leadership at its finest.

The tricky task of conveying the bad news to each consultant about his or her target revenue for the year almost proved too much for Barry. He was caught between the rock of Napier's demand that ABC should turn in fee income revenues of at least £5m (itself a pitiful fall-off from the glory years, when £20m was the minimum that could be expected) and the hard place of having to confront each consultant with an individual performance target of fees that might range between £300k and £500k. The end of the week came and went, as did the end of the month, while Barry agonised, brushing the issue aside in the vain hope that it would go away of its own accord. But it wouldn't.

Finally, in mid-March, Barry decided that the easiest thing was to give them all the same target of £400k. He sent an email to each of the consultants accordingly and sat back, congratulating himself that he had handled a difficult situation with the minimum of fuss and an equitable outcome. He was therefore somewhat surprised when one-by-one, they collared Deidre to find time in Barry's diary "to discuss the fee target". The message from them all was the same: they would have appreciated the chance to talk about the target before agreeing, and given the tightening market and the fact that they were trying to rebuild ABC pretty much from scratch, they all felt the target was wildly optimistic and were concerned about the potential lack of a bonus payment. The newcomers to search were particularly vocal.

Barry plaintively relayed the problem to Napier, but predictably received short shrift.

"They have been mollycoddled for far too long and should be glad to be in jobs," was his helpful reply. "They don't know what hard work is, so now they can find out. We cannot afford to carry any who don't perform; they must bill three times their costs as a minimum. And Barry," Napier continued ominously, "I suggest you carry on recruiting new consultants because not all of them are going to make it. They must adapt to the new world: sell, sell, sell, or die."

Barry carried the news back to the next consultants' meeting with a heavy heart. He faced an irritated crew but there was nothing he could do except use his marketing man's charm and powers of persuasion to win them all round to acceptance of their targets and the need to get out into the market to find new business. He gave another of his inspiring speeches, urging them all to pull together under the noble flag of ABC and show the market what they were made of. His brilliant rhetoric fooled nobody. They knew they were in the shit.

Noone's chill shiver of uncertainty ran more frequently down his spine. He knew he would need help to open doors at the highest level and his best year in ABS had seen him bring in £320k, decent enough for a selection consultant, but clearly way behind expectations for a search consultant. OK, his base salary had gone up to £100k, which was just about enough to live on, but what about the bonus, which is what drove the extras- the holidays, new kitchen or sports car- which gave quality of life? He already knew that it was going to be impossible to hit £400k in fees in the first year and if the bonus would only kick in at that point, it effectively meant no bonus. Napier was shafting them and Barry was too weak or stupid to do anything about it.

On March 18th, the previous year's Report & Accounts was published. It brushed over "an overall loss in recruitment consultancy" by referring to the heavy cost of "restructuring" and noting that the Board, "reflecting confidence in the future", had bravely recommended an unchanged final dividend of 5.2 pence per share. Bix Napier's statement was brim-full of positives, "viewing the previous year as a new beginning, believing that we have made considerable progress" whilst noting that "there was much still to be done". He felt that "despite the uncertainties overhanging many of the sectors of the UK economy, our own markets continue to show resilience. We have started the year well and our integrated approach has received a positive response from existing and new clients alike...I therefore continue to view our future with considerable confidence", he concluded triumphantly. Things indeed looked bleak.

25. MINGE

"We began in 2000 with a clear ambition to be unrivalled in our creative thinking, our depth and breadth of judgement and our market knowledge.

Blackwood is not the name of the Company's founders or of any of its partners; it is a bid convention in the game of bridge that means calling for Aces.

The search for excellence through excellence is at the heart of all we do."

BLACKWOOD GROUP WEBSITE

The Report & Accounts was followed by a terse internal memo from Napier:

"You may have noticed the decline in our share price. It is unjustified and a result of the sector being marked down, several inconsequential sales in a market with few buyers and the negative publicity concerning Archie Aspallan's departure." Musing with Huff over a cup of coffee, Noone remarked:

"Napier's proud boast of driving the share price to over £5 seems to have had exactly the opposite effect; I see it is now languishing at 11.5p."

"Yes," affirmed Huff, fingering the memo, "one excuse is plausible for a while, two are unbelievable, and three, quite frankly, ridiculous. It's like cancelling an appointment by saying you have flu, and anyway your car is broken and your grandmother just died."

"Do you think there is any hope?" asked Noone, knowing Huff to be an eternal optimist.

"No. Very unlikely, I feel. Certainly Barry Bargewell doesn't infuse me with zeal and confidence, and Napier wants to break the model anyway. Trouble is, his alternative solution is to go mass market and I fear we will just be driven relentlessly down that hill."

"The signs are certainly there; mind you, what do you

expect from a second-hand car dealer?"

"Yes," Huff nodded, "not the sort of chap one would invite to one's Club."

Despite that being the case, Napier could not be accused of inaction; days later, he issued a note about the reconstruction and the decision to merge the recruitment businesses into a single legal entity "to reflect the new way in which we are working". This new company was to be called AB Recruitment Consultancy Ltd (or "AB-Rec-Wreck" as it was immediately christened by Noone) and the operating businesses would "trade as its undisclosed agent." Napier's note went on to stress the benefits of the resultant need only to produce one set of trading accounts and a corresponding reduction in Corporation Tax and VAT returns, but apart from this tax dodge, Noone could see that Napier was strengthening his hand by centralising control. Further, in a separate, "addressee only" addendum written by the Group Finance Director, Noone was invited to resign his executive directorship of ABS "as it was no longer relevant in the new structure, where individual liabilities had been removed."

By now highly suspicious, Noone replied by memo to the FD, copied to Bargewell, Bly Huxford and, just to upset her, Linnet Trilby, enquiring as to the sanctity of his terms of employment. He received a further memo from the FD which loftily but somewhat blandly proclaimed:

"Please accept this memorandum as confirmation that the Reconstruction will have no effect on your terms and conditions of employment as laid out in your contract of employment. Specific provision has been made in the agency agreement to protect your employment position and you will be sent a copy of the agreement when it has been finalised." Noone knew he should have felt comforted by having such a black-and-white affidavit, but he still suspected that Napier was attempting to undermine and dislodge the Old Guard, of which he was one, even if he was "New" in ABC circles. No, in Noone's view, this was the thin end of the wedge arriving with a heavy thud.

The year unfolded unsatisfactorily. Bargewell blundered on feverishly, mangling his metaphors, failing to fulfil any leadership criteria other than being the wrong person in the wrong job at the wrong time. However, following Napier's exhortation to widen the base of fee-earners, Barry's marketing skills of bravery, bullshit and suspension of critical reasoning did enable him to succeed in hiring additional "heads" to become "hunters". By mid-year, three new wide-eyed recruits had rallied to the ABC cause, seduced by the prospect of becoming successful in one of the grand old names of executive search (even though Barry was careful to point out that "we are now a multi-platformed, multi-talented, multi-layered professional services group").

The constituents of new ABC were at least assiduous and by ploughing their individual furrows through the mire of the markets, began to achieve at least limited success in pursuit of new business. Teamwork had very little to do with it, the old tenet of always hunting in pairs tossed overboard by the need for expediency and fee revenue. Noone picked up a couple of clients that fed him three searches each at around £50k a pop, to help him towards his unreachable target. But, now approaching fifty years old, he was not happy. He reviewed a "joke" email he had received from Minge, targeted at people of his age and encouraging them to maintain a healthy level of insanity:

1. At lunch time, sit in your parked car with sunglasses on and point a hair dryer at passing cars to see if they slow down

2. On all your cheque stubs, write 'For Marijuana'

3. Skip down the street rather than walk and see how many looks you get

4. Order a Diet Water whenever you go out to eat, with a serious face

5. Sing along at the opera

6. When the money emerges from the ATM, scream 'I Won! I Won!'

7. When leaving the zoo, start running towards the car park, yelling 'Run for your lives! They're loose!'

8. Tell your children over dinner, 'Due to the economy, we are going to have to let one of you go.'

9. Pick up a box of condoms at the chemists, go the counter and ask where the fitting room is

10. You find the above amusing and forward it to your fellow forty-somethings

As he forwarded it unsmilingly to a fellow forty-something, Noone reflected that suddenly, life had ceased to be purely "fun and games". Almost certainly, he would do none of the above. Fondly, he recalled the carefree days of his twenties and thirties, with cricket nets two evenings a week followed by time in the pub to compensate for the pain, then Saturday's match, with jugs of beer and darts in the clubhouse from 5.30 to 8pm, after which girlfriends were allowed to appear and shepherd their men off to other things; either a party, a London pub with live-music or perhaps driving out to a country hostelry to continue the darts or play bar-billiards. The Rising Sun at Little Hampden had been such a pub; most Saturday nights for a period, he and Minge had joined in "Evensong", an informal two hour drinking session set up by some bright, young, northern-home-counties professionals. The Rising Sun was a classic; situated beyond Great Missenden and adjacent to the quaintly named Cobblers Hill, it was reached by the last two miles of single-track road, which promptly ended at the pub car-park in a dell of tall beech trees. It was ramblers only beyond that. A sign on the door warned: "Absolutely no muddy boots". As a participant in "Evensong", on arrival, Noone had placed a one-pound note (coin since 11th March 1988) in the permanent kitty, which sat in a battered tin box marked "Evensong" behind the Bar and drank Adnams (in those days a relative rarity beyond East Anglia) to his heart's content until 8pm, when the wives would arrive to take their well lubricated other halves to that night's dinner party. At that time in their lives, Noone and Minge did not possess wives, although occasionally and briefly they possessed other men's, so they continued drinking and playing darts until, at 11pm closing time, they would fall uproariously outside and drive home, sometimes with one eye shut to counterbalance the dizzying effect of the alcohol.

On one occasion, Noone and Minge had arrived ahead of the rest and were puzzled by their absence at 6.30pm. Cass, the all-knowing, ex RAF landlord, said not to worry, "they were at the rugby". Suddenly, there was a loud clanging of bells and the blaring of a klaxon: round the final bend to the pub chased a fire-engine festooned with men, packed inside, clinging onto the roof, hanging out of open doors. A shouted, off-key version of "Swing Low, Sweet Chariot" grew louder as the vehicle approached. The fire-engine slid to a halt across the car-park, and a drunken, motley crew, garbed with red and white scarves, hats and rosettes, cascaded out of it in an uproarious scrum and staggered into the pub, one or two of its members hauled in via an open window. Cass remained unperturbed, merely enquiring: "What will it be, Gentlemen?" as he turned to a rack of fresh glasses. Noone and Minge learned that the fire-engine belonged to one of the crowd and traditionally, on the day that England played Wales at Twickenham in the Five Nations, it would be dusted off, filled with punters and taken on a pub crawl enroute to Twickenham and back. The boys had been drinking solidly all day since 10am. Noone and Minge were impressed and resolved to buy a fire-engine immediately. They never did.

Now, some twenty-five years later, things had certainly changed. Noone no longer attended the football training sessions for a start; a dodgy knee, courtesy of a late tackle from a thug who claimed to have played for Skelmersdale United (as if that gave him the right) had put paid to that. Noone initially rationed the pain to Saturdays' matches, but of course, his overall fitness suffered. One day, when a young git of almost half Noone's age deliberately elbowed him in the stomach when the ref was inspecting daisies on the other side of the pitch and told him to "give up Grandad", Noone knew his time was up. It wasn't so much that he suddenly felt inferior and less able to compete against the new breed of callow youth, it was more that their value set was completely different. It wasn't just the constant foul-mouthed sneering and snarling on the pitch directed to opponents, the referee, even between teammates. Noone had been no saint and was not averse to calling the ref a wanker, *but not to his face.* It wasn't even the use of the arms that had crept into the game, whereby you were now seemingly able to wrestle an opponent out of the way, elbow him in the face when jumping for a header and grab armfuls of his shirt if he had the temerity to outpace you. No, the saddest thing of all was that most of them couldn't leave quickly enough after the game; some didn't even stay for a shower! It was only "The Oldies" who would remain in the Clubhouse for a few drinks and a chat with the remnants of the opposition; no bonding, no camaraderie, no darts, no late-night drinking sessions. What a waste. Noone had no idea what they did; he imagined they went home to disappear up their own jacksies in front of the telly or a computer game, or else got coked up and hit the trendy clubs of London with several floosies in tow. Lucky bastards. Perhaps he was envious after all. But of what? Not of them, really, more of his lost youth?

Reluctant to retire completely, Noone decided to play for the Veterans side, a more freewheeling crew who eschewed training but still enjoyed a drink and social patter after a game. Not all were faded refugees from the Third Eleven like Noone, so the standard was variable, but at least Noone had a purpose on Saturdays. This lasted for several seasons after his 40th birthday, but then Noone began to pull groins and hamstrings (in a non-sexual way) which took an increasingly long time to heal. He elected to appear as a second half substitute only. The nadir came when, brought on late in the game one day, he took a corner and twanged his right quadricep. He limped off in downcast embarrassment, having been on the pitch for precisely three and a half minutes. That was it: Noone hung up his boots, or rather, threw them away.

He took up golf on Saturdays instead, which passed the time but lacked the visceral thrill of a game of football. It was also intensely frustrating. The occasional perfect shot delivered two contrary results: an intense, instant high of satisfaction followed by an equally intense sense of disappointment as the next shot invariably failed to match its imperious predecessor. Still, golf clubhouses contained bars and a tradition of staying for a drink with your opponent, however much you hated the fact that he had just scored better than you. Noone approved that even in the traditional, stuffy environment of a home-counties golf club of over 100 years standing, real ale was being offered as a daring alternative to fizzy Worthington or John Smiths, the barren, banal offspring of the Watney's Red Barrel years. Mind you, quite often it was "off" and tasted of muddy, sour vinegar, because the clubs lacked the cellar and the beer turnover to keep it properly. But Noone persevered, leaving the retired grandees to their gin and scotch, and must not have been alone, for gradually, the consistency (of the beer, not his golf) improved over time. The improvement in quality allowed Noone to linger over two or three, perhaps four pints of a Saturday lunchtime, similarly on a Sunday and quite often on a Monday or Friday on the way back from work in the evening.

He developed a new circle of golfing friends, generally older than he, and although conversation lacked the edge, wit and sarcasm of his footballing days, Noone was increasingly content to sit in an armchair alongside his elders and agree with their moans about the latest outrage perpetrated on an unsuspecting public by the pernicious government of the day. As for the Rising Sun, Cass had retired and sold it to a pair of Irish homosexuals, who immediately set about prettifying it. The wonderful, worn flagstones of the public bar were carpeted over as it now merged into the lounge bar. The dart board, sadly redundant and obtrusive for the chic image being cultivated, was removed and the pockmarked wall artexed and painted cornflower blue. An extension was added and turned into a restaurant, with ruched pink curtains, candelabra, abstract pictures on the wall and daily fresh flowers. To be sure, the more feminine touch would encourage the ladies to visit with their menfolk, perhaps even attracting genteel couples from as far afield as Gerrards Cross and the Chalfonts, drawing them in with the promise of a quaint, out-of-the-way location, undisturbed, cosy warmth, intimate, candlelit dining and fine wine. Gerry and Shauny stood back and admired their handiwork, celebrated opening night with a bottle of Mumm and awaited the rush of hungry diners; it was just perfect.

So perfect was it that all the previous "regulars" avoided it like the plague. The soul of the honest boozer had been ripped out and replaced by an anodyne tweeness that appealed to nobody. It didn't help that the restaurant was launched in the middle of a particularly aggressive government advertising campaign, which, amid graphically blood-spattered pavements and the mangled wreckage of cars, warned sternly against the criminal and anti-social activities of the drink-driver. "Evensong" packed up, its demise hastened by the wives, who, armed with the zeal of the politically-correct, nagged their husbands to give up this sole remaining outlet for male-only enjoyment. The newer, restaurant clientele soon became weary of the mincing bonhomie exuded by the two owners. Usually, one visit was enough. One or two hardy souls who lived closest to what was now called the "Rising Sun Bistro" kept it going and it did attract several of the gay community by way of its new character. Minge said he "refused to participate in a remorseless and willful drive downhill led by uphill gardeners". Noone had kept away himself, but had revisited once after a decent period of mourning and self-imposed exile, in the late '90s. It was a shale padow of its former self and he had not returned.

Life, for Noone, had settled into a more mundane, middle-aged routine, although at work, the pressure was always on to develop more business and win bigger fees. Bargewell encouraged the consultants to network whenever possible, so Noone diligently attended dull CBI, IOD and Chambers of Commerce dinners as a means of delivering his business cards to complete strangers who were extremely unlikely to remember him in a week's time. On at least two of the black-tie occasions, the Chancellor of the Exchequer, Gordon Brown, was guest of honour and delivered the principal speech. Not only did he offend by turning up in a lounge suit (a scavenging skua amongst the penguins) but his speech rambled on for an hour, made incomprehensible by a scaffolding of meaningless statistics, the monotone enlightened only by punctuating jabs of an index finger. It was so crashingly boring that many of the diners had nodded off, while others with eyebrows raised in a silent exhortation for divine intervention, like Noone, sought helpless solace in the claret as a means of passing the time. Surely the grinning fool Blair and New Labour couldn't possibly elevate this man to Prime Minister, thought Noone? It would be political suicide.

In the end, it was one of these "do's" that proved to be Noone's downfall. He had kept in touch with the Thames Valley Chamber of Commerce on the off-chance that he might meet a potential client close to his home, who might provide the opportunity of a site visit and therefore an excuse not to have to go into London on that day. The pickings had been slim. One or two speculative meetings in concrete jungles of Slough or Basingstoke following a standard pattern: kept waiting in the Office Reception to emphasise his unimportance; ushered into a large office inhabited by a self-important Managing Director or, even worse, Human Resource Director, who would be twice as self-important; endure either i) a diatribe about the state of the company or parent company, or ii) an equally lengthy eulogy about how brilliant everything was; served platitudes about how he would be given a chance "the next time anything suitable came up"; ushered out within the hour by the secretary, with whom he would attempt jovial banter as a means of being remembered. Thereafter, he would phone every three months, exchange pleasantries with the secretary who would tell him that "X" was very busy and she would pass on Noone's message to call him back. They rarely did. These abortive exchanges might go on for a year or so, after which it became obvious even to one as initially optimistic as Noone, that he was being politely ignored. Thereafter, Noone would restrict contact to a Christmas card, in which he would note "look forward to catching up in due course". He religiously sent out hundreds of such useless Christmas cards every year.

One Monday in early September, Noone decided to attend a Chamber function in Reading. It was labeled a "Networking cocktail party, hosted by Jervis, Jones LLP, to celebrate its first ten years of successful business in the community" and took place within an attractive walled courtyard attached to the shoutingly modern Jervis, Jones office backing onto the canal just off Duke Street. For this smallish but ambitious regional solicitors' firm it was an opportunity to showcase its commercial "suits", almost half of whom were sharply attired, attractive young women. It was the business equivalent of "flirty fishing" except that the end game was not spiritual brain-washing but practical-financial, to hook a few local business leaders who would be impressed enough to consider using Jervis Jones as their legal representative. The Senior Partners of

Jervis Jones considered the £5k investment in a cocktail party to be well worth it.

Noone had driven into London that morning, allowing his car to be placed in the Cavendish Hotel underground car park by stepping out at the barrier and handing his keys to a valet. The £24 charge he would claim back on expenses as "business development", as he would the mileage from home to London, then from London to Reading and finally from Reading back home. After all, he couldn't possibly have completed such a round-trip on public transport. Having hotfoot out of London after a by no means unacceptable lunch at Pescatore, consisting of *filetti di triglia con fregola al limone e frittella di calamari*, washed down by a bottle of quite decent Orvieto Classico, Noone arrived well before the invited time of 6pm, and managed to convince the disembodied, tinny voice belonging to the loudspeaker at the entrance to Jervis, Jones's car park that a space had been allocated to him personally by the Managing Partner, Scott McSouthern. In fact, Noone had forgotten to confirm his attendance, but was able to convey enough authority, with the intimation that he and McSouthern were old pals, to achieve the opening of the barrier by the unseen security guard.

At Reception, he was checked against the list of attendees, issued with a lapel badge which identified him as "Alan None- ABC" and ushered by one of several nubile "receptionists" through to the marquee in the garden area, where champagne was offered by uniformed members of the catering company, Just Desserts. For the next two hours, Noone attempted to "work the room" as Bargewell would have wished: he introduced himself to a succession of total strangers, shaking hands warmly whilst holding their eye with a pointed look and open smile which signaled "I am really interested in you and want to spend some of my valuable time hearing what an interesting life/job/company you have". Of course, everybody recognised the sham sincerity, but being polite, played along. Throughout the marquee, identical shallow, forgettable conversations were occurring, with little, awkward clusters of recently-introduced folk showing mock interest in each other's inane chit-chat.

Noone achieved very little; most of the guests were, like him, trying to sell some kind of business service, although they seemed to be outnumbered by the earnest employees of Jervis, Jones, who would insinuate themselves (singly, of course, forbidden to hunt in packs) into each cluster "to help things along" and inevitably bring the conversation round to a recent example of Jervis, Jones's stunningly effective intervention on behalf of a grateful client which rescued said client from some previously unsolvable legal conundrum, which was about to drive the client out of business. Everyone was selling something to everyone else. Noone's "old friend" McSouthern, whom he had failed to meet, clanked a spoon against a glass and said a few words of thanks to all those valued guests who had taken the time out of their busy schedules to attend this proud moment in Jervis, Jones's history. It had been a wonderful ten years, with a wonderful team and they were all eagerly looking forward to the next ten years. If they would forgive him the indulgence of a quick sales pitch, he hoped that he would have the privilege of calling all those who were not yet clients, clients at some stage in the near future. Noone, by now quite fortified by the endless top-ups of champagne, was quite prepared to allow McSouthern his moment of glory, content with the thought that Jervis, Jones would almost certainly not be around in ten years, having a ninety percent chance of going bust or being taken over.

McSouthern urged them all to stay and enjoy the party for as long as they liked, but it was 8pm and Noone had had enough. He had thrust a few business cards desperately into the hands of any people he had met who appeared to be in positions of hiring responsibility in industrial firms, including, rather hopelessly, the Sales Director of a company which made caravans. The high spot had been ten minutes spent eyeing the cleavage of one of the young Jervis, Jones hot totties, whilst he flattered her shamelessly about her choice of employer, "which really seemed to be going places". She was not taken in by his pathetic, condescending, middle-aged banter. Now launched, however precariously, on the lower rungs of her career, she felt confident enough not to have to sleep with every older man who admired her intellect. She soon moved off to a more virile looking group.

As Noone made his way back to the car-park via the Gents, he congratulated himself on his self-discipline. Given McSouthern's exhortation, he could easily have stayed to the death, enjoying the free booze until it ran out (although probably moving on to the red wine or possibly a flusher of bottled beer, because "you can only drink so much champagne"). Who knows, he may even have shaken the great man's hand or made a more serious play for Little Miss Hot-to-Trot. But no, he would go back for an early night in front of the telly. Just as he reached his car, his mobile phone rang. It was Minge.

Minge had rather a complicated set of personal circumstances. He was the son of a pair of greengrocers from a rural Essex village and became the apple of their eye. They lavished care and attention on him at the expense of his younger brother and sister. They were destined for life in the village, but Minge had something special. This manifested itself when at the tender age of seven, Minge got hold of some fireworks which his parents sold as "Specials" around Bonfire Night. He carefully cut them open with his Swiss Army penknife, collected all the gunpowder, and laid it in a trail around his village primary school teacher's desk, snaking back to his own. When Mrs Gulliver was enlightening the class about crop rotation, Minge enlightened her briefly in a circle of colourful, sparkling fire. The class clapped, Mrs Gulliver didn't. When called to the school and confronted by this example of Minge's extreme behaviour, the parents resolved to send him to Boarding School in order to channel his energies more effectively and allow his obvious genius to flower. This caused considerable hardship at home, where all spare income was directed to Minge's education at the expense of holidays, eating out and new clothing for the siblings. Everything was sacrificed to the altar of Minge's brilliance. He duly emerged as just another privately-educated university undergraduate, which is where he met Noone.

Minge wasn't his real name. In Noone's hands, Simon Pringle had been turned into the anagram R.O. Minge-Nipls, and Minge had just stuck. By the time Minge reached university, although undoubtedly extremely bright, he had developed a guilt complex which caused him to become easily distracted and underachieve. An agonising affair with a clergyman's daughter took care of his middle year; she refused to have sex until they were married. Although he thought he loved her, Minge had no intention of marrying her, but he desperately wanted to partake of the treasure she kept securely within her tight jeans and pink panties. The only satisfaction he was able to achieve was her occasional agreement to help him masturbate on his bed and his pent up frustration would explode in an ecstacy of relief, sometimes ejaculating so powerfully that it would splatter the wall above the bed's headboard, at which she at least had the decency to giggle. The relationship limped along, and ended when she demanded concrete evidence of his love for her and intentions for their future together by way of a "commitment ring". When he mumbled awkwardly that he couldn't afford to buy one, she told him tearfully but coldly not to contact her again. This rejection coincided with Minge's realisation that he had mistaken lust for love, and if she wouldn't put out for him, she could fuck off, the frigid bitch.

His final university year was spent in whirlwind of romantic activity, as Minge made amends for the wasted year of sexual frustration. He was not an unhandsome fellow, and to his boyish good looks he added a self-deprecating wit, ready smile and a twinkle in his eye which charmed the ladies. He planted his seed widely amongst his fellow undergraduates, nurses from the town hospital, foreign exchange students, even local scrubbers whom he chanced upon in pubs. Passing the year in such frenetic, off-piste pursuits ensured that passing his Finals was always going to be a challenge. Somehow, his natural intelligence enabled him to scrape "a sportsman's 2:2" in Geography, although his essays were largely uncluttered by references to previous learned works studied in the Libraries, whose doors Minge had failed to darken.

Like Noone, Minge had tried a career in industry and failed, ending up as a management consultant with Cro-Magnon Man, a brash, progressive US-based strategic consultancy which specialised in telling the automotive industry how overstaffed it was. He had begun to make some decent money by becoming particularly articulate and persuasive in the black art of extending client projects by doing not very much disguised as erudite analysis. Along the way he had collected and shed a first wife who delivered him three children, both parents having failed to take precautions after the son was born second. She left him on the grounds of his unreasonable behaviour after he had reacted quite reasonably to the news of her affair with a neighbour by locking her out of the house for a week. Relations deteriorated when she called in lawyers and made astronomical demands on his finances to keep her and the children in the manner to which she had become accustomed. Naturally, the divorce-court magistrate agreed since the Law now found it perfectly acceptable for gold-digging women to marry some unsuspecting soul for a few years before making off with half his money. In the end, after a vicious mud-fight, Minge had to sell the house, buy her a smaller one, rent one himself and pay £3k a month maintenance plus all the school fees. Ironically, the boy and the eldest daughter soon came to live with him.

For a while, Minge reverted to his university days, and began to shag any female he could come across. Once again he was caught out. A dazzlingly attractive, tall, raven-haired Italian colleague at Cro-Magnon Man fell pregnant after a single after-work, late-night dinner and intoxicated coupling. It was very bad luck and Minge gallantly ignored the small voice inside his head and the loud voice of Noone, which told him he had been stitched up yet again. He married the lovely Sophia Cernusco-Lombardone quickly and quietly and went back to work while she resigned and produced little Flavia. Two years later, she became pregnant again and Minge had to endure some ribbing from Noone about his single-handed contribution to the nation's over-population burden.

That was six months ago. Now, as Noone walked through the car-park at Jervis, Jones, Minge called. He was obviously excited and spoke in a rush:

"Adam, mate, guess what? I'm at the hospital and Sophia has just given birth, quick as anything. Another girl. We are calling her Mercedes. Where are you? Can you meet me for a celebratory drink?" Noone didn't hesitate:

"Of course mate. I am just leaving a bash in Reading but I can meet you on the way home." Minge, who had not quite escaped the straitened financial circumstances caused by his divorce, lived in a semi in Lane End, outside High Wycombe, reasonably close to Noone. Noone thought briefly, then continued:

"Why don't we meet at the King's Head at Little Marlow?" With this simple invitation, Noone sowed the seed of his own downfall.

26. CRIME

"The Zygos Partnership takes its name from the Greek word zygosis, meaning the act of joining together in balance. Zygos is used to express the concept of teamwork in modern Greek.

The Founding Partners combine more than 50 years of experience in advising Boards on appointments in the UK and internationally. They recognised the benefits of creating a team of dedicated professionals who focus solely on the needs of clients without the distractions and demands of a larger organisation.

This ability to concentrate their efforts ensures that clients' needs remain the priority and clients' interests are put first."

ZYGOS PARTNERSHIP WEBSITE

As he usually did when he had taken sufficient alcohol, Noone drove fast, aggressively, yet in his opinion, very safely, from Reading to Little Marlow. Where two lanes reduce to one at the junction of London and Wokingham Roads on the way out of Reading, he successfully cut up a BMW driver by hanging in the outside lane until the last possible moment, exchanging V-signs as he forced the Beemer to give way. Very satisfactorily, he outran a second BMW on the Marlow by-pass, holding a steady 90 mph until breaking late for the roundabout at Bisham. All BMW drivers are wankers, he mused with a grim smile, not for the first time. Turning across the traffic on the Marlow Road into the car-park of the King's Head, he slightly misjudged his reverse parking manoeuvre, leaving the back-end semi-immersed in a blackthorn bush and the car at a raffish angle to the white lines denoting the parking space. It didn't matter, the car park was only half full.

Minge had already settled over a pint and had a second

ready for Noone on the table in front of him.

"I know you like Adnams, Adam, so I got us a Broadside; it tastes beautiful." Mindful that he had already downed several glasses of champagne, Noone wouldn't have chosen this strong brew as his session tipple, but what the hell, he didn't want to disappoint Minge, who was clearly on good form. Animatedly, he regaled Noone for the duration of their first pints about the wonderment of birth and the strange emotions aroused by seeing one's wife screaming in agony one minute and smiling tearfully the next while cradling for the first time the new, little bundle of joy. Noone replenished the pints, sensibly electing to trade down to a weaker, but still tasty, Timothy Taylor's Landlord, which would allow him to drink more. Noone wasn't hungry on account of the canapés he had consumed by way of "blot" and Minge was too excited to eat, so they split some helicopter-flavoured crisps and ready-salted peanuts. Noone had begun to feel a little smothered by Minge's fatherly delirium and decided to drag him back to reality.

"Y'know, Minge, it is all very well launching yet another off the production line into an unsuspecting public, but aren't you worried about the world these kids will inherit? I mean, they will be surrounded by political correctness, not allowed to eat or drink anything they like, discover that we no longer rule the world and that we haven't won the World Cup since 1966. What hope have they got?"

"Ah yes, but look on the bright side," replied Minge, who always looked on the bright side. "The technology will be amazing, women will have greater equality, they will be able to live on the moon, and they won't have to wear school uniform."

"Is that all you have to offer them? Think of the escalating energy costs, this global warming that they are all talking about, population explosions in the Third World, AIDS from Africa, the increasing bureaucracy from Brussels. It's not a pretty picture. Anyway, where did you get that from?"

"What?" replied Minge, "living on the moon?"

"No, the bit about school uniform."

"It's the latest directive from Brussels."

"See, I told you about Brussels! Let's face it, they are not going to be able to enjoy the life we have had. It's all very well to talk about the advantages of globalisation, but at a micro level there is actually far less choice. They wouldn't be let off with a caution for "misplaced student bravado" after pissing against a lamp-post, like you were, and they certainly wouldn't get away with pissing all over an hotel's freshly delivered bread at five in the morning, like I did."

"No, but that is because they are girls and wouldn't do such things anyway. They'll be far too sensible." Noone noted a certain smugness and moved quickly to disillusion Minge:

"Bollocks, they'll be drinking and shagging at fourteen, just like their father!" A concerned, thoughtful look came over Minge's face. Noone could tell he was wrestling with the actuality of his own adolescent behaviour and the idealistic fantasy he imagined for that of his two most recent daughters. Noone seized the moment, and despite Minge's protestations that it was his round, went to the bar and returned with a Broadside for Minge and another Landlord for himself. It really was excellent beer. The pub was now humming with drinkers clustered around the bar and eaters seated in the restaurant area. Noone felt thoroughly relaxed; the warm, cosy glow of the alcohol had infused him with fabulous intellectual insights of great clarity and a garrulous vocabulary with which to articulate them. Their conversation seemed to become brilliantly animated, extremely witty and, to anyone accidentally overhearing, exceedingly dull and repetitive. Minge went up for the fourth round, protesting that this would be his last. Noone therefore felt relaxed about having a Broadside: the Landlord had given him a thirst for a final burst of flavour from the more complex brew to round off the evening.

In the next half hour, the two friends solved many crises easily: Thatcher, by appealing to Man's baser nature through her doctrine of "look after Number One, greed is good" had been responsible for destroying manners carefully constructed over several centuries to protect the weak and less fortunate from our innate selfishness; the Allied troops should have pushed on to Baghdad and eliminated Saddam; Alex Ferguson and Manchester United should be banned; Arsenal weren't much better; Sepp Blatter had ruined football; Blair was a popinjay but Brown should not be allowed to succeed him as Prime Minister; petrol prices should be reduced, along with beer, wine and the cost of CDs; anyone sitting in the middle lane of a motorway should be blown up and speed limits should be raised to allow more efficient traffic flow; and, there should be a global search to find Debbie Harry, although she might be looking a bit rough by now, after all she must be nearly seventy. They literally laughed and giggled themselves silly. Then the Last Orders bell rang.

Minge still had half a glass left, Noone thought he could squeeze in a half of Broadside, since it really hit the spot and it was a shame not to take advantage while it was there. They lingered beyond the Time bell, reluctant to break the spell of the moment, of a couple of hours of shared camaraderie, laced with nostalgia and righteous good humour. They both went to the Gents before leaving, with the usual banter about "one for the road" and "better out than in" and "this is where all the Big Knobs hang out" across the urinal. Finally, they bade their farewells in the car-park, with an affectionate hug and "see you soons".

Just as Noone was about to open the door to retrieve his car from the blackthorn bush, his mobile phone rang. He was at first puzzled to see that it was his voicemail messaging system calling him; then he remembered that the King's Head was notorious for not being able to pick up a mobile signal and he had just stepped back in range of a cellular mast in walking through the car-park. He decided to listen to the message as he got in the car and turned the ignition. One-handedly, he steered out of the bush and across the car-park behind Minge's BMW. "Wanker" thought Noone, smiling, as he decided the automotive enthusiast in Minge actually believed in BMW's superior engineering. As Minge turned left onto the A4155 to Marlow, Noone's message began. He checked the road and swung right towards Bourne End, realising that the message, from his secretary about a meeting several days in the future, was essentially meaningless. Having terminated the messaging service, he contemplated calling Minge to remind him he was a wanker for driving a BMW, but in the end, threw the phone onto the passenger seat beside him. Only then did he see the lights quite close behind him. "Where did he come from" he wondered, as he checked that he was travelling only marginally above the 50mph speed limit, just in case the car behind happened to be the police. He checked the mirror again: "Shit!" he exclaimed aloud, it was the police. Still, no worries, keep cool, reduce speed to the 30mph limit just before the mini-roundabout at Sheepridge Lane. He carefully steered around the roundabout, not across it as he usually did, then equally carefully around the tight left-hander at Coldmoorholme Lane. He was just beginning to think that it was all going rather well, when the police car's blue lights started flashing. "Fuck" said Noone, "I'm fucked".

He pulled to a halt before reaching the Black Lion pub, desperately trying to remember all the stories about how to pass a breathalyser. He recalled "Badger" Brock saying he had once avoided trouble after a day's drinking at the races by breathing very deeply, so that he forced "pure" air into the mouthpiece. Darth Gwent swore that putting loose coppers in your mouth neutralised the alcohol in your breath. And Caspian Cordell had parked his MGB across the central reservation of the M40 without even being breathalysed! But the only coppers Noone had right then were parking their car behind his. Perhaps he could convince the coppers that he hadn't been drinking. He remembered he had run out of Polos, which he kept in the glove-locker for the purpose: "anti-Filth sweets", he called them. Shit. Never mind, take the battle to the enemy: he bounded out of his car and walked as nonchalantly as he could in a straight line towards the police-car, which was disgorging a male and a female.

"Any problem?" he enquired with as charming a smile as he could muster. The policeman, who looked about eighteen to Noone, replied without any of the customary pleasantries:

"We pulled you because you were talking on your mobile phone and therefore driving without due care and attention. We also noticed you driving out of the King's Head car-park. Have you been drinking, sir?" Shit, that was it, he couldn't lie to that without the Polos.

"Yes, I had a couple of pints with a friend."

"Can you recall exactly how much you have drunk, sir?" Bollocks, they were trying to get him to confess. Noone had once been breathalysed after he had been stopped for speeding at 44mph in a 30mph zone. Fortunately, on that occasion, he had been in a hurry and had only consumed two pints of Courage Best at the Golf Club. He had been let off with a warning: "You are very close to the line, sir," the policeman had said, "and this time we will let it go; but may I suggest that in future, you don't drink two pints of beer before getting behind the wheel of a motorcar?" On the contrary, Noone had used the experience as a rule of thumb thereafter: he could beat the breathalyser on two pints of beer. They had still done him for speeding, mind...

But this was tricky; he knew he had consumed far more than that, even discounting most of the earlier champagne. He stared into the scary blue eyes of the discomfited policeman.

"I'd say about three pints; but I was in there most of the evening" he offered, lamely. He knew he had given the boy-policeman the opening he wanted.

"We are going to have to breathalyse you on suspicion of driving under the influence of alcohol. Have you been breathalysed before, sir?" Noone considered answering no, to demonstrate what an upright citizen he was, but suspected the records would betray him. His second experience had been seven years before, when he had been breathalysed on his way to collect a Chinese takeaway after being stopped for speeding by a police motorcyclist. On the face of it, it shouldn't have been a problem. The problem was that it was a Saturday evening after he had played a game of veterans' football and Noone had a few jugs of beer afterwards with the lads. Once home, he had consumed another bottle of beer whilst he ordered the takeaway over the phone. Then, as usual, he had driven as fast as the conditions allowed towards the restaurant, only to be confronted by the policeman who leapt out of a bush with a speed-gun in his hands and waved Noone urgently to stop. The constable informed him that he was travelling at 42mph in a 30mph zone, said he could smell alcohol on his breath, asked the question, breathalysed him, told him he was over the limit, and called up a squad car to take him to the police station for processing. To Noone's immense relief but vague expectation, he had passed the test, and was escorted to the door of the police station by the unhappy bike policeman, who, in his annoyance, forgot to charge Noone with speeding. Noone had to make his way back to his car via minicab, in which he left his wallet by mistake. He felt that missing his Chinese dinner and having to cancel all his credit and debit cards was more than enough punishment.

"Yes," he answered brightly, instantly realising that the policeman would view him as a man who did not heed warnings and took risks with the law. Noone tried to appear unconcerned, whilst taking huge breaths as surreptitiously as possible. Got to get that pure air into his lungs.

"In that case, you will know what to do" the policeman said, opening the breathalyser kit and proceeding to demonstrate to Noone what to do. "I require you to provide me with a sample of your breath. You must fill your lungs and blow into this instrument with one continuous breath until I tell you to stop. You must blow strongly enough to illuminate the flow light and sound a continuous bleep, and long enough to bring on the analysing light and sound a double bleep. You are warned that failure to provide a sample without reasonable excuse may render you liable to prosecution."

As the policeman fitted the mouthpiece, Noone noticed that the Black Lion was offering Happy Hour half-priced drinks between 6pm and 8pm. How ironic. Pubs filling people up with booze and police waiting round the corner to collar them. It just wasn't fair. He took the mouthpiece, holding the policeman's eye momentarily to demonstrate confidence in his own innocence. This, then, was the moment of truth, when the lie would be exposed, yet he hoped against hope that somehow it would be alright. Strange that the policeman wanted him to fill his lungs with all that lovely, pure, fresh air...

Noone breathed as instructed through the mouthpiece until the policeman told him to stop. It was a good show, a strong, uninterrupted breath. He hoped he had managed to exhale all the beer fumes from his lungs and that this package of breath he was delivering through the tube was uniquely untainted. It wasn't.

"The breathalyser shows that you have a higher than permitted alcohol level", the policeman said, looking at his colleague meaningfully. Noone noticed for the first time that she had been writing in a notebook. She looked even younger and had spots. "I am arresting you as this indicates that the proportion of alcohol in your body exceeds the prescribed limit. You do not have to say anything, but it may harm your defence if you do not mention when questioned something which you may later rely on in court. Anything you do say may be given in evidence. We would like you to accompany us now to the police station." As the impact of these words hit home,

Noone suddenly felt bitterly cold and numb and became aware that his left leg was shaking uncontrollably. He nodded dumbly.

"Please give me the keys to your vehicle. We will lock it and leave it here for collection later." Noone handed over the keys and thrust his hands in his jacket pockets. Whilst the policeman went to and from his car, Noone discovered a small square of some long-forgotten restaurant's complimentary chocolate in his left jacket pocket. He knew that this roadside test was just an excuse to get him back to the police station where he would be tested again; perhaps the chocolate would help mask his breath? He quickly unwrapped it and slipped it into his mouth. The policewoman reacted poorly:

"The suspect has just put something in his mouth," she shouted to her colleague. The policeman rushed back to the police car.

"What have you put in your mouth?" he shouted at Noone.

"Just a piece of chocolate, I was hungry." replied Noone.

"If you have any more, give it to me now." Noone shook his head. "You are not to eat or drink anything, do you understand?" Noone nodded, crestfallen, his heart thumping. The policewoman opened the door and pushed him in while her companion jumped behind the wheel and gunned the engine. He executed a three-point turn across the A-road and, with a screech of tyres struggling for traction, sped off towards High Wycombe. From the rear seat, Noone noted angrily that they had hit 65mph in the 30mph zone; so it was fine for the police to break the law as they pleased. They hit ninety up the hill on the Marlow by-pass to the Handy Cross roundabout at junction four of the M40, then down Marlow Hill into High Wycombe at fifty.

"Good job you haven't been drinking, at these speeds" he observed sarcastically. He instantly regretted this ill-judged comment. The policeman gave him a long, hard stare through the rearview mirror:

"I suggest you keep quiet. If you were so clever, you wouldn't be sitting where you are now." Noone, noting he wasn't called "sir" anymore, kept quiet for the rest of the journey. Good job he hadn't asked the policeman jocularly if he were old enough to drive. The police-car screeched into the car-park at the rear of the police station on Queen Victoria Road and Noone was ushered out of the car and in through the back door by the policewoman. She led him to the Duty Officer's desk in the reception area. A burly constable was restraining a violent drunk, who, whilst he was being booked in by the Duty Officer, was subjecting everyone to a foul-mouthed tirade:

"You can't fucking do this you fucking cunts. Fuck off you cunts. Get your fucking hands off me. You fucking cunts." Derek and Clive would have been proud of him, thought Noone, quietly awaiting his turn. All his possessions were taken from him by the policewoman, placed in a bag and handed to the Duty-Officer who labeled it as he asked for Noone's particulars. He was told to sit down whilst the resident breathalyser unit, or Intoximeter, was prepared. The drunk was hauled off to the cells, still screaming abuse which the police patiently ignored. The policewoman's partner appeared and beckoned Noone though a corridor to the right of the Duty Officer's desk; he stood up and walked through, accompanied by the policewoman. He felt very sober. They turned off the corridor through a door on the right and Noone saw the Intoximeter, large, squat and immovable, on a table in the corner of a very small room. It hissed ominously and reminded Noone of an iron lung, which he had never seen, but imagined looked something like this. A heavy duty corrugated plastic tube emerged from its bowels. The policeman showed Noone a sealed packet from which he extracted a mouthpiece which he pushed into the free end of the tube. Noone noticed that the policeman's hands were shaking. Perhaps it was *his* first time? More irony...

"We will just purge the system," he said, pressing a button on the machine. It whirred, hissed and clanked for a couple of minutes, then delivered a strip of paper from a slot in its side. The policeman showed it to Noone and he was aware of a number of zeros and percentage signs. It meant nothing to Noone. He assumed it meant there was nothing: no tainted air in the machine. The policeman asked him whether he had smoked, eaten, or drunk anything in the last twenty minutes, apart from the chocolate. Noone replied that he had not.

"I require you to provide two specimens of breath for analysis by means of an approved device. The specimen with the lower proportion of alcohol in your breath may be used as evidence and the other will be disregarded. I warn you that failure to provide either of these specimens will render you liable to prosecution. Do you agree to provide two specimens of breath for analysis?" Noone had stories of men who had refused to give both breath and blood samples, causing such confusion that they had got off on a technicality, but here, in the cold, stark reality, he couldn't see it working for him.

"Yes," he meekly replied. The policeman instructed him on the blowing technique again. He wondered whether the policewoman ever got the chance to talk about blowing properly. Probably not, he decided. He then had to confirm that he had not brought anything up from his stomach before he took the mouthpiece and blew as instructed. The Intoximeter seemed insatiable and Noone ran out of breath before the policeman told him to stop. The machine was then purged again and the exercise repeated. The two police looked at both readouts together before turning to Noone. The final countdown. They offered him the readout. The first test showed 54, the second 55. He wasn't quite sure what that meant.

"So what does that mean?" he asked.

"The legally permitted limit is 35 microgrammes of alcohol per 100 millilitres of breath," replied the copper. He didn't seem particularly triumphant. "You will now be formally charged with driving with excess alcohol." Noone now knew what it felt like to have one's world come crashing down on one. It was an almost physical shock, this realisation that he had gone over the edge, and could never return to the way things had been before, the carefree days of only forty five minutes ago, as he waved farewell to Minge. Whether it was the alcohol kicking in or whether he went into a state of semi-shock, Noone only retained a hazy memory of the ensuing events until he was deposited alone in a cell. The key elements he did recall were that the policewoman took him to another room to take his DNA with a mouth swab, that he was formally charged and had to sign a piece of paper acknowledging the circumstances and that he was issued with a further sheet of paper proudly sponsored by The Law Society and Legal Aid entitled: "Remember Your Rights". Through it all he acted meekly; long gone was his affected, pained half-smile which said: "this is all a terrible mistake, I am not a real criminal". He spoke only when questioned except when he asked for a newspaper to read as the cell door was about to close on him. There were no newspapers in the police station apparently. It was half past one in the morning. He scanned through the "Remember Your Rights" leaflet, noting that he could ask the police for their Codes of Practice, which he was entitled to read but not for "so long that it holds up the police finding out if you have broken the law". The Codes of Practice were either far too long to be intelligible or the police had a lot of trouble with illiterates. Noone decided not to bother. He also noted he "must be offered three meals a day with drinks" and fervently hoped he wouldn't be incarcerated for long enough to need sustenance.

Noone took stock of his surroundings, not that there was much of which to take stock: a narrow bed with a laughably thin mattress set into the far wall, no pillow; at its indeterminate head or foot, a seat-less stainless steel lavatory, with a tiny, stainless steel sink to one side. No soap, the single concession to bodily function success being a roll of Bronco lavatory paper. Noone remembered it well from his youth: impenetrability rather than comfort was its watchword. The cell measured about ten feet by ten feet. There was no window. Escape was out of the question, then. He lay down on the bed. Suddenly, there was a rattle of keys and the heavy door swung open.

"You wanted something to read?" A different policeman came in and handed him a magazine.

"Thanks," said Noone. "Any idea how long I am going to be here?"

"We will test your alcohol level again in a few hours and when it is below the limit, you can go." He backed out of the cell and the keys rattled again. A few hours! What was he supposed to do until then? Sleep would be out of the question. He would be fucked for work tomorrow. All he had to pass the time was the poxy magazine. He looked at it for the first time. "Supercars of the Past Decade". Yet another irony: the police were endorsing very expensive, outrageously fast cars, guaranteed to break every speed limit encountered. It *was* so unfair. Why weren't the police out catching the real criminals- the murderers, rapists, paedophiles, burglars and car thieves?

Noone indignantly remembered an incident several years ago. He had been awoken at four in the morning by his doorbell ringing. Stumbling awake down the stairs, he met a policeman on his doorstep.

"Does this belong to you, sir?" the policeman had enquired, holding up Noone's briefcase. How was this possible? It transpired that an opportunistic thief had noticed it on the back seat of Noone's car, which was sat on the drive. He had forced open the driver's door with a heavy-duty screwdriver, or other such essential item of a burglar's kit, and made off with it in his own car. A late night (or early morning) walker in the neighbouring village had spotted the briefcase being tossed out of the car window (it containing nothing of value to thieves, only business documents) as it roared through the village, and called the police, who had cleverly discovered Noone's name and address from a label which Noone had attached to the handle, in the event of leaving it behind on a train when pissed. Despite the eyewitness statement recording the colour and make of car, the police subsequently displayed no appetite for solving the crime; a "forensic team" of two bored coppers had called in two days later and half-heartedly "took fingerprints". Noone had heard nothing more and had been singularly unimpressed with Britain's finest. Mind you, he never left his briefcase in the car again.

Noone tried, and failed, to read the magazine. Not even the incomparable profile of a Lamborghini Countach could hold his attention. The violent drunk had gone quiet. In the end, he lay there, endlessly re-running the events of the evening through his head. If only Minge hadn't rung and he had gone straight home from Reading; he would have been alright. That was unlucky. And what about the bastard police hanging around outside pubs at closing time, just to catch honest citizen drinkers like him? He seethed with the indignity of it all. Bound to be stripped of his licence, he would have to train and taxi everywhere. How would he get around his more far-flung clients? What about his social life? He would be reliant on lifts and taxis. It would be a nightmare.

Noone saw his watch through to three thirty but then dozed off for he was jerked awake by the rattle of the keys.

"Let's test you again, then," said the same constable who had brought him Supercars of the Past Decade. He had brought in a hand-held breathalyser kit and led Noone through the by now all-too-familiar routine. This time it delivered the desired result:

"OK, you are below the limit now. You can go." said the constable, opening the door wide for him. Noone was past the stage of feeling relieved. Everything was fucked anyway. Noone was escorted back to the duty officer's desk, where he was handed his belongings in a bag and asked to sign for them.

"Would you like a lift back to your car?" asked the duty

officer. Noone could hardly believe what he was hearing: they were now going to allow him to drive?

"Yes please," he said quickly, in case the duty officer had made a mistake.

"OK, I will ask a patrol car to pick you up." Noone sat in the reception area, marveling at the arbitrariness and injustice of it all. Just because he had been a few points over the limit he had been prevented from driving a couple of miles to his home, had been summarily (and at illegal speeds) hauled to the police station, treated like a common criminal and thrown in the cells. Now he was free to drive home as if nothing had happened!

After fifteen minutes or so, the duty officer indicated he should walk out of the front door to the police car which was waiting there. It took him back to his car at a relatively sedate pace. Nobody said a word until he exited with a quiet "Thanks". He drove home, strictly observing the speed limit, left a message on his office answerphone saying he would be in late and collapsed into bed at 5.45 am. Noone's last thought was that his world had definitely changed forever.

It was the eleventh of September, and later that day, United Airlines Flight 175 and American Airlines Flight 11 were deliberately crashed into the Twin Towers, and the world itself changed forever.

27. PUNISHMENT

"We operate as one company with high-level consultants selected from leading companies across Europe. This truly international outlook helps us form the right team for multi-country assignments. Through knowledge-sharing, our wide network of contacts with industry leaders, and a proprietary worldwide database, we offer our clients a uniquely integrated approach.

We employ consultants with broad experience and call on individuals with specialist expertise to meet the specific needs of each client situation. This multi-sector approach allows us to widen the search to include outstanding candidates with transferable skills who may otherwise have been overlooked.

It is very important to me that we maintain the highest ethical standards. We never recruit employees from our clients, maintain strict confidentiality policies and strive to always exceed expectations. This is perhaps the reason why many of our clients have stayed with us year after year."

ERIC SALMON WEBSITE

It was one of those JFK, "everyone remembers what they were doing at the time" days. Noone got to the office around midday, wondering whether he needed to tell Bargewell about his previous evening's misfortunes. He had more or less convinced himself that he could get away without telling him, when his secretary told him that according to "breaking news" channels on the internet, a small plane had hit one of the Twin Towers. Noone followed Dexter Macdangle and Henchley Longbad to the lounge of the Holiday Inn at the Piccadilly end of Berkeley Street, where they could take a late lunch and observe the unfolding ghastly drama on TV. The filthy, black, billowing smoke, the tiny figures choosing to jump to death rather than be overcome by fumes and heat, the impact of the second plane into the south tower, the virulent, angry fireball and more smoke. The towers' twin collapse, with people scattering through the streets and seeking refuge in doorways from the choking tidal wave of dust and smoke. Noone almost felt sorry for the vacuous Bush when the TV showed the moment that he was informed that America was under attack: that bewildered, haunted look of a man who had ignored the warnings of impending terrorist action and was no longer in control of his world. Thanks to the immediacy of modern, televisual media, these scenes would etch themselves onto the collective memory of the present global generation.

The lounge watched in shocked, aweful silence. Even Henchley Longbad, never short of a few words, was short of words. Noone felt that these apocalyptic events were putting his travails of the previous night into perspective. He was bruised and irritated by his predicament but although he was going to lose his driving licence, which felt as if it would be the end of his world, he found it terrible that there would be people around him in London who were forced to watch as their loved ones were consumed by fire and fumes and the collapsing buildings.

Over the next few days, Noone went mechanically about his business, trying to function as if nothing had happened while everyone else seemed convinced that nothing would ever be the same again. Flights into and out of America were halted and, as the stock markets crashed, it seemed as if the world was taking a collective breath, waiting to see what would happen next. Noone's Summons arrived through the post. Having been granted bail, it was his "duty to surrender to the custody of Wycombe Magistrates Court on the 21st day of September". No apostrophe, he noted. He would be "charged alone" that on "Monday 10th September at Bourne End in the County of Buckinghamshire he drove a motor vehicle, namely a Mercedes estate motor car index number NO5OONE on a road, namely Wycombe Road after consuming so much alcohol that the proportion of it in [your] breath exceeded the prescribed limit. Contrary to Section 5 (1) (A) of the Road Traffic Act 1988 and Schedule 2 to the Road Traffic Offenders Act 1988". Noone thought it might be time to tell Bargewell and arranged an audience in his diary through Deidre, who didn't seem to approve that he wished to see Barry alone.

"Can it wait until after the next consultants' meeting?" she enquired brusquely.

"No, it can't." replied Noone, equally brusquely. He wasn't going to flatter or charm her. Grudgingly, she allocated a 6pm slot the following Monday.

"I can let you have half an hour only," she warned, "he is going to the opera that night." Noone deduced that Bargewell was lavishing sycophantic hospitality on an important client, for Bargewell hated opera.

"So be it," he said, turning away and almost adding "my little nest of vipers". He read in the Evening Standard that on an American TV programme called the *700 Club*, TV evangelists Jerry Falwell and Pat Robertson said that pagans, abortionists, feminists, gays and lesbians, the ACLU, and the People For the American Way were partially to blame for 9/11. Osama Bin Laden, apparently a Saudi Arabian billionaire, was named as a suspected mastermind behind the atrocities, but he issued a denial.

Noone's meeting with Bargewell was short, and if not sweet, mercifully matter of fact and lacking in recrimination. After exchanging pleasantries about the dreadful events "across the pond", Bargewell played intently with the retraction mechanism of his gold Cross ballpoint pen as Noone recounted briefly his hard-luck story.

"Hard luck. Could have happened to anyone. There by the grace of god and all that. Bit of a bugger, though. I suppose you will lose your licence. You mustn't let this interfere with your work. How will you get around?" Noone was under no illusions, despite hearing apocryphal stories of people "who had got off on a technicality" or a rush of sudden leniency from a court. It was only a question of for how long his licence would be removed; received wisdom suggested six months minimum, eighteen months maximum for a first offence. Therefore, he had been giving plenty of thought to the transportation conundrum. From his house in the small housing estate of Sutton Close on the outskirts of Cookham, Noone decided he could cycle each morning to Maidenhead station and catch either a First Great Western or Thames train into Paddington. Thence, he could cycle to the office, reversing the journey in the evening. All he required was two bicycles, a season ticket and use of the shower. Client visits outside London would have to be undertaken by a mixture of cadging lifts with colleagues, trains and taxis. It would be a severe test of both Noone's patience and the abilities of Railtrack and the self-serving, passenger-unfriendly, train operating companies, which Noone would be forced to reward with his reluctant custom. He relayed his contingency plan to Bargewell.

"Sounds do-able; easy on the taxis though. We won't pick up any gratuitous fares, so try to charge the client whenever you can, there's a good chap". The unspoken implication was that Noone should not let his business development activities slacken in any way. Typical. Bargewell wasn't sympathetic at all; he was only interested in the bottom line.

"Of course, Barry," Noone said smoothly. "Rest assured it won't affect my performance in any way." That was really what Bargewell wanted to hear.

"That's the ticket; just what I wanted to hear. I know I can rely on you, Adam. Jolly hard cheese and all that. Best of luck".

"Enjoy the opera, Barry," said Noone as he made for the door.

"I will, thanks. Prospect of some work coming from it as well." Replied Bargewell, with a knowing wink. Sanctimonious, lying bastard, thought Noone, as he exited.

The day before Noone was due in court, President Bush

gave his "state of the union" speech:

"And tonight, the United States of America makes the following demands on the Taliban: Deliver to United States authorities all the leaders of al Qaeda who hide in your land. Release all foreign nationals, including American citizens, you have unjustly imprisoned. Protect foreign journalists, diplomats and aid workers in your country. Close immediately and permanently every terrorist training camp in Afghanistan, and hand over every terrorist, and every person in their support structure, to appropriate authorities. Give the United States full access to terrorist training camps, so we can make sure they are no longer operating.

These demands are not open to negotiation or discussion. The Taliban must act, and act immediately. They will hand over the terrorists, or they will share in their fate.

Our war on terror begins with al Qaeda, but it does not end there. It will not end until every terrorist group of global reach has been found, stopped and defeated."

Thus, with this show of bravado and impossible demands, the chimpanzee-lookalike President of the United States condemned the world to a bleak future, setting western democracy irrevocably against an increasingly active and militant Muslim agenda. In the years to come, this schism, like a festering scab, would be repeatedly picked open by NATO-backed shows of military might, countered by the horrific slaughter of innocent people by a seemingly endless well of terrorist suicide bombers.

Noone had confided the circumstances of his arrest and impending court appearance to Bob Ellis in the vain hope that the ex-policeman might be able to offer him advice on how to achieve leniency from the magistrates shortly due to sit in judgement on him. Bob listened to Noone relaying the whole ghastly mess.

"Well, Adam, me old cock, bit of a ghastly mess, eh?"

"Yes," acknowledged Noone gloomily. "What do you

think? Is there any way I can plead mitigating circumstances? You know, the fact I had to comfort an old friend and all that?"

"Not a chance, mate; you are bang to rights. Best chance is to get a letter from Barry confirming how difficult it would be for you to carry out your job without a car and hope they take some notice."

"Really?" Noone felt a momentary surge of hope. "Do you think they would let me keep my licence?"

"Nope; you are just the sort of middle-class professional with money and a casual regard for traffic law that they love to make an example of," Bob replied, dashing Noone's hopes instantly. "They probably want you off the road for eighteen months, but would settle for twelve and a fine if you lay it on with a trowel. Oh, and agree to take the remedial course if they offer it: it reduces the sentence by 25%." Armed with these cheering words, Noone had obtained a letter from Barry which confirmed what a decent chap he was, expressed astonishment at his lapse of judgement which was so against character and had resulted in the unfortunate circumstances of his arrest, and implied that so crucial to the performance of his duties was ready access to a car, that without it, his whole work situation might have to be reviewed. Again on Bob's advice, he had obtained a letter from Minge which spoke similarly of Noone's stoutness of heart and character and, distraught at what had befallen his old friend, took the entire blame for forcing him to the pub that night and pouring strong ale down him. No mention was to be made of Noone's Reading-based, pre-lapse champagne reception.

Minge had also agreed to ferry Noone to and from the Magistrates' Court, anticipating the inevitable, that Noone would be leaving the Court stripped of his licence and thus prevented from getting behind the wheel of a car. The day passed in a blur. They had parked in the Easton Street multi-storey, at 0945 reported to the Court Usher, a be-gowned and bespectacled busybody with a clip-board and spent an hour or so sitting in the waiting hall outside the entrances to the individual court-rooms, watching assorted human flotsam and jetsam come and go. The day's defendants, all male, stuck out like sore thumbs, mostly dressed in shiny suits and ill-knotted, polyester ties. Some had anxious-looking, pale girlfriends attached, others came armed with a mate or two inevitably sporting tattoos on bare forearms. Some were cocky and loud, obviously used to the experience, others apprehensive, nervous and downcast. Noone wondered what exotic cocktail of offences was being paraded before the courts: GBH, ABH, burglary and car-theft from the real criminals, perhaps one or two unlucky drink-drivers like himself? One fellow traveller, hands in pockets and beanie hat pulled down to his eyes, confessed compulsively to Noone that this was his second time in for driving without a licence or insurance, "unlucky or what, innit?"

Eventually, the Usher called him through to Court Two for *Regina vs Noone, Adam*. In fact, he was to be tried by a District Judge (or "Stipendary") not by magistrates, which he took as a negative. Magistrates could have been ordinary people like him and therefore sympathetic, but a county judge was clearly no mere mortal but a professional, paid not to sympathise. He was shown into the defendant's box by the Clerk of the Court, now called a Legal Advisor, and asked for his licence. The Clerk then read out the charge and asked him how he pleaded.

"Guilty," he replied, with a dry voice. Then the Solicitor from the Crown Prosecution Service read the circumstances of the case as described by the police officers. Noone noted indignantly that they had recorded that he had driven erratically and without main beam headlights, both untrue, presumably to embellish the fact that he had been incapable through drink. He was hardly in a position to dispute the claim. The judge asked whether there were any factors to be considered before sentence was passed and the two letters were read out. The judge delivered his verdict: suspension of licence for twelve months and a five hundred pound fine plus costs of seventy "in view of his circumstances". Fuck me, talk about soak the rich, which I'm not, thought Noone bitterly. As predicted by Bob Ellis, the judge asked him whether he would consider attending a drink-driver rehabilitation scheme, to which he answered yes, and the sentence was duly commuted to nine months. As the Legal Advisor escorted Noone from the stand, she kindly asked him whether he would care to pay the fine and expenses now by credit card "as it was probably easier that way". Yes, and a sure-fire way of getting the money off him quickly, Noone thought, as he duly gave up his credit card; still, at least he would get that back sooner than his licence. He signed a form which confirmed his change in status with a bold statement in capital letters: **YOU ARE NOW DISQUALIFIED FROM DRIVING**. He was favoured with a copy of this, as if he needed reminding.

And that was that. Noone was now a fully paid up member of the registered criminal fraternity. He was yet to see it that way, though. His cathartic journey to enlightenment came through the drink-driver rehabilitation scheme on which he now embarked for three whole, successive Mondays. Bargewell generously turned a blind eye to Noone's absence from the office "as long as he made the time up in his own time". The course onto which he had enrolled was staged by a Thames Valley non-profit-making (so they said, although Noone had to send a cheque for £120 for the privilege of attending) organisation snappily monikered Convicted Recently Or Almost Convicted Drivers Education Against Drink. Noone immediately noted the lack of apostrophe and the forbidding acronym. It ran courses throughout the Thames Valley, sweeping up the newly-convicted drunken drivers spewed out by the courts. Handily for Noone, one of the locations from which it practised was a small community centre off St Luke's Road in Maidenhead, an easy cycle ride from his home. CROACDEAD proudly boasted that although national statistics showed that 9.6% of convicted drink-drivers re-offend within 36 months, only 0.22% of people who undertook its sixteen-hour course, did so. Studying its website in anticipation of the first session, Noone read that the objectives of the course were to:

-Increase knowledge about alcohol
-Improve health-related alcohol behaviours
-Promote change in risk-taking behaviours
-Consider the need for change in attitudes to drink-driving

What a load of bollocks, Noone thought. He wasn't looking forward to being preached to by a bunch of teetotal do-gooders who aimed to interfere with his lifestyle. His immediate problem was how to continue his lifestyle without the aid of a car. He had already received a letter from the DVLA acknowledging his driving disqualification and warning him that although his breath test reading was less than twice over the limit, which would have necessitated a medical check before the re-issue of a licence, nevertheless, if he were to incur a further disqualification for an alcohol-related offence within the next ten years he "would be required to undergo medical tests before consideration would be given to issuing a new licence". The letter continued soberly:

"This policy was first introduced in 1983 and extended in June 1990, following a review of road traffic law. It is the department's aim to reduce the number of road casualties by 40% and children by 50% by the year 2010." These were things about which Noone had been completely ignorant, in particular that the Government wanted to reduce children by half. The letter ended rather condescendingly, Noone felt: "As a significant number of accidents are alcohol-related, I am sure you will appreciate that positive steps need to be taken to reduce the number of incidents arising from drink/driving offences." Noone noted the interesting use of a slash, rather than a hyphen, which seemed to suggest that the Government wasn't quite sure whether both drink and driving needed to be reduced, or drink, or driving.

Returning to the CROACDEAD website, Noone became even more suspicious of its non-profit-making status by the warning in bold letters: "PLEASE NOTE- if you do not attend session one, having booked a place, you will have to pay half the course fee again in order to book another course." The testimonials by former attendees were predictably cheery: "It is not as bad as it sounds", "Everyone should go on this course", "I enjoyed it and learned so much. Thanks!", "I am so pleased I did the course, everyone was so friendly" and "Well worth the money". Yeah, right, thought Noone, we will see.

The small community centre was certainly small, nothing more than a large room in what originally had been a small commercial or office building. Noone, armed with his Drink-Drive Rehabilitation Scheme referral order issued by the Clerk of the Court, became one of an anonymous and furtive group eyeing each other up self-consciously. He seemed to be the only cyclist amongst them, judging by the lack of lurid yellow jackets and helmets, other than his own. Noone wondered how many had driven here. A large, rotund chap in a scruffy, maroon sweat-shirt encouraged everyone to help themselves to coffee, tea and biscuits from a table in one corner. Considering its immediate inhabitants, the room was inappropriately and gaudily decorated with children's pictures and learning aids: garishly coloured stick people interspersed with giant letters of the alphabet, rakishly stuck to the walls. A second man, thinner and in a blue sweat-shirt, who was smiling around at everyone rather inanely, suddenly clapped his hands and asked the inmates to find a seat from the chairs arranged in a loose three-quarter circle. Noone spotted a quite attractive blonde in a faux fur jacket and made a casual beeline for the chair next to her. Ignoring the fat, ugly woman on the other side, he smiled encouragingly at Blondie who fleetingly offered a nervous smile in return. Noone too was feeling nervous.

Looking round, he counted a dozen silent people, all equally edgy and strangers to each other, avoiding eye-contact, waiting for the session to begin.

"Welcome everyone," opened Blue Sweat-shirt, "my name is Dave and this," he indicated Fatty Red Sweat standing beside him, "is Brian. We are your course leaders." (At least they are not 'facilitators', thought Noone).

"We are not here to judge you. In fact, we have sat where you sit now. In my case, it was driving home after 'a quick one on the way back from work' and Brian will speak for himself in a moment. You don't even have to tell us your stories if you don't want to. Our job is to explode a few myths about alcohol and show you how little it takes to get to the drink-drive limit, how long alcohol takes to leave the body, how alcohol influences your judgement and driving skill and what strategies you can use to avoid drink-driving in the future. In short, we are here to separate your drinking from your driving, not prevent you from drinking. Brian?" As Dave turned to introduce his mate, Noone was relieved to hear his last few words; he had feared that the course was to be a relentless finger point and tut-tutting about drinking with the aim of turning them all into rabid teetotallers.

"Exactly Dave," said Brian in what Noone took to be a Mancunian-type of accent. "I am an alcoholic. I was caught driving with over double the legal amount of alcohol in my blood having parked the front of my car in the back end of a bus, which I had failed to see. During my eighteen-month ban, I realised why I was out of a job, why my wife had left me and why I had crashed my car: alcohol had taken over my life. I resolved to stop drinking and haven't touched a drop since, although as you probably all know, we recovering alcoholics can never say never and have to take things one day at a time. I don't ask you all to stop like me, but I want to make sure you understand how to keep away from the wheel of a car when you have had a drink." Fair enough, thought Noone, the guy has been through the wringer; as long as he doesn't become too 'preachy'.

Dave then collected all their referral orders and took a roll call; it seemed that two people had failed to appear, which Dave said was standard, probably sick or frightened or both. He asked them to introduce themselves in turn and say what their alcohol level had been when tested, but emphasised that they didn't need to reveal the circumstances of their being apprehended, since they were all probably feeling very embarrassed, even ashamed, about the incident. Noone realised this was spot on: whilst he had told close friends and Barry Bargewell, who needed to know, he had been reluctant to spread it further. Of course, word 'had got out' in the office, and everybody knew; Deidre Fettle had made sure of that.

Over the three sessions of the course, Noone's life changed. On that first day, they completed a quiz about alcohol, which revealed how little they knew, and learned how to measure alcoholic drinks in units. Noone was surprised that a pint of Adnams Broadside at 5.5% ABV represented three units. A large glass of wine, which all pubs thrust at you these days, could set you back 3.5 units. He therefore saw how ridiculous it was to say to a policeman "I've only had a couple of pints", or "a couple of glasses of wine". Worse, drinking a normal 75cl bottle of claret or rioja of 14% ABV would infuse his body with 10.5 units of alcohol- and he could easily get through two bottles at a dinner party, after an aperitif (usually at least two units if poured at home) and washed down with a "flusher" or two of beer, probably two to four additional units.

In the second session, they learned about tolerance and intoxication and how long alcohol takes to leave your body, relating this to how long before you become alcohol-free and are therefore safe to drive. In the dinner party scenario, Noone realised that he would often have been over the limit until well into the afternoon *of the following day*. They constructed a diary of their daily alcoholic unit intake, encouraged by Dave who admitted to 21-28 units per week. Noone seemed to average around 50 units per week, which he had never really bothered about or counted before, but was now forced to acknowledge put him in the 'heavy drinker' category. Several of the more artisan males in his group drank even more; the exception was mousy Dawn, who said she, like Brian, had given up 'the alcohol' as a result of 'her incident'.

The third session reached a crescendo: Dave showed them how to find the cheapest quotes for car insurance from brokers sympathetic to their situation and the mechanics of how to apply for a new licence. They considered risk-taking behaviour and peer pressure, which naturally led on to talking about what happened in each of their particular situations and now, responding to Dave's question asking who would like to tell the group about 'their incident', they were all eager to talk, perhaps sensing that the unburdening before a sympathetic peer group would be therapeutic.

Their stories were manifold, interesting and shocking. Ron, after an evening drinking in a pub, went to move his car from the car-park, which was due to be locked at closing time, to the road outside so that he could carry on drinking courtesy of a 'lock-in'. Unfortunately, the car, which had previously been written off in an accident and resurrected, Lazarus-like on the quiet by a mate 'in the trade', sheared its steering bolt and, in front of a passing police car, Ron was unable to prevent it sailing into the gate-post where it expired. Pete was stopped by the police for 'weaving across the road' on his way back from comforting a friend whose wife had just died. The comforting involved sharing a bottle and a half of scotch, which Pete had considered perfectly normal.

Gary had driven friends from his home in Slough to a party in North London, where he had partaken lavishly of the hospitality before falling asleep in a bedroom with a bird he had just picked up and managed to shag (the group nodded knowingly and gave him approving, even jealous, smiles). At about five in the morning, his friends had woken him up and demanded he take them back home. The bird didn't look too good at that time in the morning, so he agreed. With his mates snoring in the back, he made it to the outskirts of Slough before falling asleep at the wheel and bouncing off several cars parked along the street. This sent his car broadside across the road and he had been attempting a twenty point turn when apprehended by a passing patrol car.

"The bleedin' annoyin' thing was, like, I was only 500 yards from me 'ome" he complained to the group.

Mark had been at a wedding in the country. The reception had been held in a village hall with a coach laid on afterwards to ferry the slaughtered guests to their hotel about three miles away. It had made one trip and was due back to pick up the stragglers like Mark, who had elected to stay 'for one last drink'. However, four of them had become impatient and wanted to take their drinks with them to the hotel, where they could have 'one last drink' with whomever was still standing in the hotel bar. Mark offered to drive, so they piled into his car and promptly got lost in the country lanes. Spotting a police car parked at a crossroads, Mark had the brilliant idea of asking the way to the hotel and, betrayed thrice by his slurred speech, unfocused eyes and beery breath, was duly nicked.

Alan, a rough-looking Tottenham supporter who worked in a warehouse and had "Spurs" creatively tattooed on each forearm, always went to the pub with a colleague or two during his lunch-break 'for a couple of pints'. On this particular day, he had got into an argument with an Arsenal fan over whether or not Sol Campbell was a 'treacherous bastard and a bloody great poof'. Lapels were grabbed and blows threatened but not delivered; the air was ripe with language. Alan was bought a third drink by his mates to calm him down before they returned to his car in the car-park, where on taking the driver's seat, Alan found a policeman tapping on his window. His erstwhile adversary in the pub had been an off-duty police officer who, after their liberal exchange of views, rather meanly had called up his chums to interview Alan. It wasn't Alan's fault that he had a penchant for Carlsberg Export which gave him a pleasingly sharp and argumentative edge, but the off-duty Fuzz knew that three cans of the stuff at 9% ABV equated to over 12 units, placing Alan satisfactorily well over the limit.

John had been to watch an England World Cup qualifying match at Anfield with four mates and had volunteered to drive since he, a jobbing decorator, had the largest car, a clapped out Volvo 940 GLE Estate. Despite a boot filled with paint paraphernalia, it could contain five large girths with relative ease. 'Old Wembley' had been demolished and the new white elephant was in the process of construction, so the home qualifying fixtures were passed around the leading football cities. They had driven up early on the Saturday morning, parked up near the stadium in Lower Breck Road and taken a liquid lunch of 'a couple of pints' at The Cabbage Hall pub on Breck Road. From one of the factory bars in the stadium, they crammed in another round of gassy and overpriced fizz at half-time, and on the way back from the match, had celebrated the 2-1 England victory (Owen and Beckham) with a quick one back in the Cabbage Hall on the way to the car. The journey down south had been high-spirited but uneventful until John had had to brake very suddenly because of a sudden tailback on the M1 near Toddington. The car behind failed to react as quickly as John and buried its nose amongst the paint pots in the Volvo boot. Several other cars then joined the fun and it took half an hour for the mess to be sorted out from the safety of the hard shoulder. Although nobody was hurt, the arriving police wanted statements from all witnesses and, unluckily for John, breathalysed all the drivers. John was caught over the limit and armed with his new-found knowledge about units, admitted proudly to the group that he had probably consumed twelve or more units during the course of the afternoon.

Mike and Pete had similar stories: both had committed a minor traffic offence which was observed by an unobserved (by them) police car. Mike had jumped a red light, Pete got stuck on a yellow box junction and when pulled over, had breathed alcohol fumes over the Fuzz, causing the fateful enquiry: "Have you been drinking, sir?" They both had, admitting to the group that each had just left a lengthy session and couldn't remember how much liquid they had shifted.

The most shocking was Dumb Dick, as Noone was forced to call him. Dick had already lost his licence twice before, but cause and effect clearly didn't register with him. He was returning 'from a session', lost it on a bend, and sent the car through a hedge, across a garden and embedded it in the wall of a house. Fortunately, there was nobody at home, and amazingly, despite losing a front wheel, Dick was able to reverse the car out of the front room. Unfortunately, however, several sets of neighbours had heard the crash and pulled Dick out of the car as he unsuccessfully tried to turn it round to drive off. For this, he had been sentenced to six weeks in jail, commuted to three with the instruction to attend this course. He was deemed a 'High Risk Offender', had been banned from driving for four years, and would have to retake a driving test as well as pass a medical before being allowed back on the road. Given that this had been Dick's third known offence, Noone felt little sympathy for the bloke who was clearly so thick that he probably shouldn't be given responsibility for anything more complex than a paper bag.

And then there were the ladies: fat, ugly Christine was a very sad case. She lived with her mother, an alcoholic who was rapidly dragging Christine down into the same mire. One evening, sat watching telly, they had run out of fags and booze and mother ordered Christine to 'the Offie' to replenish stocks. In the shop, she had dropped and smashed a bottle of wine and got into an argument with the shop-keeper about not paying for it. He had called the police, she stormed out and was caught by a squad car on the way home. She admitted to the group that she and her mother had earlier drunk three bottles of wine between them, more or less a daily occurrence. Also rather sad was mousy Dawn, a post-woman. Having finished her round, she had joined some fellow 'Posties' in the pub where she had consumed several barley wines. She had then mounted her scooter, fancying some fish and chips on the way home. Having successfully completed the purchase, she set off for home, only to fall off while negotiating a roundabout. The resultant traffic chaos attracted the eyes of the Old Bill who, in assisting a distraught Dawn away from the roundabout, noticed her reeking breath and asked the inevitable question. Her scooter remained forlornly parked at the side of the road for ten days, she said, the fish and chips secure but increasingly smelly and inedible in the under-seat storage.

Blondie Sharon had been completely stitched up by a love-rival. Sharon had divorced her abusive husband, who had repeatedly beaten her before leaving to shack up with Sharon's 'friend', who lived a couple of streets away. This woman had subsequently called Sharon to share that the man had taken to beating her as well and Sharon had been sympathetic. One night, during a party which Sharon was holding in her flat, her phone went and it was the woman, apparently hysterical, screaming that the man was threatening to kill her and could Sharon rush round to help her? She agreed, hopped into her car and was greeted outside the woman's premises by a pair of policemen who told her they had reason to believe she had been drinking and would she breathe into the dreaded device? As the proceedings reached their inevitable conclusion, her 'ex' and the girlfriend had emerged laughing from their flat.

"That'll teach you, you fuckin' ugly slag," were the last words Sharon heard from her former husband, as she was eased into the back seat of the police car.

Noone reflected that they were all united by two common themes which had caused them to commit their crimes: firstly, peer pressure had been a factor, in that they were all responding in some way to the bidding of others; and secondly, the alcohol which they had drunk caused them to make the poor decisions which had led to the situations of their arrest.

Finally, they completed another alcohol quiz (Noone was pleased to get all the answers right this time) and then Dave stood before them for the last time:

"Well that's it everyone. Thanks very much for being an attentive and interactive group. We hope that the things that you have learned here will prevent you from placing yourselves in high-risk situations in future. Remember, keep your drinking separate from your driving: the police will target drivers returning from a Drink-Drive conviction through increasing use of number-plate recognition technology. Brian and I wish you all the best; your certificates of attendance are on the table by the door on the way out. 'Bye."

28. REFLECTIONS

"Established in 1973, the Corporate Consulting Group (CCG), part of the Oxinia group of companies, is amongst the leading consultancies for executive search. We have sustained a record of quality and achievement, and have an unrivalled fund of knowledge in the course of helping companies with leadership and senior appointments. We are highly selective in the choice of our consultants and researchers. They have the knowledge, experience and ability to deal with complex and sensitive issues at board level; to understand all elements of corporate culture: values, strategies, systems, organisation and accountabilities; and, critically, to make judgements about people. We operate internationally and work with a relatively small number of clients in any one sector, thereby ensuring the greatest possible choice of management talent."

CORPORATE CONSULTING GROUP WEBSITE

The CROACDEAD course, far from being a video-nasty of horror scenarios and bloody car smashes, had proved incredibly informative and beneficial. It had a profound effect on Noone and changed his life. While the world around him was adapting to the new enemies decreed by George W Bush's "Wrr on Trrr" post "9/11" (as the Americans now euphemistically called the attack on the Twin Towers) Noone adapted to a car-free existence and found some new enemies of his own. His wife bore a lot of the burden, handling all the driving to and from social functions, except when she refused and they had to engage taxis. She normally refused after Noone had been critical about some aspect of her driving. Generally speaking, she seemed blissfully unaware of all the other road-users around her. Her use of the gears was sporadic, random and unconnected to their true function and she seemed focused on hitting every pothole or piece of debris in the road. She was ignorant of the width and length of the car and therefore terrified of reversing, during which manoeuvre she without fail failed to use the mirrors, hopelessly craning her head over her shoulder instead. All four corners of the car had been scraped or dented by malevolent forces unseen by her. She was not averse to driving off with the parking-brake on, despite a warning sign on the dashboard; indicators were operated belatedly and then only after she had slowed to make a turn. Noone tried desperately to ignore all her routine cock-ups and sit silently beside her, but the friction in the air would be palpable by the end of each journey and having to endure helplessly in the car while she murdered yet another journey seemed to Noone the hardest punishment of all.

He carried out his commuting plan, cycling every day to Maidenhead station and taking a train into Paddington where he had positioned a second bicycle to transport him into the West End. He became a cycle hooligan, developing a deep hatred for any car or pedestrian which caused him to slow down, and ignoring red traffic lights whenever possible. His rationale was that when faced with a red light, he could dismount and push the bike across the junction, so why not stay on it and ride across? With the braggadocio of the hardened criminal, he dared the authorities to challenge him, but nobody ever did. Noone did, however, draw the line at cycling on pavements, which he felt was probably a bridge too far; pavements were indisputably pedestrian territory, whereas the road was his and pedestrians encroached there at *their* peril. When absolutely forced to stop by red lights on busy junctions, such as those across Oxford Street or around Hyde Park Corner, Noone would shoot forward on yellow and harangue any laggardly pedestrian who had failed to make it to the other side in time. Once, he was embarrassed to have delivered a few choice observations about the speed of his walk to a man whom he subsequently noticed was carrying a white stick. Ah well, an urban cyclist takes no prisoners.

On the whole, despite the rain and the condition of London's roads, for which he blamed the mayor, "Red" Ken Livingstone, Noone's cycling regime worked well. It was interrupted briefly when his Paddington bike was stolen, despite it being a rusty, old beast and attached to a bike-rail by two padlocks, albeit cheap and obviously useless ones. Noone was able to make a claim for £500 on his household insurance which enabled him to invest in a decent Ridgeback hybrid and a Kryptonite New York D-lock, which the man in the shop said was "as hard as a Chinese word-search; hard enough to deter even hardened criminals". He certainly lost weight and felt fitter and made a determined effort to cut down his alcohol intake, religiously keeping count of his units consumed.

The subject of alcohol was also where his life had changed: he could now bore for Britain, and indeed did bore his friends with his new-found knowledge, most of whom, like him, were socially dependent on alcohol. He now knew that, contrary to his previous belief, everyone's judgement was impaired by alcohol. Not wishing any of them to experience the humiliation that he had felt, he became a fervent evangelist for "separating drinking from driving", in particular crusading against the often neglected perils of driving "the morning after". He knew that, like him, all his friends had driven while over the drink-drive limit at some point, and many were serial offenders like he had been. Like him previously, most had no idea how to calculate their intake and clearance of alcohol. He warned that 100,000 motorists were convicted of drink-driving every year in the UK and that 17% were undone "the morning after" and that percentage was rising steadily and would soon reach over 20%. He told them that how they felt when drinking was useless as a guide to whether to drive or not, merely an inevitable journey from jocose, through bellicose and lachrymose to comatose. And that eating first or drinking milk "to line the stomach" simply delayed the onset of the feelings of drunkenness, not the speed with which the alcohol entered and coursed energetically through your bloodstream.

The high risk situations into which people placed themselves when "under the influence" tended to stem from one of three sources: negative emotional states (such as anger, sadness or boredom); interpersonal conflicts (ie family, partner or employer); and social pressure (either direct, from someone, or indirect, from somewhere such as a party). Noone lectured on coping strategies that one should put in place in response to a high risk event, ranging from the £20 set aside for emergency taxi rides to handing over one's car keys to one's partner on returning home ready to pour a "sundowner snifter". He advocated the "driver rota" for nights out whereby there would always be a designated non-alcohol-drinking driver (or "the man called Bob" as the Dutch put it). He revealed that there were cases in which people had been "done" for driving whilst impaired through alcohol, *even though they had passed a breathalyser.* That being caught three times over the limit could cause a custodial sentence; that for four times over, as Dumb Dick had discovered, prison would be automatic. It was important to move from the natural mind-set of "it will never happen to me" to the more alien "it *will* happen to me" and use this mantra to prevent drinking and driving; but that, despite all the warnings if you were going to drink while in charge of a car, it was better to drink the glass of alcohol first, so that the liver could get to work on its disposal, and then have a soft drink, rather than the received wisdom of the other way round. He burned with embarrassment when he recalled the alcohol-induced driving transgressions of his previous life.

Noone sent off for Unit Calculator discs which the Department for Transport had helpfully printed in their thousands and issued free-of-charge to an ignorant and indifferent public. These he passed round his acquaintances. In a fit of extra missionary zeal, he even took some to his local pub and left them on tables until the landlord had a quiet word in his ear:

"I don't appreciate you interfering with my customers. We don't want any guilty consciences, thanks very much, so just fuck off, ok?" Noone sighed at the industrial-strength tide of denial that pushed against him, a solitary beacon to temperance adrift in a storm of ignorance. He knew how Jesus must have felt, preaching to the sceptical unconverted or even David Icke, the one-time respected BBC sports presenter turned reptilian conspiracy theorist and figure of public ridicule. He nearly said "Forgive them Lord, for they know not what they do", but stopped himself just in time. A convert he may be, but it was important not to become self-important about his mission.

Back at work, things were no easier. Noone still held the sympathy vote for his drink-driving conviction, for most of his male colleagues felt that "there by the grace of God went they". Sabra Termigniogni and Amber Reddie, both with well established flats in fashionable parts of London, took taxis everywhere and only drove occasionally at the weekend to visit friends "in the country". Fastidious about the Underground ("we never take the Tube, it is so unclean") they were equally fastidious about drink-driving and even at their weekend escapes, would only drink in moderation ("not for me thanks, darling, must keep a clear head for the drive back to London tomorrow"). They thought Noone a buffoon for ignoring the repeated warnings, especially around Christmas, when even the BBC carried graphic, Government-sponsored "advertisements" on the horrible consequences of drink-driving (despite statistics showing that there were more alcohol-related car accidents in June). Of course, Noone's offence hadn't been at Christmas, but that wasn't the point: he had been a fool.

Noone didn't particularly care what they thought. Self-serving Sabra he had always thought a loose cannon who was bound to explode once too often. She felt her vivacious personality and sexy style were winning her many friends. In fact, people found her dangerous and tedious. Her previous success with La Femme Qui Chante had not repeated itself recently and she was therefore cosying up to Bargewell, in the hope that he would favour her with some crumbs from his table. The trouble was, he was too intent on making as much bread as possible for himself to throw out many crumbs for anyone else. Skittish and nervy Amber had proved Noone's assumption that she would be high maintenance, many times over. In the first six months, she had run through three secretaries, two of whom had fled in tears back to their agencies on the back of a severe tongue-lashing from Amber. The agencies now took care to ask first for whom their girls might be working before committing to providing further cannon-fodder. Amber was well networked, narrow-minded, shrewish, self-centred and driven by a burning ambition to reach the top of her new tree, knocking off those on the branches around her as she powered upwards. These were excellent traits for a would-be headhunter, as Noone now recognised. She name-dropped infuriatingly, but equally infuriatingly, seemed to be able to pick up the phone to her high-level contacts who were pleased to see her retail knowledge being applied in the field of executive search. After all, there were far too few genuine retail specialists who really understood the whole complex mix of the four Marketing "P"s, topped and tailed by branding and the supply chain. Amber had "been on the shop-floor and got the t-shirt", as she liked to put it. She worked hard to differentiate herself in this way and it was undeniable that, one-on-one, she could dominate a conversation by talking loudly and rapidly, denying anyone else a say. Clients, who only saw this public face were impressed by her confidence and knowledge of the subject, and allowed themselves to be battered into submission by her motormouth. She was becoming a highly effective business-developer for Aspallan, Bane, and all her colleagues and subordinates hated her. Slightly puzzled that she was never invited to impromptu informal social get-togethers, she carried on climbing the slippery pole regardless.

Henchley Longbad was very strange. He was a country bumpkin who felt ill at ease in the company of suave, sophisticated, cosmopolitan Londoners where he had found himself, almost by accident. He wasn't stupid and had made his parents extremely proud by gaining a second class honours degree in Geography, albeit, as Barry rather uncharitably used to say "from some provincial ex-Poly University of Double-Glazing." Thence, he commenced work as a salesman in a company making and selling wire-rope, and through the dogged persistence of one with an inferiority complex, who refused to let others "get one over on him", had proved surprisingly successful. Always a loner and lacking the people skills to make it into management, he ploughed his lonely furrow, always beating his sales targets and earning his modest bonus. Then one day he saw a Daily Telegraph advertisement placed by a US-firm of so-called search consultants which was expanding in Europe and wanted hungry, aggressive, sales specialists. The promise of an egalitarian meritocracy where riches beyond his dreams could be earned from over-achieving targets appealed greatly to Longbad. In turn, his pugnacious and prickly style appealed to the US company President, a self-made millionaire "from the wrong side of the tracks" who had been fighting the cosy status quo of the Establishment all his life. Longbad was hired and thrived; sure, he had to be creative with retainer fees and sail close to the contingency wind on occasions, but cutting deals was in his blood. If his assignment completion rate wasn't as high as some, it didn't matter because his new business rate was much higher than most and his hopper was always full.

The "hire and fire" American way suited him and he earned the respect that was due to him by his own efforts. He quickly appreciated the need to specialise, to "find his market franchise" and discovered that dealing with emerging technology companies was sufficiently obscure and undiscovered for him quickly to become a recognised recruitment expert. As his fee and activity levels rose, he was feted by the Americans to whom shiny suits, button-down shirts with no tie and brown shoes were perfectly normal and by whom he was held up as an example of "a limey who got it". He understood the simplistic, performance-driven culture and in return, the Americans misunderstood Longbad and rewarded him financially. They assumed he was driven solely by money; but in fact, whilst that was indeed a major consideration, it was merely part of his status issue. Money allowed him at least the trappings of social equality, but inside, he still felt inferior. He decided that joining one of the old-established UK search businesses would provide the final stepping stone to the peer-group acceptance that he craved.

Numerous tacky "rec-to-rec" recruitment agencies had sprung up in the boom years of the Nineties and "post 9/11", all were scrabbling for business from a largely indifferent client group of search consultancies which were busy cutting costs and heads to meet the bleaker reality of redacted life in the long shadow of suicidal Muslim extremism. One of the pond-life from such an agency had been ringing round trying to pinpoint the up-and-coming talent in the search world; Longbad's name had been mentioned and his contact number furtively elicited. Longbad was flattered to be called and told that he had been recommended as an upcoming star for a perfect role ("for which we have been retained exclusively as consultants" whispered Pond-life smoothly down the line) in the UK's finest search business, Aspallan, Bane Consultants, where he would be able to double his earnings and reap the benefit and kudos of working within such a prestigious brand name. It was all bollocks of course. In reality, Pond-life was fishing, and intended to reverse-sell Longbad as a mercurial talent that needed to be snapped up quickly, into ABC via Bly Huxford, whom he had been courting via a quarterly trencherman's lunch at The Gaucho Grill.

Strangely, as happens once in a while, he struck lucky. Longbad was seduced enough by the weasel words to allow his name to be mentioned; Huxford, following Napier's mantra that the Group was now "one big happy family" and knowing Bargewell to be desperate to hire, recommended him, and a deal was eventually done. As times were hard, Pond-life grudgingly in public, but delightedly in private, accepted a one-off fee of fifteen percent of Longbad's initial salary of £100k. Longbad was delighted as this gave him a twenty-five percent salary increase. Huxford was delighted as he added an extra five percent as his personal kick-back and charged the company twenty percent for Pond-life's introduction. Bargewell was delighted as he gained some eagerly needed new blood, even if it was attached to a brown shiny suit and scuffed brown shoes; he assumed that emerging technology people all dressed that way.

Now, nearly a year later, Longbad was too focused on his own steps up the greasy pole to be too concerned about Noone's slide down it. He was superficially chummy to Noone, while secretly thinking he deserved to be taken down a peg or two. Noone seemed to him too smug and lazy, wrapped in a public school cloak of careless invincibility that all those self-satisfied bastards seemed to possess. Well, Longbad was doing better than Noone now, so he could put that in his pipe and smoke it. As for that upper-class twit Ughyngton-Fitzhardinge, Longbad knew that he could never aspire to rub shoulders with one who possessed such a grand lineage, and he hated him for it. But what he lacked in castles, real-estate and blue-blooded contacts he made up for in fee revenues and in this he had become of superior value compared to Huff.

Stephen Addergoole and Dexter Macdangle were sympathetic to Noone but were also preoccupied with building their own track records and reputations. The former continued to farm a network of dull, old-fashioned manufacturing people who had reached MD level in dull, old-fashioned, manufacturing companies, of which there was still a surprising number. The latter had a similar network of FMCG HR types that were his friends and had no difficulty in giving him business since he sympathised with their daily struggles, having previously been there himself. Although a little dour, he revealed a dogged persistence in assignment management which meant that invariably "he got his man" and his stock was rising accordingly.

The brutal fact was that Noone was falling behind. The prime cause was his failure to pick a specialist sector and stick to it, developing both expertise in that sector's practices and knowledge of its leading players. It always impressed potential clients if you could spout a few relevant clichés and imply that you knew barrow-loads of the "movers and shakers" of that arcane world. He had actually been quite impressed with the unimpressive Addergoole, who, in a meeting to which he had invited Noone ("Nobody else is free, would you mind Adam?") had completely convinced an admiring client of his all-pervasive knowledge by repeating only a few negatives.

"So do you know anyone who would fit this role?" the client had asked at the end of a long and tedious briefing. Addergoole paused for a long time, then looked out of the window as he replied:

"Well, that's an interesting question. An interesting question. Rencher Gropeshit from Apex would be good. But he wouldn't want to leave his big bonuses. No, he is definitely too expensive. 'Bombs' Borret is a possibility; you know, Borret at Ramsets? But I can't see him moving from the North. No, he wouldn't move his family…six kids, y'know, six kids…amazing, but quite a tie, quite a tie. There is always Axel Wildwood at Foster-Gurvitz. Yes, Wildwood. He could do it, but I am not sure he would fit your culture. He is a little soft and you need a real driver here, a real driver." The client was by now hanging off every word.

"What about Rape-Ramhorn?" he threw in, hopefully.

"Rape-Ramhorn at Snelling? No, moved around too

much. He'd be gone inside two years. No, I really feel the best way forward is to conduct a full search assignment using our extensive network of sources, contacts and candidates." And that was that, sold to the admiring client behind the big desk and computer screen.

Noone no longer found any of the email jokes funny, mainly because the internet's immediate, inclusive and expansive nature meant that every known joke had now been circulated to everyone on the planet at least three times. The art of oral joke-telling was dying. Even quotations allegedly uttered by reliably thick footballers had lost their power to amuse, he thought, as he surveyed a list which he had received almost simultaneously from four different sources:

"My parents have always been there for me, ever since I was about 7." **David Beckham**

"I would not be bothered if we lost every game as long as we won the league." **Mark Viduka**

"Alex Ferguson is the best manager I've ever had at this level. Well, he's the only manager I've actually had at this level. But he's the best manager I've ever had." **David Beckham**

"If you don't believe you can win, there is no point in getting out of bed at the end of the day." **Neville Southall**

"I've had 14 bookings this season - 8 of which were my fault, but 7 of which were disputable." **Paul Gascoigne**

"I've never wanted to leave. I'm here for the rest of my life, and hopefully after that as well." **Alan Shearer**

"I'd like to play for an Italian club, like Barcelona." **Mark Draper**

"You've got to believe that you're going to win, and I believe we'll win the World Cup until the final whistle blows and we're knocked out." **Peter Shilton**

"I faxed a transfer request to the club at the beginning of the week, but let me state that I don't want to leave Leicester." **Stan Collymore**

"I was watching the Blackburn game on TV on Sunday when it flashed on the screen that George (Ndah) had scored in the first minute at Birmingham. My first reaction was to ring him up. Then I remembered he was out there playing." **Ade Akinbiyi**

"Without being too harsh on David Beckham, he cost us the match." **Ian Wright**

"I'm as happy as I can be - but I have been happier." **Ugo Ehiogu**

"Leeds is a great club and it's been my home for years, even though I live in Middlesborough." **Jonathan Woodgate**

"I can see the carrot at the end of the tunnel." **Stuart Pearce**

"I took a whack on my left ankle, but something told me it was my right." **Lee Hendrie**

"I couldn't settle in Italy - it was like living in a foreign country." **Ian Rush**

"Germany are a very difficult team to play...they had 11 internationals out there today." **Steve Lomas**

"I always used to put my right boot on first, and then obviously my right sock." **Barry Venison**

"I definitely want Brooklyn to be christened, but I don't know into what religion yet." **David Beckham**

"The Brazilians were South American, and the Ukrainians will be more European." **Phil Neville**

"All that remains is for a few dots and commas to be crossed." **Mitchell Thomas**

"One accusation you can't throw at me is that I've always done my best." **Alan Shearer**

"I'd rather play in front of a full house than an empty crowd." **Johnny Giles**

The only thing of note, Noone mused, was that the England captain, David Beckham, had three entries in the 23 examples of footballing intelligence. Did that make him 13% thicker than your average footballer, Noone wondered?

The distractions of the drink-drive conviction, the embarrassment and diminishment he felt because of it and the daily struggle on train and bicycle had sapped his confidence and drive. In his last year at ABS, he had been one of the highest billers, with personal fee revenues of around £320k and introductions which arguably took his contribution beyond £600k. As his first ABC year-end approached, Noone's total fee contribution had fallen to around £350k. He had not quite hit the holy grail of "covering his costs times three", which was when you became socially and collegially acceptable as a headhunter. Significantly, he had "eaten all that he killed" and had not found any spare engagements to pass on to any of his colleagues, the mark of a truly useful search consultant. Mind you, none of his colleagues had introduced him to any work either. Yes, it was becoming a dog-eat-dog world again and Noone began to fear for his own ability to avoid becoming dead meat.

29. LOSING TOUCH

"The Rose Partnership was established in 1981; we have a strong reputation within the industry for the quality and professionalism of our work. Our brand, derived from 29 years of delivering excellence to top companies and financial institutions, gives us an edge in our marketplace. We represent clients convincingly and powerfully because we are specialists and know our markets inside out. We are in a position to recognise what our clients need and we have the quality of people and process to deliver it."

THE ROSE PARTNERSHIP WEBSITE

Noone's gloom persisted into the palindrome of 2002, when all the fee-clocks were reset back to zero and each consultant had to begin the climb all over again. With the exception of Sabra Termignioni, all of them had qualified for some degree of bonus. Amber Reddie and Dexter Macdangle had completed excellent years from standing starts and billed over £500k each, as had Longbad. Barry Bargewell had somehow delivered £750k. The rest, save Sabra, had produced between £300k and £400k. The bonuses had been trimmed by the Group skimming off its "share of profit" and Bargewell skimming off his "management bonus". Bargewell trousered £75k, not up with the glory years but enough to pay for the school fees and a couple of luxury holidays to Gstaad and St Lucia. Of the consultants, at the top end, Amber and Dexter each qualified for a bonus of £50k, paid after the tax year-end in April, and the rest somewhat less. Noone and Huff got £15k each.

Bargewell asked Sabra to take a pay cut, as she "wasn't covering her costs". Deidre Fettle confided to Bix Napier's secretary, with whom she felt on a level, that Sabra had exploded in fury and had screamed some extremely unladylike things at "poor Barry", only some of which had been in Italian and the rest "in all too plain English, if you know what I mean", she said, arching both eyebrows. Strictly speaking, she arched one eyebrow, since she possessed a deeply unattractive, black, conjoined "monobrow". Napier's secretary wondered why Deidre didn't shave a gap which could then be dabbed with foundation: it would disguise Deidre's Neanderthal leanings, she thought, unkindly.

Shortly afterwards, Sabra cleared her office and flounced out for good. When Bob Ellis reported to Bargewell that her PC and keyboard had had red wine poured over them and were damaged beyond repair, her client lists had vanished and certain hardware items such as a dictation machine, mobile phone and a limited edition print were also missing and a fire had occurred in the waste-bin, Barry tried to issue an injunction against her. However, this proved impossible as she had apparently quit her rented flat and, according to her former landlord, "had left to go sailing on a yacht". Nobody ever saw her again.

Bob Ellis, aware of Noone's darkening mood, sought to cheer him up with some black humour on the hot topic of fanaticism. He emailed an offering from one of his former copper colleagues, which contrasted the joys of living in a western democracy with the alleged privations of submitting to Islamic law. Exaggerated for effect and illustrated by sharply contrasting pictures showing life on both sides of the idealistic divide, it nevertheless concluded with a telling tract from deepest America:

FANATICISM

"A man whose family was German aristocracy prior to World War Two owned a number of large industries and estates. When asked how many German people were true Nazis, the answer he gave can guide our attitude towards fanaticism.

'Very few people were true Nazis,' he said, 'but many enjoyed the return of German pride, and many more were too busy to care. I was one of those who just thought the Nazis were a bunch of fools. So, the majority just sat back and let it all happen. Then, before we knew it, they owned us, and we had lost control, and the end of the world had come. My family lost everything. I ended up in a concentration camp and the Allied bombing destroyed my factories.'

We are told again and again by 'experts' and 'talking heads' that Islam is the religion of peace, and that the vast majority of Muslims just want to live in peace. Although this unqualified assertion may be true, it is entirely irrelevant. It is meaningless fluff, meant to make us feel better, and meant somehow to diminish the spectre of fanatics rampaging across the globe in the name of Islam. The fact is that the fanatics rule Islam at this moment in history. It is the fanatics who march. It is the fanatics who wage any one of fifty shooting wars worldwide. It is the fanatics who systematically slaughter Christian or tribal groups throughout Africa and are gradually taking over the entire continent in an Islamic wave. It is the fanatics who bomb, behead, murder, or honour-kill. It is the fanatics who take over mosque after mosque. It is the fanatics who zealously recommend the stoning and hanging of rape victims and homosexuals. The hard quantifiable fact is that the 'peaceful majority', the 'silent majority', is cowed and extraneous.

History lessons are usually incredibly simple and blunt, yet for all our powers of reason, we often miss the most basic and uncomplicated of points: peace-loving Muslims have been made irrelevant by their silence. Peace-loving Muslims will become our enemy if they don't speak up, because like my friend from Germany, they will awake one day and find that the fanatics own them, and the end of their world will have begun. Peace-loving Germans, Japanese, Chinese, Russians, Rwandans, Serbs, Afghans, Iraqis, Palestinians, Somalis, Nigerians, Algerians, and many others have died because the peaceful majority did not speak up until it was too late.

As for us who watch it all unfold; we must pay attention to the only group that counts; the fanatics who threaten our way of life."

Armed with that bleak assessment of the threat to humanity, Noone went to the pub with Huff.

"I mean, what's it all about?" he ruminated morosely into his favourite pint of Scruttocks. Even its familiar and normally welcoming, fragrant, hoppy aroma and strong, first taste failed to set his taste buds racing in anticipation of the golden-hued, honey notes softening the dryness of the bitter hops and the gentle malt background, which would linger throughout.

"You and I were part of making ABS the best firm of its kind in the country. We were both successful managing consultants who billed plenty and introduced our clients to our colleagues as appropriate, for the greater good of the firm, as was drummed into us by Hugo. Now, through the management incompetence of our supposed superiors, we have seen two great businesses fall apart and are rewarded for our loyalty by being lumped together with imbeciles such as Bly Huxford and Barry Bargewell." Huff nodded sagely in agreement.

"And," said Noone, continuing his rant, "they bring in the likes of Macdangle, Longbad and that cow Amber Reddie who completely lower the tone, and selfishly pursue their own ends to bill as much as they can, sod the rest of us," he ended, slightly jealously. Huff nodded again and said:

"All presided over by the Prince of Darkness, Bix Napier. The problem is that he doesn't feel part of or like our world. He believes it is too old-fashioned and he wants to change it. Just so long as the fees are rolling in, he doesn't really care about how. The watch-word of 'quality' which we had to live, breathe and embody on pain of death from Hugo, Archie or Giles, has gone out the window. Macdangle, Longbad and Reddie are the new search-world order. It all about is fees, fees, fees and the devil take the hindmost."

"i.e. Sabra," observed Noone.

"This time, yes, but it could be you or me next," warned Huff, but Noone knew this only too well and didn't need reminding. He was already beginning to wake up in the night and fall into a muck sweat just thinking about the consequences of failure, something he had never even contemplated before. Quality and customer service should be paramount, yet these tenets had been pushed aside in the drive for the "bottom line." Noone had heard of candidates being sent to the wrong client interviews; Longbad and Reddie had almost come to blows in a Consultants' meeting over a candidate whom they each wanted to headhunt; Macdangle quietly solicited someone from an off-limits client; one of the researchers pretended to be the Chairman of a major corporation in order to get a target to talk; Stephen Addergoole interviewed a candidate for fifteen minutes on Platform 1 at Slough station, while Intercity trains rushed by to and from London and the West; Longbad boasted of arranging over the phone a blind date with a client's PA ("She turned out fat and pig-ugly. The dinner was expensive, so I *had* to pork her after; just the once, mind.").

Everywhere Noone looked or listened, there were the signs of the decay and decadence which had preceded the collapse of the Roman Empire. Regurgitating shortlists became usual. At the weekly consultants' meeting, anyone commencing a new search would ask: "has anyone got any good candidates?" and try to work them into the shortlist. There was an increasing reliance on pulling candidates from the database, rather than undertaking truly original, telephone-based research. The aim was to short-cut, to fit the search to the available candidates, rather than the other way round: anything to alleviate the drudgery of delivery. In this way, promoted by Bargewell ("get ten good CVs in front of the client as soon as you can, guys,") consultants could concentrate on developing new business rather than the chore of actually delivering a full search. After all, it was much more cost-effective.

Increasingly, with the responsibility of running ten or twelve engagements at any one time, the Consultants found themselves too busy to be bothered with the fag of writing candidate reports for clients; researchers sat in on interviews and then reprocessed the shortlisted candidates' CVs with a few lightweight introductory and summary paragraphs. This was called "topping-and-tailing", but always, the consultant's name went as the byline on the report. As a minor protest, a researcher working for Longbad slipped in a sarcastic sentence: "If anyone takes the trouble to read this report, you will find that candidate Snooks has bad breath and wears a wig." Neither Longbad nor the client spotted it.

For Longbad, search was entirely about the thrill of winning new business; he hardly cared about completion, for by then, most of the fee would normally have been paid. He picked up an American client, the CEO of a smallish bio-tech business keen to establish a footprint in You-rap. Longbad was to find a European CEO to kick-off the international expansion. After two months of desultory and half-hearted effort, he cobbled together a database-driven shortlist, which he presented proudly over the telephone to the client. The client decided to send over his VP HR to conduct the initial interviews; he would select one or two candidates to fly to the States for final selection and to finalise the offer. An archetypal, cowboy-booted Redneck duly arrived, set up shop in the Park Lane Hilton and met the four finalists one by one. Longbad, who was by now concentrating on winning business elsewhere, realised that all was not so hunky-dory when his candidates individually fed back to him that during the interviews, Mr Redneck had asked them to relate their family history and then stared out of the window, hardly asking another question. All felt awkward with this unusual approach and Longbad sensed that persuading any of them to accept an offer may prove difficult. The debrief with Mr Redneck did not go well.

"Did you enjoy the meetings," asked Longbad insouciantly, but fearing the worst. The worst came.

"Nope. Furst was a faggot, secon' a hippie, thurd a ree-tard and nummer four a fee-male."

"But she is highly intelligent, with a great record," offered Longbad, weakly.

"I done care if she brighter than George Dubya Bush, the President of the You-nited States of America. She gonna have chillun one day soon. Ain't no good t' us. Nunnuvem any good t'us. You bin wastin' arr tahm." And with that, he showed Longbad the door of his hotel room and returned to the US the following day. Much to Longbad's relief, he never heard another word from the company.

On occasions, Amber Reddie couldn't even find the time to interview candidates, so her poor, put-upon researcher, a young graduate with no experience of business, became responsible for the entire assignment transaction and fed Amber the personal titbits about candidates which enabled Amber to pretend to her clients that she knew the candidates intimately. By now Amber had two PAs (or "EAs", Executive Assistants, as she liked to call them) working for her and two researchers. She had also managed to avail herself of the services of a limousine hire firm, and would be picked up from outside the office, swept in private luxury to her meeting, and would exit the car grandly, the chauffeur holding open the door, with a throw-away "wait for me here dear," over her shoulder.

Rodney Shakeshaft had taken to hiring a room in the Berkeley Street Holiday Inn every Thursday afternoon ("It helps my chronic back problem and enables me to continue to function"); Henchly Longbad had observed to Noone that, coincidentally, a succession of "professionally-dressed" women were interviewed by Shakeshaft in his hotel room. At six o'clock one Thursday, Longbad had spotted him propping up the hotel bar.

"I have just drunk a bottle of champagne by myself to

celebrate clinching an offer which I made from my bath," he reported proudly, unaware of the lipstick smudge on his collar.

Bargewell turned a blind eye to such excess since he too had his nose firmly embedded in the trough. He had managed to pick up a search for a US-based client which apparently necessitated him flying Business Class every month for six months to demonstrate progress (or "keep the client updated and close to the action" as he put it). It was just about possible to justify, but somehow Barry managed to take his wife and dog with him on every trip and dined out in New York's finest restaurants at the client's expense. Noone could only shake his head in wonder at Barry's brass neck and the gullibility of the Septics.

Noone was also curious to observe that Bargewell, despite having a mobile phone permanently in his hand, when not in the USA or elsewhere "away on business", would make a daily sortie from the office to one of the public phone boxes on Berkeley Square. He tackled Bob Ellis on the subject.

"So why does our dear friend need to make calls from a public urinal when he has the latest technology permanently strapped to his ear?" he asked.

"Ah, you don't know? I shouldn't be telling you this, but let's just say he is talking to a horse trader about some white lady to rail," Bob winked as he said this. Noone raised his eyebrows quizzically, so Bob tried again.

"He is on the blow, bump, yak, Columbian marching powder, if you see what I mean." He leaned back knowingly.

"No, I don't see what you mean; I haven't the foggiest idea what you are talking about," said Noone, becoming exasperated. Bob leaned forward conspiratorially.

"Bloody hell, Adam, you are supposed to be a man of the world, squire; our friend Barry likes to take a daily sniff of celestial sugar, coke, cocaine…got it?"

"Shit. I had no idea."

"Obviously," said Bob, wryly.

"How long has he been doing this?" asked Noone.

"Certainly while he has been head of ABC, probably way before that," replied Bob. "I have had a shufti through the drawers in his office, but he is careful to keep them clean. Mind you, the bog seats are probably coated with the stuff." If he was fuelled with cocaine, Bargewell's increasingly extravagant behaviour, the shouting match with Sabra, his disorganisation to which Deidre Fettle constantly had to attend, his flaky but obsessive approach, suddenly began to make sense.

"I have a high octane, coke-fuelled junkie as my boss. Perfect," muttered Noone, despondently.

"Look on the bright side," said Bob, in his inimitable, sardonic way, "he is bound to slip up one day and Napier will have him for breakfast. If I were a betting man, which of course I am, I'd say he probably won't last long." As usual, Bob proved right.

Outside in the market, the customary lurid stories came and went, just as they always had. At an investment bank, a favoured candidate was sent for a final interview with the CEO for the Head of Mergers & Acquisitions position. Imagine the mutual surprise when each shook hands with his own brother: the CEO had changed his name years ago and both had neglected to keep in touch. Another investment bank seeking a Head of Sales decided there were only six possible candidates in the world and offended the lead candidate by offering him a bacon roll at his first interview. He was Jewish. After a long and agonising time, the bank managed to secure the services of the Head of Sales from its leading rival. Within six months, his entire sales team had crossed the border and joined him. The bank blew its entire annual recruitment budget of £5m on this exercise alone. But it was a win/win/win situation: the search firm made £5m, the hires gained hundreds of thousands of pounds in sign-on bonuses, and the investment bank made hundreds of millions in new business, poached from their rivals.

A third international bank was served handsomely by a headhunter who happened to be the brother of the Head of the Commodities trading team. Handily, one of the headhunter's colleagues knew the trading team at a rival bank, and between them they persuaded the entire team of 200 to move across. The same search firm was reputed to have won a mandate from a US bank to "business-build" in the UK by hiring four revenue heads and the teams underneath. It was a complex and time-consuming project, but all went well to the point when some thirty senior folk had been lined up to commence work at this new enterprise. Then abruptly, the US pulled the plug. What a complete waste of effort, money and goodwill. Such were the monumental ups and downs of headhunting in Financial Services, which largely passed Noone by.

The market did lick its lascivious lips at the antics of an all-female search boutique, the Powder Partnership, which had quickly earned the disparaging sobriquet, The Killer Bimbos. Formed and ruthlessly managed by Paella De Ville, rumoured to have once been a brothel-madam, their aim was to outdo the men in this unfair men's world, by any means at their disposal. No holes were barred and Paella positively encouraged them to sleep with their clients. Women who applied to join the firm, first had to be attractive, and were asked bluntly at interview by Paella: "Would you sleep with a client if it was necessary for the business?" Those who said "no" or who prevaricated were given short shrift; they simply did not have The Right Stuff. Paella understood that sex sold and tits were a competitive advantage. The female form, feminine charm and the body itself were vital strategic elements in the battle that needed to be won over men, who started with all the advantages: the weight of history, the expectation of the parents, the expensive education, the Old School Tie network and men's ineffable kinship, confidence and smugness: all these paved the way to a man's success and had to be overcome by a woman's personal determination to best arrogant, conceited male opponents with her alternative weapons of flirtation and seduction. Every woman held this key to unlock a man's weakness, if only they knew it and were prepared to use it. The Killer Bimbos knew it and were prepared to use it.

To help "Her Girls", Paella allowed them "pampering hours", when she would pay for them to be groomed, waxed, even botoxed if necessary, in the best London salons. They could also take time off to shop for expensive and alluring clothes, with a thousand-pound monthly allowance which took the place of a company car. Tights were banned, since men literally went weak at the glimpse of a stocking-top. Armed with such drive and determination, they could only succeed, and rapidly gained a reputation for "service" which won more than their fair share of assignments. Paella even had the foresight to employ a couple of lesbians to pander to the occasional lonely, frumpish, dyke HR Director that everybody mischanced upon every once in a while.

Of course, over time, The Killer Bimbos developed fierce internal rivalries just like any other consultancy. When two of the consultants fell out over a client, the market was titillated by the leaked reports of each consultant's determined efforts to sleep with the other's husband by way of revenge. Both succeeded, for what man could resist a female friend demanding a quiet dinner at which, with close and meaningful eye-contact, she sadly, occasionally tearfully, unburdened herself about her current partner's complete lack of interest in "bedroom games"; who on being escorted home, shyly invited her escort in for a nightcap, as husband was away on business; and after slipping off to change into something more comfortable, returned in a dressing gown which she triumphantly opened to reveal her assets encased in gossamer material which inflamed the male imagination with lust and the single thought: "I have to have her now"?

The Killer Bimbos embraced sex as a legitimate tool of the trade, but more often it was men taking advantage of their positions of power to bed lesser female mortals. One notorious lothario who owned a mid-market boutique, lived with his Financial Controller until she reached her fortieth birthday. She was unceremoniously evacuated from his home and replaced with a younger secretary, who lasted for a while. By the time the lothario reached sixty himself, he was recycling ever-younger models from an agency on a weekly basis and was heard to remark, like "Col" Ned R. Porage, that "women over forty are no good at sex". This was code for "I can only get it up when I can order a young girl to flash her tits and give me a blow-job whenever I want one", if only he knew it.

2002 ground on depressingly for Noone. He had still failed to specialise and his fragmented contact base was providing too occasional and disparate assignments. His numbers were looking sick compared to those of his colleagues. Then one day, the whole firm was called to the boardroom to hear an important announcement which Bix Napier wished to make. It was standing-room only and as they assembled and jostled for position, Noone noted that although Huxford was standing self-importantly alongside Napier, there was no sign of Barry Bargewell. Bob Ellis's prophecy had come true.

30. NOONE

"Apart from an expert knowledge of the talent available, we believe a Partner at JCA needs five crucial assets: the first is empathy, an instinctive understanding of what the client really wants, even if at times they don't fully know themselves - an ability to "listen between the lines". The second is an almost obsessive diligence, to examine and re-examine every possible solution, being thorough, yet also creative. The third is honesty, with the courage to give people, both clients and candidates, straight, candid and constructive feedback. The fourth is a sense of fun; this is quintessentially a people business, people are its only product, and people by and large work better when they enjoy themselves. The fifth is about passion. As a team, we share a common belief that we really can make a difference."

JCA GROUP WEBSITE

"Thank you all so much for breaking your busy schedules to come here," began Napier, condescendingly, as if they had a choice. "I wanted you to be the first to hear some exciting news." This was an obvious lie; they clearly weren't the first. "To begin, I want to thank Barry Bargewell for all he has done for the firm, initially as a consultant in ABC and latterly leading ABC's rebuilding and recovery programme." Noone knew this was shorthand for saying Bargewell had failed.

"As you see," continued Napier, "Barry is not with us. He came to me recently and openly admitted that the stresses and strains of running one of the UK's top consultancies were keeping him away from home too often. It is a sacrifice we all have to make from time-to-time, but eventually, perhaps, we must make a choice where to compromise. With great reluctance, I accepted his resignation." Noone didn't believe this for one moment. This was boardroom jargon for the classic ultimatum: go "voluntarily" or be pushed. Napier had paused while he surveyed the room, perhaps judging the collective reaction; then he continued:

"However, as they say, where one door closes, another always opens. The exciting news is that I am delighted to announce a truly exceptional replacement as Managing Director of ABC." Napier paused again for effect and looked around the expectant room. "Ladies and Gentlemen," he said in the voice of a true showman, "I am pleased to introduce to you, Calliope Brown." The door at the end of the room opened and a blonde-bobbed thirty-something with a face full of flashing white teeth entered and made her way to stand beside Napier.

"As some of you may know, Calliope helped build and then ran the Consumer Practice at Overy, Cutt & Dribble and after its trade sale, took on the Industrial Practice as well. She is a very experienced and highly regarded search consultant with a tremendous network and track record; for example, she recently found Philip Ball for BA," Napier nodded approvingly towards her as he shared this information, acknowledging her badge of honour. Noone had never heard of her.

"We are extremely lucky to have her," (Noone wondered grubbily whether Napier had had her, as part of the hiring process) "so please welcome Calliope warmly to ABC. Under her astute and inspirational leadership, I expect the great name of Aspallan, Bane Consultants to strike fear once again into the hearts of our many lesser competitors." There was lukewarm applause from some of the more sycophantic in the room; Noone believed in never applauding until someone had achieved something to justify the applause. Calliope Brown stepped forward, smiled, and spoke:

"Thank you Bix for your kind words and to you all for being here to welcome me. I have heard great things about you all and how team-orientated things are. It was one of the reasons I chose to come to ABC rather than Russell

Reynolds or Egon Zehnder and I look forward to meeting you all individually from Monday onwards. I know we can do fantastic business here and put ABC right back at the top where it belongs."

"Thanks Calliope, and I wish you all the best of luck," said Napier. "I have another meeting, but you may like to get acquainted with Calliope; there are some drinks and nibbles on the side there." With that and a toss of his long hair, Napier swept out of the room. Soon there was a gaggle of people milling around ABC's new, prized asset, but Noone grabbed a drink first, choosing a glass of over-oaked Australian chardonnay in preference to the canned lager. Slowly, the fawning crowd around Calliope thinned as people introduced themselves, shook her hand, said how thrilled they were to have her onboard, ran out of things to say and excused themselves to go home. Eventually, Noone stood before her and when she caught his eye, extended a hand and said his name. Her handshake was curious: at once strong but not completely engaged, as if she wanted to convey the Masonic bond but didn't quite know the key. Her bright blue eyes should have been attractive and engaging, but Noone found them cold and defensive. She smiled warmly at him and a shiver ran down his back.

"I have heard a lot about you, Adam, and I really look forward to working together." She had a surprisingly low-pitched voice with a northern accent (was it Manchester, Noone wondered?).

"Me too," he mumbled, and was saved from having to utter any other inanity by Calliope's attention being taken by Henchley Longbad, who immediately engaged her in a conversation about a client whom they both knew. Noone drifted off, ditched the chardonnay in two gulps and left.

The following Monday, after Calliope's first formal royal address to her new troops, Noone sought out Bob Ellis, the fount of all information, be it scurrilous gossip or home truth.

"So what do we know about our young starlet, Bob?

Napier must have had her lined up well before he shafted Barry, but I have never come across her before."

"Lucky you. Yes, she was courted for weeks and then had her gardening leave from OCD to work through. Depending on who you speak to, she is either ruthless, an egomaniac, a slime-ball or all three; of course it goes without saying that she is a control-freak. She is called 'Poison Dwarf' out on the street." Noone's sense of foreboding increased.

"Sounds charming. Why did she come here, I wonder?"

"Simple," replied Bob. "Don't believe all that bollocks about choosing between us and the Tier Ones; she didn't have a choice. Napier was the only one who would touch her because he doesn't care how awful she is, just so long as she is better than Bargewell."

"And sod the rest of us," mused Noone aloud.

"Yes. Apparently clients in the HR community love her, because she was one of them, and she charms all the old-school Chairmen and MDs with her pretty-girl flirting and flattery. They all think there may be a chance of getting into her knickers."

"And is there?" asked Noone dubiously. She certainly wasn't his type.

"Reportedly yes; some say she has had more jumps than an army surplus pommel-horse, but all in the line of business, of course."

"Of course." She clearly understood that feminine wiles were a great asset in headhunting. "She says she is going to take her first ninety days to review everything before making any changes."

"Don't bet on it," said Bob, "this one is in a hurry." Of course, he was right.

During the first month of Calliope's reign, Noone's run of bad form continued. A week before taking up his new job, a candidate Noone had successfully placed was killed on a zebra crossing by a bus, the driver of which was haranguing a standing passenger for obscuring his view and failed to notice the pedestrian until it was too late.

Another, whom he had placed nearly a year previously, imbibed too vigorously on a transatlantic flight, physically attacked his boss, and on landing was escorted both from the plane and from his job. The client had declined to follow Noone's recommendation of making the job offer subject to a medical, so Noone felt he was in the clear. Thank God it was past the guarantee period, so he didn't have to do the whole assignment again for free, but there was a whiff of taint, the client didn't return Noone's calls, and no more assignments were forthcoming. He did start work with a new client where the omens seemed good; the briefing was precise (meaning that for once, the client had a decent idea of what he was looking for) the job specification accepted with minimal fuss, the long-list reviewed positively, the short-list accepted and interviewed appreciatively and an offer was made, *subject to the candidate investing £50k in the business.* Neither Noone nor the candidate had seen that coming, and the candidate understandably walked away. The client then turned on Noone, refused to pay the third tranche of the fee, demanded the rest of the fee back and stated that he would never do business again with ABC. It was indeed an unfair world.

However, a brief moment of humour was provided when an advertisement for a senior position at the Serious Fraud Office (public sector appointments had to be advertised "for openness and to encourage diversity") produced an application from an inmate at Her Majesty's Prison High Down, Sutton. "In conclusion," the covering letter ran, "having been at the sharp end of GBH and currently imprisoned for fraud, I know what it takes and am ideally equipped to help regulate the Financial Services industry."

By the second month, Calliope's colours were emerging clearly. If this generation was the "Me" generation, Calliope was the ultimate "Me". She had to be involved in everything and her management style was unattractively school-marmish. She brought her two OCD

Executive Assistants with her; one covered internal administration, the other, client-facing stuff. She laughingly referred to them as "her slaves". Nobody laughed, but thanks to their dedication, Calliope's work rate was phenomenal. Her philosophy for creating a successful business was simple: maximise the input at the top of the hopper and you will maximise the output flowing from the bottom. The business of search became a mechanised process, which, if fed with the correct ingredients, would surely create a tangible and satisfactory end-product. X amount of BD calls would produce Y amount of meetings which would produce Z amount of new business. Simple as that, you know it makes sense, so just do it.

There was no doubt that this approach worked for Calliope. Her two slaves had soon uploaded all the contacts she had stolen from OCD and arranged numerous meetings stretching way into the future. Every couple of weeks, Calliope held "one-on-ones" with each consultant and in her chats with Noone, she used this example to browbeat him into becoming more consistently active in looking for meetings; "after all, darling, it's not rocket-science is it?" She also demanded that he specialise, once and for all.

"You may have been in the business for twelve years, but quite honestly, you cannot afford to be a Generalist any more. You must specialise to survive." Noone had to accept it was true. He didn't like it, but his widely fragmented, largely SME client-base was producing too wide and fragmented results. It wasn't consistent enough for Calliope's new mechanistic approach to search. Her approach was about ensuring that the client danced to her tune. It was about controlling the client. Philosophically, Noone came from a different school of thought: you put the client first and responded to his or her needs, delivering customer service to the best of your ability. It was evident from the few assignments which Calliope had already won that the process of delivery didn't interest her at all: she delegated as much as possible to her researchers, with instructions that she could only afford fifteen minutes to meet each candidate invited for interview "to take a view". She hired two more researchers to support the Calliope machine.

She also announced she was changing the bonus scheme. When discussed, analysed and dismantled by the consultants, two things were clear about Calliope's new scheme: firstly, there would be a higher percentage of credit awarded to the person introducing a piece of work (60%) than to the person transacting the work (40%); secondly, given her "modus operandi", it was designed to line Calliope's own pockets. She had also announced that she expected all consultants to bill at least £400k and whilst the threat was not explicit, the implication was that failure to do so would not justify their continued existence at ABC. Naturally, there were rumblings of discontent, with Amber Reddie, who saw Calliope as a threat to her own assumed "Queen Bee" status, particularly upset.

"Who does she think she is, coming in here and upsetting everything without consultation? At least we knew where we stood with Barry. I am going to raise it with Bix."

"I am not sure that's wise," advised Huff. "After all, Napier did bring her in to shake things up and that is exactly what she is doing."

Huff was right. Given that Huxford now seemed to be operating as Napier's right hand, Amber decided to approach him first. He advised that it was nothing to do with him and that Amber should raise it with Napier, who was conveniently on holiday on some remote Greek island and incommunicado. Huxford rang him anyway to warn him of a potential rebellion, but Napier predictably reacted in Marie Antoinette *"Qu'ils mangent de la brioche"* style, although not in those same words: "they can fuck off if they don't like it; and I am not going to intervene," was his response to Huxford.

"I have tried to call Bix, but it is impossible," Huxford

relayed insouciantly and untruthfully to Amber. "There is no mobile signal on the island and the line to the hotel seems to be down. Besides, he went there precisely not to be disturbed," he warned. By the time Napier returned two weeks later, Calliope had strengthened her hand by showing weekly fee progress charts, onto which were plotted monthly targets. It was quite obvious who the stars were and who was struggling. She was at the top, proving beyond all doubt that her system of delegated activity and process management worked best.

Huff was the first to go. After a particularly long "one-on-one" motivational meeting with Calliope, he emerged downcast and empty. He pulled Noone to the Running Horse on Davies Street for lunch. He looked shattered and waited miserably at a table while Noone brought them London Pride from the bar.

"I've had it Adam. Can't stand her bossy, prissy little self-centred mind. I'm leaving."

"Whoa, hang on Tiger; let's not rush into things," replied Noone. "Granted she is evil, obnoxious, divisive, but we can survive. We just have to play the game her way a little."

"It's too late; I leave with immediate effect. I've just got to pack my things this afternoon and go. I expressed my concern at her management style and she indicated it was probably time for me to move on. She didn't quite accuse me of being a dinosaur, but her sarcastic, offhand manner made it clear that I have no place in her brave new world. There is no use fighting it. Anyway, I am rather relieved: she is destroying what was left of everything in which I believed." Noone noted with approval that even in his hour of extreme provocation and stress, Huff still spoke in grammatically correct sentences. Perhaps he (and by association Noone) really were dinosaurs, only good for uselessly upholding "the old ways" and the Queen's English, two fast-eroding rocks of rectitude awash in an overwhelming tide of dumbing-down, personified by Calliope Brown.

Later that afternoon, packing done, Huff came to Noone's office to bid him farewell. They had been through a lot together, shared good days and now bad, but they shook hands and manfully looked each other in the eye. They promised to keep in touch, as everyone always does. That was it, the end of an era, thought Noone, as Huff turned and left with a final, terse warning, leaving him alone with his fears and few remaining hopes:

"Watch out, Adam, you will be next."

Noone reflected on how it was possible that such a monster could be unleashed in their midst. Of course, the industry was set up to reward the biggest egos. The most successful players were those who gained ownership of key relationships and refused to relinquish them. Bitterly, Noone recalled over the years the number of clients to whom he had introduced colleagues who had been more appropriate to handle a specific piece of business. He had been too trusting. The Calliope Browns and Amber Reddies of this world would do no such thing: in their view, they were always the best option for their clients. It dawned on him dully that what many preached and he always practised, *doing the best thing for the firm,* was not followed by those at the top of the pile; they always did what was best for themselves. He had been naïve, stupid even, to believe in the party line and not put himself first all the time. The big egos needed to be seen not to fail and for this they needed to own relationships. Fees came from these relationships, not the other way round. The nice guys, of which Noone fondly imagined himself to be one, were either averse to behaving like this or didn't understand the necessity. Therefore, they would never be judged to be truly successful by their peers. Only personal fee income mattered. Foolishly, he had missed that trick and could see how exposed he had become.

He realised now that the reward structures of recruitment businesses prevented the right people from becoming inspiring team managers. The only important thing was the amount of fee revenue you could generate, which was why MDs were either self-serving, like Calliope, or incompetent, like Bargewell. Often they were both. Surely it didn't have to be that way, did it? Executive resourcing was not complex: you identified a client with a need and then you found the best solution you could; it should be *win, win, win,* as Giles Bane had told him when he first started in 1990. But somehow it had become sullied and Noone now saw the industry as petty, squabbling, bragging, indiscreet, self-promoting and an over-complication of a beautifully simple business. This was particularly true of executive resourcing businesses which had become plcs; the demands of annual growth forecasting, quarterly reporting and providing increased returns to shareholders were incompatible with working in the best interests of both client and candidates. Feeding the plc machine demanded growth at all costs which matched Calliope's production line techniques, not Noone's. The bigger a search firm became, the more its emphasis was on winning, rather than delivering, business, and the biggest could afford to lose clients through the back door by poor service because the power of their brands would always bring in new clients through the front door. Despite the familiar and all-too-repetitive mantras on their websites about specialist expertise, commitment to clients and quality, how appalled would the clients be if they realised that most major search firms' successful assignment completion rate was barely 80%? Could firms win new business if they didn't lie to clients and instead said honestly: "we fail in one in five of our engagements"? Of course not.

Yet instead of concentrating on delivering the one simple thing they have been paid to do, the insatiable appetite of shareholder-return drove them to embellish still further to "add value" and build market share; all the major firms now offered psychological profiling, succession planning, organisational development, performance management, Board assessment, executive coaching and other trivial HR services. Christ, one of them would offer outplacement soon, and there was a conflict of interest if ever there was one! Yet none of these so-called value-added services was delivering a meaningful return, so what would everyone do next? It seemed to Noone that search worked most smoothly when pared down: a sectorally or geographically focused firm which genuinely set out to serve the clients and candidates best.

Armed with this sense of disillusionment, he was no match for Calliope in their subsequent "one-on-ones". She bullied him into agreeing to specialise in pharmaceuticals, or "Life Sciences" as she put it, because it was a relatively unserviced niche in the market and was recession-proof. With an ageing global population, demand for drugs would only increase; it could be very interesting indeed. Noone acquiesced. He had no interest in it whatsoever. She lectured him how she would approach the market and open it up, commencing with thorough research to find out who the major players were and what the issues were.

"Get a researcher to help identify the names, write a mail-shot, send it out and let's review progress in two weeks' time," she suggested brightly. Noone nodded grimly. That was the winning formula: cram the hopper full at the top and something would be bound to fall out the bottom. Over the following weeks the process ground remorselessly on: review the number of mail-shots, how many follow-up calls, how many follow-up follow-up calls, the number of meetings, further follow-up calls, the number of meetings, do the grunt-work, *do the maths*. It was relentless, soul-destroying stuff in which Noone was destroying his soul. He developed a deep hatred of the Poison-Dwarf and dreaded the regular one-on-ones, where Calliope sat in judgement as he attempted to persuade her of his wholehearted efforts to win new business. His heart just wasn't in it, and he suspected she knew, if her ill-concealed impatience was anything to go by.

He began to fantasise about her sudden demise: she might slip from a platform, fall tragically into the path of an incoming train, and become one of those "passenger action" statistics; a tyre blow-out on the motorway might catapult her across the carriageway, down a steep embankment and into a river; a building site crane might lose its load of scaffolding poles just as she walked by underneath. This mushroom cloud of hate grew and grew, poisoning Noone's days and nights with its miasmic, bitter fog. He became obsessed with finding a final solution and gradually realised that he would not be able to leave it to chance. He would need to take action. Instantly, he was appalled at that thought: was he seriously considering killing someone? Good old easy-going Adam Noone, contemplating murder? He couldn't be, could he? He searched deep within himself and found, shockingly, that he was. How far was he prepared to go with this horror-thought? He discovered that he didn't possess either the courage or psychopathic leanings to take premeditated, direct, violent action by confronting her with a lethal weapon. No, that was clearly madness. It would have to look like an accident. The problem with accidents was that they tended to be accidental. Planning one was difficult. He would need to be carefully opportunistic, always on the lookout for possibilities. Once firmly decided on this nebulous, nefarious course of action and inaction, amazingly, Noone didn't have long to wait for just the right opportunity.

Although, inevitably, the work-process sledgehammer began to crack a few nuts and Noone achieved a number of meetings with his target companies, it was Calliope who came up with the first real piece of potential new business. One of her "darling" HR contacts had recently moved to a FTSE 100 pharmaceutical giant as Head of Resourcing and had called Calliope about a senior hire the company wished to make. As Calliope would take the lion's share of the credit if the business was won, per her new bonus scheme credit system, she was happy to ask Noone to accompany her to the pitch. She would introduce him as her assistant on the project; it would gain him some traction in his chosen specialisation and he could handle the delivery side, leaving her free to forget about this and move on to winning more business elsewhere. She so loved the thrill of the chase; it was, well, gusset-moistening.

So it was that they found themselves striding purposefully along Jermyn Street to the client HQ round the corner in Lower Regent Street, she towards the glory of another successful pitch, he entranced by the huge wing-mirror advancing towards them at accelerating speed. He could see it was exactly the right height to collect her head just above the shoulders. Perfect, it would smash her fucking face in. Level with Lewins, Calliope checked the groundwork with Noone as she strode unknowingly towards it.

"You've got the presentation pack, the assignment stats, our track record and the sources list?" she demanded.

"Of course," Noone answered obediently. The large, shiny mirror loomed appealingly.

He had manoeuvred to the inside of the pavement, and as the UPS van reached them, he would accidentally slip and nudge her into the path of that magnificent mirror. It was that easy; his troubles would be over and so would she. Forty, thirty, twenty feet, the van continued to accelerate and was closing fast. Noone stumbled into Calliope. She lurched sideways into the path of the mirror. It was all over.

ACKNOWLEDGEMENTS

- My headhunting mentor, Richard Boggis-Rolfe and my friends and ex-colleagues who have contributed reminiscences, memos and stories, in particular Elisabeth Marx, Eric Price, Gareth Davies, Iain McNeil, Robert Hutton, Camilla Arnold, Phil Peters and James Hervey-Bathurst and Eastnor Castle
- Kevin Fitzgerald for advice on publishing and Mike Knox for encouragement
- Sean Duggan of the Surrey Comet for allowing me to adapt material for my chapter on Email
- The Week magazine for report on Robin Cakes
- Australian TV channel for interviews with Americans
- US State department for info on Oman
- The Economist for analysis of Mao's poor management techniques
- Tom Davis and Seth Katz, the creators of Bullshit Bingo
- Viz Magazine's "Roger's Profanisaurus"
- Daily Telegraph for "Most Boring Postcard Competition"
- Department of Forensics, University College London, for the Tube seat analysis
- Directory Enquiries, Samsung Electronics, RAC Motoring Services and Word Perfect for technical support conversations
- Israelnationalnews.com for the essay on Fanaticism
- For information on castles: www.castlexplorer
- Unknown journalists for newspaper headlines, street argot and statistics
- Anonymous creators of the Shoppers' Prayer, the Four Ages of Policing, the Book of Corporate Life, schoolchildren's exam responses, email statistics and one-line funnies and any other inadvertently unattributed quotations

- Last but not least, my chum Bob Ellis, for the policing background and lending his name to a character